The screams and howls of dying humans, half-orcs, elves, and halflings sounded in a mad chorus. Drow war cries screeched and echoed in the hellish light. Through it all, a strangely beautiful female voice managed to shout at the Justicar.

"You cannot see, human! You are doomed!"

Jus closed in upon the voice, deliberately keeping himself turned slightly away as though unable to find his enemy. He moved his sword point uncertainly.

"I know enough. You have been *judged*."

"You are the Justicar—the hand of justice!" Sneering, the drow high priestess shifted, moving to one side.

Jus flicked his head and turned, again slightly out of line.

"You cannot see!" she screamed in triumph as she attacked.

Jus threw himself flat, spinning with his sword scything across the ground. The blade sheared through ankles, and the ranger heard a scream of agony. He rolled, rose, and slammed his sword through the stunned priestess, killing her instantly.

"Justice *is* blind."

AGAINST THE GIANTS
Ru Emerson

WHITE PLUME MOUNTAIN
Paul Kidd

DESCENT INTO THE DEPTHS OF THE EARTH
Paul Kidd

THE TEMPLE OF ELEMENTAL EVIL
Thomas Reed
(MAY 2001)

THE KEEP ON THE BORDERLANDS
Ru Emerson
(SEPTEMBER 2001)

Descent into the Depths of the Earth

Paul Kidd

DESCENT INTO THE DEPTHS OF THE EARTH
GREYHAWK CLASSICS
©2000 Wizards of the Coast, Inc.
All Rights Reserved.

Distributed in the United States by St. Martin's Press. Distributed in Canada by Fenn Ltd.

Distributed to the hobby, toy, and comic trade in the United States and Canada by regional distributors.

Distributed worldwide by Wizards of the Coast, Inc. and regional distributors.

Cover art by Jerry Vander Stelt
Map by Dennis Kauth
First Printing: June 2000
Library of Congress Catalog Card Number: 99-69447

9 8 7 6 5 4 3 2 1

ISBN: 0-7869-1635-4
620-T21635

U.S., CANADA,	EUROPEAN HEADQUARTERS
ASIA, PACIFIC, & LATIN AMERICA	Wizards of the Coast, Belgium
Wizards of the Coast, Inc.	P.B. 2031
P.O. Box 707	2600 Berchem
Renton, WA 98057-0707	Belgium
+1-800-324-6496	Tel. +32-70-23-32-77

Visit our web site at **www.wizards.com**

For Alexandra—damaged for life, but enjoying the ride!

With thanks and love to my wife Christine—reader, editor, partner—who has the patience of a saint.

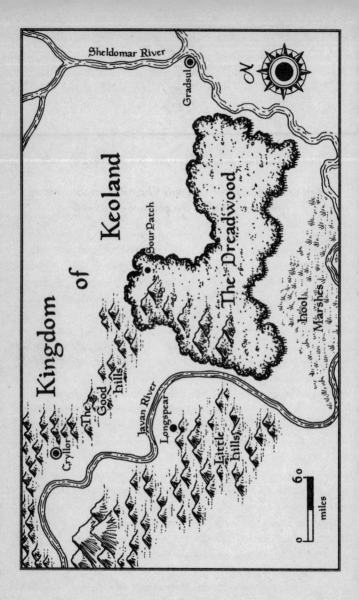

Prologue

Clan Sable had an eye for spectacular locations, and in a court jaded by centuries of tinsel and frippery, the talent had a certain dark appeal. At the very least, their choices would spark off a frenzy of one-upmanship as the other faerie clans sought to offer wilder, madder thrills.

Acheron had been a choice of genius. On this plane of existence, the entire universe seemed to be trying to smash itself to pieces. A vast infinity of air suspended countless turning cubes of iron. The sepia-tinted atmosphere sizzled with electricity as lightning arched insane shapes between the cubes, leaving brilliant violet trails scorched on the eye. The cubes were tiny worlds, and the worlds tumbled like dice. Here and there the cubes collided, the noise ringing through space like titanic bells. Fragments of iron and helpless little bodies went tumbling free into space while far away, wars and violence went ever on. The place stank of lightning strike, of the hammer-and-forge reek of the smashing cubes, and the rusty stench of blood.

The Seelie Court was unconcerned. They were the faerie, the deadly sword point of a secret world. Although Queen Titania and the sylvan powers held state in distant planes, they used the faerie as their hands, their eyes, and their ears. Sinking deeper and deeper into their introverted world, the sylvan powers now scarcely knew fantasy from reality and left the power of the Seelie Court in the hands of the clans.

Faerie control over the sylvan powers was absolute, and with power came intrigue—plots and plans, schemes and dreams.

Wrapped in glorious isolation, the Seelie Court posed and schemed in a frenzy of activity that filled the centuries with the comforting illusion of activity.

Sitting languidly upon outcrops of jagged iron and rust, today's gathering had eyes only for the conflict being fought at the bottom of a crater just below them. Two combatants, both male faeries, fought and posed in the battlefield. Small, lithe, and winged like dragonflies, the creatures battled viciously with sword and magic. The duelists were slim and elegant, with clothing gleaned from a dozen exotic planes. Holding absurdly thin little swords, they stood and flung spell after spell at one another in a display full of flash and glory but rather empty of blood. Spellfire lit and stained imperfections in the metal of the crater, making it glow brilliant green, lavender, and orange. Here and there a faerie gave an appreciative patter of applause, while mortal servants poured out tinctures of faerie wine.

Today's duel served as a welcome little diversion. Ushan, Lord of Clan Sable, sat beneath a fan waved by one of his servants. It amused him these days to be attended by female orcs, their bestial forms draped in courtly finery. A man much in love with his own image, Ushan raised his glass to another faerie, who wandered over, keeping his eyes upon the fight.

Ushan's comrade drew himself up on a stool that had been covered with a leucrotta skin. He accepted wine from a serving girl and said, "My Lord Ushan."

"My Lord Faen." Silver haired, Ushan had today dressed in robes of animated flame. "I trust Acheron suits you well?"

"Well enough, well enough." Lord Faen affected spectacles and a pointed beard, considering himself to be the greatest scholar of the Seelie Court. He gave a quiet flutter of his wings. "Can you recall the reason for this duel?"

"The usual—insults, women . . ." Lord Ushan seemed more interested in watching the slow tumble of a distant iron cube than following the duel. "Who remembers?"

"The participants, perhaps?" Carefully watching the nearest

duelist, Faen slowly stroked at his antennae. "Your man Tarquil has quite a touch. Do you have hopes for him?"

Watching the boy, Ushan appreciatively sipped from his glass. "His technique has improved. I believe him to be the best duelist in the lower court."

"He is your sister's son?" Lord Faen steepled his fingers, carefully watching the two faeries below as they stabbed spell and counter spell at one another. "He likes killing too much."

"Not a bad thing in a noble. We see too many milksops in the current generation, too little thirst for blood."

Ushan relaxed. All about him spread the Seelie Court, the nobility of faerie. Small, winged figures—some remaining elegantly in form and others changing shape as they pleased—lay scattered languidly about. The inhabitants of Acheron had wisely fled. Few creatures ever mistook a faerie for one of the lesser forest folk and escaped to tell the tale.

In the crater, spell followed spell. The two battling faeries flew and circled—invisible one moment, then outlined by detection spells in the next. Etiquette demanded non-lethal spells, yet Ushan's nephew stabbed these spells home with vicious intensity. He slammed his opponent back against the ground, sending the faerie skidding along hot rusted metal.

Lord Faen narrowed his eyes as he watched the combatants. "Splendid isolation is an illusion. We have wasted our intellects on self aggrandizement."

"A superior being is allowed aggrandizement." Ushan shot a dark glance toward Lord Faen. "Our intelligence makes us strong."

"The mark of intelligence is the ability to adapt to unseen changes."

"The mark of intelligence is to prevent the occurrence of any unseen changes." Ushan's lavender eyes sparked. "Events are merely sculptures of action made in the medium of time. We can control and shape events to meet our own needs. We are not mere butterflies to be blown along in the winds of any random storm."

Matching cold anger with disdain, Lord Faen smoothed his

beard. "We have already produced one dark goddess from our ranks. She too believed that events could be controlled."

"All it won her was an eternal prison." Ushan made a sharp motion with his hand. The Faerie Queen of Wind and Woe was not a topic for open discussion. "Clan Nightshade saw to it, and good riddance to her . . . and them."

A heavy sigh escaped Lord Faen as he sat back in his seat. He took more wine and swirled the amber liquid slowly in its glass as he said, "We must speak of Clan Nightshade."

Ushan slowly turned a frosty gaze upon the other faerie. "They played for power, and they lost. The lesson has kept the lesser houses in line." Once the greatest of faerie houses, Clan Nightshade had been exiled for centuries. "Clan Nightshade is no more."

Faen speared Ushan with an acidic, mocking gaze. "Clan Nightshade is alive. Your Clan Sable is aware of it. We are *all* aware of it. Only a fool would remain ignorant of a potential ally—or a potential enemy."

"They are no longer of the Court." Lean and elegant, Lord Ushan held out his glass to his towering serving girls. "They have adapted to other worlds. Why should we care for what Nightshade does?"

"Clan Nightshade now has a great deal of experience in the outer worlds—in the material plane, in particular. Experience and knowledge are *weapons*, Ushan. Without weapons, the universe may overtake us, intelligence or no." Lord Faen set his glass aside. "Clan Nightshade clipped the wings of the Queen of Wind and Woe. It is a skill we may soon need again."

"Faen! We have no need to go chasing demons in the outside world!"

Faen tapped his index fingers carefully together and replied, "Yes. We are all too skilled at breeding them from within." The faerie tugged straight his long goatee. "If we do not curb the habit, it will be the death of us."

In the crater below, Ushan's nephew scored a hit, smashing his opponent from his feet. Ignoring the duel, Faen rose to leave. Ushan immediately shot to his feet, his wings spread in fury.

"Clan Nightshade are outsiders! They are not of the body!"

"Then we need ties." Faen turned away. "A means of welcoming them truly back into the family of faerie."

"It cannot be done!"

"It *must* be done. The council meets before the Queen Titania tomorrow. I shall propose exactly this: that Nightshade be brought back from its exile in the wilds."

Ushan flexed his fists only to feel Faen's voice derisively caressing his rage.

"Truly, Ushan, turn your intelligence to the task. A new age is being born! Faerie must survive it." Lord Faen rose into the air. "We need *tools*, Ushan. We need weapons."

The faerie scholar faded into invisibility and then departed. Left alone with his serving girls, Lord Ushan sat in stony silence. In the crater below, Tarquil wiped his blade above his kill and looked up to meet his uncle's eyes. His thin mouth twisted into a smile.

CY 588

I

Autumn had stripped the maple trees of their green leaves, carpeting the forest in a deep, damp carpet of flame red and russet brown. The smell of damp and mold was everywhere, strangely fresh and enervating.

A man dressed in armor made of black dragon scales plodded silently along the road that meandered through the trees. A shimmering black hell hound pelt hung down his back, the canine's head sitting atop the man's helmet and grinning madly with bright white fangs. The man's hand rested upon a huge sword that jutted through his belt. Heavy hiking boots, a backpack, a coil of rope . . . it was the equipment of a man who marched fast and slept rough. Shaven headed, powerful, and suspicious, the Justicar marched his tireless march, his eyes watching the forest for the slightest stir of life.

Hovering gaily in mid air beside him, wearing an outfit to make a mother scream and a father reach for weapons, Escalla the faerie whistled a tune. Two feet tall, her long blonde hair shining straight and free, the faerie travelled without a worry in the world.

Along the road behind them rumbled a mule cart driven by a little man with an axe-beak nose. On the cart hung a banner reading: TRANSPORTS TO ADVENCHER. Polk the teamster drew in deep breaths of satisfaction as he looked about, as if the forest were a personal construction project in which he took huge pride. Beside the cart padded Enid the sphinx—brown haired, smothered in freckles, and enjoying the dappled forest sun immensely.

They followed an old overgrown road lined occasionally with the heads of sunken statues, the granite faces of ancient kings frowning down at the travelers. Sparing the statues a brief glare of annoyance, the Justicar adjusted the fit of his hell hound and gave a seething growl.

Their road map had finally been found. Polk had been using it as a wrapper for a greasy pile of ham sandwiches. As it turned out, their destination, Hommlet, was not in Keoland as Polk had claimed. Instead it lay three hundred miles to the northeast. Jus was lost, bruised, battered, and had almost been eaten by a hydra a few miles back. This was not one of his better days. Nursing righteous indignation, Jus shot a dire glance back at Polk where he rode upon the wagon.

"Keoland indeed!"

Happy as a clam, Escalla simply shrugged and said, "Get off his case! So he got the map upside down. It's the Flanaess! With these kind of place names, anyone can make mistakes." Escalla happily fluttered her wings. "We'll just go north for a few hundred miles and *bam!* We'll be in Hommlet."

Unperturbed by the detour, Escalla, Polk, and Enid simply seemed to look forward to the journey and enjoyed the views. More concerned with safety, food, shelter, and keeping his companions alive, the Justicar looked about the forest and *seethed*.

"Keoland. I've never been to Keoland before."

"Well, these autumn leaves are neat." Flying backward, Escalla plucked at a huge red maple leaf. "Feels kind of homey, like I've been here before."

The fact that they were totally lost had made no impression on her. Jus looked at her with one raised brow and asked, *"Have* you been here before?"

"Ah, I dunno. Trees . . . yeah. Leaves . . . yeah. One patch of forest is really pretty amazingly like another." Escalla turned around in midair as she flew. "But this"—she gestured at the slowly crumbling remains of a long fallen statue—"*this* could be familiar! I know I've seen statues like this somewhere before. I mean kinda similar . . ." She darted forward down the road. "Hey! I know! Let's follow the road! It must lead to a town!"

"Escalla, we *are* following the road."

"Oh. Hoopy!"

The road turned a bend, and a row of thatched roofs suddenly met the travelers' eyes. It was a village long deserted and left to the weeds. In a wilderness of deserted buildings, only the squirrels reigned. Cottage doors hung open, some creaking slowly like the sagging bones of the dead. Other houses simply lay cold and empty with thistles sprouting from the thatch roofs. The squirrels sped and flitted from roof to roof, wall to wall, perching atop rusted wagons and twittering atop abandoned ploughs. They even perched on the faded sign of an old tavern, making the painted boards sway slowly in the wind.

War had come and gone. The village lay abandoned, the inhabitants having been wise enough to retreat before powers they could not resist. The buildings were still intact but were now home to only an occasional nest of stirges.

As Enid padded her way down the weed-ridden street, Polk the teamster reined the cart to a halt. The sudden silence was deafening.

Grim and tired, the Justicar plodded over to the tavern and prodded the door open with his black sword. The gloomy taproom was deserted, all except for a family of voles.

"Cinders?"

The hell hound searched with senses far sharper than any mortal's. *Stirges, tree hoppers, moss, mold, mouses with tailses, rain puddles, little spiders.*

"No movement?"

No monsters, no magic.

Jus knelt to carefully examine the street. The hard-packed earth was carpeted with weeds, none of which seemed bent or broken by the passing of feet. "And no tracks."

"Hey! Look at this! It's a dead elephant!" Escalla hovered over a broken cottage. "Wow! Ivory! We could find a fortune in ivory!"

Jus walked over to the girl and looked at a row of crushed and shattered houses. Lying sprawled amongst the fallen walls was a huge skeleton easily three times the size of a man. The skeleton's feet were wrapped in moldering boots. A tree limb had served it for a club. It lay long dead, furred with moss, and with dandelions growing from the sockets of its eyes.

Escalla darted above the houses and rubbed her hands in glee. "There's another elephant over here! And another!"

"They're not elephants, Escalla. They're giants."

"How do you know?"

"A remarkable lack of elephant-like properties." Jus levered a flaking piece of bone from the top of a giant's shin and passed it up to Cinders. "I judge them about sixteen feet tall. They must have driven off the villagers."

Sitting on a rooftop, Escalla went into a sulk. "Well, they *could* have been elephants."

"Escalla, there are no elephants in the Flanaess."

"How do you know?"

"I'm a ranger. Trust me."

Whatever had happened to the village, it had happened many years before. The place was clean, no dangers, no enemies. With a heavy sigh, the Justicar unfastened the paws of the hell hound pelt from his neck and drew Cinders from his shoulders to shake the dust out of his friend's fur. The big man walked back and sat down on a mounting block outside the tavern, unfastened his helmet and let it crash down into the grass, then began to carefully brush the hell hound's fur.

Cinders's tail thumped as the dog skin grinned its mad piranha grin. *Camp? Start fire?*

"Yep. Guess we can." The Justicar, a ranger who had fought a savage war against injustice for more years than he cared to tell, spread his friend out across his lap. A big currycomb brushed the hell hound's fur to a brilliant shine.

Tired and with his ribs aching from a hydra's bite that had failed to pierce his armor's scales, the Justicar and rose heavily to his feet. New territories meant new work. There would be towns here, meaning inequality and injustice. More than enough labor for a mortal man to do . . .

"Night's coming," he announced. "We'll stay in the tavern. It's big, and we can block the doors. Polk, get the mules under cover before the stirges get them. Enid, see if there's any water down that well." The ranger retrieved his helmet and his hell hound skin, then shoved open the tavern door. "Check every room. Keep your eyes open. If there's trouble, call me."

Inside the tavern, heavy ceiling beams were still hung with bunches of dried herbs. A single iron pot lay overturned beside the hearth. Jus strode ahead of Escalla, checked the kitchens with their pot hooks and empty pantries, then clumped upstairs to check for lurking terrors. A single stirge—big as a small dog, feathery, and shaped like a mosquito—fled in terror out a window of the master bedroom. Jus banged the shutters closed then turned to make his way back downstairs.

Escalla sprang into view beside him, shedding invisibility with a barely audible pop. Her long blonde hair shimmered like golden silk as the faerie toyed with it nervously in her mouth.

"Hey, Jus? Good fight with the hydra back there, huh? Really livened up the day. I mean, you look at a place and think, 'Gee, now here's a dead spot.' "

She wavered nervously, keeping out of reach. Bone tired, Jus sat down on the steps, wincing as his bruised side twinged. He unclipped the shoulder fastenings of his dragon scale cuirass, unbuckled his sword belt, and let the whole ensemble crash heavily to the ground.

"You and your hydra! Damned thing almost stove in my rib cage."

"Yeah, but you're not mad about it or anything, are you?" The girl hovered back and forth like a nervous bee. "I mean, it just lets you see how cool this journey is! Danger everywhere! And I'm sure we can find some injustice just dying to be, um . . . re-justiced and stuff."

The Justicar pierced Escalla with one dire eye and said, "Escalla, we just found a twelve-headed hydra in a watchtower. That's enough activity for today."

Going into a magnificent sulk, the faerie kicked at a dead

woodlouse on the floor. "You're mad about the hydra. I knew it. Why does it have to be *my* fault?"

Unamused, Jus looked levelly at Escalla. "You swiped scrolls from its treasure horde, didn't you?"

"Only one!"

"I thought we had decided not to go haring off on our own?" Jus's words had the damning weight of common sense. "What did I tell you about wandering away where I can't protect you?"

Stung, Escalla proudly sat her little bottom on a broken stool.

"I wasn't *wandering*. There was a plan." Sniffing, Escalla tried to weasel her way out of making an apology. "I'm a ruin exploration professional. Do I want my comrades to be burdened by useless side trips?" Escalla placed one hand loftily upon her breast. "I was merely attempting to add to party assets without slowing your travel time. The presence of the hydra was simply an unforeseen variable!"

"You screwed up."

Escalla regarded her friend through leveled lashes. "I am a faerie. Faeries do not screw up. We just have occasional bouts of adverse results production."

"Uh-huh. Well, at least you got a spell scroll out of it." Jus found a dried apricot in his pouch and gave the girl the bigger half. "Are the rest of the pixies in the forest just like you?"

"Nah. I'm the cute one, one of a kind, and I'm sure as hell no pixie!" Escalla stood, turning to clench her rear. "See those lines?"

"Pure thoroughbred." Jus lifted one arm experimentally and gave a wince. "I think I hurt."

"You think?"

"All right, I *do* hurt." The man planted a hand beneath his sweaty tunic and shoved a healing spell into himself, the magic crackling like a pine cone in a fire. "That damned hydra almost killed me!"

"He never laid a glove on you. This is just a trail sore." Escalla whirred up into the air. "Hey! We found a tavern. I bet there's a bathtub here!" The girl called out of a window. "Hey, Enid! Was there water in that well?"

The sphinx was sitting in the tavern yard eating a freshly killed stirge. She guiltily hid her meal and cleared her throat. "Um, yes there was!"

"Well, find a bucket! We've got work to do!" Escalla hung her head out of the window and frowned at the sphinx. "Are you snacking between meals again?"

"No!"

"Enid, stop it! How are we going to land you a nice androsphinx if you won't listen to your fashion advisor?" The faerie leaned through the windowsill. "Check my bags on the wagon. Have we got any faerie cakes left?"

"One."

"Hoopy! We can have it with dinner!"

"Ah," Enid peered into a leather bag. "It's a bit green."

"I like 'em green!"

"Ah, it's a bit greener than you like it." Enid tilted her head. "Actually, it's really kind of *furry*."

Escalla opened up her arms. "It's fungoid enriched! Just bring it in!" The faerie turned happily to Jus. "See J-man, you just relax. Auntie Escalla will take care of everything. A nice bath . . . and I kept a faerie cake! Enid can walk on your back. She'll keep her claws in this time, I swear!"

The Justicar expectantly raised one brow, waiting. Escalla turned, muttered beneath her breath, looked at him sourly, and finally sniffed in irritation. "All right, all right! I'm sorry about the hydra! Not that it was my fault!"

✳   ✳   ✳   ✳   ✳

Evening in the abandoned village had a certain picturesque quality that soothed the soul. The quiet roofs and empty streets caught the light of sunset just *so*. The plaintive hoots of stirges echoed through the trees. Woodsmoke drifted beautiful blue curls against the evening sky. Somewhere in the background, a delicious smell of cooking stole through the tavern, making mouths water and all thoughts turn to supper.

In a stone room at the back of the kitchen, a giant wine barrel had been converted to a makeshift bath. Sitting like a ponderous leviathan, the Justicar let his shaven head jut over the barrel's rim. Hot water steamed, heat soothed, and he seemed uncertain whether such luxuries really befitted his role as defender of the weak.

Escalla sat in a copper pot, seething like meat in a stew. The faerie, who always read in the bath, was flipping through the scorched pages of a book rescued from the hydra's lair. It hovered in midair, held by the effects of one of her spells. The book was ancient. Escalla became more and more fascinated by the pages and even managed to lose interest in the delicious smell of frying meat coming from the kitchen a few feet away. After several long minutes of relaxed reading, she set the book aside and used an old toothbrush to scrub at an itchy spot between her wings. With her foot drumming the bottom of her bath like a well scratched dog, she looked over to where the Justicar's head floated amidst the steam. She gave a satisfied sigh and swam closer for a better look.

"Hey, Jus! Do you have to shave your head a lot? I mean, is it just a once a week thing? Once a day?"

"Whenever." Jus moved and a vast swell of water spilled over the edge of the gigantic barrel. "It's not important."

"You know, I could wax it for you—smoother finish than shaving."

"I just shave it to be practical."

"Yeah right, and in no way to project a monastic, ruthless appeal." Escalla dipped her brush in her bath and scrubbed at something beneath the waterline. "But hey, there's candles and stuff here. We can do wax."

"Escalla, there aren't enough healing spells in all the Flanaess to let you wax my head."

Trying to get on with the business of his bath, Jus sniffed suspiciously at a piece of soap—flower scented and taken from Enid and Escalla's private stores—then awkwardly began to scrub his feet.

"Good book?" he asked.

"It's a spellbook," she replied. "High level. There's only one or two bits I can understand." Escalla made a little sign with one finger, retrieved her book, and turned a page. Little flakes of burned parchment showered onto the floor. "I might be able to salvage something useful and get a few new spells out of it."

Jus raised one shaggy brow and said, "How do you get more spells? Will you have to go see your teacher?"

The change in Escalla's countenance was infinitely subtle. Only someone who knew her well would ever have noticed the pallid stiffness of her hands.

"I don't have *teachers.*" Pages closed with a cold snap. "I work alone."

The subject lay where it had fallen. Jus had hounded countless clues to ground before now, but he knew when to leave well enough alone. Escalla's past was a line drawn across her soul. The period before she had taken up with Jus and Cinders was something she preferred to forget.

Jus threw a wash cloth at her. It hit with a satisfactory *splat.*

"Spell copying is expensive. Don't you need gems to grind into ink?"

"It's no problem!" Escalla peeled the wet cloth away from her face and looked into the kitchen. "Hey, Polk! Do we have any gems?"

Enid and Polk had just pulverized gems in a pestle to make Enid's next stun symbol papyrus. Freezing guiltily, Enid covered the pestle with one paw and said, "Ah, no."

"Damn!" Escalla rested in her tub with her pretty pink feet steaming out in the open air. "Polk, go look in my bags, will you?"

Indignant at being disturbed, Polk slammed pots and pans about the kitchen table, putting the powdered gems dangerously close to the seasonings for the night's meal.

"We spent 'em, girl!" shouted the teamster. "That's what treasure's for! Supplies! Essentials! Gifts to the needy and glory to the gods!"

The faerie pursed her mouth. "You spent it on booze, didn't you?"

"Essential exploration assets!" Polk waved his hands. "An evening drink by the campfire is a prime piece of any adventure! Just read the literature!"

"Polk, one of these days, you are going to get such a pinch." Escalla irritably went back to her book. "All right, I'll use the burned version for now, but we need some gems—just little semi-precious ones."

Jus reached out with the point of his sword and tugged a hanging blanket back into place, sealing the bathroom off from the kitchen.

"If I find any lying around, I'll let you know."

With an expressive little sigh, the faerie slung her hair down the back of the cooking pot. She leaned her head against the rim of her bath and paddled with her toes.

"My water's getting cold. Can we get Cinders in here to warm it up?"

"Near a bath? Remember last time?"

The last time had been in the city of Trigol about two months before. The trouble of dunking a wailing hell hound skin into an unwanted bath had been amusing, to say the least. Escalla chuckled, then suddenly discovered that she was sitting on her scrubbing brush. "You know, for a refugee from the Abyss, that dog can be a real coward!" The girl lay in her bath and smiled. "Do you think they ever replaced that ceiling?"

"Remember the noise he made?"

"I remember." Rolling her head, Escalla slyly regarded her shaven-headed friend. "Hey, J-man! That was the first time I saw you getting out of the bath."

Jus decided not to comment. He propped his sword within easy reach and reclined once again.

Unperturbed, Escalla leaned over the rim of her pot and gave a feline little smile. "You have two cute little dimples in your rear."

Jus glowered. "That is called 'muscle confirmation.' "

"That just happen to be shaped like cute itty bitty dimples!"

Jus nursed his pride with a sniff and rearranged his sword again.

There was something odd about the village. Something *disquieting*. Jus knew Cinders had sensed it, though the hell hound had seen nothing invisible. There were no traps and apparently no creatures lurking underneath the floors, yet there was a sense of imminence, as though something dark and sinister had the place on its mind.

For her part, Escalla had no suspicions. She seemed to have other troubles on her mind. Coming to the edge of her bath, she looked out of the cooking pot at the Justicar.

"This is kind of a nice place though, huh?" The girl waved a nervous hand about the room. "It's a convenient little stop. Did you see all the squirrels? Those things are really cute!"

"Very."

"I like them. Too bad we can't stop. We should get out of here first thing tomorrow." Escalla sighed and sniffed the delicious smell of frying in the kitchen. "I thought we only had hard tack left. What's for dinner?"

"Just eat it. You'll love it."

The faerie squirted water through her clasped hands. "So are we leaving at dawn?"

"Maybe." The Justicar heaved a sigh. "Polk's gotten us lost. We'll have to circle around, find a settlement, and figure out just where we are so we can plan a route."

"Will it take long?"

The Justicar rose half out of his barrel, stretching and cracking his shoulders. His skin was pale where his armor always covered him, but his head and hands were tanned. "You're very keen for us to keep heading for Hommlet."

"Yeah." The faerie shrugged, sat up, and began to wring out her long blonde hair. "There's something weird about these woods, something . . . I don't know. It makes me feel creepy. I just want to get out of here." The girl sighed. "I wanna go to Hommlet. We've got the deeds, man! Still, I want to make sure no one's really unhappy about it or anything."

"No one's unhappy." Jus watched Escalla for a long moment, strangely pleased by the efficient way she wound her wet hair into a towel and tied it into a turban. "Most everything has good in it. You just have to know where to look."

With her slim, naked back to him, Escalla's little wings gracefully fanned themselves dry. "I've never really been told that I have much good in me."

Jus knew when to listen. He rose out of his bath and sat with a towel wound about his middle, leaning forward onto his hairy knees and watching her in silence. Slim and strangely graceful, Escalla quietly wound herself inside a towel. She turned to look over at him, her face thin, her shape tiny and vulnerable.

"I lived alone for a long time, Jus. A long, long time." The girl turned away and pulled her towel tight. "Thanks. You know, just for . . . for stuff."

Jus studied the faerie for a long, quiet moment. She fidgeted with her towel, staring at a puddle of bath water on the floor. Jus had never gotten on particularly well with people. He did what he had to in order to follow clues, sift information, and feel the pulse of a town, but his days and nights were spent in the company of his own thoughts. First Cinders and then Escalla had come to knock on the doors of his citadel, and now his days of solitude were over.

Trudging damply over to Escalla's side, the man took her small hand into his fingers, squeezed softly—and then turned to wander off and find his clothes.

"Dinner's done."

Escalla looked down at her hand and gave a rueful little smile. Wavering up into the air, she flew off in search of Cinders, hoping he hadn't eaten too much brown coal before blowing her hair dry. Polk ran past her through the kitchen holding plates of surprisingly glittery-looking meat. There was whiskey in the jug and a fire in the grate. All in all it seemed the village offered them a cheery night.

✿   ✿   ✿   ✿   ✿

With the kitchen now deserted, an eerie quiet fell. Outside on the roofs, the stirges hooted plaintively for blood. Ashes hissed in the stove, and an old brown tea kettle leaked steam into the breeze. Above the stove, there was a subtle stir of motion. A wisp of smoke in the chimney swirled then crept out into the light to hover just above the floor. A single eye solidified in the smoke, and then a long trunk-like snout sniffed and snuffled at the table top. The smoke creature drifted carefully along the table then flowed down onto the floor. It sniffed at the giant wine barrel with its cloudy water.

A scent caught the trunk's attention. The eye swiveled, blinked, and the creature hovered above Escalla's deserted bath. The trunk sniffed deeply at the water while the eye carefully examined the old rusty pot.

A single golden hair lay floating in the water. The smoke creature carefully picked up its find, examined it carefully, staring at it inch by inch, then gripped the strand tight.

A sudden noise came from the door. The smoke creature made a splash as it tore across the room and shot back up the chimney, fleeing into the night. Padding into the kitchen with an empty bucket hanging from her mouth, Enid blinked, then put down her bucket and frowned. She lumbered into the room, sniffing carefully and following a smoky trail that wound across the table and over toward the baths.

Escalla's voice pealed in from the taproom behind her. "Enid! Come on, hon! We have to rinse all this gem powder off the food before it sets!"

Her freckled nose snuffling, Enid creased her pretty brows into a frown. "Wait! There's something here!" The cat-woman peered suspiciously at the chimney. "Something's up the chimney."

"It's just a stirge. Don't worry. I blocked the chimney with a metal grate." Escalla, still resplendent in a pair of little towels, popped into the room. "Come on. Let's clean off this fried rabbit or whatever it is, then we can beat Polk with a stick!"

Reluctantly Enid filled a bucket from Jus's bath then turned to go. With a last look behind her, she padded back to the taproom to join her dinner and her friends.

2

Morning stole over the old, bleached giants' bones and crept cat-footed through the tavern windows. Ashes cracked in the tavern fireplace. Huge and fuzzy, Enid slept beside the fire, flexing her huge talons in a feline dream. Polk snored like a sawmill, curled protectively about a big stone whiskey jug and muttering occasionally in his sleep.

The Justicar opened his eyes slowly, carefully searching out the room. Curled against his ribs and bundled in an old beaver skin, Escalla slept happily. She made little chipmunk noises, unwilling to keep quiet even in her sleep. Propped above them on the back of a chair, Cinders grinned his crocodile grin, keeping watch over the room. All seemed quiet. All seemed still.

Something was wrong.

Cinders's ears stiffened. In perfect rapport, Jus and the hell hound listened to the air currents in the quiet room. Jus could sense no movement, no presence hovering in the room. Cinders had given no warning of illusions, invisible creatures, mysterious scents or noises, yet—

There was a sudden sense of movement. In a blur, the Justicar's sword hissed through the air above Escalla. The black steel clove emptiness, and the room seemed still once more.

"Cinders?" Sitting in bed, his huge sword gleaming in his hand, the Justicar breathed slowly as he sensed something strange in the air.

The hell hound sniffed at the air, his red eyes gleaming dangerously.

Magic!

"Where?"

Gone.

Jus rose and began jamming on his clothes. Beside him, Escalla rolled into the warm space of his abandoned bed. Jus slid into his black armor, the straps simple, well tended, and efficient.

"You were asleep?"

Cinders snooze. The hell hound cautiously searched the room, seeming annoyed at himself for sleeping. *Magic soft. Didn't smell.*

"That's all right."

It might have been a scrying spell. Certainly there was no physical presence. No creature mortal, immortal, or undead could sneak past Cinders. Jus buckled his helmet into place, swept the pelt about his shoulders, and settled the hell hound's head atop his helmet.

The big man nudged at Escalla with his foot and whispered, "Escalla?"

"No one wears underwear with these, Dad! I swear!" The little faerie sat upright, a look of blank wonderment upon her face.

With his attention on the windows, Jus moved carefully over to one wall. "Escalla, there's something spying on us. I'm going to investigate. Wake the others and stay alert."

Silent and grim, he went hunting.

"Yeah," replied Escalla sleepily. Her eyes were wide open as she sat in her bed of beaver fur. Jus gave her a glance, nodded as he saw her awake and alert, then slipped stealthily into the dawn like a wolf upon the prowl.

Behind him, Escalla stayed upright in bed, eyes staring blankly at the wall.

". . . but if it was orange, how would they put wheels on it?" The faerie fell backward, continuing her rather strange little dream. At her side, a fresh bouquet of flowers suddenly gleamed in the light— delicate champagne roses, still frosted with dew.

Escalla turned over in her bed and breathed the scent of roses. Tucked into a ball, the little faerie smiled and hugged her pillow in her sleep.

❖   ❖   ❖   ❖   ❖

In the cold light of dawn, a soft mist filled the village streets as sunlight warmed the night's dew. Even the old gray thatch on cottage roofs seethed with steam as the warmth of morning set in.

The Justicar stalked carefully, scanning for the slightest marks upon the silver frost. He walked only in the lee of the buildings where the dew lay thin and unfrozen. He kept low, moving as stealthily as a rustle in the breeze.

To the north, somewhere along the old weed-grown road, smoke was rising slowly in the dawn—light, clean smoke, probably kitchen fires. Jus filed the information in his head, never once ceasing his careful search of the ruined village. Pausing at the huge skull of a long-dead giant, Jus watched the empty streets.

Magic. Cinders let the air run across his nose, his ears pricked up into wicked points as he searched for signs of life. *On the roof, one house to left. More magic—house roof on right.*

The grass outside the tavern dripped. Something had brushed the frost and set it melting. The Justicar knelt, scanned the roofs above, then carefully examined the grass.

One shutter had been opened—just a tiny slit scarcely large enough to admit a cat. Caught on the wooden shutter, a thin silken thread drifted in the breeze. Blue and almost metallic in color, the tiny thread now hung like a microscopic banner. Jus left it where it lay, narrowed his eyes, then faded behind a stand of dead, dry weeds.

On the rooftops above, nothing moved, but he could feel something there. Traveling with Escalla had taught him the knack of seeing the faint ripples where an invisible creature passed. On the thatching, the neat array of straw wavered slightly as an unseen creature shifted its stance.

It could not help but have seen him. Jus deliberately rose, passed his gaze across the rooftops as though seeing nothing, then went walking slowly down the open street. Above his helmet, Cinders grinned a gleeful, manic grin. The two partners moved quietly down the street. Obligingly, the attack came from the roof just above.

A blinding light stabbed downward. The Justicar whirled, put his back to the blast, and hunched as a fireball exploded all about him. Cinders's black fur took the heat of the blast.

The Justicar was already on the attack. Burned and streaming flames, the Justicar leaped through the dissipating fire, his black sword already clearing its scabbard. Cinders's head swung, and a vicious column of flame shot from the hell hound's jaws to blast the rooftops above.

Something screamed, and suddenly a shape materialized. The tiny blue figure staggered, beating at itself. It shifted shape, changing even as it dropped out of view.

Leaping across broken roofs, the blue-clad figure seemed nearly human, but it was only two feet tall and sported a pixie's wings. Long black hair streamed in the wind as the creature landed on its perch and turned a look of hatred at the Justicar. The creature wore a cloak that had been sliced almost in half—a cut long and precise. Scorched blue threads trailed from the damaged cloth.

Cinders fired again before the creature could finish the spell half woven on its lips. It dodged aside, taking a painful blast of fire. The creature turned invisible and fled, speeding so swiftly through the leaves that twigs shattered as it passed.

Thatching gave a single tiny crack. Jus dived through a cottage window, just as a spell thundered down from another roof farther along the street. The second visitor had opened fire, missing Jus but collapsing an entire row of houses. The assassin leaped from roof to roof, invisible and fast, then sped over to the rubble. Mud and wattle steamed. Thatch burned. Hissing, the assassin pounced upon a rooftop and tried to catch sight of its prey.

A black sword blade erupted through the thatch, ripping a line of blood from the invisible assassin. The creature screamed a feminine scream, rolling aside as the black blade stabbed through the roof again.

The Justicar burst upward through the straw, roaring like a mad god as he ploughed the black blade through empty air, trying to cut his invisible assailant down. Visible at last, the assassin briefly took the form of a pixie and then suddenly became a spider with butterfly wings. The winged arachnid managed to tumble sideways and stab out a spell that filled the street with shards of flying ice. The Justicar disappeared in the hissing torrent of razor-sharp frost, and a triumphant laugh rang out. Seeing its spell strike home, the intruder hovered and laughed viciously, peering through the ice clouds and looking for its victim's corpse.

Streaming blood, the Justicar flung himself upward from the ice cloud, scything his black sword downward at his enemy. The spider-creature screamed and tried to leap aside. The sword tip narrowly scored a cut across its back, springing blood into the air. The spider-creature sped aside, landed on a roof ridge, and cocked back its limbs to summon energy for another savage spell.

"Jus!"

The entire house the creature stood upon exploded. Hovering outside the tavern clutching her beaver skins about her shoulders, Escalla snarled and blasted energy into the distant hut. Her enemy dodged, spider eyes wide. Blinded by the power discharge, Escalla ripped her spell sideways in pursuit of her unseen enemy, gouging stones from walls and sending thatched roofs tumbling in a cloud of straw.

As the flying spider fled into the ruined cottages, a swarm of little golden bees sped out from Escalla's hands. The magic insects swirled in a mad shield all about the Justicar. As a lightning bolt stabbed out from a ruined house nearby, the bee swarm darted and swatted the energies aside. Escalla snarled in glee as she saw a dark shape run flitting through the weeds.

"Hey, spider! Suck on this!"

Escalla slammed her hands toward the ground, and a savage ripple tore the earth toward her enemy. Black tentacles writhed upward from the street, lunging for prey.

With a curse, Escalla's enemy dived through a garden archway. Light flashed, and the assassin disappeared. The hungry tentacles slammed against the archway and tore it to shreds in a petulant burst of anger.

Stones cascaded to the street. Maddened tentacles thrashed. Clutching a bleeding shoulder, the Justicar hunched in the street, his face savage, golden bees still weaving about him in a dancing shield. Magic flashed as he shoved a healing spell into his shoulder, then another into his left hand. Burns and wounds closed over. Ignoring the hurt, the big man straightened and looked toward the thrashing tentacles.

"Thank you."

The dancing bees faded and disappeared. Escalla settled down to land upon Jus's unwounded shoulder, pulling her beaver pelt about her naked skin.

"What was that?"

"Spies." Jus lifted his sword. The tip showed a brief sheen of blood to which a fine metallic blue thread adhered. "There were two of them, shapeshifters."

"Shapeshifters?" Escalla carefully lifted her hand and spellfire shone. She coldly and efficiently scanned the village. "Nothing. They've gone now."

Jus examined his black scale armor where an ice bolt had punched a ragged hole through the shoulder and into the flesh beneath.

"Small. Magic using. One of them looked like you."

"Like me?"

Dismissing it with a quirk of her brow, the faerie gave a superior little smile. "That's *really* unlikely."

"Small humanoid. Wings."

Escalla turned to take a sharp look at where her foe had disappeared. She stared for a moment in puzzlement, then shrugged and dismissed the whole idea.

"If it was a shapeshifter, then it could be anything." The girl shivered in the cold and tugged her beaver skin tight. "Are you all right?"

"It will pass. It's only pain."

"J-man, did I ever tell you that you're my hero?" Escalla ruffled Cinders's fur, patting both of her friends on the head. "Let's get indoors. I forgot my wand."

"And your clothes."

"Hey, man! I just woke up!" The girl opened her hands in protest then made a grab for her beaver skin. "I rescued you!"

"So you didn't rouse the others as I told you?"

"Sure I did!" Escalla rolled her eyes. "They all fell back to sleep. You know those guys—not a dedicated bone in their bodies."

"Right."

The Justicar took a careful look at the weeds, frost, and buildings. Hell hound flame, magic spells, and tentacles had combined to obliterate any hope of tracks and evidence.

"Cinders, anything still here?"

Gone. All gone. The hell hound watched a cottage roof burn and happily wagged his tail. *Burn bad guy! Funny!*

Jus reached up to pat the hell hound and said, "Good boy. You just keep burning them."

The threesome trudged back up the street, Jus stepping over the ruins left by Escalla's tentacle spell. The big man looked at the spell's remnants and gave a grunt. "Good spell."

"You like it?" Escalla preened. She sidled closer, waggling her brows. "Hey, Jus! I finished reading that spellbook."

"And?"

"We got *stoneskin.*"

"Stoneskin?"

"A spell! Oh, it's hotter than a volcano. This one you're going to love!" Escalla rubbed her hands together. "I just need a teeny eeny little ingredient or two. You reckon we can find some diamond dust anywhere?"

The Justicar looked at the girl and said, "We have exactly eleven gold pieces left."

"Ack." Escalla crossed her legs as she sat on Jus's shoulder. "Well if you see any diamonds, give me a yell."

"We will not steal diamonds."

"Steal?" Planting her hands at her breast, Escalla goggled at the mere thought. "Would I steal?"

"Yes."

"What!" Escalla puffed up, feeling her honor impugned but lacking evidence or moral ground to stand on. "For your information, when faerie girls take something, it's loveable! It's not stealing!"

"No diamonds."

"Well, unowned ones then! You know they grow in the ground somewhere."

Escalla, Jus, and Cinders stared once again across the quiet roofs.

The faerie drew her brows into a frown. "Shapeshifters, huh? We must have pissed someone off mightily."

"Someone has plans we must be interfering with." Jus flexed his hands. "Be careful."

✳   ✳   ✳   ✳   ✳

Outside the tavern, the open street offered the best view of the surrounding land. Smoothing Polk's map under his hands, the Justicar looked thoughtfully at his painted lines and squiggles. The map was hopelessly inaccurate. The party's position could be virtually anywhere dozens of miles from where he imagined them to be.

To the southeast lay the sea. To the west lay a ruined castle in which Escalla's hydra had made its lair. Northward, many hundreds of miles away, lay Furyondy and Hommlet. Keoland was a broad kingdom. The forest supposedly served as its southern border, although the map seemed to be made mostly from wishful thinking and pure guesswork.

The road through the village seemed old and abandoned, yet perhaps it led to another settlement where they could find directions and purchase food. The smoke he had seen earlier in the morning seemed to suggest that there was some sort of settlement nearby. Jus amassed his information swiftly and methodically, while behind him ash cakes baked in the tavern's hearth for breakfast.

Blowing through his scraggly moustache, Polk watched disapprovingly from afar. He finally marched out of the tavern and took position behind the Justicar's map.

Jus folded the map without bothering to look up. "Polk, shut up."

"What are you readin' for, son? You're addled! Touched in the skull!" Polk squared his silly hat upon his head. "This is a time for action, boy! A time for sword and blades and magic!" Polk stamped in impatience at a student who seemed to be eternally dim. "Never mind the maps. Let instinct be our guide!"

"Polk, you have *personally* managed to put us at least three hundred miles off course." The Justicar's voice rumbled in an ursine growl. "Let me tell you just how much I respect your instincts."

Cinders lay spread across the table, his shark-toothed grin gleaming with a piece of coal between his jaws. The Justicar borrowed a coal flake to draw on the map.

"May I?"

Welcome!

"Polk!" Jus drew a circle around the supposed location of distant Hommlet. "We have just been attacked by something that seemed really annoyed." The ranger tapped a finger on the map, guessing at the possible flow of local rivers. "I'm in favor of moving very carefully and fairly swiftly, looking for inhabited villages and keeping our heads down while we see who might want us dead."

Enid had found a tall stone tower at the edge of the village. On tables dragged from a dozen houses, she had begun laying out scrolls, riddles, books, and parchments found on an eventful journey from Trigol. More loot from the ruined castle's library gave her even more toys to play with. Plain and sweetly curious, she was reading through her books and thoroughly enjoying herself. She looked over the edge of a scorched volume, raised her brows, and said, "Aren't we staying here, then? I was so looking forward to catching up on a book or two!"

"Someone apparently doesn't want us to stay."

Jus stored the map, patted Cinders, and then cocked one brow as a strange noise came drifting from the tavern door.

Light-hearted, happy singing astounded one and all. It came pure and sweet, a girlish voice without a trouble in the world.

Through a window, Escalla could be seen hovering in mid air. She had fixed her hair and wore a beautiful silk costume bought in Trigol. She primped herself happily in a mirror, then turned a little pirouette.

The faerie drifted lightly out into the morning air, twirling merrily as she came. On seeing Jus she paused, made a knowing little smile, and then hovered at his shoulder with her head tilted to one side. She smiled secretly at him for a moment. Finally, to everyone's shock, Escalla kissed him on the ear and said, "You're *most* welcome."

Jus stared in wonderment. The faerie hovered, looking at him with a strangely satisfied smile, and then fluttered back into the tavern.

Cinders's red eyes gleamed. *Faerie give a kiss! Faerie give a kiss!*

Jus's ear tingled. He actually turned a strange shade of reddish pink. Polk joined him in staring at the tavern door. The teamster cleared his throat into the silence.

"Spring?"

Enid blinked and said, "Autumn's only just begun."

"Maybe faeries get it early?"

"Oh, dear."

Jus wonderingly touched his ear—still red hot from Escalla's kiss. He blinked, shook himself, then swept his maps efficiently underneath his arm.

"All right! Let's get fed. There's smoke about three miles to the north. We'll leave in ten minutes, head north, and investigate. Enid, if you want to organize your books, you might want to stay here while we go to town and fly after us in a"—Jus sniffed at a strange odor—"in . . . in a . . ."

Something was frying, possibly bacon, possibly honey. A sickeningly sweet stench redolent of dental cavities coiled about the village roofs. A pan banged noisily from the tavern room, and Escalla's voice pealed into the street.

"Breakfast! Come on, adventurers! Get it while it's hot!"

Enid and Polk uneasily looked at one another. The sphinx looked a little pale as she said, "Escalla cooked?"

"She cooked." Polk bit his lip in trepidation "Well, ah, she is a girl. I kinda guess all girls can cook."

Escalla had a metabolism like a hummingbird. Her concept of a happy breakfast had enough sugar in it to turn grown men into gibbering loons.

Jus gave a sigh and tightened up his sword belt. "This could be interesting."

Enid blinked and said, "I wouldn't miss it for the world."

Inside the tavern, Escalla had laid out a dented old serving platter full of food. She hovered above the table, pleased as a cat swimming in cream, and very ostentatiously primped a vase of champagne roses at the center of the table.

"There was honey in a pot in the pantry, and we still had sugar, so I made cakes and bacon!" Breakfast gleamed beneath a sweet glaze of sugar crystals. "Eat hearty!"

Everyone stared at Escalla's creation, which sat there gleaming under an ocean of syrup. The faerie personally made sure that everybody had a helping. She put extra syrup on her own plate, dipped waybread into the mixture and crammed it straight into her mouth.

" 's good! Try shome!"

With painfully polite expressions, the faerie's companions all tried the meal one by one. It had a jolt like an electric eel. Everyone made a great show of swallowing and nodding, making Escalla beam.

The faerie had brewed tea in a big rusty kettle she found in a cupboard. The resulting brew was colored half by rust and half by tea leaves. She happily poured the mixture into tin mugs for one and all. Polk sniffed at it, looked at the Justicar with the eyes of a man who had just been handed hemlock, and watched Escalla as she went about her chores.

"Aren't you drinkin' any, girl?"

"Oh no. Tea makes me hyper!"

Sitting beside her bouquet of roses, Escalla sat on her hands and happily watched Jus as he ate. In his time, the man had been stabbed, cut, burned, bashed, bitten, clawed, and gnawed upon, so this seemed comparatively mild torture. He stoically drank the tea and ate the food, consuming it slowly and carefully without batting an eye.

Escalla primped the roses again, looking about and hoping that everyone noticed the flowers. She then came whirring over to land at Jus's side. She looked at him with a wry fondness and then chucked him on the chin.

"Jus, about the rescue thing . . . that's . . . that's just so sweet. You never thanked me like that before."

Jus frowned, wondering why women had to fix upon the most strange little things.

"I've thanked you before."

"Yeah, but you never made it so obvious you meant it!" The faerie giggled then chucked him on the chin again. "Well you didn't have to go to all that trouble."

Jus bit his lip. All he'd said was thank you. He wondered how she would act if he'd given it to her in writing. With a shrug, Jus turned back to his tea, managing to ignore the strange deposits floating on the top.

Escalla leaned forward and lowered her voice so that only he could hear. "Ah, Jus, I'm aware that I sometimes cause a few . . . *difficulties*, so I'm going to try and think a little more about how you feel from now on. I promise." She crossed her sleek cleavage with a finger. "Partners?"

Jus looked at her, fond but puzzled. He held up his finger so that the faerie could clasp it in her hands. "Partners."

She seemed relieved to be free of the burden of true confessions. Escalla slung her ice wand over her shoulder, dragged her collection of scrolls and spell lists over to Jus's backpack and stuffed them inside. Her roses were carefully taken outside, where Polk helpfully installed the vase upright between the blanket bundles. Escalla tidied the blooms, clapped her hands and rubbed them together, and seemed eager for another challenging day.

"Right! So we're off to look for locals. Should I go invisible and take the point?"

"No need yet. Just stay close." Jus intended to walk into town in as non-threatening a manner as possible. "Enid, are you staying here?"

"I think I might. There are ever so many books to organize." The sphinx padded over from her work tables with a little rolled papyrus in a tube. She dropped it into Escalla's lap. "Here. Stun symbol. My last until we get more gems. Sorry that it smells of squirrel!"

Escalla blinked. "Squirrel?"

"She means rabbit." Jus had already hidden all evidence of last night's feast. "Enid, be careful. Follow the road to catch up."

"Have fun in town!" The sphinx waved goodbye as Polk's wagon rumbled off down the trail. Enid's freckles shone like stars as she smiled. "I might find you a stirge for dinner!"

* * * * *

Three hours later, the Justicar lay against a tree trunk carefully surveying a crumbling pile of stones. A fountain poured sweet water into a broken moss covered font. A chapel lay half crushed beneath the weight of a fallen tree. With Cinders on his back, Jus lay hidden in the shadows carefully testing the area for any hint of danger. The hell hound's red eyes gleamed as he thoughtfully sniffed the air.

Magic. Very recent.

"Same scent as this morning?"

Same type. Fancy. Cinders sniffed the air. *Gone now.*

Leaves shifted as the Justicar came out of cover. Stealth had long served as his deadliest weapon. Moving to circle the fountain, he scanned carefully for tracks.

A tiny scuff marked the fountain's moss. The moss oozed water. Jus touched it with his fingertips and thoughtfully sniffed before raising his hand up to Cinders's nose.

The hell hound thoughtfully savored the air. *Elfie-faerie-pixie smell.*

A patch of empty space over the far side of the clearing shimmered as it dropped down through the trees.

"Hey, guys! You see anything?"

"Nothing." Jus shrugged. "Yet."

"Hoopy!" Escalla popped into view in midair.

At a loud summons from Jus, Polk's wagon came rumbling down

the road. Now mostly empty, Polk insisted on dragging the vehicle behind the party in the hope of filling it to the brim with jewels and gold. While the vehicle arrived, Jus spread out his maps at the rim of the fountain and rubbed at the harsh stubble on his chin.

"All right, according to the milestone, this is Agnes's Fountain. The map puts that just at the north end of the Dreadwood." He folded the map away, then uncorked his drinking flask and took a swig of beer. "That smoke we saw is about half a mile away. Escalla?"

Jus held out his beer flask and swirled it, expecting the girl to take her share. After a minute he frowned and looked at the flask.

No Escalla.

The faerie stood on the fountain's edge with her hands clasped behind her back, her head tilted and her face in a knowing smile. She walked artlessly on tip toes, making a pair of prancing little steps towards the Justicar.

"Oh Ju-uus!" Escalla's voice slyly sung. "Look what I just *happened* to find over by the fountain!" The girl held out a small package all tied up with ribbons and waved it in the air. "A box of sweets."

Puzzled, the Justicar and Cinders recoiled. The hell hound sniffed suspiciously at the package, stiffened his ears, and wagged his tail.

Sweeties!

Escalla waggled the box slyly in mid air. "Aren't I the lucky one? Let's share them, shall we?"

Throwing his mule's reins aside, Polk landed beside the fountain with a thump. "Sweets!" The man instantly took one from the packet. "Best Tegel toffee!"

The faerie shrugged gaily and said, "I just found them. Guess we might as well share!"

Jus raised a brow as he inspected the package. "It was just lying there?"

"Of course it was! How strange it should be right there where I could find it." Escalla shot a sly, amused look at Jus. "I'm beginning to feel a little spoiled. Or a little pampered."

Jus took a morsel and let Cinders sample it. The hell hound

smelled no poison or magic in the sweets or on the box. Walking aside to suck on one of the morsels and puzzle over events, Jus found himself pacing back and forth beside the ruined chapel.

"Cinders, did you see a box there when we arrived?"

No box! The hell hound grinned his manic grin. *Maybe faerie keep as present. Give to friends for treat!*

"Yeah." Jus rubbed at his bristly scalp. Why was she being so full of gifts and song today? If she'd bought treats all the way back at the last town, why save them for this exact moment? Was she planning something? Had she screwed up again?

Jus paused.

Was she going to leave?

The thought caused an instant hollow pit in Jus's stomach. He turned, but there sat Escalla, laughing with Polk. Irritably jerking his usual grim persona back into place, Jus marched back to his companions and stood with them by the fountain.

"Right. We found sweets."

Escalla tilted her head to look at him out of the corner of her eye. "Right."

"So it's just lucky." Jus kept his eyes on the forest. "There's no reason to read anything into it at all."

The faerie steepled sticky fingertips. "Yep. Quite right." She bit her bottom lip and peered across her shoulder at the Justicar. "Unless someone wanted to say something special?"

Jus folded his arms. "No."

"Fine!" Escalla twiddled her wings. "Fine. Guess there's nothing to say."

"Nothing."

"Good."

Polk was busily stuffing sticky sweets into his pocket for later. "I've got something to say!"

"Shh!" Escalla shot the little man a glance. "Silence is golden."

Grandly dusting herself off, Escalla drifted up into the air. She bowed, ushering Polk, Jus, and Cinders onward, slipping the uneaten treats into the back of the wagon for later use.

Taking the lead, Jus marched on down the trail, his brows drawn into a heavy frown. He looked back across his shoulder and saw Escalla riding between the ears of the wagon mule. She slyly waved her fingertips at him and gave a very knowing smile.

Annoyed, Jus hunched forward and kept his eyes searching for trouble on the road. Above his helm, Cinders contented himself with making sucking sounds and mumbling a strange little tune into the ether.

Jus cocked an eye toward the dog. *"You're eating one?"*

Scorched almond.

"It figures."

3

A shabby assortment of heaped stones masquerading as a town sprawled across the forest path. A substantial settlement had apparently been razed to the ground and then rebuilt by people big on enthusiasm but small on engineering skills. There were hundreds of shabby tents and lean-tos in the shelter of the older ruins. The sign outside the village had been painted upon an old, scarred shield. It read: SOUR PATCH. GOOD FOOD AND LICKER.

The village had been cobbled together out of rotten canvas and old scrap. Bark huts half tumbled into open sewers, and hundreds of dispirited peasants shuffled down the dirty streets. More and more people were arriving, all of them ashen, dressed in rags, and carrying everything they owned upon their backs. Long lines formed at wagons that were dispensing bread and gruel. Children were crying, and the air stank of human misery.

The streets seemed overcrowded with the hungry and the poor. A gibbet hung empty at the center of the village, attended by two guards with rusted armor and faces redolent of brutal stupidity.

As the Justicar stood looking at the squalid, crowded camp, a figure bowed down with wood trudged close nearby. Dropping his load, the newcomer looked from Jus to the village and back again.

"Don't go, friend!"

Jus looked at him and asked, "Where?"

"Sour Patch." The woodcutter had a donkey, and the donkey carried a hundredweight in fresh cut wood. "Bad luck. Don't stop. Turn back."

"And go into the woods?"

"No. Turn back to Keoland!" The woodcutter gave Jus a sharp look of panic. "You mean you came through the *woods?*"

"From the coast."

"Friend, you're mad." The man worked solidly to make a pile of timbers. "I'm here because the baron paid me. He paid me because the king paid him. We're running supplies here to the refugees. If they're fool enough to settle here, then they have to have a chance."

Standing and carefully looking over the crowded shantytown, Jus fingered his sword. "Refugees from what?"

"Raids. Something's been clearing out all the villages in the river valley, sweeping them clean. No one left. No warning. No trail. It's like the gods just up and took 'em." The woodcutter finished his work and wrenched his donkey around. "Everyone's fled the valleys. Some merchants offered free land to refugees, but no one thought to ask 'em where the land might be. But the Dreadwood. . . !" The man looked at the forest and shook his head. "Even the valley's better than that! Only a fool goes near the Dreadwood."

He made to leave. Jus extended one big hand and held the donkey's bridle. "What's wrong with the Dreadwood?"

"Cursed. Bad luck. Was never meant for mortal man. It's a haunted wood. People see things in there. People disappear." Agitated, the woodcutter looked in fear at the trees. "Five, six years ago, giants wiped out all the villages, killed everything that moved! Now it's happening again, you mark my words! Bad luck in the Dreadwood." The man wrenched his donkey free from the ranger's grasp. "Bad luck!"

The woodcutter left, fleeing down the road at the best speed his little donkey could manage. Emerging from her hiding place in Polk's cart, Escalla rubbed thoughtfully at her little freckled nose as she watched the woodcutter depart.

"What was *he* drinking?"

"I don't know." Jus hitched his belt. "Someone's running this camp as a scam, maybe trying to repopulate some junk land. Keep a lookout for trouble."

Half-orcs and slovenly humans kept watch over the refugees. The guards ate meat and drank wine while refugees lined up for stale bread. Jus took one look at the village and seemed to swell with predatory energy.

"Cinders?"

Magic. Cinders's fur lay low, and his fangs shone evilly. *Old food. Raw hides. Smelly stuff. Hot iron. Half-orcs. Bugbears. Ogre-stink. And elfie-pixie.*

"Elves?" The Justicar used his thumb to loosen his sword in its sheath. "Keep your eyes open. There's work to do."

Choosing invisibility as her best option for sneakiness, Escalla hovered in the air nearby. "Keoland looks like a good place to be well away from. What's that awful smell?"

Jus shrugged. "Half-orcs, ogres, bugbears, raw hides, hot iron, an open sewer, and some elves or pixies."

"Elves?"

"That's what Cinders says."

The Justicar felt the faerie giving a happy shrug.

"Hoopy! Well, he should know." The girl's wings buzzed. "Any idea where we look to find our shapeshifting spies from this morning?"

"If they're here, we can find them." Huge and brooding, Jus scanned the streets. "Stay invisible. You can rest in the backpack if you need to." Jus settled the hell hound into place upon his helm. "Are you all right, Cinders?"

Burn! Burn!

"Later. Don't annoy the locals until we have to."

Jus turned around, but Polk's wagon already stood abandoned at the edge of the road. Moving at an astonishing rate, Polk had already mounted the steps of a rubble pile that masqueraded as the local tavern. Ignoring the sounds of a fight from inside, Polk tightened his belt, slapped his hands together, and rubbed his palms in glee.

Jus gave a heavy ursine growl. "Polk!"

The teamster turned, incredulous that the others were not following him to the tavern. "Son, it's a tavern!"

"Polk, we are not here to drink!"

"But it's a den of iniquity, boy!" Appalled, Polk waved his hands in the air like a maddened bird. "We can't just pass it by! Dens of iniquity are part of being a hero! Here's where you defend a maid, find a clue, buy a treasure map, start a brawl. . . ! Think of the possibilities!"

"Polk, the only adventures that ever start in taverns are usually ones that involve puking or collecting genital lice." Jus tied the wagon in place and took a long, hard look at passers by, making sure they knew that he would remember their faces. Glowered at by a six foot tall man wearing a hell hound skin, most pedestrians elected to walk hurriedly away. "We are going in for one drink while we skim for information." Jus sniffed the scent of roasting meat and gave a prim lift of his chin. "And perhaps a bite of something savory."

"And then a fight?"

"One fight per day is enough."

Jus shouldered his way in through a door made from an old blanket. As he passed, Polk gave an unhappy sigh. "That boy has no idea of how to be a hero. It just ain't in him."

Escalla's voice laughed from empty air. "He gets the job done."

"I tell him again and again! It ain't *what* you do, it's *how*." Polk swept the blanket aside to allow Escalla to pass. "You know, it's high time that boy took a grip on his responsibilities!"

✤ ✤ ✤ ✤ ✤

The Sour Patch tavern sold only two types of food: raw and burned. The beer smelled like old laundry, but Polk drank it nonetheless. Escalla contented herself with lounging inside the Justicar's backpack as it sat beneath the table. The ranger's wineskin had yielded a last few drops of decent beer, and there were still sweets aplenty. The girl reclined with her little feet crossed and her arms behind her head, thinking sly, warm little thoughts as she watched the Justicar.

Jus loomed at the bar, shaking down the locals for information. This was where the guards lived and drank. Teamsters bringing food to the shantytown and sharks keen to fleece refugees of their cash all came here to spend their coin. The crowd was loud, the room smoky, and the jokes were rich with filth.

A half-orc seemed to be giving Jus trouble—probably not the best choice the half-orc had made in his career. The Justicar's patience was remarkable but would eventually wear thin. Enjoying the interval between the disappearance of rational, talkative Jus and the appearance of wrath-of-the-gods Jus, Escalla smiled.

The ranger had an endearing habit of tugging his grim persona about himself like a cloak. He enjoyed it like an actor living for a good role in a play, but from time to time, Jus could be persuaded to drop the façade, and then a rather interesting man began to emerge. Escalla had rolled onto her belly amidst the warm depths of the backpack, when quite suddenly a hand began groping at her rear.

Escalla jerked away, whirled about, and scowled.

A hand had snuck into the backpack. The hand was attached to an arm, and the arm had somehow ended up affixed to a pimple-smothered thief with protruding teeth. The thief groped about in the backpack, looking for anything valuable, and kept himself hidden under the table.

Escalla gave an amused little smile. She watched the groping hand, cracked her knuckles loudly, and then went to work.

Working carefully and with his eyes peering under the table toward the Justicar, the thief frowned as something touched his wrist and then jerked tight. He scowled, looked down at the backpack, then almost expired as he saw that the bag now had evil eyes and horribly sharp teeth.

With a noise like a whip crack, a long, rough, rope-like tongue wrapped around his arm, holding it in place. Talking with its mouth full, the bag gave an evil little roar. "Me magic bag of gnawing! Now me feed! Feed good!"

Serrated fangs gleamed, the thief screamed, and quite suddenly a flash of magic sparkled in the air. With a bang, a weasel appeared beside the terrified thief. The weasel wrung its paws and pranced in concern.

"Don't move! One wrong twitch and *pow!* It'll rip your arm off!" The weasel moved to hastily survey the thief's arm. "It's all right. I'm the magic wishing weasel. I've got the bag held in a spell. Don't make any sudden moves, and you might get out of this alive."

Pale with fright, the thief held his arm rigid, the bag's tongue holding him trapped. He stared at the backpack's fangs in fright. "M-magic wishing weasel?"

"Well, you wished for a way out of this, right?" The weasel opened up its front paws. "So what are you complaining about? I happened to be passing, so I'm on the job . . . unless you want me to go?" The weasel snapped its fingers, and instantly the backpack roared and yanked the thief's arm deeper into its maw.

The thief gave a pathetic bleat of fright. "No! Stay! Just get it off me! Get it off!"

"Sure! Fine!" The weasel clicked its fingers again, and the snarling backpack subsided. The magic wishing weasel leaped onto the thief's frozen arm and inspected the backpack's hairy tongue.

"Hmm. All right. Simple to fix. You've got one hand free, right?"

"You want me to cut the bag?" The thief groped hastily for a knife. "Fine!"

"No!" The weasel hurriedly waved its paws. "You'll enrage it! No, in a case like this, you have to make use of natural strategy."

"Natural strategy?"

"Trust me, kid. I'm a weasel."

Traveling in a sinuous round-about route, the weasel ended up upon the thief's shoulder. It tapped its paws together and gave a brief flip of its tail.

"All right, kid. We have to make nature work *for* you, not *against* you."

The bag shifted its grip, trembling as if about to break its restraining spell, and the thief swallowed in fright. "Magic weasel, help me!"

"All right, kid, now listen." The weasel looked down at the thief's bulging purse then stood aside. "I've got it held for a while. To escape the bag, you have to trigger its gag reflex, but not by putting a hand or a tool in there! Oh no. That thing senses anything big in there, and it'll rip your arm right outta its socket!" Drawing a brief sketch in the dust, the weasel chattered on. "There's one patch at the back of its throat that can trigger the gag reflex. You have to hit it with something heavy—something small, dense, and solid—to make it spit out your arm."

The thief immediately threw an empty beer stein into the backpack. The magic weasel gave a tired sigh. "No. Something *small* and heavy. Very small, very dense." The weasel rapped on the thief's head. "You understand dense, yeah?"

"What?"

"Nothing. You want brains, don't come to the Flanaess." Sketching out a diagram in midair, the weasel tried to educate the thief. "Look. There's a little tiny slot at the bottom of the bag. All you do is drop little heavy things in there in the hope they'll go through the slot. Little flat heavy things—small, flat, round, heavy things."

The thief blinked cluelessly, and the weasel gave a snarl. "Look! Just drop coins into the bag, or it'll nibble your knuckles off!"

Fumbling in haste, the thief grabbed for his purse, undid the drawstrings with his teeth, and sent a tumble of gold coins spilling down into the backpack's toothy mouth. The carnivorous backpack scowled, mumbled, then suddenly gave a great cough. Feeling his arm held in a briefly loosened grip, the thief jerked his hand free. He immediately threw himself as far away from the backpack as possible.

Frustrated, the backpack gnashed its fangs and grumbled. Meanwhile, the wishing weasel slapped the panting thief on the back in congratulations.

"There you are! Free as a bird!" Grinning, the weasel began to prod the thief out from under the table. "Now go on. Scram! Off you go. Borrow some money, have a drink to celebrate, and maybe consider a change in career."

Pale with fright, the thief still had eyes only for the gnashing backpack.

"Th-thank you, magic wishing weasel!" The man withdrew into the tavern light. "How can I repay you?"

"All in a day's work, kid! No need to thank me. Just naff off!" The weasel suddenly bit its lip and scuttled closer. "But if anyone was to ask—say, just for argument's sake, if a really big shaven headed guy in black armor wearing a hell hound skin—if a guy like *that* asked what happened to your money, you'd say that you *chose* to put it in the backpack, right?"

The thief rubbed his bruised wrist in fright and said, "Right!"

"Great, kid. Now scram!" The weasel crept onto the table beside an incredulous Polk. "Nice kid, but a brain the size of a peppercorn."

Polk looked at Escalla the weasel in confusion and asked, "Was that boy a thief?"

"Nah. He came to make a donation. I think we must have made about fifty gold pieces outta him." Escalla dropped her illusion spell from the backpack, which returned to being a plain old leather pack. The "tongue" of the beast—a disreputable length of chord—was stuffed back into the darkness of the pack. Escalla shifted back into her usual form and rummaged about inside the backpack to find her discarded clothes.

She was tugging her leggings into place when a heavy presence made itself known outside her sanctuary.

"Escalla?"

"It was an unsolicited gift!" Escalla jammed her head out of the bag to face the Justicar. "Ask him! He gave it to us on his own initiative!"

Jus squatted on his heels beside the backpack and scowled. "What?"

"Oh. Nothing." The faerie saw Jus's look of confusion and gave a nervous twiddle of her wings. "Nothing at all! Did you get any information?"

"Enough to know we don't want to eat whatever that is cooking over the fire." Jus slowly cracked the knuckles of his left fist. "This town needs justice."

"Well, I've been redressing the balance and doing my bit." Escalla finished tugging her long leggings onto her feet and wriggled her elegant bare toes. "So, are we staying or going?"

"Going." Jus tried not to breathe the tavern stink. "These are lower level predators. The disaster in the valley's giving them the chance to prey on these refugees." The man's face was a shadow beneath the jet black hell hound skin. "Kill the head, and the body has to die."

The Justicar swung the pack onto his back, and Escalla stayed inside for the ride. Above her, Cinders's tall ears stood proud. With her hands folded behind her head, Escalla wriggled on her bed of misappropriated gold and sighed.

"That's the man!"

Walking heavily through the tavern, Jus heard the excited yell from the door ahead. He stopped and saw a skinny, pimple-smothered man backed up by four huge half-orcs dressed in rusted armor. The leader of the armored brutes seemed strangely hunched and bestial. Part bugbear or part ogre, he had a skin covered in scabs.

The smaller man swelled in righteous fury and roared, "That man there! He has a carnivorous backpack! He uses it to extort people!" The thief waved his hand. "He's in league with the *Takers!* He's here to scout for the pale lady!"

The four half-orcs instantly started forward. Polk immediately took a big step to one side, carrying himself away from the Justicar as he opened up his chronicles and dug out a fresh pen. Behind him, the whole tavern crowd arose. At least twenty thugs, mercenaries, brigands, and rogues surged to their feet.

Jus walked toward the huge, misshapen figure of the senior guard. The big ranger scratched his stubbled chin and scowled. "Who's the pale lady?"

"She runs the Takers! She clears the valleys." The half-orc hissed and flexed its claws. Yelling to his men, the guard began to draw a scimitar. "They're Takers! Hang 'em!"

Jus felled the beast with a lightning fast left jab. The half-orc flew backward into his men, sending weapons flying and armor clattering.

Another soldier grabbed his comrades by the shoulder and hurled them to the floor.

"Down!"

The half-orcs threw themselves flat. Behind them stood two more bestial soldiers, each leveling a crossbow straight toward the Justicar. Fangs spread into grins as the men swung their weapons onto target.

Cinders's huge teeth gleamed.

Hello!

Flame blasted through the doorway, slamming the crossbowmen back into the street. Cinders's flames sheeted across the half-orcs on the floor. The hell hound screeched in happy bloodlust as screams filled the air.

Burn! Burn!

A sword hissed toward Jus's head. The big man ducked and landed a massive kick into the swordsman's guts, folding him in two.

Inside the tavern, men scattered aside in terror as Cinders's nostrils trailed little flames. One man hammered a spell at the Justicar, a charm spell that twisted aside from the shielding influence of the ranger's magic ring. Jus strode forward with a roar, and tavern goers scattered and fled out the back door.

Escalla popped her head out of Jus's backpack, looking toward the open street. She paused for one thoughtful moment, then opened up her hands and molded an arc of sizzling electricity between her palms. She sped the spell through the door. A lightning bolt flashed into being just outside the doorway, sizzling perpendicularly left and right. Unseen voices screamed and wailed. Escalla dusted off her hands, having eliminated an ambush party waiting just outside the doors.

Flattened against one tavern wall was the thief. The man quaked in terror as he stared at Escalla and the Justicar. He took one long look at Escalla, shook his head in absolute terror, and slid to the ground with his eyes rolling upward in a faint.

Unused to her beauty being so sadly reviled, Escalla dusted off the smoking palms of her hands and said, "Next time, just listen to your friendly neighborhood weasel!"

The tavern seemed deserted. Escalla flew out of the backpack and went to search her victims for loose change

"Are we done yet? I hate taverns like this!"

Jus shook his stinging left hand. The half-orc's jaw had felt like it had been drop-forged out of steel.

"Let's go."

"Sure. Just a bit!" Escalla surfaced from amidst a pile of smoking half-orcs. "Hey! A gold tooth! You got any pliers?"

"Escalla . . ."

"Your dagger will do in a pinch."

"Escalla!"

"Just kidding!" The faerie waved her hands in innocence. "Lighten up! We came, we saw, he toasted butt—just another typical day."

Jus snared her by the wings and dragged the girl outside.

"Let's get moving before their pale lady takes an interest." The ranger shot a look at Polk, who was taking a hasty body count. "Polk, *move.*"

Jus strode onto a street that now seemed deserted. A last few people were fleeing into their homes. Jus threw Polk into the wagon and wrenched the mule into motion, whacking the creature into a trot and running heavily alongside.

Still busy with his books, Polk totted up numbers and beamed in delight. "Not bad, son! Not bad!" Polk tried to make a note in his ledger. "I make it sixteen at least!"

Jus clung onto the mule's mane as he lumbered down the road. "Shut up and drive the cart."

Polk closed his book with a loud bang. "One punched, one kicked, six burned, and eight fried."

Escalla clung onto the sides of the cart, her hair streaming in the breeze. "And one just kinda fainted!"

"So that's *seventeen!*"

Jus looked back over his shoulder and said, "Polk, what are you doing now?"

"Keeping score! Every group of heroes has to have a score!"

4

A side trail led off the main track. Forced to slow down, the Justicar cursed the mule and cart for the thousandth time as he swung them onto the new route. Hanging back as the cart blundered onward, Jus swept the new trail with a severed branch and retreated away from the main track.

Escalla sat atop the cart counting a little pile of gold. She smiled at Jus, holding up one of her glittering trophies. The Justicar growled under his breath, swept the trail clean of cart tracks, then walked irritably along at the wagon's tail.

A mile down the track, Jus allowed the mule cart to slow to a halt. Wheezing like broken bellows, the mule staggered forward to a little stream where it stood hock-deep in water. Polk took the chance to uncork his whiskey bottle. The little man took a swig, sighed, sealed his bottle, and then sat up in his seat.

"When do we go back to town? Your ruse must have worked, boy! The soldiers will be out searchin', so now's the time to head back and face down their leader with cold, hard steel!"

Annoyed, Jus glared at the little man, half tempted to harness him next to his own mule. "Polk, we are not fighting anyone!"

"But they said they knew a pale lady! Were she good, she'd be the 'fair lady,' but 'pale lady' . . . she just *has* to be evil!"

"They thought *we* worked for her, Polk. Shut up and drink."

The glade seemed peaceful, deserted, and quiet. Little birds twittered amidst the brilliant red autumn leaves while the cups of fallen acorns shone twinkling in the sun. Water flashed and sunken leaves lined the streambed with red and gold.

The Justicar stood, feet planted wide apart, and his gaze speared Escalla. The little faerie raised one brow and pointed at herself in inquiry. Jus answered by crooking a finger in her direction.

"Escalla. A word."

Deliberately innocent, Escalla drifted into the air and kept pace with Jus as he stalked beside the stream. Already guessing virtually everything he needed to know, the Justicar turned toward Escalla.

"The tavern. . . ?"

Rubbing her hands together and looking a tad embarrassed, Escalla shook her head in wonder. "Yeah, some place, huh? Sad how some people just take an instant dislike to you for no reason at all!"

Unamused, Jus held her in place with a scowl. "You promised not to cause any more trouble."

"Aw, but it's an *endearing* kind of trouble!" Escalla made a sheepish grin, then pranced in midair in front of the Justicar. "It's lively! It's fun! You'd miss it if it wasn't there every day of your life! How's your hand, by the way?"

"Hurts."

Escalla took his hand and gave it a little faerie kiss, light as a feather and strangely warm. "Well, it was a good punch."

Jus flexed his hand and winced—then remembered that he was supposed to be cowing Escalla beneath the weight of his indignation.

"You promised no more scams! You lied to me!"

Escalla sighed miserably and suddenly seemed the heart and soul of guilt. Her long antennae wilted, and her pointed ears fell. "I'm sorry, because you know, when you think about it, when we lie, we murder the truth."

"Yes." Puffing up with righteousness, Jus gave a dire nod. "Well put. I agree."

Escalla put on her most gentle, wise, and sorrowful face. She laid one hand on the Justicar's shoulder and used her other hand to show him the glory of the trees.

"Autumn leaves falling, branches stark and withering, and within it all, the acorns send green shoots into the soil. Beautiful, aren't they?" The girl floated like a spirit of the wilds, while overhead tall oak trees soared. "Each new green shoot springs from the loam, but do you know where that loam comes from?"

Jus stood his ground and folded up his arms. "Do tell."

"It comes from the dead leaves and trees that have gone before." Escalla seemed full of an infinite, quiet motherly love as she floated amidst nature's timeless wonder. "New life springs from the death of old, and ideas are the same! Truths are just preconceptions, ideas trapped and put into a box! Sure, lies murder the truth, but when we kill truths, it allows new ideas to spring up in their place! A glorious profusion of nature. Intellectual freedom! Art and science and light and love!" The avatar of a glorious future, Escalla turned a pirouette up in the sky. "Jus, we *owe* it to future generations. They deserve that intellectual freedom! And it's all in our hands, Jus! I say we owe it to the future to lie through our teeth *right now!*"

He stopped and stood there, arms folded, and watched her patiently. Escalla hovered in front of him, coyly biting one finger.

"Not buying it?"

"Not really."

"Still . . . pretty hoopy speech, huh?"

A warrior for justice should not be amused at falsity. Jus sniffed and kept a straight face. "One of your better ones."

"Ha! Sorry, man. I drive you nuts." Escalla flipped a finger as though tipping an imaginary cap. "If you didn't love me, you'd never put up with me."

"Yeah."

Jus's face cracked into a fond smile despite itself. Suddenly Escalla met his eyes and matched his expression. The girl suddenly blushed, then paled and hastily whirred backward, thoroughly flustered. Aware that his ears were glowing an uncomfortable red, Jus cleared his throat, scowled, and turned to look along the stream.

Escalla cleared her throat and sped off to the wagon, busying herself by tidying an already neat pile of coins. Jus decided to walk along the stream and look for nonexistent tracks.

From his perch atop Jus's head, Cinders sniggered and hissed smoke. *Funny!*

Choosing not to comment, Jus tugged his armor straight and went about the serious business of being the Justicar.

* * * * *

Back at the wagon, Escalla meandered in midair like a humming-bird surveying her domain. With a sly, self-satisfied little smile, she blew a strand of hair from her eyes, pushing her long cornsilk locks behind her pointed ears. Remembering a hand mirror tucked into dark recesses of her baggage, the faerie fluttered down to pull at the satchels stored upon the cart, spilling her embarrassing collection of lingerie, old scrolls, and stale faerie cakes into the sun.

Gold sparkled amidst the bric-a-brac. Busily propping up the mirror against the baggage, Escalla flicked the gold a single annoyed glance. She stood before the mirror and turned sideways to admire her little figure, tidied her hair . . . and then frowned as the golden glimmer caught her eye once more.

There, lying amidst a colorful scatter of underwear, was a tiny little necklace on which a single clear stone shone and glittered in the sunlight. Escalla approached it, looking at it in startled disbelief. She touched it. The gold work was impossibly fine and fashioned perfectly for the scale and delicacy of a faerie.

Incredulous, Escalla lifted up the jewel and watched it sparkle. With the prettiest of little blushes, Escalla quietly put the necklace on. She admired it in awe, unable to believe just what was happening.

The gold was a dark, rich orange that showed her hair to be of a far more precious hue. The clear stone hung between her breasts and seemed to shimmer and flow with all the colors of the forest sky. It caught the green of her eyes and turned it from a sly glimmer to a shade innocent as forest grass. Escalla turned and gazed at her reflection in the mirror, looking at herself in blank astonishment.

It had been custom made for her—custom made with infinite care.

Escalla turned and looked toward Jus. The man knelt beside the stream, carefully examining fallen autumn leaves in the mud. The faerie felt something akin to a tear well in her eye, even as she swelled her breast like a puffer fish about to burst.

A blush spread from her eartips to her toes. Suddenly girlishly shy, she found herself unable to move or even speak. The necklace hung fluid and gleaming about her neck, while Jus artlessly managed to avoid watching her.

Polk corked his jug and gave a loud, satisfied sigh. He had given his astonished mule a slug of whiskey, and the poor animal now stood with its knees knocking and its eyes staring into different dimensions of space and time. Turning, Polk saw Escalla's necklace glistening about her alabaster throat.

He creased his brows and exclaimed, "Jewels!" The teamster scratched his head with a noise like sandpaper. "Is that treasure?"

"Oh, *definitely*."

Escalla floated quietly into the air, feeling a strange, numb sensation. She hovered indecisively for a long moment then tugged her skirt straight, took a deep breath, and flew over to the Justicar.

He knelt, examining a fallen maple leaf, one of untold thousands that carpeted the banks of the forest stream. This particular leaf showed a tiny mark on the moist dirt that sheened its upper surface—a mark like a tiny footprint only a few inches long. Escalla landed softly on the mold nearby, her hands behind her back and her body swinging from side to side like an embarrassed child called up before her school.

She cleared her throat. Jus contrived to carefully lever up the fallen maple leaf and examine the indentation left in the mud below. The footprint could not have been made by a creature any heavier than a modest house cat.

Escalla took a step closer, and the sheer radiance of her blush made Jus look up into her coy smile. Looking at him from the corner of her eye, Escalla held her necklace stone in her hands.

"It's, aah, a beautiful necklace."

Jus knelt in the leaves before her, and Escalla cleared her throat.

"It's slowglass. It sees everything I do and filters it out the back in a fortnight's time." She blushed a deeper shade of cherry pink. "They're called newlywed stones."

Jus bared his head, slipping Cinders down onto his shoulders and letting his unhelmeted head gleam in the light. Escalla ventured a little closer, suddenly feeling an urge to pat the velvet stubble of Jus's skull. She instead bit her lip and smiled down into the fallen leaves.

"This is just too too sweet!"

Blinking, Jus looked at her from her tight little leggings up to the roots of her hair. "The necklace suits you."

"Well, it is *gorgeous*. It's tailor made." The girl half turned away, hugging herself and casting one eye back across her shoulder. "Jus, I can't! This is, like, *really* expensive!"

Looking a little confused, Jus sat back on his heels. Muscles moved under his shirt, making Escalla's heart flutter in strange ways.

Jus scratched thoughtfully at his chin and said, "It does look expensive, but if it's what you want . . ."

"Oh, oh, I want!" Escalla whirled, paled, blushed, and hid her face behind one hand. "I mean . . . it's really appreciated. I know you think, well, that maybe I didn't understand. I just wanted you to know . . ." Escalla bit her finger, struggling her thoughts past her embarrassment. "I just wanted you to know that, well, I've been *thinking*." Her cheeks were aflame. Escalla pressed the backs of her hands against her face to cool them and felt a lump in her throat. "I've, ah, been thinking it through. I know that's what you'd want me to do." She felt her hands shake and hid them behind her back. "I mean, we have to be careful about all of this. It's a change—not a bad change!—but it shifts everything into . . . well, you know . . . a new light."

Jus rubbed at his nose, his confusion growing. He raised one brow and asked, "What have you been thinking?"

"Um, well, I've been thinking that it's all right. You've sort of grown, I've sort of grown . . ." The girl swallowed. "I . . . I think it's time."

Jus's brows creased. "Time?"

"Oh, I know what you're saying!" Escalla whirled, all-of-a-passion. "I know size differences might seem a . . . well, you know, a bit of a problem! But, ah, I think there's a spell somewhere that can help! You know, I could make myself a better scale. More able to, ah . . . to share . . . ah . . ." The girl suddenly blushed beet red and began prodding the tips of her index fingers together. "Well, it just opens up possibilities, but we can wait. We have to wait. We might just have to be patient. You know—for a while . . . until we find the means . . ."

Sucking on a tooth, Jus crossed his legs, collected the faerie and arranged her on his knee. He hunched down to meet her eye in concern.

"Escalla, are you all right?"

"I'm fine!" The girl almost jumped out of her skin. "Just fine!"

"Good." Jus tilted his head to examine her as if she might be mad. "Escalla, what are you talking about?"

Escalla felt the blood drain out of her whole body and go into storage somewhere on another plane. She wilted like a boiled lettuce as she stared at the Justicar.

"You didn't give me the necklace, did you?" Still mystified, Jus shook his head. Escalla felt her whole life sliding into a horrible pit of embarrassment. "You didn't give me roses, and you didn't give me the sweets either."

"Ah, no." Jus scratched his head. A mind used to sifting tiny clues and solving crimes struggled with the events of the last five minutes. "What was all that about *scale?*"

"*Nothing!*" Escalla jumped to her feet in fright. "Nothing at all! It was—" The girl looked for something neat and glib to save her face. "It was wing scales! Like butterflies! I need to change my scales! Dust them off, polish them! And it will all take time!" The girl fluttered like a mad moth in a bottle. "Yep! Time! Which implies anticipation! Lots of anticipation, all working toward, ah, fruit. No, not fruit. Cherry picking!" The girl whirled and grabbed Jus by the armor. "No, *not cherries!* Bananas! Apples! Yes! Gotta have my wings ready by apple blossom time! Faerie tradition!"

Suddenly Escalla stopped, stared at Jus, and leaned away. "You gave me none of those gifts?"

"Nope."

"Not roses, not my favorite sweets, not this tailor made necklace just for me?"

The Justicar spread his hands in innocence. "Escalla, really!"

"Shhh!" The faerie's face went blank. She lifted a hand for silence as horrible thoughts skittered through her mind.

"It wasn't you . . ." Sudden cold fear griped Escalla, and she whirled to stare around at the forest in fright.

She fired off a battery of spells—an anti-scrying shield, then an illusion of herself and Jus still sitting talking by the stream. The girl grabbed Jus by the shirt and dragged him into a run, yanking him back toward the cart.

"Run! Come on! *Run!*"

She snatched her ice wand, Enid's stun scroll, and her spellbooks all in a single mad second. Polk began wrenching his cart around to follow as she dragged Jus out across the stream. The girl took one look at the cart and fired a swarm of little magic bees that slashed the mule's traces and cut them in two.

"Polk, get on the mule and ride! Hurry!"

"My cart!" Polk stared at the abandoned vehicle. "My cart!"

"Lose it!" Escalla whacked the terrified mule across its rump. "Go!"

With a bleat of fear, the mule sped into the trees, plunging Polk through a bramble bush. Jus backed away from the stream, his hand on his sword, trying to cover Polk and Escalla's backs.

"What is it? What's there?"

"Just *run!* Just do it!" Escalla felt tears of panic flood her eyes. "Come on, man. I don't want to lose you!"

The girl dragged Jus away, and he broke into a run. He led the way past Polk and the mule, twisting sideways down a deep gully filled with leaves that helped cover their trail. They fled past fallen statues, past another giant's skeleton, and sped out onto an old road with weeds jutting up between the cobblestones. Escalla danced in a cold fright, keeping her companions in the cover of the trees.

They ran for a mile. Breathing hard, Jus stopped beneath a broken oak to look behind him. Nothing moved. The world seemed still. Escalla shot out of the skies, her eyes roaming in fright across the leaves.

"Jus, if we get separated, meet me at the Hydra's lair! Just wait! Wait as long as it takes!" She half tore out of his hands, surged forward, gave him a kiss, and broke away. "You're my friends! I'm not losing you!"

Something unseen flashed through the leaves high above. Escalla whirled, stabbed a spell into the treetops, and blasted a web across the trees. Something small and invisible struck the web, kicking and cursing. Escalla shot aside, invisible again. A line of golden bees hissed from midair to show her position as she passed. She blasted the branches and tops from trees, sending a cascade of debris tumbling through the forest.

Something invisible hovered in the falling leaves—something that cursed and threw up a shield to ward away the debris. Stabbing upward from below came another spell, and another of Escalla's webs hit something full force and plastered a struggling shape against an old dead tree.

Leaves jerked as Escalla sped invisibly away—until a vast wall of fire suddenly thundered upward in her path. Escalla's voice could be heard cursing, then cursing again as another fire wall blocked her escape off to one side. In a sudden flash, Escalla's invisible body was somehow outlined in sparkling light as an unseen enemy neutralized Escalla's camouflage.

Jus was already running to her aid. He tackled the girl, balling himself about her as he leaped through the fire wall. Cinders's pelt shielded them from the heat. Rolling to his feet, Jus released the girl. Breaking away, she sped hard and fast through the underbrush.

"Jus, keep back!"

A spell stabbed at her from above. Escalla rolled aside, but the magic had never been intended to hit her. Instead it lanced into the fern beneath, which instantly sprang into life and caught the girl about the waist. Struggling, Escalla became visible as she fired a shower of little missiles into the plants and blew them apart.

She flung out a hand and scythed a spell into a patch of empty space. A female scream echoed in the woods, and a small form smashed into the autumn leaves, flickered, and instantly became visible.

It was Escalla in mirror-image: small, lithe, blonde, and winged like a dragonfly. Dressed in white lace, the faerie had a face and hair that could have been Escalla's own. With a vicious screech, the newcomer scrabbled to her feet and threw a killing glance at Escalla.

Escalla hissed, whipped open her hands, and the blinding sizzle of a lethal spell flashed into life. The other faerie snarled at her, matching Escalla's motion and wreathing herself in dancing electricity. The two girls were about to open fire, when a sudden imperious voice pealed out from above.

"Enough!"

It was a voice that hit with a tidal wave of matronly power. On the forest floor, the two young faeries jerked sullenly back as though struck a blow. Unused combat spells leaked off into the ground.

"Escalla! Tielle! Cease this at once!"

A regal presence shimmered into being above the two glaring girls. Lean and arrogant, blonde and beautiful, it was a female faerie dressed in icy splendor. Her body had a wild hauteur that almost stung the eye.

Other figures shimmered into view—faeries, male and female, in hunting costumes and in gowns. Their fashions were exquisite, their faces arrogant. Here and there, tiny dragons buzzed and hovered at a faerie's side.

Looking stark in her black leathers, Escalla stood and coldly wiped the spell taint from her gloves. Standing proud and arrogant amidst her peers and keeping a good grip upon her battle wand, she stared at the magnificent woman floating above and gave her a look that dripped poisoned icicles.

The woman looked down at Escalla as though examining a slug found beneath a log.

"Hello, Escalla."

Escalla matched the woman gaze for gaze.

"Hello, Mother."

5

It was a world where dreams had taken shape into reality, a place of strange colors and spaces that shone like alien stars. A titanic tree stump made an island, and above the island, the sky shimmered with little drifting points of light. A dark, cool pool stretched off into the distance. Wooden stepping blocks stretched off across the lake to other islands, far and near.

The light-motes reflected in the water, showing the shapes of fish and giant water beetles far below. Bullfrogs pealed from the shadows, while nightingales flitted between strands of alien flowers. All about the pool, nature had been put into good order, arranged as a careful piece of art.

It seemed to be night. The sky was dark and starry, and yet everything shone as clearly as in the light of day. Sitting sourly on a pillow at the center of a little isle, Escalla swatted at a nightingale as the stupid creature twittered by.

The garden upon the tree stump isle had been sculpted perfectly. Plants had been shaped into tables, chairs and couches, all overlaid with silk brocades. A satyr daintily served tea and scones, while plates of food and flasks of wine stood gleaming in the light. Surrounded by dream-like plenty, Jus, Polk, and even the mule all remained frozen in shock.

The satyr bowed, proffering jam and cream. Escalla ignored the creature until it went away. Sitting alone with her knees hugged to her chin, the faerie kept her eyes carefully away from the scenery. She tossed a glance at the feast then turned away.

"Don't drink the wine," she said without looking up, "and don't eat the food."

Polk jerked his hand back, already reaching for a scone. "It's enchanted?"

"Polk, don't drink the wine. Don't touch it. Don't sniff it. Don't even touch the damned cork!" Escalla sat with her knees hunched beneath her chin. "Unless you're a faerie, faerie wine's instant suicide. Makes you drunk as a pickled thought-eater in seconds three."

"Oh!" Polk eyed the wine glass nearest him, half tempted to give it a try. "Really?"

"The hangover comes about ten minutes later, Polk. Rumor says it's like having a pair of exploding wolverines mating inside your skull."

Even Polk, inveterate drinker that he was, shrank away from the wine. "Wolverines?"

"Yeah, especially the vintage sixty-three. Gives you violent tremors and convulsions in less time than it takes to scream."

Polk kept a distance between himself and the nearest plate of scones. "How about the food? Poison?"

Escalla shrugged and said, "No."

"Should we eat it?"

"No."

Blinking, Polk scratched his skull. "Why?"

"Because we don't want to give my mother any leverage!" Escalla sat back against a rock and tossed a pebble at a nightingale. "If she feeds you, she can ask for a favor in return. When she comes back, watch what you say. Don't give her any information she can use."

"But she's your mother!"

"Killer amoebas have mothers, Polk. I'm not going to embrace any of *those*, either."

The faeries had opened a door in the empty air of the forest and had led Escalla and her companions into this eerie fantasy land. They now sat amid the songbirds and the frogs, surrounded by a ring of ghostly elf hounds that kept them trapped in an unwinking gaze.

Jus reached into his belt pouch, brought out a chunk of hardtack and split it three ways between himself, Polk, and Escalla. At his side, Cinders lay nose to nose with an elf hound. The hell hound leaked sulphurous steam from his nostrils, and the elf hound bristled, bared its teeth, then broke into a vicious growl. The growl turned into a yelp of panic as Cinders's spewed a jet of flame that scorched the elf hound's back.

Of all the travelers, Cinders was the only one with a grin.

Funny!

Kicking at the scenery, Escalla stood and paced, watched by a dozen elf hounds as she walked. She stood at the shore of the island and stared off across the dark, reflective pool.

"They redecorated."

Jus joined her, sitting at her side, his hand resting too casually upon his sword and aware that the walls could have ears.

"So this is the Seelie Court?"

"Ha! They wish!" Escalla gave a flick of contempt. "This is just a pocket above the forest, a tiny alternative realm. Tons of places have them. Think of it as Flanaess plus one. It runs about, oh, a mile wide." Escalla looked about. "The forest is still there. Any tree you find in here with an arch of branches is a gate to somewhere or other."

Jus weighed the information, still wondering just exactly where they were. He carefully scanned the starry sky, checking the constellations.

"Does time move differently here?"

"No, although on other planes it does." Escalla used her hands to show her friends the horizons of the eerie faerie world. "This is just a citadel. Thirty faeries, three hundred servants, and a ton of these damned hounds." Eyes narrowed, the girl carefully watched an elf hound that slunk watchfully nearby. "Try not to look straight *at* anything. Try to look past the surface. Most of it's an illusion. You can get the knack of telling." Escalla sounded sour. "Careful of the wildlife. Anything about the mass of a faerie probably *is* a faerie. No trout is a trout, no cat's a cat. The bored ones can get pretty strange. Don't stare, or they'll try and get pushy."

"Hmph," the Justicar grunted. "What if we're attacked by one?"

"Cut it fast and hard. Give it time to throw a spell, and you're dog meat. But don't do it. I'm almost out of spells." The girl shrugged. "They have a dueling code—one on one fights are your own affair if you make it a formal challenge."

"Are they all magic-users?"

"Yeah. *All* of them."

Jus rippled his finger tips along the hilt of his sword. "Should we try to bring in Enid and have her bust us out of here?"

"Not yet." Escalla's antennae stayed stiff and high, testing magic currents in the air. "I need a way to get you guys clear of here before I do anything cute."

Heaving a frustrated, angry sigh, Escalla paced, drawing Polk and Jus down beside her. Polk had filled his moustache with hardtack crumbs. He seemed to regard Escalla with newfound awe.

"So this is a faerie palace! A gateway to adventure!"

"Yeah." The girl gave a sneer. "And I'm a princess." Polk and Jus both gave her an appraising look. Escalla angrily waved her hand. "I told you that when we first met! A faerie princess, I said! No one believes me! No one ever believes me!"

"Can't imagine why." Jus scratched his head and left it at that. "All right, so what's the story? Why are they after you? Why are we here?"

"Well they weren't shooting to kill, so that means they want to talk." Escalla ran her fingers through her hair in frustration. "I hate this place! I hate these people!" She turned her face away. "Here's the run-down. This is Clan Nightshade, my clan. They're exiled from the Seelie Court over some crap you and I could care less about, so Clan Nightshade is a rogue. Fought their way through three different planes and ended up here, holed up on the Flanaess." Her voice was toneless. "Faeries usually live in a sealed society—the Seelie Court. It straddles several planes of existence—very old, nine clans always stabbing one another in the back. Spawned a dark goddess once and has kept out of mortal affairs ever since."

She leaned closer, her voice dropping to a whisper.

"Nightshade is *trouble.* They are my clan, so don't underestimate them. We learned magic the hard way." Escalla kept her face neutral and guarded, her eyes flicking left and right for signs of scrying spells. "The Seelie Court clans are a lot more inbred, more reclusive, more formulaic."

Jus slowly stroked his fingers through Cinders's hair. "But these are all faeries like you, right?"

Escalla gave the man a sharp stare. Small, slim, and somehow sinister with her pointed ears and tilted eyes, she suddenly seemed no joking matter.

"Clan Nightshade is personally responsible for neutralizing and imprisoning a goddess." The girl narrowed her eyes. "You're still thinking of elves and pixies. *Don't.* Faeries are the *true-folk.* Imagine a race of magic-using, flying creatures that can change shape and go invisible at will." The girl bitterly pitched a piece of grass into the wind. "Elves are to faeries what skinks are to black dragons. Don't make the mistake of thinking that just because something's short, it can't splay your lungs all over the grass."

Polk recoiled, looking Escalla indignantly up and down. "But you're not nasty! You've got honor and guts and good intentions!"

"Polk, I'm the girl who didn't fit in and ran away."

She hunched over, cradling her head in her hands. The Justicar dragged Cinders over beside Escalla. Heaving a tired sigh, the little faerie reached out to scratch the hell hound's ear.

Cinders look after faerie.

"Thanks, man. You're my favorite pooch."

Sensing that some of the plants were clearly spies, Jus looked at Escalla as he spoke. "What happens now? Why are we here?"

"I have a few suspicions." Escalla's hand tightened on Cinders's fur. "I'm eldest daughter to the clan head. Whatever they want, it's no good news for me."

"Are you in danger?"

"Not immediately. It's not like I broke any laws. Plus I've already taken down some of the clan's best spell slingers twice today. They know I'm not quite the same little girl who ran away from home."

A fanfare of trumpets pealed out across the lake. An instant later, a row of brilliantly clad little creatures popped into view. They seemed to be a type of pixie—shorter than Escalla and far, far sillier, with long cricket's legs and eyes like an insect's. The creatures blew on heraldic horns then tittered with mirth as they rolled their eyes at Polk and Jus.

"Summon come! Summon come! Come to biggie lord! Leave mortals to play game with happy grigs!"

Sharing a look of seething annoyance with Jus, Escalla rose to her feet and said, "Grigs. I hate these guys." The faerie planted her fists on her hips. "Now hear this! These are my blood companions. A spell cast on them is a spell cast on me." The girl turned dire eyes on the shocked little grigs. "I mean it! Tricksie-tricksie, pay back doubles!"

The grigs scuffled their feet and pouted.

"Mean!"

"Yeah, well I'm *that* one! Remember me? The mean lady is back again!" Escalla swatted at the little sprites, who scattered sullenly away. "Half-wit relatives! You can bet your butt they don't have to put up with these little buggers in the *real* Seelie Court!"

Peeking out of cover all around the island were a host of tiny little shapes—all pixie-like, all small, all less formidable that the pure faeries Jus had seen. Jus settled Cinders securely into place upon his helmet and looked at the forest sprites.

"These are all related to faeries? Why so many offshoots—pixies, sprites, grigs, atomies. . . ?"

"Chaos wars." Escalla led her way through the ranks of hiding sprites. "Lotta pure bloodlines were split up. Goblinoids, giants, dragons. Faeries took the brunt of it. That's why we turned reclusive." The girl had reached the shore, and here a party of lean, elegant faeries awaited them. "We're summoned. Come on. Let's go meet the family. Keep your eyes open and your mind straight."

Jus and Escalla both flexed their hands, each feeling for the rings that kept them safe from charm spells.

At the water's edge, Escalla's twin awaited them.

The newcomer was pure faerie. The lean lines, the aristocratic face and air of cool intelligence instantly marked her. In shape and face, she could almost have been Escalla. A little rounder in the eyes, far, *far* plusher in the bosom, but as alike as two sisters had a right to be. She had dressed herself in tight white lace with a glint of silver on her hand. Escalla's leathers looked stark and almost primitive in contrast to the other girl.

The lace-clad figure sketched a mocking little bow and said, "Sweet sister."

"Yeah, whatever." Escalla turned and jerked her thumb toward the other faerie. "Guys, this is Tielle, my little sister. A total bitch."

Polk doffed his cap. Jus merely gave a brief nod of his head. Turning back to her sister, Escalla stared the other girl up and down. The two females exchanged looks that dripped with pure disdain.

"So Tielle. You porked-out."

"Yes. They're called *breasts.*" Tielle looked at her sister with a sour laugh. *"Love* the outfit. Is it uncured leather, or is that smell all your own?"

"Ha! You kiss so much butt, I'm surprised you still have any sense of smell."

Looming like a vast black giant above the faeries, Jus cleared his throat in a bass rumble. It brought the exchange of insults to an end as both sisters flicked a glance up at the human.

Tielle gave a wrinkle of her nose and said, "You're summoned to the clan council."

Escalla gave a sniff and replied, "Why do I give a damn?"

"Daddy's asking nicely. And we have visitors." Tielle clicked her fingers to summon more faeries. Male and female spellcasters closed in to surround Escalla and her friends. Tielle's fingers gleamed as the light fell on a tiny silver ring shaped like a spider. "Oh, you'll like it. Mummy and Daddy have you foremost on their minds . . . as always."

Escalla sniffed at her sister and looked scathingly at the faerie warriors.

"I'm soooo intrigued." Escalla shrugged. "Nice ring, by the way."

Tielle raised a mocking smile and used her other hand to indicate a line of stepping stones that stretched into the distance. "Get moving. They're waiting."

At least a dozen faeries served as escorts. Escalla scowled. On a good day, she could cream almost anyone in the clan, but with her spells depleted from three combats in a single day, she no longer stood a chance. Whatever happened, Jus and Polk would catch most of the damage. Seething with hate, Escalla tried to crush the helpless feeling of being dragged back into Daddy's house as she flew out over the lake.

"Come on, guys. Let's get this done."

The Justicar shrugged his armor into place then strode forward on his strangely quiet boots. Behind him, Polk refused to move. Instead, the teamster turned to Escalla with a vacuous smile.

"My dear, I really don't think this is any business for mortals."

Escalla planted her fists on her hips. "What?"

"Why, I think I'll wait here. Thank you, Escalla. Gosh, but the weather is nice!"

Turning her dire gaze upon the faeries, Escalla snarled. "Oh ha ha ha. You blitzed an idiot with a charm spell."

Something flickered in the air. A charm spell shot from a faerie toward the Justicar and shattered on the shield thrown up by the man's magic ring. Cinders hissed, Jus jerked his head around, and the hell hound's red eyes focused on an invisible shape lurking behind a tree.

There!

Escalla threw up a hand and shoved a single spell toward the hidden faerie. A reeking cloud enveloped the culprit, sending him reeling and retching off into the bushes. Escalla watched the faerie go, unshipped her ice wand, and noisily pumped the activation slide. "What did I tell you about my friends? Try it again, and I'll get nasty!"

Grinning happily, Cinders wagged his tail. *Burn!*

"Not yet!" Escalla looked at the stepping stones. "Cinders, some of the stepping stones are illusions. Just keep your eyes open."

Looking bored with it all, Tielle hovered over the surface of the lake and said, "None of them are illusions. We have better things to do with our time."

"Good. Then let the Justicar carry you and hold you tight."

Tielle looked annoyed. She made a pass with her hand, and half of the stepping stones disappeared, leaving only blank water in their place. Escalla flew out to lead the way, hovering protectively close to the Justicar.

"Polk, come on. Follow me."

"Why yes. What a lovely suggestion!" Polk beamed vacuously, his voice vapid and formal. "May I just say how pert you look today?"

"Polk, spell or no spell, nobody ever uses *pert* in normal conversation, all right?"

Jus jumped and strode awkwardly from stepping stone to stepping stone, his heavy bulk strangely graceful, his armor and sword quiet through long habit of stealth. Polk bumbled along in his wake, leaving his mule staring forlornly after them. Escalla flew along in silence, flanked by a dozen faeries and refusing to so much as even glance at her sister.

In the deep waters of the lake fish swam—giant cuttlefish and little stingrays, all faeries shapeshifted into animal form. In the trees overhead, animals watched the travelers, each creature showing intelligent faerie eyes. Watched from a dozen directions, Jus, Polk, and Escalla made their way across the lake toward a giant garden that glimmered with bright flowers.

At the shore stood a circular grove of gnarled, ancient fruit trees. Escalla jerked her thumb at the fruit trees as Jus passed them by.

"Plane trees."

The Justicar turned. "Plain trees?"

"No, plane trees—like a tree of the various planes of existence." Escalla shrugged. "That grove leads off to other planes—primal energy, negative energy, fire, water, that sort of thing. You need a key taken from the plane you're heading to—amazingly useless."

The garden made a ring of light about a faerie palace, an airy thing all made from pearl-gray wood. A long path led toward the palace doors. Beside the path, a lawn hosted a dainty party attended by a dozen faerie folk. The faeries mingled, gossiped, and intrigued. Fawn and satyr servitors poured drinks, while animated plants played music upon lutes. A bevy of female orcs knelt servilely about a faerie lord who was wreathed in fiery robes. All conversation stopped, and all eyes turned as Escalla marched out from the trees.

A faun approached and bowed, ushering Escalla along the path. Escalla waited for Jus and Polk, keeping them at her side. Surrounded by guards and stared at by faeries and servants alike, the three companions walked slowly through the party and headed for the palace doors.

The silence was nerve wracking and irritating. Whirling, Escalla turned to face her peers.

"Yes, it's me! I'm back! You all seen enough? And you? And you?" The girl pivoted in mid air, tugging her skirt tight.

Escalla sped forward in anger, shoving past two beautifully liveried centaurs and throwing open the palace doors. A vast hall stretched before her, a place of moving murals and carpets that shifted shape and form. A hundred faeries lined the way, most of them dressed in brilliant, alien finery. There were guards dressed in bright red mail and faerie dragons fluttering through the rafters eating flower arrangements. Escalla took one look at the crowds and sagged back toward the ground.

"Oh *bugger.*"

Tielle whirred forward to whisper to a scowling major domo. Faerie maids in exotic fashions eyed Jus and whispered sourly behind their fans.

Escalla pulled in close to the ranger and whispered quickly in his ear, "This is not Clan Nightshade! This is way more than Clan Nightshade!" The girl suddenly spied a slim, hypochondriacal faerie surrounded by rings of courtiers. "Oh futz. It's the Erlking!"

Jus pulled at his nose and asked, "The who?"

"Oberon! Hen-pecked consort to the queen bitch herself." Escalla quickly looked for avenues of escape. "I think this *is* the Seelie Court!"

Turning, Jus regarded his friend. "Escalla, just what exactly did you do when you left here?"

Escalla managed to look both annoyed and evasive all at once. "Well I *may* have requisitioned more than I was strictly allowed to." The girl waved her hands in outrage. "Hey! Faeries don't age, man! So letting your kids know they have an inheritance is unfair. So I just prematurely requisitioned what was mine."

Jus regarded her with leveled brows. "You stole daddy's wallet and ran away from home?"

"There was more to it than that! You had to be there!"

Polk beamed good will at the whole universe. "Why, it seems to be a splendid place! Why ever did you leave?"

Cinders flattened his ears, scowling at the fripperies and gave a growl. *Illusions. Old magic.* The dog almost sneezed in disgust. *No fun here. All spells.*

Escalla applauded. "Thank you, pooch! Polk, we'll have a little shared lesson on mind/body phenomenology later on, if we're all alive."

"But it's so pretty!"

Escalla glared. "Polk, say, 'I am an idiot.' "

"I am an idiot."

"Great! Now shut up and enjoy your charm spell before I make you take off your pants!"

Jus looked disapprovingly about the room. It was pure luxury and opulence, and much of it pure illusion designed to stroke the senses. Dour and spartan, Jus was the antithesis of the entire faerie way of life. Faeries kept well away, staring at the mortals as though they carried a disease.

Tielle emerged from the crowds and looked her sister up and down. "They want to see you. Do you care to dress properly first?"

"Just tell me why I'm here."

"Oh no! Little surprises are always such fun." Tielle gave a nasty smile. "This way to daddy-kins. Hop hop! And *do* tell your mortals not to scuff the rugs."

Today Jus's boots had trampled through muddy streets, forest streams and dirt, and he could not care less about the rug. Escalla girded herself and flew through the parting crowds, finally finding herself confronting her mother, her father, and a host of unfamiliar faces.

Her father turned. Powerful and solid—for a faerie—his poise was somehow similar to the Justicar. His hair was long and steel gray, his beard pointed, and his eyes sparked the same green fire as his daughter. He took one look at Escalla, split his face into a rough smile and crushed Escalla in his arms.

"Honey blossom!"

He wrestled the girl from side to side, making her eyes bulge. With a great bass roar of a laugh, the lord of Clan Nightshade hugged Escalla for all that she was worth.

Trapped in her father's arms, Escalla struggled upward until she could catch Jus's eye. "Guys, this is my dad."

Overjoyed, Escalla's father ruffled the girl's hair. "And this, this is my Silly Scellie!"

Cinders sniggered, thump-thump-thumping with his tail. *Silly Scellie!*

Jus looked amused, and Escalla spiked him with a snarl.

"Just keep laughing, *Evelyn.*" Escalla gave a long suffering sigh. "Gang, this is Charn, Lord Nightshade, my father. Daddy, this is Polk, a transport consultant; Cinders, a sentient hell hound skin; and here"—the girl cast a look longing for help toward Jus—"is my friend, the Justicar."

Big, solid, and rough cut out of pure honesty, the Justicar bowed to Escalla's father. The faeries scarcely came up to his knees, but he managed to bow toward them with vast dignity.

"My Lord Charn."

"Capital! Capital to meet you!" Escalla's father took one daughter under each arm—Escalla suffering patiently, and Tielle coldly smiling. "So you are the ones who have served my daughter so loyally while she roamed in the worthless wilds!"

"They're not servants, dad."

"Of course not, dear!" The man gave his girl a shake. "But she's home! She has returned to home and duty at last."

A silken movement came from the crowds. Escalla's mother appeared, cool as ice and regarding her prodigal daughter much as she might regard an insect specimen.

"Escalla."

"Mother."

"You decided not to dress." Escalla's mother took a drink from a tray proffered by one of the scantily clad orc servants. "No matter. For our purposes, nothing could be better."

"Purposes?" Escalla's voice lowered the temperature of the entire hall. "Someone tried to kill my friends this morning, then some imbecile tried bribing me with candy and flowers." The girl ignored her father and faced her mother. "Do tell me all about your little *purposes*."

"It is called *obligation*."

"I don't care to be obliging." Dusting herself off, Escalla disengaged herself from her father's arm. "Dad, why am I here?"

"You are here because a great day is here! A *family* day!" The faerie lord beamed. "The court has rescinded our exile. Clan Nightshade is to be brought back into the fold!"

The news hardly hit Escalla like a thunderbolt.

"Oh whoopee."

"It's provisional." Escalla's father took hold of her elbow and propelled her through the crowds. Scowling faeries made way as Jus and Polk lumbered in Escalla's wake. "But here, you see? Old comrades all together once again. Old faces to rediscover!"

Escalla made a wry little expression. "I've never seen any of them before, Dad. We were exiled about a zillion years before I was born."

"But comrades still! Kith and kin! Even representitives from the inner court itself!" Charn spread his hands to show his daughter that the palace halls were filled to overflowing. "Many of them will be staying here with us while a few formalities are handled, but it's a new beginning for you. They want us to take the lead in wonderful new plans. It will be time for *you*, girl, eldest child of the clan head! Think of all the changes you can make!"

"Nothing changes, dad." An old bitterness and nightmare shone through Escalla's words. "You make castles out of clouds, mountains out of molehills, and nothing ever happens."

Lord Charn looked left and right, used a spell to shield him from prying ears, and whispered cautiously in his daughter's hair. "There has been a change in the power balance, and Nightshade holds the key. The clan that defeated and imprisoned the Faerie Queen of Wind and Woe, the clan that knows where she is hidden . . . we are about to become a *power* once again."

The man clamped Escalla on the back, his voice picking up as his spell faded. "And so! Faces for you to know! New relatives! Kith and kin! Here is Faen, Lord Half Moon. Lord Faen is knowledge-keeper to the Seelie Court and advisor to Queen Titania herself."

A thin faerie with a long wisp of a goatee gave Escalla a courtly bow. Several mages of the Half Moon clan stood with him, all sharing a conspirator's smile with Escalla's father before appraising the girl. Her outlandishly stark clothes and aggressive air seemed to meet their secret needs. They inclined their heads and turned to one another with significant little smiles as Escalla passed.

Jus trod carefully behind Lord Charn. Escalla was aware of him covering her back; she could feel the ranger watching her mother and her sister. Cinders's tail wagged. Towing her through the room, Escalla's father dragged her from one knot of courtiers to another.

"Ah! Escalla, here is Fareel, Lady Mantis." A sorceress and her entourage bowed in a rattle of outlandish insectoid costumes. "Here is the priestess of Corellon and her acolytes. This is Jenna, princess of Clan Raven." Suddenly his eye lighted on his true quarry. Escalla's father seemed to swell with new energy. "Ah, and here is someone just for you!"

Waiting at the foot of a fountain stood a faerie cavalier, a youth eel-slim and armed with a delicate silver rapier. His black silk shirt had ribbons bound about the upper arms—kill ribbons from a dozen duels. The cavalier looked Escalla up and down. Her leathers were tight as a second skin and showed an astonishing amount of breast and thigh. She half turned, her figure svelte as a velvet cobra, and raked her audience with a haughty glare. The faerie cavalier preened his moustache and whispered approvingly into a neighbor's ear, reaching out to take a tiny goblet of wine.

Jus had seen the faerie cavalier before. He had worn a blue silk cloak torn by Jus's sword.

Beside the cavalier waited a dark haired faerie, the same flame robed lord she had noticed in the park outside. Kneeling orc slave girls made a bizarre, outlandish backdrop as they awaited their master's word of command.

Lord Charn brought Escalla forward to the flame robed man.

"Ushan, Lord Sable, I present my Eldest Daughter, Escalla Brightflower, the Heiress Nightshade." Escalla sniffed, looking dangerous, disdainful, and positively alien amidst so much splendor. "Escalla, Lord Ushan is chancellor to Queen Titania. Clan Sable is the right arm of the throne."

Escalla shrugged. Her father happily dragged her past Lord Ushan and into the middle of Clan Sable. The young cavalier posed, smoothing his moustache as he awaited to greet her.

"Finally Escalla, the best comes last! This is the valiant Tarquil, cavalier of the Order of the Sunset, scion of Clan Sable, and nephew to Lord Ushan."

Eagerly paternal, Lord Charn faced Escalla and Tarquil off against one another.

"Tarquil of Sable, I present Brightflower Maid, Princess Escalla." The man gave a vast, expansive smile. "Your bride to be."

6

It was amazing just how long polished wood could burn. One entire corner of the palace had gone up in flames from Escalla's fire-ball. Walking over the deserted lawns, Jus came over to the edges of the blaze. He pulled a choice coal out of the ruins of the palace and popped it into the hell hound's mouth. Cinders mumbled happily, making contented little noises.

Polk sat beaming happily into the empty air. Jus sighed, sat down facing him, and carefully removed his protective ring. He slipped the ring onto Polk's finger then slapped the man hard across the face.

Polk's eyes rekindled with wits. He turned a hurt expression on the Justicar. "Hey! Son, that hurt!"

"Good." Jus relieved the teamster of his ring and put it back on his own hand. "You were under a charm spell."

"Who me, son? Never! I was lulling, making a false impression, quieting their suspicions!" Polk swelled like a turkey in heat. "I've been freeing you for action. What are the faeries' plans? Do they have a quest for us?"

"No." Jus pulled his sword half from its sheath and inspected the weapon's edge—sharp enough to shave hairs and flawlessly polished. "They're trying to take Escalla."

Polk stared in shock. "Will she go?"

"I don't know."

The thought of there being no Escalla seemed like a chunk torn out of Jus's heart. Cinders fell quiet. Polk seemed to shrink. All three looked over the far end of the gardens, where a distant summer house lay beneath a giant cherry tree.

Jus looked away, slamming his sword back into its sheath. Aware that hundreds of faeries spied on him from afar, he pulled Cinders into his lap and silently brushed the hell hound's fur.

*   *   *   *   *

In the summer house, Escalla stood facing her mother. The older woman kept her hands folded in her lap, her slanted eyes cold and serene. The woman had the same thin face and long, straight golden hair as her daughter, but there the resemblance ended. Escalla was a creature of pure passion, and she paced like a leopard in a cage.

"What the hell were you thinking—that I'd be a good daughter if you asked, that I never meant to run away?" Escalla whirled in a rage. "What? Are you totally stupid!"

Escalla's father and sister stood by the windows. Tielle looked over at the burning north wing of the palace and smiled. "The prodigal returns."

"You can shut up for a start! You spend about as much time at home as I do!" Escalla flung a bitter jab at her father. "If she wants to play at being the good girl, then have that Sable idiot marry *her!*"

"It must be the heir." Lord Charn paced, no longer the happy father as he glared at his willful child. "To seal our return, we must marry our heir into the Seelie Court."

"I'm not doing it!" Escalla flexed her fingers as though wanting to choke something. "I can't believe you thought you could round me up like a wildcat and just marry me off!"

Escalla's mother looked down her nose at the angry girl. "If necessary, a spell might calm you."

"Just try it!"

Lord Charn chewed his moustache. Escalla had moved to a far window where she stared angrily out at her mortal friends. The faerie lord paced toward her, raising a spell to keep away curious ears and eyes.

"Daughter, this is the marriage of dreams. Clan Sable is at the pinnacle of the Seelie Court."

"Well those are not *my* dreams!" The girl turned, and tears stood out in sharp green eyes that seemed so suddenly vulnerable. "Not *my* dreams!" Tired and trapped, Escalla ran fingers over her little skull. "It's been five years. For Erythnul's sake, how did you find me?"

"You happened to fall in range of our scrying spells just when your mother needed you." The faerie lord twiddled his fingers. "It's a big world. If you wanted to stay lost, you should have kept your distance and kept your shields up."

"I have other uses for my spells. I *do* stuff these days! Important stuff! Stuff that matters!" Escalla rubbed her eyes. "Five years, Dad. Surely that was a clue that I'd gone for good."

"A mayfly flicker." Lord Charn waved a hand at the gardens. "Escalla, the council is almost at war over this. Clan Half Moon has convinced the queen to reprieve us. Clan Sable is furious. When Nightshade left the court, it was Sable that seized power. By welding Sable to Nightshade, we prevent a rift in the court! It is the only way to return and bring peace!"

"Why do they want us, dad? Why now?"

"Because they need what we can do." Lord Charn paced the room beside his daughter. "We are the only clan with experience on the primal plane. We have spied and studied, intermingled and co-existed with the powers peculiar to this layer of the universe."

"It sounds thin." With the slowglass necklace clenched like brass knuckles in her hand, Escalla turned away. "Who's this Tarquil, anyway? A damned duelist?"

"He's a sorcerer and a swordsman."

"A *murderer.*" Escalla tugged her clothing tight about her little frame. "I won't do it."

Escalla's father put a denser shield between himself and his wife, then leaned quickly closer to his child. "Escalla! Your mother *knows* how much you value those mortal friends of yours. You refuse to do this, and she *will* kill them."

The little faerie turned pale. She swung about to face the window. Behind her, Escalla's father hissed quietly in her ear. "Escalla, do not underestimate your mother's ambitions for power.

The court means everything to her. Nothing else matters! If you want your friends to leave here alive, do exactly what she says. She will watch you, Escalla. Every word you say, every person you meet will be spied on. Your mother wants the Seelie Court in her hands." Escalla's father took the chance to kiss his daughter hurriedly on the ear, fearing his wife's ability to break his spell. "It will be all right. You'll get used to it. I'm doing what's best for you."

The moment passed. As Lord Charn's spells faded, Escalla found herself staring blankly at a windowpane. Outside in the gardens, music and laughter sounded as alien and distant as the surging of a sea. Numb, Escalla flexed her hands, her mind blank of anything except her friends. Escalla's mother waited. The girl bowed her head and looked blankly at the floor.

"I will marry Tarquil."

*　*　*　*　*

Jus and Polk rose from the grass where they had sat waiting for a long and silent hour. Finally they saw two small figures approaching them from the garden path. Dressed in sheer white lace, Tielle drifted coyly above the ground. Beside her, a little figure in mother-of-pearl silk flew in quiet misery.

Escalla landed before Jus and Polk. She wore her shimmering gray dress demurely. Her blonde hair had been pulled back, and her leathers were bundled in one hand. The girl dropped her clothes at Jus's feet and stared palely at the grass.

"Justicar."

"Lady Brightflower."

Jus's voice was hoarse and quiet. He looked down at the delicate little faerie before him and felt infinitely sad. Escalla curtsied to him slowly, unable to meet his eye.

"Justicar, there is a time in all lives when . . . when a change must come." The girl's voice caught in her throat. "For the good of those we love, we have to . . . to accept what has to be."

"Yes, my lady."

Escalla's head bowed. A tear fell to speckle the back of one daintily gloved hand.

"We . . . we have spoken of philosophy, you and I. Remember what we once said about what we owe to future generations? Can you picture it *clearly* in your mind?"

"Yes, my lady." The Justicar remembered. "You showed me the way that new ideas grow."

"Then you will know how much I owe to my family and my clan. You know that I now wish to leave my life of wandering and embrace the court. I must leave you and do what is right and proper."

Jus bowed his head and slowly closed his hands. "Yes, my lady."

"I . . . I will be married in three days time. I do not think we will meet again."

Escalla jerked away and hid her face. Bored by the tedium of it all, Tielle clicked her fingers and summoned a serving girl.

"Justicar, Clan Nightshade wishes to thank and reward you for your services as guard and guide to our daughter." Tielle seemed in a hurry to be elsewhere. "Escalla has indicated suitable gifts."

The girl allowed her servant to pass out the items one by one.

"Polk. To you, we offer this magic wine bottle. Speak into the bottle's mouth, and it will refill itself one thousand times with whatever liquor you care to name."

Looking desolate and appalled, Polk numbly accepted the bottle. Tielle took another gift from the serving girl behind her.

"For the hell hound, we offer this. It is a vial containing all the scents we have found in many worlds. A toy, but you may have some pleasure from it." Escalla's sister turned a measured glance at the Justicar. "For you, Justicar, we offer these scrolls. We are told spells are something you can utilize. Also, Escalla says you have need of diamond dust."

The huge man bowed slowly and said, "I thank you."

"Escalla asks that you take her old clothes with you when you go. She never wishes to see them again."

Escalla slowly walked over to stand before the Justicar. Still unable to lift her face, she held out her tiny hand. "Good-bye, Justicar."

"Good-bye, my lady." The Justicar knelt, closed his eyes for a long moment, and quietly kissed her hand. Faerie tears stung salt into his lips. "It has been a privilege and a pleasure to serve you." Faerie fingers squeezed Jus's hand. "May justice forever be yours."

He rose and bowed. A servant held out a hand to show him to a gate that led back to the world of summer rainstorms and morning frost. Escalla turned away, unable to watch him go. One hand covered her face, and the other clutched tightly against her heart.

* * * * *

Dawn in the faerie lands was an arbitrary affair. If it had been inconveniently pale, bright or rainy, one or more faeries would have been sure to smooth it over with illusions. The illusions were easily seen through by those who could be bothered, but few bothered. The faeries drew few lines between illusion and reality, preferring to discuss the virtues of real versus unreal for long hours over steaming cups of tea. Or possibly cups of *not-tea*. Illusion had a way like that.

Sitting in a room decorated for a good little daughter, Escalla propped her elbows on her knees and sighed. These were not her old rooms. Those had been turned into guest apartments long ago, and Tarquil now snored in Escalla's old bed. Mother had created a new room for her errant daughter, one more suitably fashioned to her image of the perfect child.

The decor was mostly fuchsia pink. Escalla felt her entire intestinal tract rebel.

She sat looking into the slowglass gem. A white wedding dress as big as a whale hung from one wall—a dress covered with seed pearls and beautiful enough to stop any normal woman's heart. There were paintings on the wall, *real* paintings. There were color shifting rugs upon the floor—*unreal*. The view from the windows showed any one of a dozen illusory scenes of imagined grandeur. It all had the grainy, almost greasy quality that Escalla had come to associate with all her childhood memories.

All of her memories before she escaped into the real world . . .

Wearing a dress simply felt weird, but Escalla bore it. She sat staring at the fantasies conjured by the windows, until a knock at the door brought a presence sweeping into her room.

With a flurry of servants and a flutter of gorgeous wings, Cavalier Tarquil stood at the entrance of Escalla's apartment and sank into a rather oily bow.

"Brightflower Maid! How much more refreshing than the dawn is your brilliant smile."

Escalla rose, flipped out her wings, and made a curtsy carefully measured to keep the suitor at bay. Even so, she felt his eyes travel down her cleavage as she bowed. Escalla hissed, caught herself, and pulled part of her face into a smile.

Her mother had spies all around. A scrying spell would be on her, and there would be an invisible creature lurking in every room. In a society of shapeshifters, any object of the right size and mass was instantly suspect. Escalla had already kicked most of the furniture and felt tremors of pain in reply.

They were watching her for spells, for any attempt to escape. They would be reporting Escalla's right behavior to a mother who was as deadly as a dracolich. Escalla kept her face stiff and her thoughts to herself as she turned to invite the cavalier onto her balcony.

"Cavalier."

The man had a bodyguard, a scarred duelist from his own clan that clandestinely cast a detection spell. Leading the way to the balcony, Escalla caught the motion from the corner of her eye.

"Oh, I can assure you we are being watched. There's no point in wasting a spell."

"Ah, dear maid. It is not whether there is a spell, but *who* has thrown the spell." Tarquil's voice was polished and as silky as his silver sword. "Sad to say, a man can sometimes acquire enemies."

Cavalier Tarquil wore twelve kill ribbons on his sleeves—mementos of duels gone by. Escalla gave a sarcastic lift of her eye and said, "I can't imagine why."

"You disapprove of dueling, dear?" Tarquil snapped his fingers. A servant ran forward to supply him with wine. "It is a righteous sport."

"Sport?"

"Of course." The cavalier gave a mocking smile to Escalla. "Shall the pot call the kettle black, my dear? You have an impressive kill record of your own—monsters, creatures, brigands. It sounds like quite the little crusade."

Escalla bit back a savage reply, half turned away, then flew over the balcony railing to land in the garden. Today, her father's gardens were a fantasy of roses. Even the grass seemed to be fashioned out of tiny little flowers, all illusory, all slightly false to an eye that loved the glorious imperfections of the real world. Escalla walked onward for a way then stood still as she felt eyes running over her from behind.

She turned and glared at the cavalier.

"Quit looking at my butt!"

"Your pardon, maid, but it is a most noteworthy rear." The cavalier toyed with his sword. "When my father informed me of this match, I never once thought that it might prove to be so . . . *beneficial.*"

Escalla flicked her shirts out to hide the benefits in question.

"The benefits aren't yours yet, bub!"

"No? A shame." The cavalier took a swift, searching look across the open garden. "Shall we move into the shade?"

"You mean into cover." Escalla looked a the man in sudden intuition. "Who's trying to bump you off?"

"Perish the thought. A mere habitual precaution, nothing more."

She took him into a rose bower—a bower carefully searched by Tarquil's bodyguard before he entered. Standing in privacy with Escalla, the man visibly relaxed. He leaned against a towering rose trunk and looked Escalla appreciatively up and down.

"A flower in the wilderness."

"Yeah, that's me. Bloom bloom bloom." Escalla lifted up the slowglass necklace that hung about her throat. "This is yours?"

"Of course. Slowglass is rare. Slowglass is beautiful—almost as rare and beautiful as you."

"Oh, your clan must want me somethin' awful. Where the hell did you find the slowglass? This stuff is rarer than hen's teeth."

Tarquil twittered his fingers and replied, "Your sister found it for me. Your family was keen to help me pursue my suit."

"I'll *bet*."

Escalla sniffed and turned away. A moment later, she felt a very unwelcome presence behind her. Tarquil set his hands upon Escalla's bare shoulders and leaned his face into the curtain of her hair.

"I am in your own old rooms. The mirror, the bed . . . places where you must have dreamed so many restless adolescent dreams." The man nuzzled at Escalla's ear. "Dreams can be so much tastier when we snatch them secretly. Perhaps you want to sample a little piece of the cake before eating it becomes simply a duty to be done. . . ?" Tarquil leaned much, much closer. "Your old mirror might show you something you might like."

He slid his hand onto her breast. In one blindingly fast movement, Escalla whirled, balled her fist, and struck him in the face—the force enough to send him staggering.

"Touch me again, and I'll kill you!"

With a look of private amusement on his face, Tarquil touched at his cheek. "You had best get used to it, my dear." The faerie hissed as he probed the bruise on his cheek "Yes, you are exactly as we thought. How *gratifying*."

In a whirl of his blue cloak, Tarquil turned and left the bower. Escalla watched him go, flexing her hands and trying to hide the fury in her eyes.

"No one touches the faerie."

A slither in the shadows behind Escalla told her that mother's invisible spy was still at hand. Without looking at it, Escalla angrily picked up her skirts and passed it by.

"Go tell Mother: no free samples until the deal is signed and sealed!"

❖ ❖ ❖ ❖ ❖

Beneath a flame tree in the gardens, Lord Faen quietly approached Lord Ushan. Ushan of Clan Sable stood stroking his chin, his eye on the distant rose bower that held his nephew and the bride to be. As Tarquil walked silkily forth, dusting at his clothes with a smile on his face, Lord Faen came to stand at Ushan's side.

"You seem agitated, colleague."

"New alliances always bring birthing pains." Ushan's flame robes made colors dance within his quiet eyes. "Still . . . romance makes interesting viewing."

"Quite so." Faen smoothed his goatee, his eyes on Escalla as the girl walked disdainfully through an illusory bridge and stream. "An interesting creature."

"She's a savage." Ushan glared at Escalla as though she were an unwanted scientific specimen. "She wallows in the real like a beast in mud."

Faen made an exasperated sound. He turned on Ushan with his antennae held low and said, "Ushan, the drow are moving. There is a dark Seelie, my friend, a reflection of all that we are. The old court of the Queen of Wind and Woe has been approached by the dark elves, and with the dark elves comes the demon Lolth, the Spider Queen!" Faen's voice hissed low in Ushan's ear. "We have enemies gathering, Ushan. We need allies on the material plane if we are to protect our flanks."

Lord Ushan clicked his fingers. Two of his serving girls brought a sedan chair to his side.

"The Queen of Wind and Woe was once Lolth's mistress. If we handled the dark queen, then we can handle her pet spider well enough."

"*We* did not handle the dark queen! It was Nightshade. Only *they* have the secret!"

"Then if we give Nightshade what they want, we can trade. You have made your point, Faen." The sedan chair turned away. "The wedding will proceed. Prepare your list of which court positions you want Clan Sable to abandon to the barbarians and present it to me tonight."

Ushan's servants bore him off, leaving Faen standing upon the flowery grass. With an irritated sweep, Faen banished the illusion. He now stood upon honest moss, pacing up and down as he furrowed his brows.

Two days until the wedding. Faen walked and watched the Nightshade palace, his brows permanently creased into a scowl.

7

In the abandoned village amidst the giants' bones, the morning seemed miserably quiet. Outside in the frost, the Justicar practiced with his sword. The huge black blade made fast slices, thrusts, and parries. Stripped to the waist, Jus rehearsed his savage combat style, matching blade work with kicks, punches, head butts, and elbow strikes. His breath steamed as he worked, coming in harsh puffs as he repeated his movements for the eleventh time. Sitting on a pile of stones beside him, Cinders hung limp and desolate, sniffing softly at a tiny little faerie vial.

Inside the tavern stables, Polk and Enid leaned on a windowsill, the human dwarfed by the freckled sphinx. Both looked equally miserable. Both sighed listlessly and stared blankly into the morning air.

Polk sighed yet again. His usual bluster was faded and gone. "I left my bacon to cool this morning. No one stole the crunchy end bits while I was gone."

Enid's tufted tail hung limp as an old wet rope. "There was a dirty ditty folded up in one of these old books, but there's no one to explain it to me."

Both companions sighed unhappily, feeling as though a vast weight were crushing their souls. They could hardly bear to look as the Justicar fought shadows in the tavern yard.

His hard work seemed sad and futile. He was using action as a substitute for grief. Enid and Polk both nodded wisely, then turned away from the window with a sigh.

On the tavern table lay a little bundle of goods—a tiny leather dress, gloves and leggings, plus a bundle of papers. Rather than magic scrolls, Escalla's gift to Jus had simply been her own spellbooks, and wrapped within them had been her battle wand.

Polk reached for Enid's currycomb to brush her pelt, but instead fell into apathy as he saw the sad pile of papers on the table.

"I guess she's really gone for good."

Out in the courtyard, Jus could be heard sluicing himself down with water. He stomped into the tavern dripping wet, breathless, dark and brooding. He dropped his sword on the table and proceeded to dry himself vigorously with a villainous piece of old sacking. The Justicar's heavy body showed a pale network of scars. Magic healing left few traces, although reknitted wounds looked less weatherbeaten than the rest of Jus's skin.

He took the small silver mirror that always hung about his neck and propped it on a windowsill. Taking a razor from his pouch, Jus warmed it briskly in the tea kettle, then squatted down to peer into the mirror as he shaved his head.

The harsh *scrape-scrape-scrape* of the razor set Enid's nerves on edge. The big sphinx arose and began pacing back and forth, swishing with her tail. She sighed in agitation. Jus shot the sphinx a look, turned back to his shaving, and finally knocked his razor clean against the windowsill.

Perfectly calm, Jus drew in his breath, looked out the window, and then drew his brows into a frown.

Smoke smudged the skyline.

Jus shrugged on his tunic, keeping his eyes on the skyline. He found his armor and tugged the black dragon scale cuirass into place. He tied his sword belt with one hand and swept Cinders about his back with the other.

The distant smoke had a broad base, deep black and unmoving. It was a village burning, not a forest fire. Jus had seen enough towns destroyed in his time to know the signs. The big man checked the edge of his sword and then flung open the door.

"I have to look at something. Stay here and get ready to move. I'll be back by midday."

The Justicar slammed the door behind him as he left. He took a deep breath of forest air and looked about the abandoned village. Only the birds and squirrels were stirring.

This was how it used to be—alone except for Cinders, alone in the silence. Jus closed his eyes for a moment and tried to savor it. The cool, the quiet, the isolation . . . He held it in his mind, but the old perfection of it had gone.

The ranger turned and strode down the trail toward Sour Patch, moving at a grim and silent speed. Still a ways from the village, he sank into the woods, feeling the breath and movement of every tree.

Autumn had left the trees stark. Leaves lay in deep drifts, wet and heavy, muffling every footfall in the gloom. Jus moved fast. In the damp, sound carried badly, and few ears were sharp enough to hear him coming. He crossed three miles in brisk time, keeping his eyes on glimpses of the smoke cloud that smudged the sky.

A scent struck him, and he dropped. The wind had changed, and with it came a foul bestial reek. The stink of it hit like a hammer, and Jus lay instantly invisible among the leaves.

Nothing moved in the forest. There were no footfalls, no bending twigs. Even so, the stink seemed to come from an animal—or a vast swarm of animals. It smelled like a thousand putrid menageries, like rotting flesh and rotten fish and unwashed bodies festering with slime.

"Cinders?"

No moves. The dog winced. *Smells bad!*

If it moved a hell hound nearly to tears, then the reek was bad indeed. Rising into a half-crouch, Jus sped forward from cover to cover and followed the source of the breeze.

A towering hill of manure steamed in the chill. It marked the edge of Sour Patch, a town that now stood beneath a haze of smoke made from burning homes. Jus slithered on his belly though a patch of leaves, raised his head, and looked at the ruined village in silence.

The tumbledown refugee cottages were all gone. Here and there, flames leaped high, but most had already slumped into a sullen smolder. The fires had burned for at least two hours—time enough to sink into ashes.

Every roof had gone. Most of the shacks were burned, though damp and rain had kept the fires miserably small. Doors in the crowded shantytown lay smashed where something had battered its way into every hiding place.

Nearby, a body lay face down in the mold with a feathered javelin jutting from its back. Jus took careful stock of the silent village, then slithered forward and inspected the corpse.

It was one of the half-orc guards. Jus rolled the body over, looked at the obsidian javelin head that stood out from the corpse's chest, and then let the body lie.

From here, he could see other bodies. These had been physically torn apart, their heads and organs splayed in shocking patterns all over the mud. Jus moved silently from cover to cover, then squatted down to stare into a dead face.

It was an old woman. Beside her lay an old man. The other corpses all seemed to be the aged, the crippled and infirm——here, a boy on crutches, there a veteran warrior missing a leg. Someone had culled the villagers with an obscene, callous brutality, discarding those that failed to meet their needs. The hundreds of survivors had been taken . . . where?

There were tracks in the mud——human and . . . something else. Jus knelt and inspected his find. The non-human tracks were long, clawed, and smeared occasionally by what looked like a heavy tail.

Lizards.

The bestial stink filled the air. Jus approached a broken door and carefully inspected a smear of oil that smudged the wood. The oil gave off a strong whiff of the stench. It gleamed slightly, showing where a large oily creature had shouldered open the door.

Inside the burned house lay the charred skeletons of babies. The Justicar breathed deep and slow, feeling the old, cold fire spreading into his soul, filling his very essence. Cinders growled, deep and feral. Jus narrowed his eyes and lay a hand upon his sword hilt, looking back across his shoulder as he backed into the street.

There were no tracks leading into the village from the woods. Jus walked slowly around the village, finding nothing but the body of another man who had tried to run. The woods were free of the lizard stink. Frowning, Jus returned to the village and stared at it in thought.

Prisoners had been herded together in the street, culled, then marched toward an ancient apple orchard. Jus followed the river of tracks—perhaps two hundred prisoners with half as many captors—and then the tracks suddenly seemed to stop.

The tracks simply shut off as though a line had been drawn across them. Jus looked carefully at the tracks and then stared upward at the crooked apple trees.

Something seemed strange about the bend of two trees up above. The boughs leaned inward to form a perfect arch, almost as if deliberately tied in place.

The arch rested directly above the tracks. Jus circled it, passing a hand carefully into the empty space defined by the archway. His hand tingled as if expecting to find a door, but his fingers met no resistance. He touched only empty air.

Something flickered in midair. Before Cinders could shout a warning, Jus had already turned, his sword a blurring arc of black steel. A javelin split in two as Jus sliced it from the air. He ran roaring at an apple tree that suddenly tried to blunder to one side.

Jus jammed his black sword through the bark and heard a scream. Blood jetted as he ripped the steel free, parried a claw, and hacked a savage blow straight down. His sword cleaved into a reptilian skull, and a reeking creature fell writhing on the dirt.

Colors shifted. What had once looked like the trunk of an apple tree now lay sprawled over the leaves. It was reptilian, a huge bipedal lizard with a chameleon's skin. Colors faded as the creature died, its thick skull split open. Oil oozed from its hide, filling the air with its foul stench. Jus kept away from the creature's reach as it died and wiped his sword on a handful of wet leaves.

"Troglodyte."

The secret of survival was knowledge. Jus had made it his business to study every creature in, on, or under the Flanaess. Troglodytes were a carnivorous lizard species—savage, cunning, subterranean dwellers. Hating sunlight, they would scarcely be likely to venture far away from their caves.

Caves beneath this sort of soil seemed unlikely. Jus looked at the apple tree arch, knowing it was a faerie gate, and wondered just how far away it led.

Intensely stupid, troglodytes would normally have killed and eaten their prey. Were they intelligent enough to herd their meat on the hoof? Perhaps, but no troglodyte could ever puzzle out a magic gate. Jus cast about the orchard carefully then began inspecting every tree.

A flicker of motion caught his eye on a bough high above. Jus scowled, sheathed his sword, and climbed into the lower boughs.

Motion flickered again, and he found it. A single black silk thread had snagged upon the bark. Jus inspected without touching, then brought Cinders's snout close to the treasure.

"Can you smell it through the stink?"

Little bit. Cinders snuffled unhappily. *Is faerie smell.*

Jus sat in the tree for a long moment of silent thought. He carefully retrieved the fallen thread and stored it in a folded paper inside his pouch.

It seemed he had work to do.

* * * * *

Half an hour saw him home again. He passed a giant's crumbling bones and then walked into weed-strewn streets. Outside the old tavern, Polk's cart stood hitched to his rather nervous mule. Enid stood amongst her saddlebags and scrolls, awkwardly trying to fit them across her own back. Jus appeared silently, hitched the sphinx's bags into place, and tied the straps. She beat her huge, heavy wings to test the load and then looked back at him in alarm.

"Heavens, what's that smell?"

"Troglodyte." Jus went to a rain barrel and took a handful of ash to scrub his sword and his hands. "Polk! We're leaving! Move it or we'll be late!"

Bustling out of the tavern and looking as though he had been seeking the solace of his magic faerie bottle, Polk winced as he walked into the light.

"What is it, son? What's happening?" Polk's bluster was weighed down by misery. "We ain't late. There's nowhere we have to be, nothing we have to do."

"We have to get to the ruined castle." Jus tightened his sword belt, settled Cinders properly in place, and then fastened a hand into Polk's tunic and lifted the small man onto the driving seat of the cart.

"Why the castle?"

"The day's wasting." The Justicar began leading the way down the road. He could feel his two companions staring at his back. "We have to get back to where I killed the hydra. If we're not there by midnight, we'll be late."

Enid hurried along, drawing anxiously level with the Justicar. "Late? Whatever for?"

"To meet Escalla." Jus felt a nasty inward glow of satisfaction at a secret well kept. "When she comes, she'll be coming fast. Have you got her gear?"

Polk and Enid both sat in place. The cart stopped. The two travelers stared at Jus as he looked at them with an artfully raised brow.

Polk blinked like a stunned owl. "B-but she said she was staying with the faeries!"

"It was all a pack of lies! It's what she does, Polk. Escalla says she owes it to future generations." The big man pulled a coal from his pouch and popped it into Cinders's mouth. He breathed deeply, filled with new energy. Suddenly it seemed to be a brighter day.

"She'll be escaping in a couple of hours. Come on! Looks like we'll be on the run from the whole Seelie Court."

Cinders grinned like a mad piranha and energetically thumped his tail against Jus's backside. *Faerie coming back! Faerie coming back!*

The Justicar marched down the road with a new energy in his step. Polk and Enid exchanged one brief glance of joy and then hastened after him.

"Son! Hey, son! But her father's wishes! Ain't you breaking a law or something?"

"Law?" The Justicar walked onward, his face wreathed in a smile. "Polk, forced marriages are unjust." The big man hitched his sword. "Don't you remember? No one touches the faerie."

Polk suddenly grinned, flicked out his reins, and drove happily off along the road.

"Hurry up, son! Quit yer dawdlin', or we'll be late!"

8

The morning dawned bright. It always did. Illusion spells saw to it, and if winter shadows seemed at odds with a summer sun, then a flick of the imagination whisked all one's troubles away.

Escalla rose from her bed and felt the air flicker with spy spells as her mother's agents kept a tight watch on their prey. The girl washed and dressed nicely in gray silk. The slowglass necklace had been thoughtfully placed to record her every movement in her sleep. Escalla looked levelly at the thing, then dropped it over her neck before turning to the business of the day.

She spent her first hour of the morning painting upon a papyrus—a painting rich with colors, if a little scant on skill. She propped it up to dry, paced agitatedly about the room, and then fluttered into the morning sun.

Mother awaited her on the lawns. They looked at one another—one lean and sculpted, the other lithe and sharp. Escalla's mother finally turned and signaled for her daughter to walk with her.

"You have been very curt with your betrothed. I expect you to treat him with more cordiality."

"He wanted to sip something, but it wasn't cordial." Escalla proudly held up her hems as she stepped over the lawn. "Are you pimping me now, mother?"

The woman glared coldly at her daughter. "This clan has plans that reach far beyond mere woods and fields and streams. Tielle realizes it, but the gods have cursed us with having to seal our deal through you."

"Thank you, Mother. I love you, too."

"Lord Ushan is still fighting the bargain. He wants none of his power lost to Clan Nightshade." Escalla's mother could have been talking to the wind. "We need the nephew's interest. Go to him tonight."

"I will not."

"You *will*. You father may have forgotten the way you left us, but I have not." Escalla's mother turned a bitter glance upon the girl. "If this alliance fails, if you deny me the Court, then I shall seal you to keep the Queen of Wind and Woe *permanent* company."

"I'm sure you know the route."

Escalla's mother had given her birth—but merely to bind Clan Nightshade's lord to her in marriage. There was no love lost between mother and daughter. In Escalla's view, detonating her mother might be the best favor that she could ever do for her father.

The walk led about the house to the stables. A peculiar reek escaped the attention of faerie spellcasters, making Escalla frown. With her mind fixed upon her plans, Escalla's mother scarcely seemed to care.

"Go to your old rooms tonight," her mother said, "but mind you don't give him the whole cake! Enough of a nibble to prevent him wriggling out of the marriage tomorrow. Men are always fools enough to be caught by the glands."

Escalla gave a scornful sniff at her mother. "As I'm certain Father could tell me."

At the stables, Tarquil stood admiring a prime young faerie dragon. Tarquil sketched a bow toward Escalla. Watched by her mother, Escalla gave the man an interested appraisal and a smile.

Mother approved. She retired from the field, leaving Escalla to turn away . . . and give a secret little smile.

❖   ❖   ❖   ❖   ❖

By evening, Escalla's preparations had been made. Her mother had kept her well away from any spellbooks. Any attempt at magic would bring the spies running, and all the main gateways to the Flanaess were set with alarms. But to a creature who had grown up here, who had played here and languished through a frustrated adolescence right here in the palace, there were countless other secret doors.

As night fell, Escalla walked to a particular patch of orchids beside a pond filed with swans. She waved the illusions away and found a little patch of dandelions closing their petals to the slowly sinking sun. She plucked a flower and tucked it carefully into her cleavage.

Escalla had dressed with care. She wore her slowglass necklace to please her mother's spies and wore a dress of white silk that fit her like a second skin. She posed, feeling a shift in the air that told her that her mother's invisible spy was pleased. With a last moment's thought, she picked up the little painting she had made that morning and tucked it underneath her arm.

The palace lay quiet—deliberately quiet. Mother had cleared the way, using her own spells to shield Escalla's tryst from view. Escalla fluttered quietly onto her old balcony. Her sister's room next door still showed a little gleam of light. Escalla sneered, then quietly sensed the way ahead for any spells.

From the gardens, Tarquil's bodyguard saw her. The faerie gave an oily smirk and deliberately turned his back, hiding his view of the room and balcony. Escalla seethed then dropped lightly down to make her way into her own loved and hated haunts.

The room had been repainted but remained the same otherwise. A great arched mirror along one wall reflected the rock garden and a sumptuous bed. Lying face down, Tarquil seemed to be sleeping rather easily for a man about to be married, although the reek of alcohol in the room apparently told why. If anyone expected much activity from Tarquil tonight, they had sadly miscalculated.

Escalla looked at the figure sprawled unmoving on her old bed and gave a laugh of contempt. She hung her painting above the balcony door, looked at it, frowned, set it straight, then turned back to the bed. It was time to get to business.

Escalla hung her slowglass necklace from a door handle where it could overlook the bed. Mother must have her evidence!

Moving with a deliberate, slow sensuality, Escalla stripped away her outer clothes. She started with her gloves, doing a little dance for the inevitable audience. Next came her slippers, and then the dress. Finally, she stood in stockings and sheer underwear. She whipped the gauzy curtains closed over the balcony and walked sensuously over to the bed.

Escalla looked slyly back across her shoulder. The gauze curtains twitched and parted as something invisible stole softly into the room behind her.

BOOM!

Enid's stun scroll, now framed and reversed with its back turned into a bad watercolor landscape, blasted magic downward as the spy crossed under it. A body jerked and thudded to the ground.

"Gotcha!"

Escalla laughed, jammed her gloves into the invisible spy's mouth, tied him up with stockings, and shoved him beneath a pile of Tarquil's laundry in the far corner of the room.

Tarquil was still asleep, and Escalla had thirty seconds to spare. What girl could resist?

Escalla took position in the eye of the slowglass necklace and gave a little wave. Whispering to the necklace, she slapped herself upon the rear.

"Hey, Tarquil! Here we go. Look and weep into your damned liquor!" Escalla made a face into the slowglass gem, gave a traditional sign with her finger, then threw her dandelion flower at her old mirror.

The mirror flashed, shimmered, and a new gate opened into another world. Escalla took a running dive at the mirror and disappeared, the gate closing an instant after she plunged through.

This was the route she had used for countless secret trips to the Flanaess in her teenage years—a route her mother had never been able to pin down. Escalla emerged half-clothed in a stream. It was pitch dark and cold as ice. The girl screeched, sending bubbles to the surface, then turned herself into a very long and wriggly eel.

A pipe still led down into old irrigation drains. The eel sped

along the waterway, stopping only to snatch a copper coin from a
pile hidden in a sunken flowerpot many years ago. The eel whirled,
sped past a row of sunken archways, and reached a deep, dark pool
inhabited by a giant pike. The pike made a lunge, but Escalla the eel
sped nimbly away. An archway of fallen rock stood out in the filtered
underwater light. The eel used its copper coin as a pass. The coin
flashed and disappeared, the gateway opened, and the eel sped
through—

To find itself falling freely through a forest sky.

The gate exited from the arches of an ancient aqueduct. Escalla's
body flashed as she shifted shape. An instant later a rather large and
fluffy owl flapped its way into the cold night air.

To the south lay the seashore with its towns and boats and taverns—the world Escalla had spied upon as a little girl. To the north
there lay nothing by the empty forest. With a smirk, the owl sped
northward, scanning downward for a landmark it might recognize.

There.

A road with big statue heads. Escalla swooped downward, lofted
over a village scattered with giants' bones, and saw a distant castle
with a teetering tower.

Light glimmered beneath her as she turned a victory roll above
the castle courtyard. She changed into her normal form and
streamed down to be caught in a pair of waiting arms.

"Ta-daaaaah!" Cradled in Jus's grasp, Escalla threw her arms out in
triumph. "She's back, and she's here to sta*aaaawk*—*!"*

Escalla felt herself crushed in a bear hug. Jus held her in silence
with his face pressed into her hair. Escalla felt her ribs creak but
clung to him with glad ferocity. Above her, Cinders's white teeth
gleamed, and his red eyes shone.

Hi!

"Hey, pooch! I'm back." Escalla managed to make herself some
breathing room in Jus's grasp. "I'm back."

Jus and Escalla stood clasped together for a long moment. Finally
Escalla drew a breath and looked into the night.

Polk had warmed a blanket for her at the fire. The teamster swept it around her, grinning like a maniac, and puffed with pride—clearly giving himself credit for having arranged the entire escape. Escalla opened her mouth to say hello and instead found Polk's bottle jammed between her lips.

"Drink, girl! It'll warm you! Good for the blood, the adventuring blood!" Polk pulled the bottle free as Escalla turned green and gasped for breath. "Amphisbanae double-snake's head whiskey! That pixie bottle of yours is a gem!"

The faerie coughed as though trying to wrench her esophagus out of her throat. With tears in her eyes, she gave a thumbs up to Polk and Enid. Purring like a cage of satiated lions, Enid paced about in the background putting out fires and cleaning up the camp.

Jus handed Escalla her cherished leather clothes, her battle wand, and her books of spells.

"How long have we got?" he asked.

"Maybe an hour—until morning, tops." The girl dressed swiftly and efficiently, keeping one eye on the sky. "There'll be faerie dragons, elf hounds, and faeries. Mother will probably summon eagles and stuff."

"What do we do?"

"We head for a bolt hole and sit tight for a week."

The group walked out of the castle and followed Escalla toward the old moat. The girl hummed happily, hugging her ice wand tight against her heart. Behind her Enid politely fluffed her wings.

"We're terribly glad to have you back. How did the wedding preparations go?"

"Oh, pretty good. Shame to miss it. They made a cake and everything!" Escalla turned and eagerly waved her hands. "You should have seen the dress! Pure white and bigger'n a landshark!"

Walking at Escalla's side, Jus flicked her a glance bright with secret delight. "A *white* wedding dress?"

Hovering indignantly, the girl bridled. "Hey! I'm entitled!"

"*Oh?*"

Everyone turned to stare in amusement at Escalla, who instantly panicked as she felt her reputation fall to pieces.

"N-n-not to say that I'm not experienced!"

Jus's teeth gleamed. "Yeah, how about with another person?"

"Keep it up, baldie!" The faerie had turned a shade of scarlet. "Right now I'm thinking you'd look pretty good as a size eleven frog!"

Flying haughtily on her way, the faerie swept down to the castle moat, trying to ignore the amused looks from behind her. She tugged her clothing into place, sniffed importantly, and hovered beside the pond.

"If you people are *quite* finished, shall I show you how a true master's escape is done?"

Cinders looked at her and sniggered happily. *Funny!*

"Cinders, I don't think a hearth rug with teeth has any call to be mocking *my* love life!" Escalla shook out her wings "Right. Now can we please get going?"

Jus looked up at her and stroked his chin. "The faeries can fly, have magic faerie hounds, and use scrying spells. What's the best way to evade them?"

"Dunno." Escalla gave a happy shrug. "We're lucky! They'll miss us somehow. Don't worry about it." The girl snapped her fingers. "Trust me. I'm a faerie!"

Polk, Enid, Jus, and Cinders all simply looked at her. The Justicar sucked on a tooth and said, "Trust to luck? That's your whole escape plan?"

"Look. I just escaped from the whole Seelie Court! I can't be expected to handle everything!" The faerie waved her hands in indignation. "Some of the details I have to leave to *you!*"

The Justicar looked at the forest and gave a tired sigh. "Are all your escapes like this?"

From a tree overhead, there came a sudden weary sigh. "Most of them."

Jus whirled, his hand on his sword.

Escalla's father sat on a tree bough, looking old, tired, and glum.

Everyone stared up at the faerie lord. An uncomfortable silence reigned for long moments. Putting on her best innocent grin, Escalla gave him a timid little tinkle of a wave.

"Hello, Dad. Ah . . ." Escalla gave a hopeful little flip of her antennae. "Why all the excitement in the forest?"

"My dear, I believe they have come to ask you why you murdered Tarquil." Lord Charn looked at his daughter and gave a heavy sigh. "This time you've really managed to outdo yourself."

9

When you wanted a fire in a hurry, Cinders was always ready to oblige. Sitting happily in the cellar of the ruined castle, the hell hound breathed little licks of flame from his nostrils to warm Jus's battered old camp kettle. The brew steamed, and Jus loomed above the kettle to pour himself another serving before seeing to his guests. The Justicar patted Cinders on the head as he passed, making the hell hound thump his long tail against the floor.

"Thanks, Cinders."

Welcome!

Above the castle, an illusory light blinked and flared. It matched the movements of real faeries searching for the fugitive Escalla. For a while at least, the magic would keep the faerie hunt at bay.

Deeply annoyed by events, Escalla sat high up near the ceiling on a jutting stone, her knees beneath her chin and a look of total annoyance on her face. She was in a magnificent sulk, seething and muttering as she shot clandestine looks at her father.

Answering the implied question, Lord Charn snorted as he settled by the fire. "It's *my* realm, girl. I picked it because of all the damned gates I found here." Frowning in annoyance, the faerie lord sipped tea from an old tin mug. "I just thought of what route I'd take if I was trying to avoid the wife. The pike fish told me the rest."

Finding a stone big enough for him, the Justicar sat down. "Pike? What pike?"

"Carnivorous fish. Big one. Wife can't stand them." Lord Charn made a face as he tasted Jus's abominable tea. "I put no end of things near gates to stop the wife going through." The faerie lord gave a snort. "I have to have somewhere quiet to go."

"You stay in the woods here?"

"Rather than the palace? When I can. Lets me get a bit of peace." Carefully setting his tea aside before it could poison him, Lord Charn fluttered his wings. "Now there'll be no damned peace till all this nonsense is done."

Perched upon her stone, Escalla shot a petulant look at her father. "Dad, I did *not* kill that stupid cavalier!"

"Don't be dense, girl!" Lit by the hell hound's nostril flames, Lord Charn's face took on sharp, wicked shadows. "If I thought you'd killed him, I wouldn't be sitting here with you drinking tea!"

Tired and annoyed, Lord Charn made the mistake of sipping the tea again. Wincing, he put the cup far away and turned to carefully regard the Justicar. The faerie lord's eyes sparked as he measured the big warrior across the fire.

"You went to White Plume Mountain? You were the one who did in Keraptis's disciple?"

"Escalla, Cinders, Polk, and myself."

"Yes." The faerie lord sipped tea again, which distinctly tasted of the onion soup that had been made last night in the same pot. "Is my daughter any good?"

Jus made a gruff noise, shifted his dire shadow in the gloom, and said, "She's damned good, one of the best I've seen."

Above them, Escalla beamed.

"Well, she'll need to be." Charn gave another sigh, then kicked irritably at a pebble. "She doesn't belong with us." The faerie lord spoke a spell, opened up his hands, and provided bottles of decent wine. "Here. It's not faerie wine and certainly not the sixty-three." That particular vintage seemed to have scarred some lives forever. "Sit, drink, and let me tell you a tale or three."

Polk immediately shot forward, ignored a glass and took a bottle for himself. Enid the sphinx sat down to clumsily nurse a glass between big furry paws, sneezing as the bubbles tickled at her nose. Jus waved the wine away and contented himself with his awful tea.

Lord Charn swirled his wine inside a tiny thimble glass and began.

"We need to come out into the world. My daughter is the test. Faeries could be an instrument for good or bad. I suspect we might verge toward the bad. We've spent too long looking after our intrigues." Lord Charn heaved a sigh then leaned toward the Justicar. "Intrigues have a way of excusing evil. Tarquil's dead, and in my own house."

Clambering over Enid's head to fetch a glass of wine, Escalla shot another angry look at her father. "I told you, I didn't kill the bugger!"

"But there's evidence enough to slam you right into the hands of the Faerie Council."

Jus leaned forward, listening. Polk leaned forward, thieving more wine. Sitting beside the Justicar, Lord Charn laid out the situation for his daughter's companions.

"Lord Ushan's valets came to Tarquil's room to summon him. Tarquil was discovered dead, lying on the bed. There was an empty cup—looks like the man was poisoned. When the palace was searched, it was discovered that Escalla had gone. My wife's maids knew that Escalla had arranged a secret tryst with Tarquil in his room."

Jus stroked at the harsh stubble of his chin. Beside him, Cinders listened with pointed ears, his red eyes gleaming.

"No spies in Tarquil's room saw anything?"

"His own alarm spells had been disabled. However, Escalla had apparently spent at least two days making sure that she would be unobserved. Scrying shields in place, careful blanking of spying spells . . . Her mother had a spy following her. Escalla knocked him out when he tried to follow her into Tarquil's room." The faerie lord leaned closer. "What's more, Tarquil's bodyguard saw Escalla sneaking into the room just before the body was discovered. He remembers that she seemed stealthy."

Escalla remembered the bodyguard and gave a vicious curse. "He knew why I was supposed to be there!" Escalla leaped to the ground and paced in anger. "That bastard! I'll—!"

"In good time." Her father turned to the girl. "Did you see anything? Any evidence you can remember?"

Escalla planted her hands against her heart and squawked in indignation. *"I didn't do it!"*

"That's not going to be much of a defense." Father glared at daughter. "You had motive. You had opportunity. You blanked out scrying spells and knocked out the spy who followed you, then you fled off into the wilderness to escape!"

Escalla sank into nervous anxiety, then suddenly shot up, filled with energy. "Ah! The slowglass! I hung the necklace from a door handle overlooking the bed!" Escalla smacked her fist into her palm. "Ha! There you go! It'll show him alive and me leaving—everything you need to know!"

"Just what we need," Lord Charn shrugged, "but no one reported seeing a necklace in the room. Still, we can search for it and see."

"What about spells?" The Justicar's meat and bread came from investigating injustices and crime. "Can you speak with the deceased?"

"No ghost is present. It must have already fled."

The faerie lord rose to his feet and paced in agitation, his head level with Jus's thigh.

Escalla sat irritably down by the fire and cursed. "Poop."

"Poop indeed." Lord Charn made a rock float over to serve as a chair for the girl, bringing her to sit between himself and the Justicar.

"Now listen. Your mother is going to use you as a sop to Clan Sable. They want a murderer, and by slinging you to them, she will be able to save her ambitions. Through sacrificing her own daughter, she shows that she is a true member of the court, and she will still have your sister to marry off to the Sable Clan." Charn's antennae slanted. Apparently there was no love lost between himself and his wife. "Your sister and mother have great plans. This is almost better for them than having you and Tarquil safely wed. Meanwhile, Clan Sable screams out murder and assassination, calling for our eternal barring from the Seelie Court."

Jus thought upon the situation, his face its usual mask of sharp intelligence. "You want Escalla's name cleared."

"Of course I do! She's my girl. *My* girl!" The resemblance between father and daughter in mind and spirit was certainly remarkable. "I let her go to the world because it was what's best for her."

"*Ha!*" Escalla gave a sour sniff. "Don't talk rubbish! If you'd known I was skiving off in the first place, you would have stopped it. Mother must have given you hell." The girl gave a sniff and sipped her tea "Probably took you a whole week to realize I was gone."

"By failing to pay attention, I was obeying unconscious higher motives." Lord Charn clearly shared a heritage of glibness with his daughter. "I knew it was right and proper that you take your place within the world"

"Oh bosh!"

"Bosh yourself." Charn dusted imaginary crumbs from his tunic. "Who was it that showed you where the dandelions grew in the first place?"

Miffed, Escalla sat crosslegged on her stone. "Fine! So I'm too incompetent even to run away from home by myself, and my own mother is conspiring to have me executed. Anything else?"

Speaking for the benefit of the ever-patient Justicar, Lord Charn refilled his glass.

"Lord Faen is with us. He is chief advisor to the Erlking and is in charge of the investigation. He will let us clear Escalla's name if it can be done. If we show a love of justice, that will be better evidence of goodwill to the court than throwing a scapegoat to the dogs." The anxious father glanced at Escalla, running his fingers through his hair. "Justicar, I know you have experience here. I am at a loss! As you love and value my daughter, please help us clear her name!"

Jus nodded slowly and thoughtfully. Rising from his seat, his vast bulk loomed like a giant above the faeries. "Is it possible for me to see the body and the murder site?"

"It can be arranged, but it must be *now*, before the faeries return to the palace from the first hunt!" Lord Charn rose quickly from his seat. "There is a gate at an archway high above, but we'll have to run!"

Escalla, Polk, and Enid all rose together. Lord Charn looked at them in alarm.

"No! Escalla, stay hidden. This must be fast. If your mother's spies see visitors, she'll follow you and strike. I'll take the Justicar alone. If we're not back here in an hour, then go wait for him in your spider bubble in the pond!"

Lord Charn kissed his daughter, gripped her shoulders, and then whirred up into the air, his wings sparkling. Behind him, the Justicar seated his sword in his belt. Cinders swept about him like a cloak, the hell hound's grin gleaming as the creature was fastened in his rightful place. Following him to the cellar door, Escalla anxiously wrung her hands then came to hover in front of Jus face.

"Jus, I didn't do it."

He looked into her frightened green eyes for a long moment, then reached out to touch her cheek. "I know."

He nodded, then turned and walked away. Once he was gone from the room, Escalla's night seemed suddenly frightening.

✳ ✳ ✳ ✳ ✳

The ruins of the keep yielded an arch, and the arch had long been overgrown with ivy. Lord Charn hovered nearby as Jus hauled his powerful frame up the sheer stonework toward the magic gate.

"There are gates everywhere, of course, sir Justicar. People just can't see them. This forest is a nexus, a place where dozens of them congregate. It's why we settled here in the first place." The faerie lord plucked a sprig of fennel from his purse. "There! This should be the one!"

Hanging from a sheer stone wall thirty feet above the ground Jus paused while searching for a handhold.

"Fennel?"

"A key for the gate." Charn put his other herbs away. "Each one is triggered by a different herb or token. A copper coin, a dandelion, splash of wine . . . You can trigger them by accident if you're unlucky enough. That's why mortals think the whole forest is haunted."

As Jus reached the rough stone precipice below the ancient stone arch, Lord Charn gestured toward it with his herbs.

"This gate leads to the palace lands, but I don't quite know where. Stay hidden until I can find Lord Faen, and we'll bring you to the murder site."

Jus nodded.

Lord Charn hovered before the door, then tapped the blank space of the archway with his sprig of dried fennel. The fennel flashed and disappeared. Suddenly the archway shimmered.

"Now!"

With a heave, Jus shoved himself upward. He stepped though into a soft gray light and found himself on all fours upon a fragrant forest floor. Illusions were transparent to Cinders's eye. The dog sniffed and then hissed in Jus's mind.

Trees is trees. Leaves is leaves. Flower bushes is illusion.

Jus chose the real concealment of the leaves over the illusory comforts of the bushes. An instant later, he lay in a drift of leaves, perfectly still and quite invisible with only Cinders's black nose showing above the mulch. When Lord Charn appeared, he looked about in brief confusion, then shrugged and whirred off on his way.

Jus saw that he was lying amongst the plane trees—the gateways to universes of fire, flame, and antimatter. The faerie lands were no place to wander carelessly; one wrong turn might be your last.

Lord Nightshade returned long minutes later with another faerie at his side. Cinders sniffed the scent of them long before they arrived.

Escalla's father. One other faerie, a male.

Jus heaved upward, shedding leaves like a leviathan shedding the ocean floor. Two faeries hovered nearby, impressed as the big man emerged from total invisibility. Jus brushed wet leaves from Cinders's fur and looked levelly at Lord Charn and his guest.

The newcome faerie was slender and affected long gray hair and a wisp of a goatee. He sketched a bow as Lord Charn made the introductions.

"Justicar, you remember Lord Faen. My Lord Faen, the Justicar is something of a specialist. The elves of the Celadon trained him."

The elegant, calm Lord Faen looked coolly at the Justicar. "What temples does he favor?"

The Justicar's dark, dire voice seemed to fill the wood. "Justice flows from the heart, not from gods."

Nodding noncommittally, Lord Faen turned in midair and said, "Come then. We have cleared all eyes away for a short time. We will show you what we can."

Jus strode like a dark giant, the black hell hound skin wreathing him in shadow.

"You have interviewed everyone who might have been near the room at the time of death?"

"We did what we could. Truth spells are seen as an insult, and at the moment, insults are something we cannot afford." Lord Faen flew pace by pace with the Justicar, detecting a kindred spirit in the mortal's mind. "A certain amount of conspiracy has taken place. Maids and servants have contrived to be absent. There is only the bodyguard, who identified Escalla. Indeed, she left her dress in the murder room, and he could describe it to us exactly."

"Escalla's mother organized a tryst."

"And might have reached the Sable clan guards and servants." Faen ushered the way toward a balcony. "It is here. I'll tell you nothing. Your own untainted impressions will carry better force."

The palace had not been made with human scale in mind. Still, there were enough humanoid servants to require high ceilings and large doors. Jus carefully approached the balcony, eyeing a place where he could use a tree to leaver himself up and over the fragile-looking balustrade. He then knelt in the leaves below and let the hell hound go to work.

"Smell anything?"

Faeries. Cinders thoughtfully sifted scents. *Male once walked here— two-three hours ago.*

There were tracks consistent with a single faerie waking slowly below the balcony—probably the bodyguard. Since faeries could fly, tracking was hardly likely to reveal real clues. Jus looked carefully at the eaves and railings then heaved himself up the tree and onto the balcony.

The room had a wide window screened by curtains of silken gauze. The curtains had been thrown open and the room trampled by enthusiastic, clumsy investigators. Even so, there was much to see.

The body had been moved, but where it had lain, the bed was indented. The pillows and sheets seemed otherwise undisturbed. If Tarquil had come here to sleep, then he had lain down and found no time to toss and turn.

Beside the bed was a table that seemed a little like doll's furniture. Jus knelt carefully on the carpet, going onto all fours to examine the half-sized furnishings. A wine bottle stood open beside a pair of glasses. One glass stood untouched and full, while the other seemed half empty. Jus sniffed the cup, and Cinders confirmed his suspicions.

Bad smells! Wine poisoned.

Holding the half-empty glass up to the light showed a faint oily film down one side. Poison had been trickled into the glass from an outside source.

The wine was poured carefully back into the bottle, and Jus surveyed the results. Nodding, he put the empty glasses aside, then cast carefully back and forth across the room.

No necklace hung from any doorknob. Various hands had wrenched open cupboards and curtains looking for would-be assassins. Yet a gleam came from the carpet, and when Jus bent down to examine it, he found the tiniest of tiny golden links—a piece of delicate chain from a necklace that had been broken clean through.

Cinders breathed a scent and shivered his long black tail. *Escalla's skin.*

"Just so."

The Justicar looked carefully at the door that led through the apartments and into the palace. He opened the door and looked into a passageway lined with brilliant animated murals. Searching the empty corridor with a long, hard glance, Jus turned away, returned into the room . . . and caught sight of a single black thread hanging from the doorjamb.

He trapped it, laid in in a folded paper, and put it in his pouch beside the golden link. Rising, Jus carefully dusted off his hands.

"Where have you put the body?"

"We are about to take it to the chapel." Lord Faen swung open the door to the passageway and looked carefully out into the deserted palace. "We have lain him out in the drawing room down here until then. Come quickly."

One man, one hell hound skin, and two faeries swept quietly out into the corridor. They moved three rooms down and edged into a room guarded by a faerie warrior. The warrior looked studiously away from the Justicar, ignoring his presence entirely but nodding to Lord Faen.

In the long, cool room beyond lay the body of the Cavalier Tarquil. The corpse seemed pathetically small, like a child sleeping in the grass. They had laid him on his back, with his hands out at an angle from his body. Jus knelt beside the corpse and removed its cover sheet, looking at the clothed body in professional, dispassionate chill.

"Is this how you always lay out a corpse?"

"No, but the body stiffened in death rigor, and we could not cross his hands decently upon his breast."

Nodding, the Justicar inspected the body's mouth. The lips were not inflamed, nor the inner mouth burned.

Jus opened the cavalier's shirt and pulled up his inner clothes. The blood had pooled on the body's belly side, leaving a purplish color, but it was already on the move again now that the body was laid out. Soon the corpse would be as pale as ash.

"How long ago did you find him?"

"One hour."

"Lying on his face." Jus levered the body over on its side and then began methodically to strip it naked. Shocked and reluctant, the two faerie lords half started forward before leaving the man to his work.

Jus inspected the corpse's skin inch by minute inch, then looked beneath its nails and through its hair. Finally the big man sank back onto his heels, looming vast as an ogre as he nodded slowly in thought.

Jus let out his breath and spoke. "He was poisoned, but not by wine."

Lord Charn raised his brows in silence, but Lord Faen chose to speak. "Not by the wine?"

"No. Here on his scalp and hidden by his hair is a puncture wound."

The faeries leaned in to see. The Justicar parted the black hair of the dead cavalier to show a small hole in the scalp, far broader than a needle puncture. It had oozed a clear fluid, and the hair strands beside it were silvered with a dried mucous or glue. Jus let the hell hound's nose nestle close to the puncture hole.

"Cinders?"

Cinders smells fish.

"Yes." The Justicar sat back in cold triumph. "Cinders smells fish."

The two faerie lords looked at him in silence, and the Justicar enlightened them.

"See the dried slime? It's from a cone shell—a venomous mollusk that uses a puncturing tongue to kill. Instantly lethal. Small, concealable in the palm on anyone gloved and confident enough to use it. Even a faerie."

Lord Faen scowled. "And where might a cone shell be found in a forest?"

"Nowhere. This is a kuo-toan assassination technique—right down to hiding the wound in the hairline."

"You have encountered it before?"

"I've read about it." The Justicar wiped his hands. "This is my profession. I am the Justicar."

Sitting back on his haunches, the Justicar thoughtfully regarded the corpse. "Cone shells come from tropical reefs. This has been carried a long, long way with the intention to murder." Jus stoked his chin, black stubble rasping in the quiet room. "The wine glasses were a decoy. When the wine was put back in the bottle, it made the bottle totally full. There was not even half a mouthful missing. It reached the stain line inside the bottle neck."

Escalla's father grinned a predatory grin, apparently extremely pleased to witness the Justicar at his work. "Yes, lad. Now what else was in that room? What didn't other eyes see?"

"There is one link from the gold chain that held Escalla's slow-glass pendant. It was by the windows, probably where Escalla tore the necklace off and broke it. The necklace itself is gone. Is it valuable?"

"Perhaps a thousand times the value of a similarly sized diamond."

Jus made a soundless whistle. Such a necklace might conceivably buy an entire castle, garrison it, and pay the troops' wages for a year.

It was time to retire from the room. Jus found a balcony and leaped over it, then let the two faerie lords follow him into the woods. Hidden by the trees, the big man sat and laid out tiny paper packets on his knee.

"The body has been dead longer than two hours. There was rigor. I'd make it three or four hours dead, meaning he'd been dead before Escalla was seen entering the room."

Stroking his goatee, Lord Faen nodded. "A hostile mind might argue that the effects of the poison caused the muscles to freeze in spasm."

"Yes. It's not proof." Jus stroked his chin. "But the mouth was red at the back of the tongue. He was orally poisoned and then stung later by the cone shell. The shell wound hadn't bled, not even a bead. His blood was already cold when the puncture was made."

Pacing carefully back and forth, Lord Charn cleared his throat in thought.

"Was someone making certain of his kill? A poison draught then the more definite poison administered at a later time?"

"Possibly. The poison glasses were a decoy, though. There was no burning of the victim's mouth tissues. I find that interesting." Jus opened up one of the tiny packets of paper on his knee. Inside, carefully pinned in a slot of the paper lay a single delicate piece of black thread. He gave it to the faeries, who leaned over it and thoughtfully stroked their beards.

"A thread from clothing?"

Jus shook his head. "It seems too clean. Threads ripped from clothing show furred surfaces from the abrasion." Jus leaned in closer. "This is a thread I found elsewhere. Identical to this second thread, from Escalla's doorjamb. They're the same length and neatly cut, like threads bunched and all cut to a length."

There was a sudden cool flood of understanding from Lord Charn. "Gateway tokens."

"Gateway tokens." Jus held up the threads. "Keys used to travel through the forest's magic doors."

Escalla's father sat on a tree stump that had been colonized by orange fungi. The fungi gleamed like fruit peel as the faerie lord used the shelves to rest his boots.

"I have a master list of the gates and keys we know of. I will look and see which ones require black silk."

Jus nodded and asked, "Where do the gates go?"

"From here? Only to the forest. Within the forest, there are gates to other places across the Flanaess. The forest seems to have served as a travel nexus." The man rose to his feet. "What are we looking for? Who killed Tarquil?"

"A faerie—a faerie who travels through a gate triggered by black thread, a faerie who could not resist taking the slowglass necklace for his own. The murderer had access to a marine cone shell and knew how to handle it and had the means to keep it alive. And he was able to pass your guards without suspicion."

Unhappy, Lord Faen plucked at his beard and said, "I cannot use this to clear Escalla's name. There is evidence enough to convict her if Sable presses for a judgment. We must catch the murderer and link the cone shell, black threads, and motive to them."

"It can be done." Jus kept the tiny golden link broken from Escalla's necklace in his hand. "This gold link was part of the slowglass necklace. We can use it for a location spell to find the rest of the necklace, if you have a mage capable of casting it."

"We have mages capable of casting it." Charm arose on whirring wings. "I will arrange it, and I will fetch the master gate list."

"Then we will find your murderer." Jus arose, his knees cracking and autumn leaves drifting from his clothes. "We have the tools. We merely need the time."

❖   ❖   ❖   ❖   ❖

Back at the castle cellar, Enid, Polk, and Escalla were busy stuffing themselves with a favorite delicacy—ham sandwiches made with fresh white bread and butter. With all due seriousness, Enid sat holding a little sandwich between her great paws. The mule stood in one corner, its eyes nervous as it listened to creatures hooting in the night.

Meanwhile, Polk slathered butter upon more bread and let his voice boom into the gloom. "Don't worry, girl! False accusations are all part of the deal! Without false accusations, you don't get righteous indignation! Without righteous indignation, you don't get mighty oaths! Without oaths, you don't get gods interfering with heroic souls, and we can't have heroic souls running about doing stuff without being guided by the gods. Stands to reason!"

Worried and annoyed, Escalla looked at him across the surface of a titanic sandwich. "What are you on about now?"

"Gods, girl! Heroes are heroes because they're tools of the gods!"

"Polk, what's heroic about being a theological hand puppet? Anyway, have you seen the names these gods give themselves?" Escalla took a mouthful of bread and ham. "Ne'fer fo'ow a god whosh name reads like shomefing from an apothecary's shelf!"

Her freckles living a life of their own in the gloom, Enid licked butter from her paws and said, "I made a glove puppet once!"

Stones shifted at the door. Without looking up, Escalla made another sandwich filled with extra ham. "Hey, Jus!"

The big man loomed in the blockaded door, checking that all was well. "We're moving out. You're ready?"

"Yep. Spellbooks read, and I'm all charged up!"

"You didn't set a guard?"

"Invisible servant. You just passed him. If it was anyone else, he'd have smashed a bottle on the castle wall." Escalla rose and looked at Jus, handing him the sandwich and trying not to appear as anxious as she felt.

"So did you go and . . . you know . . . see the dead guy and all?"

"Yes." Jus looked levelly at the girl. "Tell me: were you quiet when you went into the room?"

"Ah, maybe?"

"You never noticed he was dead?"

"Um, well he did seem a little subdued." Escalla blinked. "So he was dead all the time?"

"Looks like it." Jus helped shift rocks aside, clearing a path into the castle. "Your father's here. The murderer took your slowglass necklace, and we have a locator. We're going to look at a gate we've found. It's the one the murderers used to escape."

"Oh, hoopy!" Escalla instantly cheered up. "So you can get me off?"

"Nope. Unless we get the slowglass necklace back, you're toast." Jus ushered everyone outside. "Come on!"

Lord Charn awaited his daughter and her friends, keeping a worried look upon the nighttime sky. The distant sound of elf hounds could be heard off to the south. It signified nothing. Hunters could be lying invisible almost anywhere. Escalla's father took his daughter's hands and drew her up into his arms.

Jus began to mount the way back up to the magic gate above the castle courtyard. He called down, "We have to get the murderer before the hunt gets Escalla. She's safest on the move with us. Polk, get climbing!"

The archway above the castle yard was a small window—too small for a sphinx. Enid eyed it unhappily and tested her wings. "Can I fly and meet you where the gate empties out?"

"Best not." Jus cursed and then jumped down to rest a hand on the sphinx's soft brown hair. "Look. Set up shop back at that old deserted tavern. Take Polk's mule with you. Read your books, eat stirges, and make it look like you, Polk, and I have set up camp. We'll be a while. Just wait. We'll come back quick as we can." Jus shoved Polk onward and pressed a sprig of fennel into his hands. "Polk, go through the arch and just stay put!"

"Son, maybe I should stay with Enid and—"

"Enid will keep *her* mouth shut if any faerie hunt comes by. *You* get to come with us!" Jus propelled the man skyward. "Now hurry up!"

Escalla fluttered over to the unhappy Enid, kissed her on the nose, and then shot up toward the gate. As the arch flashed with light, the fugitives slipped through in haste, ending up in the forest near the palace in the faerie realm.

Lord Faen awaited them. He quickly ushered the way to a stone gazebo just out of sight of the family wing of the palace. An archway showed the recent scuff of boots. Jus ushered his party together then turned to lift a hand in farewell to Lords Faen and Charn. Lord Nightshade held out a piece of silver wire and thrust it beneath the gazebo's arch.

Magic flickered. Jus stepped through, dragging the wailing Polk underneath his arm. Left with her father and Lord Faen, Escalla fluttered unhappily. She flew to the gate, stopped, rushed back to give her father a kiss, and then shot through the arch an instant before the gateway flickered shut.

Standing alone with Lord Faen, Escalla's father suddenly felt his world turn a little dim.

10

In the dark of night, the stink of corpses hung foul and sickly sweet. There was a reek of smoke, and a stir of rats and night creatures fleeing from gnawed carrion. Standing beneath an ancient stone archway, Escalla, Jus, and Polk looked about, listening to awful, furtive little noises in the dark.

"Sour Patch."

The shanties were burned, and the bodies of slain refugees were hanging rat-gnawn in the gloom. At least the stink would have driven away any faerie courtiers. Surveying the wreckage, Jus rested his hand on his sword and pointed the way over to the apple orchard.

"This way."

Escalla looked around, appalled by the half-seen corpses in the gloom.

"What the hell happened here?"

"Massacre before dawn this morning. It was a slave raid. They killed the old and weak, then took everyone else through a gate over there in the apple trees."

Escalla had found the body of one of the familiar half-orc guards. She flew slowly backward, trying not to stare at the corpse.

"Wh-who did it?"

"Troglodytes."

"Yeah." Escalla looked bitterly at the stinking dead. "Troglodytes led by a faerie."

The Justicar looked over at her with his steadying dark eyes. "You all right?"

"I'm all right." Escalla blurred her wings and headed for the apple trees. "I'm getting sick of this. Let's get 'em."

A dead troglodyte lay near the gate tree. As Jus fished the carefully folded black threads from his pouch, Escalla wincingly drew close to the bisected troglodyte. A javelin lay glittering in the grass nearby, the head severed from the shaft in the tell-tale sign of Jus's celebrated parry technique.

"Ick! It stinks like an orc's outhouse!"

"Oil." The Justicar wrinkled his nose at the stink. "They excrete an offensive oil when roused."

"It worked. I'm offended." Escalla looked at the hideous splay of troglodyte organs lying on the ground. "Do you have a key to this gate?"

Jus held up a glimmering black thread and said, "I'm pretty sure I do."

"Then try this locator spell thing of yours. Let's see where the slowglass necklace is hiding."

Lord Charn had cast the spell on the necklace. The broken link of Escalla's necklace had been glued to a small sliver of enchanted wood, and the wood had been hung from a length of thread where it could quiver and swivel like a compass. Holding her battle wand casually beneath her arm, Escalla hovered in midair and watched intently as Jus dangled the little charm and let it slowly twist and settle.

The needle pointed south and hung quite still. The Justicar looked at it intently, then bundled the charm back up again.

"You father said it would start to quiver as we got closer."

"Well it's pretty damned still." Escalla ran her fingers through her long blonde hair, letting it spill like a waterfall down her back. "Damn! That was one greedy piece of work, snitching the necklace!"

"We're lucky they seem to value it." Jus settled the faerie into her accustomed place, setting her on his shoulder. "How long until the light passes through the slowglass jewel?"

"Fourteen days. We'll have plenty of time!" Escalla shrugged. "We're only an hour or two behind them. How far can they get?"

Walking around and around the dead troglodyte, Polk heaved a sigh then unshipped a heavy ledger from his pack. He licked his pen—forgetting it was a pen and not a pencil—and took notes with blue ink now staining his tongue.

One trawglodite, the little man scrawled awkwardly, using spelling he invented on the fly. "Was it a mighty battle? Fierce?"

"It chucked a spear at me, and I cut it in half."

"I see. I'll put it down as a mighty blow, then." Polk sniffed, partly from troglodyte stink and partly in annoyance. "Son, do you have any idea how hard it is to keep accurate records around you?"

"Look into my eyes and see how much I care, Polk." Jus jerked his thumb toward the gate. "Now come on! Let's get out of here before the faerie hunt finds us!"

"Wait! Hold on." Escalla hovered with her spellbooks open. She dusted herself in diamond powder from her kit packs and sent spell syllables twisting through the air. Her skin took on a brief gleam of magic, which faded cleverly from view. "There we go!"

Jus glowered. "What was that?"

"Stoneskin! It's brand new. You'll love it!" The girl posed, admiring her perfect, pure white little arm. "Protects you from cuts, punctures, bites, and swords!"

"Can I have one?"

"Tomorrow, man! What? You think I'm made of high level spells?" Escalla ushered the way to the apple tree gate. "You've got armor, muscles, and stuff. Now come on. Let's get weaving!"

Jus held out one of his pieces of black silk thread. As it passed beneath the arched apple boughs, a gateway shimmered into life. Polk immediately walked past Jus into the gate, his quill pen behind one ear and a half eaten apple in his mouth. Jus made an annoyed noise and stepped after the man, Escalla flying along at his side.

* * * * *

They stepped out into a wilderness of charred, dead bones.

It had been a town once, a healthy place with earthen walls

topped by a palisade. Wooden houses and temples now lay burned and broken, making shocking silhouettes against the night stars.

An ancient dolmen made an arch overhead—an arch tall enough to shelter a giant. Jus straightened up, Cinders glistening like new iron in the starlight. He listened for sounds, then strode into the ruins, surrounded by the moan of wind traveling through the weeds.

As Polk crunched on his apple, a voice suddenly echoed from the dark.

"Hold!"

The voice was very excited and very, very young. Jus, Polk, and Escalla turned.

A young man slithered down from the earthen ramparts, holding a crossbow in his hands. Chain mail rattled, and a long sword on the boy's belt threatened to spill him head over heels. He stumbled in his eagerness to keep his captives covered as he yelled out into the dark.

"Sergeant! Sergeant! I've found them! I've got the Takers!"

Escalla instantly turned invisible. Jus held his peace until three more men arrived in a clank and clatter of chain mail armor.

One of the newcomers took one look at the youth and bellowed in rage, "Private Henry! Do these individuals look in the remotest way reptilian?"

"N-no, Sarge, but—"

"Do they perhaps have claws or scales of a lizardlike persuasion of which I am unaware?"

"Uh—" The recruit waved a hand in vindication. "But Sarge! See! The big one's wearing black!"

"Private Henry, you are a pustulous canker on the hallowed butt of the border patrol!"

Annoyed by his recruit as only an old soldier could be, the sergeant looked Jus and Polk carefully up and down. He kept his voice loud and his hands resting near his weapons.

"Gentlemen! Geltane is a strange place to be taking a stroll in the dark."

The Justicar made a bass growl in agreement, then nodded slowly in the dark. "I'm on a private commission, hunting a murderer." Jus looked about at the ruined town. "Someone raided the refugee camp of Sour Patch. The whole adult population's gone."

With a bitter huff of breath, the sergeant relaxed. His martial fury gone, he revealed himself to be a very tired soldier. The man shook his head and pointed across the ruined town.

"Well, I guess they must have come through here. Gods know how. It's at least twenty miles from here, but someone did see movement in the ruins just before dawn." The man turned and led the way along through the ruins. "Found a trail. Looks like a couple of hundred people. The trail just seems to start right about here, and we lose it about half a mile farther on."

"Lose it how?"

The sergeant gave the helpless shrug of an angry, frustrated man. "You got me beat. Come and see." The man clicked his fingers. "Private Henry, you light one field lantern in the approved fashion! Now, boy!"

It took Private Henry a good three minutes to manage the mysteries of his tinderbox. As he worked furiously away in a corner, a little patch of svelte perfection popped into existence beside Jus and produced a brilliantly glowing stone upon a string.

"Hey, J-man! Hey, guys!" Escalla waved to the soldiers. "In the interests of the preservation of social skills, I'm Escalla, the one with the big nose is Polk, and the man with the dog skin is your pal and mine, the Justicar!" Escalla produced her packets of sweets and began to hand out all around. "Here you go. Good for the soul. Private Henry? Good tinderbox, man! You really know how to strike those sparks!" Stared at by astounded soldiers, Escalla slapped her hands and rubbed them together. "So what have we got?"

The Justicar laid a level glance upon Escalla and said, "My partner, Escalla." Jus bent down, producing his own charmed light stone—a gift from Escalla many weeks ago. "Did anyone see who made these tracks?"

No one answered. These were the same tracks as those in Sour Patch—troglodyte footprints flanking a horde of human tracks. The line of march headed straight toward a gap in the ruined walls of the town.

The Justicar stood, looking carefully over the burned ruins nearby. "What happened here?"

"Old history, my friend. The Takers came here a month ago! The town began missing its people five by five, ten by ten. They sealed the gates and gathered together in the temples. Then the Takers came and got 'em in one go." The Sergeant gestured to the dark. "Must have burned about two hundred folk alive in the temples. The rest were just gone. Six hundred folk lost without a trace."

The Justicar turned a slow survey of the ruins. "These 'Takers' . . . you know what they are?"

"Reptilian chameleons. Vicious. They're like troglodytes, only smarter. They have magic. They hit fast, they have brains. No one sees them come or go. No trails ever last more than three miles." The sergeant flexed his hands. "All over Keoland it's the same. Ain't seen anything like it since the giants."

"Giants?"

"Three, maybe four years ago. Giants raided the whole kingdom. Killed hundreds." Walking along beside the trail left by the Takers, the sergeant beckoned Escalla, the Justicar, and Polk to follow. "The forest march is in ruins. We must have lost—what?—two thousand people in the last two months."

Polk ceased crunching on his apple and goggled. "Two *thousand* people! Son, *you've* got a problem!"

Escalla drolly raised one alabaster brow. "Thanks man. They may have picked up on that one by now."

The trail led straight through the shattered town ramparts and then into overgrown fields. Old cabbage crops had gone to seed, and the trampled plants showed the path of the prisoners and their reptilian guards as they headed off toward a wilderness of scrub. The sergeant motioned toward a flat patch over to one side of the trail.

"Found us a dead one there. Half-orcish boy, about ten, maybe twelve. Shot in the back."

Bending carefully over the indicated spot, the Justicar searched carefully amongst the cabbage stalks. "You buried him?"

"Yep. Buried him at midday."

Turning to the sergeant, Jus suddenly tilted his head. "You said *shot*. Not hit by a javelin?"

The sergeant shrugged. "Could have been a javelin. No weapon left in the wound."

"But you said *shot*." A soldier's instincts were not to be ignored. Jus knelt down over the trampled patch of earth and leaves. "Was he found on his front or his back?"

"Lyin' on his, ah, on his back."

Escalla and Polk crowded close, watching in interest as the Justicar combed the dirt with bare fingertips. It was soft black loam, well seasoned with manure by patient gardeners. His fingertips struck something buried in the muck. He brushed dirt aside, and then carefully began digging down into the soil.

An arrow lay buried in the dirt point-upwards. It was a short shaft, the point snapped off by the victim as he spun and fell.

The arrow shaft was ludicrously small and fine, like a scale model of a crossbow bolt. Escalla looked at the thing and gave a little frown.

"It snapped off right down at the end?"

"No. I think it was made this short." The Justicar carefully blew dirt from the business end of the shaft. "See? There's a metal shank in the shaft where the point broke away. This arrow was made this long."

It only measured six inches in length. Escalla picked up the arrow, examined the wood, the feathers and the nock, then pitched it away from her in disgust.

"It's from a hand crossbow."

Drow. The dark elves. Only *they* used such weapons, and drow haunted the dark places of the earth where troglodytes might dwell. Jus and Escalla looked at each other in perfect shared knowledge, then stood up and flanked the sergeant.

"Where did you lose the trail?"

The soldiers hurried them through the brush, looking left and right to scan the darkness.

"Half a mile ahead. It just vanishes." The sergeant waded over tall cabbage stalks and broccoli. "We've seen it before. Do you know how they do it?"

"I can guess." Jus pitched the broken crossbow bolt away. "Take us there."

Jus's voice seemed the one iron-hard, dependable thing in all the world. The soldiers had never once asked for proof of his identity or authority. The big man moved with a solid, tireless step, his eyes scanning for danger and his thoughts kept to himself. The sergeant followed close behind like a pup trailing a wolf.

Half a mile's walk in the pitch darkness was no laughing matter. The scrub land seemed full of roots and stumps designed to trip a man over on his face. As the terrain separated the party out from one another, Jus beckoned Escalla over to his side.

"What do you know about drow?"

"Usual stuff." Escalla sat on Jus's shoulder, where she could whisper in quiet to Jus and Cinders. "Evil, live underground, slave takers, spider obsessed . . . Females are more powerful than males. Oh, and the females have a dress sense that makes *me* look like Saint Cuthbert's maiden aunt!" The girl stroked her chin—a motion unconsciously copied from the Justicar. "They're poison users, too. Can we handle that?"

"It's no problem." Jus mentally counted through the spells and powers at his command. "I can neutralize it with a spell."

"Hoopy. So as long as you're not the one that gets hit, we're all in clover." Escalla sighed and rested her chin on her hand. "No one's tied the drow to this before? Why hasn't there been any sign of elves?"

A bright, mad grin shone in the darkness

Cinders smelled! The hell hound seemed immensely pleased with himself. *Cinders smelled them—yes! Elfie-pixie-faerie smell. Smelled at Sour Patch, first time!*

"Yep. Got me there." Escalla nodded acceptance and patted the dog. "You sure did, pooch. We just forgot to take note." Escalla gave a sigh. "Sorry. I owe you a tail rub."

Welcome.

The scrub thinned. Just ahead of Jus, the sergeant stood in the light of Private Henry's lantern, wearing the triumphant look of someone about to share confusion and perplexity.

The trail of crushed and broken bushes ended on a broad, roughly circular patch of grassy ground. At the middle of the huge clearing stood a ring of standing stones.

The stones were massive slabs of granite, moss covered monoliths that seemed to have sprouted from the Flanaess itself. Each pair of stones was topped by a capstone to form a titanic arch. The trail ended at the base of one archway, the footprints once again cut off as though sliced with a knife.

It was a familiar enough sight. Escalla looked the offending archway up and down as she hovered before it in midair.

"Jus? Check the locator thingie."

The ranger opened his pouch and duly produced the charm. It swiveled, settled, and hung pointing south without making so much as a twitch. Escalla looked at it in interest then paced busily up and down.

"Damn! They're still miles away!"

"No matter." Storing away the charm, the Justicar arose and looked at the stone circle. "The murderer must be linked to these slave raids. It looks like they might be following the same route."

"Yeah." Escalla's frown faded then suddenly was replaced by a look of sly, brilliant joy. *"Yeah!"*

Sidling past Polk, the girl ended up beside the sergeant.

"Sarge? Saaay, this king of yours . . ." Escalla tapped the fingers of her hands together, suddenly the heart and soul of avarice. "If we were to free these poor lost citizens of yours and maybe detonate whoever's behind these raids, do you feel the king might express his joy in a physical, maybe *fiscal* type of way?"

"Huh?"

"You know, in a material fashion." The girl excitedly waved her hands. "An openhanded expression of esteem. Royal pleasure demonstrated though means of treasury assets."

The sergeant scratched his head, giving a confused look at the little faerie girl. "You mean is there a reward?"

"Yes! If you want to get all uncouth about it!"

"Well, Ma'am, that is, Miss, I believe the reward stands at ten thousand gold pieces."

"Ten!" Goggling, Escalla waved her hands, almost lost for words, then came racing up to shake the sergeant by the hand. "Kick back, man! Relax! We'll deal with it!" The faerie halted suddenly. "Does this king of yours have a name?"

"Umm . . ."

"Great! Tell King Um that Escalla's on the job!" The girl turned a back flip, ending up beside Polk, who was sneaking yet another drink from his faerie bottle. "Polk, let's get busy! Time to show these guys that their worries are at an end!"

Always happy to see activity, Polk corked his magic bottle. The man had apparently been sneaking more than just a wee drink or two to sustain him on the march. He wiped his mouth and gave a happy, addled cry.

"That's great! Well, come on. Time's a-wastin'!" The little man picked up his feet. "Lezz go!"

Jus wearily uncoiled the magic rope from his belt—a shortened, somewhat scorched souvenir from a battle with an erinyes—and whipped it out to entangle Polk. The Justicar hauled Polk in like a flapping fish, took one sniff at him and gave a huge, threatening growl.

"You're drunk!"

"Never, son!" Polk seemed far happier than any man on a murder investigation had a right to be. "It's just high spirits! Glad we're on the job!"

Jus growled. There were too many things to occupy him. Looking at the stone circle, the ranger called, "Escalla! Just tell me how we're supposed to trigger these damned gates! Is there a spell to tell us what the keys might be?"

"Sure there is!"

"So throw the spell."

"I can't. I don't know it." Escalla waved innocently. "Like we use it every day! Come on, man, we're going into battle! I just tanked myself up with shields and fireballs!"

Jus pried the ever-full liquor bottle away from the complaining Polk and asked, "So how do we find the key?"

"Hey, J-man!" The girl circled, taking possession of the ever-full bottle. "You've got to think practically! The trick with these gates is that sometimes you might get here and not be carrying the right key, so you always hide a few spare keys somewhere you can reach 'em. Our murderer came here about an hour or two ago, so just look for any place real close that looks like a hiding place!"

Escalla searched the column tops and the crowns of a few nearby trees. The sergeant, Private Henry, and their unnamed companions spread out with lanterns to look beneath toadstools and stones. Jus dragged Polk along by the scruff of his neck as he set about searching for anything out of place. The pure white of his light-stone showed his face grim and seething.

Polk struggled, and the Justicar snarled in dark, dire anger, "Polk, don't you ever, *ever* get drunk on the job again!"

"But son, I'm making your chronicles! It's to help my creative flow!" Polk waved his hands. "It was the kelp, wasn't it? All right, I can change to beer when we're actually on the job!"

"Polk, you get the bottle back at rest stops. One cup at lunch, one cup at night, and nothing more!"

The hapless teamster wailed like a child deprived of his only toy, but Jus dragged him on.

Ten minutes of fruitless searching yielded no surprises except one edible truffle and a family of voles. Annoyed and still battling with Polk, the Justicar yelled up to Escalla as she flew amongst the monoliths, "Escalla, did you find anything?"

"No." The girl seemed miffed. "I looked in all the good places! It's always somewhere close! I mean, what if you were in a hurry?"

"You're supposed to be an expert!"

The faerie lost her temper. "I *am* an expert! You people think you can do a better job, then just fly up here and do it yourself!"

Losing patience, Jus stood and bellowed, "Just tell us what the damned key's likely to be!"

"It could be anything!" Equally annoyed, Escalla flew backward as she spoke. "It could be a herb, a fruit, a rock, a flower, diamonds, silver, a flute, a dead rat . . . For all we know, it could be the golden hairs from a virgin's—!"

Escalla passed through the arch above the tracks, and suddenly magic flashed in a sharp, white light that lit the entire hilltop. For a split second, Jus saw a look of astonished embarrassment on Escalla's face—and then the girl was gone. The gateway still shimmered with magic.

With only seconds to act, Jus picked up Polk, ran toward the gate, and bellowed over his shoulder, "Sergeant, thank you! We'll be back!"

Jus leaped through the gate, Cinders swirling about his back. There was a flash, then Jus landed on dry soil that stank of sulphur. Cinders made an appreciative noise, sucking in the stink of smoke and flame. The night sky above was lined by the vicious teeth of a mountain range, teeth back-lit by hellish volcanic flames. A natural archway of rock formed the magic door behind them. Polk sat blearily looking at the volcanoes. Leaping about like a mad locust doing an interpretive dance, Escalla clutched at her groin and pranced about in pain.

"Damn it! Assa frassa fragin *dammit!*" The girl made a mad little dance in the dark. "Holy Hanali, that *stings!*"

Jus rose, disoriented by his passage through the gate. "What stings?"

"Mind your own business! Ow! Ow! *Oooow!*"

Jus poised himself to investigate further, when suddenly there came a flash, and fresh light flooded through the gate.

Private Henry sat up in the dust, blinking in fright. The young soldier sat up, then yelped as Jus hauled him to his feet with one mighty heave of his hand.

Too late. The gate snapped shut, its eerie light cutting off to leave the archway dead and dim. Jus planted himself before the young soldier and roared, "What are you doing here?"

"Sir! Um, well, sir . . ." Terrified, the boy looked up at the vast, grim figure looming over him. He helpfully offered his lantern "I . . . I brought a light, sir!"

"That's wonderful." The Justicar turned to the faerie. "All right, Escalla. Send him back."

"No."

Jus turned to look in astonishment at the faerie, who hovered unhappily nearby.

"Jus, I *can't*." She looked embarrassed, pained, and evasive all at once. "I haven't got any key material left! The gate took it all!"

"The gate took it all?"

Jus blinked, recoiled, and for two heartbeats his countenace froze. Then his whole face lit into a smile. The big man suddenly folded forward and bit his fist. Huge shoulders shook, then a laugh escaped him to shake and shatter the night. He laughed for the first time in public memory, laughing all the harder once he saw Escalla's face. The Justicar laughed so hard he cried.

Escalla stood flapping her mouth in indignation, then turned away, her ears flaming bright. "Oh right! Sure, sure. *Now* it's funny! What happens when we need to go back?"

Cinders snickered like a mad thing, his tail whirling madly round and around. *Funny!*

Jus was having trouble breathing. One look at Escalla set him off laughing again. "A white wedding dress. . . !"

The girl swelled up in righteous anger. "All right! Yes, I admit it! I qualify. I qualify for a white wedding dress! Right! *There*! Are we all happy now?"

Jus almost choked. *"No one* touches the faerie!"

Escalla seethed, folded her arms across her breasts, and turned away. "Oh, go bite a purple worm's butt!"

* * * * *

In the pitch dark world of the Dreadwood, tiny lights dipped and swirled though the treetops. The forest floor glowed the sickly colors of dreams as savage little shapes tore through the woods in search of prey.

Beside a burned and ruined village, among corpses and old apple trees, an elf hound ran sniffing wickedly at the ground. The creature leaped up to land upon an upper branch and found a scent clinging to the bark. He gave a long, flute-like howl.

Two faerie warriors flashed into visibility. They flew up to the branch and joined the elf hound, then pulled out a hunting horn and blew a low, moaning note that echoed above the trees.

Long minutes later, Lord Ushan arrived.

The faerie lord still wore his robes that swam with all the colors of flame, but now the fire ran blue and white instead of red. The lord knelt beside his hunters and fingered a single strand of perfect golden hair that had caught upon the apple bark.

He breathed a long, slow breath of triumph and turned his face toward the waiting apple trees.

The warriors watched and waited while Lord Ushan of Clan Sable let his thoughts drift with the wind.

The gate could lead almost anywhere and pursuit was no longer the top priority. A great many plans had worked well tonight.

It was enough.

Lord Ushan made a slashing motion with his hand. The warriors sheathed their swords then flashed back into invisibility, their wings whirring as they shot off into the gloom.

✵   ✵   ✵   ✵   ✵

Twenty minutes after their arrival, the group stood at the lip of a chasm that plunged deep into the earth. Volcanoes lit the distant horizon, ebbing and pulsing like blood. The red light made the shadows seem darker and more filled with menace, and the whole landscape seem to shift and move in hunger. The air held a stink of sulphur, ash, and acidic rain. Cinders breathed it in like a breath of holiday air, while his companions' noses snorted from the hellish stink.

The tracks of hundreds of feet led down treacherous paths toward the chasm floor. Skeletons and corpses glimmered in the ebbing volcanic light, showing where some captives had slipped and tumbled to their doom. In this grim scene, the only sounds were the distant hiss of steam from the volcanic range and a sudden snicker from the Justicar.

Stung and indignant, Escalla shot the man a dire glare.

"Will you stop it with the laughing already? Enough!" The girl tossed her golden hair. "I just happen to be saving myself for Mister Right."

"While dressing like Miss Wrong!"

"No one likes you, Jus! We took a poll!" The faerie waved her hand toward the chasm. "Now if we are all *quite* ready, would you take a reading with the locator spell?"

Jus and Polk were utterly incapable, their hands still weak and shaking from their suppressed laughter. Seething, Escalla relieved them of the locator needle and stood at the precipice, unraveling the needle's string. As she made ready, Private Henry stood over her, looking skinny as a bean pole and about as dangerous as a mouse. Escalla saw the lantern quiver and shot the boy a glare that could have shattered stone.

"Kid, don't you say a frazin' word!"

"No, ma'am!" The young soldier blinked in the lantern light; his face seemed to be mostly composed of freckles, and he seemed to be in absolute, worshipful awe of her. "Not one word. Not one!"

For once, someone seemed to be treating her like the legendary sylvan overlord she really was. Escalla sniffed importantly, absurdly soothed, and smoothed her long gloves.

The girl let the locator needle dangle, taking a reading on the whereabouts of the slowglass necklace. The needle pointed straight down the canyon at a good, sharp angle. The needle actually quivered, wavering happily from side to side as though excited by the proximity of the prey. With a professional sniff of disdain, Escalla put the locator needle away and flew over the path.

"This way." Escalla magnanimously gave Private Henry a magic light. "Here, Private. I will lead, and you may light the way."

Having been given a magic light by a real faerie was apparently the high point of the young soldier's life. He looked up at Escalla in amazement, held up the magic light, and proudly began walking down the path, crossbow in one hand and magic light in the other. Escalla made to go after him, when Jus suddenly lumbered over to the trail.

"Escalla, we can't take him with us!"

"Well he can't stay here. He'll get eaten." The faerie gave an expressive shrug. "He's safest with us."

With a sigh, Jus acknowledged the point. Finally composed, he unsheathed his sword, the blade long, black, and comfortingly lethal, and walked to the path.

"All right. Have him bring up the rear behind Polk. He can be rear guard. You take the point, and I'll be right behind you." The Justicar looked up at the faerie girl. "You got your spells memorized?"

"Sure! And you?"

"Healing, anti-poison . . ."

"So it's all hoopy! We go in, kick troglodyte tail, release a few thousand prisoners, catch that murderer, and retrieve the evidence!" The girl gave an airy wave of her hand. "What could be simpler?"

The trail seemed long, the chasm deep. Back-lit by volcanic fires, Jus stared down into the depths. "We only have a few days of rations and about one gallon of water."

"Don't worry about it! It's a *dungeon*." The girl flew backward without a care in the world. "It's just a hole in the ground, Jus! How deep can it possibly be?"

II

Through a darkness so absolute that it hung like velvet folds, the party descended into the depths of the earth.

It was a well traveled route, a tunnel partly natural and partly carved by hand, that formed a roadway plunging into the heart of the Flanaess. The tunnel floor had been leveled roughly flat, but the jagged roof dipped and soared into vaults and dripping ceilings. A reeking little rivulet led the way ever deeper, twisting left and right, then splashing down into a limestone cave.

The tunnel descended down, down, down . . . first a hundred yards and then a thousand. Soon all memory of the outer world, all breath of sulphurous air, all light of sun and moon, had almost vanished. The long, cautious descent plunged the party half a mile below the earth. Neither Escalla nor the Justicar suffered from delusions of collapsing walls or crushing roofs. Even so, the sense of so much rock above and the infinite earth to either side made the tunnels seem horribly oppressive.

Finally, a wide limestone cavern opened before the party. Escalla flew with her little light out into a massive void. Long stalactites hung down like spears overhead, while drips of water fed into trickles that joined into the single stream. Jus held up a hand to halt Polk and Private Henry, then lifted his magic light to spill its glow into the cave. The light shone as brilliant as day, flooding into the cave to strike sparks and highlights from countless outcrops of wet stone. While comforting, it was also a trifle blinding.

Escalla swirled up toward the roof and tried to peer down into the maze of shapes below. "Hey, Jus!" she whispered, "there's a dead guy down here!"

Her voice carried strangely, the strength of it lost amidst muffled echoes. Jus lowered himself down a gigantic limestone shelf and frowned.

"What killed him?"

"Dunno. I can't see." Escalla flew to hover above the corpse. "Oh wow! Hey, guys! I see a—*whoa!*" A stalactite detached itself and plunged from the ceiling, almost spearing her. Escalla sped aside, and the stalactite missed her by a country mile. It fell to the floor with a heavy thud, righted itself, and fixed a beady eye upon Escalla above. The creature seemed to be a tall, thin mollusk with a shell shaped like a razor-sharp stalactite. It began to make its way slowly across the cavern floor toward a wall, traveling with the glacial, bubbling pace of a gastropod.

There were other stalactites near Escalla. The girl eyed them with clear suspicion, readying her wand. "The ceiling's alive with these things."

"Don't get under them!"

"Thanks, Jus. I don't know *where* I'd be without your constant good advice." Escalla swerved to the ground, where a human body lay. It had been pierced from the neck into the abdomen. Nearby there lay the empty shell of one of the stalactite mollusks, still smeared with blood and lined with goo.

"I think one of these shell-critters killed a captive. The trogs must have eaten the shell creature." Escalla hastily backed away. "Eeew! And ate most of the dead human, too. Damn!" Appalled and angered, Escalla circled the body.

She had found the main exit from the cave—another huge tunnel that led due north. Moving to join her, Jus thumped down to the floor, sliding down the rock slope in a pool of light. He caught Private Henry and helped the boy to the ground, steadying his crossbow with one big hand.

"Son, do you really know how to shoot that thing?"

"Sir yes sir!" The teenager blinked. "Well, kinda. I scored thirty out of fifty on the target range."

"At what distance?"

"Um, thirty yards."

"Wonderful." Jus set the boy to watching the rear, then caught Polk as the teamster came sliding noisily down the limestone slope. Still annoyed with the man, Jus dragged him onto his feet. "Don't fall behind. Keep between me and the boy, and keep your eyes open!"

"Sure, son! They're open!" Polk still reeked of fermented kelp. "I jus' stayed back to watch the lights—real pretty! Now that's what adventure should be all about. Pretty things and the unexpected! Surprising vistas, boy! A fitting backdrop to heroics!"

Jus fixed the man with a suspicious glare, while Cinders leaked a wisp of smoke and flames.

"Are you still drunk?"

"No, son! Jus' look behind us! See! The whole place is real damned pretty!"

Jus knelt and waved a hand. Private Henry, Escalla and even Polk all settled down in silence. Jus covered his light and waved the others to do the same.

With the light gone, the eyes were shocked into blindness, but it was a blindness that slowly filled out with little points of light.

Bands of minerals on the walls slowly began to glow in blues and greens. Lichens on the ceiling gave off a weird yellow light. Piece by piece, as their eyes forgot the brightness of day, the underworld began to come alive with light.

The air felt dank and cold, moving with slow breaths from tunnels and caverns in the far off dark. The only sounds were subtle, far off twitterings—bats, rats, or worse. The drip and echo of distant water filled the huge tunnels with a quiet stir of sound. Dung made a foul stench along the tunnels. Some of it seemed to be human, some reptilian, and some came from creatures best left unidentified. Toadstools grew in the compost, their caps shining with a sickly green and yellow luminescence. Clinging to high tunnel roofs, other lights shifted and moved in the gloom—luminous beetles, slugs, and worms going about their daily grind.

Jus hid his magic light inside a pouch and shoved it through his belt. Escalla followed suit. The light spells were brilliant enough to blind creatures used to this pale phosphorescence. It seemed best to keep them as weapons, moving through the tunnels with more stealth.

Over at the new tunnel, Jus looked carefully at the dim, dark shadows and touched a troglodyte footprint still fresh in the mud. He thoughtfully dried his fingertips.

Escalla inspected her friend's work and asked, "Recent?"

"About half a day's lead."

"Know what we're going to do when we find 'em?"

"Play it by ear." The Justicar arose. "Locator?"

Escalla produced the magic pointer. The little compass swung to point straight north down the tunnel. The pointer no longer quivered; the quarry had gained many miles of lead. With a curse, Escalla put the thing away and unslung her battle wand. The Justicar nodded. Escalla turned invisible and took the lead position, scouting far ahead of her friends. The Justicar settled Cinders on his helm and felt the hell hound lift his ears and begin carefully scanning the gloom. Moving with a stealth that was perfection to behold, the big man paced down the wide tunnel on Escalla's trail, his hand poised on his sword hilt for a lightning draw.

Polk watched his companions, reached for his whiskey bottle, and then remembered that his drink had been confiscated. With a concerned look at the tunnel, the man ran to catch up with the Justicar.

"Son, this is no lair! This ain't a dungeon!" Polk's voice carried shockingly far in the gloom. "Are you sure we're on the right track?"

Jus never spoke a word. He turned, glared, lifted a finger to his lips, then swung about to keep up his silent march.

Polk went into a huff. With his hands jammed into his pockets, he stomped along ten feet behind his friends, kicking at any toadstools that came in his way. Behind him, Private Henry kept a nervous rear guard, chain mail jingling with every step and his pace slowed as he turned constantly to point his crossbow at empty shadows far behind.

The party walked cautiously onward into a tunnel that never seemed to end.

✿   ✿   ✿   ✿   ✿

Long hours of walking went by. The massive passageways were a squalor of life and violent death. Great phosphorescent beetles preyed upon the slugs. Slugs chewed into glowing fungi, which in turn grew on compost left from dead beetles, old bones and dung.

Other things lived and ate here as well. The gnawed bones of humanoid creatures had been left here and there on the passage floors—sometimes elf bones, sometimes human, always gnawed clean with skulls left grinning in the dark.

There were frequent alcoves, side caves, and sink holes all along the way. The party sat down in one such alcove as they shared hard bread and rested their feet. Polk's magic bottle was produced, and much to his pain, all the travelers were served a measure of good whiskey carefully monitored by Jus before the bottle was sealed away again.

Sipping prime aged whiskey from a tin mug, Escalla kept a watch upon the corridor. Escalla had long since given up her invisibility on the march, coming to hover close to Cinders and the Justicar. After half an hour, invisibility wreaked havoc with her hair.

Swigging back her whiskey, Escalla turned to the task of gnawing upon a rock hard piece of bread. Daunted by the task, she finally used the bread chunk as an elbow rest.

"Jus, how far do you reckon this tunnel runs?"

"Honestly?"

"Yeah."

"It's a road." The Justicar was repairing one of his boot laces, working with big, efficient hands. "The trogs must have a nest down here. Probably a drow settlement, too. The thing must run for miles."

Escalla gave a sigh and idly dangled the locator needle on its string. It pointed north, straight down the tunnel, and gave not a quaver of life. The opposition must have zoomed at least ten miles ahead.

"Bugger!" The girl sighed. "How much food do we have again?"

"Not much." The Justicar finished fixing his boot. "Fancy slug stew?"

"Pass." The girl took a long look down the tunnels. "There must be something big enough to make a meal of down here."

Rising to his feet, the Justicar looked into the gloom with a growl. "That's what I'm afraid of."

The tunnels had been eerily empty so far, but it couldn't last. The Takers would hardly leave their gates unguarded. Somewhere farther along the tunnels, there would be a guard post. Beyond that lay the horrific kingdom of the underdark. Jus pondered the trouble they were sinking deeper and deeper into and looked about the dripping cavern walls.

"Any ideas who the murderer might be?" Jus asked.

Deep in thought, the faerie sat shadowed by the bright splay of her wings.

"I've been trying to narrow down my list." The girl hissed. "My mother. My sister. My mother *and* my sister. Or Lord Ushan? Or even Lord Faen? Or perhaps my mother, my sister, Lord Ushan, and Lord Faen." Escalla sat sifting her relatives and their allies through her mind. "Do you see now why I fled to the real world?"

"Yep."

The Justicar sighed, shook his head, and made a tour of the alcove. He walked past Private Henry and patted the boy on the shoulder as he passed. Having been set to thread thin strips ripped from his own cloak through the bottom layers of rings of his chainmail hauberk, the young soldier looked anxiously up for approval of his work. Jus knelt down to inspect the results, shaking the armor to make sure that its noise had been reduced.

"Good job. You did it just right."

"Th-thank you, sir." Private Henry seemed pale, but his eyes were awed as he looked up at the imposing figure of the Justicar.

"Is there anything else I should do? To make my gear better I mean?"

"How do you fight?"

"Um, just with a sword, sir. Kind of . . ." The boy looked pale. He had been given a long sword as part of his equipment, and its weight still felt awkward on his belt. "We haven't really done much practice with it."

Huge and solid, the Justicar rested a hand upon the boy's shoulder and said, "If we get into a fight, just shoot, go to ground, and leave the battle to us. If you get caught at sword point, fight defensively and call for help. We'll cover you." The big man stood. "When we get the time, I'll teach you how it's done."

Jus looked over the gangly boy's equipment. He sniffed at the sword belt, a typical botched affair—good for horsemen and useless for everybody else. Taking up the worn leather, Jus showed the lad how to wear his sword horizontally through his belt.

"You get a faster draw this way. You might need it." He helped the boy to don the heavy equipment, then shared a last drink of beer from his canteen. "All right. Let's go."

Escalla took a careful look out of the alcove, ducked back, looked one more time, and then fluttered up into the air. Jus strode out into the corridor, his heavy boots strangely quiet. With his cherished friend at his side, he moved into the tunnels with Polk and the teenaged soldier traipsing behind.

Polk automatically reached for his water bottle, discovered that for once it actually did contain only water, and almost choked. From up ahead, Jus turned and glared at the little man, silently ordering him to close the line of march. Shooting seething glances at Escalla, Polk hauled out his book and wrote awkwardly as he walked. He scribbled down scathing paragraphs on the subject of teetotalism, tyranny, and the mental benefits of alcohol.

The whole process kept him occupied for at least the next two long, slow, and silent miles.

❋   ❋   ❋   ❋   ❋

To an eye attuned to the sinister pulse of the underdark, the tunnels ebbed with life, echoing to the endless drip and flow of time. Water trickled, creatures squeaked, and deep crevices sometimes carried sounds that rang with terror.

Hidden amongst rock outcrops and stalagmites, two figures sat silent in the gloom. They were drow—the ebony skinned, silver haired elves of the underdark. Each wore a long cloak made to conceal them in the dark. They sat several paces apart, each facing in the opposite direction—sentries halfway through a long, tedious watch. With hand crossbows at their sides, the two elves passed the time. One was chewing on some sort of meat, while the other carved patterns in a piece of knuckle bone.

Around them, the tunnel echoed, time dragged by, and water dripped like blood seeping from a dying world. Into this tedious quiet came a shockingly familiar sound. A coin fell tinkling upon stone. It echoed from the southern tunnel, ringing faint but clear.

The southern-most sentry jerked his head up, covering the passageway with his crossbow as he scanned the darkness. The weapon's sharp bolt gleamed sickly black with poison.

Heat images swam in the eerie shadows of the tunnel. The wall mold glowed sometimes hot, sometimes cool, but amongst the smallest of small shapes upon the floor, a figure appeared—a little creature moving fearlessly down the corridor.

A coin rang yet again, and now both guards craned forward to look, the northern guard standing up to peer past his partner.

A rat—a very large, well muscled rat—was scuttling along the edge of the southern tunnel. Thirty yards away in the gloom, even drow eyes could scarcely pick out the slightest detail. The rat moved away and disappeared into the dark. Moments later the sound of busy digging came, a sound very faint against the tunnel noises. Soon the rat returned, seeming extremely pleased with itself. Gold glittered briefly in the tunnel. The rat dropped a coin that it had held in its mouth, making a pile with other flecks of gold in the corridor, then pranced off to continue with its digging far away.

The watching sentries leaned forward, staring in amazement. The gold was real. The drow looked behind them at the entrances to the guard rooms in the tunnels behind them, wary to see if they had been missed. There was no point in sharing treasure with too many other grasping hands.

Gold clinked again. The rat could be heard digging, and flecks of dirt and bat dung scattered out onto the floor.

The two drow raised their hand crossbows, the bolts glistening with venom. With short swords in their other hands, they advanced side by side up the passageway. They glared at one another with no love lost, then stalked forward, walking over the rat's little pile of coin. Both moved faster and faster in pursuit of the busy rat. They passed outcrops of rock, passed loose soil and gravel left over from a crumbled wall, and watched the rat as it flitted toward its treasure horde.

The elves saw the rat stop to dig at a half-buried skeleton. They gave a grin, hefted their crossbows, and strode toward the rat. Behind them, buried underneath the gravel, a pair of red eyes suddenly gleamed.

There was the softest whisper of sliding gravel, then the two sentries seemed to fall apart. One heartbeat they were half-turning as movement flickered in the dark behind them. The next instant, one elf's body stood without its head, and the other jerked as the Justicar's sword blurred down through his skull and into the torso below. Without even watching his victims fall, the Justicar swept his blade free, flicked it clean, and sheathed it all in one smooth curve. The two dead drow fell to the tunnel floor, their blood pooling into a gruesome mud on the floor.

Jus shook himself free of dirt and gravel. From far down the tunnel, Polk and Private Henry peered out of hiding, looking pale.

The rat came out into the middle of the corridor and waved them closer, turning to look up and whisper to Jus, "Think they heard?"

Jus shook his head, then knelt to drag the twitching corpses out of sight.

The big rat shimmered, changing from its furry form and into a very naked Escalla. Her clothes had been stuffed out of sight in a rock crevice. She dragged on her leggings, then wriggled her bottom into her undergarments. At the sound of a little noise behind her, she looked archly across one shoulder to see the shocked eyes of Private Henry.

Already pale, Private Henry hurriedly turned to face the wall. Escalla gave a wry smile and began pulling on her long gloves.

"Whassamatter, kid? Never see a girl before?"

"Yes." The teenager looked a tad unsteady on his feet. "Well, sort of, but you're a *lady!*"

Escalla paused, brightened, and instantly radiated a glorious goodwill to all creation. She jerked on her dress and fluttered up to kiss the boy upon the cheek. "Now *you're* a gem! Where have you been all my life?"

The boy came forward with Escalla, his crossbow at the ready, but the two drow were most deeply and sincerely dead. The Justicar, spattered here and there with dark blood, had relieved them of small pots of venom sheathed beside their crossbow bolts. He tossed these to the young soldier. Henry stared aghast at the corpses.

Escalla looked at him, and for once without any laughter in her eyes.

"They're drow. Don't waste time feeling bad for them. These bastards are worse than orcs." She jerked one of the drow's clothing aside. "Check it out. Their boots are made from human skin." Escalla let the clothing drop. "They skin girls to make the softest boots. The longer the victim stays alive and screams, the better the boots are supposed to be."

Henry took a tighter grip upon his crossbow and choked, "My gods."

"Kill them. Kill them any way you have to." The faerie nodded her chin at the Justicar's back and gave a grim smile. "It's a bad day to be a drow. Justice is coming."

After hiding the bodies in the gravel scrape and covering the blood with dirt and gravel, the Justicar turned to watch the dangerous spaces down the tunnel. Just past where the two sentries had sat their watch, two caverns opened out from the main tunnel, each most certainly housing more guards. The party intended to move down the corridor to creep silently past the two caves on either side of the passageway. The destruction of the entire drow nation, although desirable, was *not* their current mission.

Escalla patted gravel in place over the corpses, started after Jus, then stopped, reversed, and hovered directly above Private Henry, her newest admirer.

"Hey, kid! Here!" The girl sprinkled powder across Private Henry, her eyes closed as she spoke a powerful charm. He jumped as he felt his skin ripple with strange force, and an eerie glow seemed to soak into his skin. Escalla breathed out a sigh, then dusted off her hands. "There you go, kid. Stoneskin. Keep you safe." The girl rapped knuckles on her own skin. "Best insurance policy in the world!"

"B-but what about the Justicar?"

"He'll get one tomorrow! You're a bit spongier than he is!" The girl put her finger to her lips. "Now creep along quietly, and we'll sneak past the guard rooms."

The Justicar stole slowly and carefully forward, his sword held ready. He walked with cat-footed care, his boots touching at the heel, then the outer sides, then planting flat and sure. Escalla kept behind and to one side, her battle wand ready.

Jus reached the cave opening on the left, lay flat against the stone, and let Cinders's ears and nose search the air inside. He then carefully crossed the passage to the cave on the right. Cinders slowly waved his tail and sampled the damp, dull breeze.

Drow here. The hell hound's voice echoed softly in the minds of Jus, Escalla, Polk—and also now to the startled Private Henry. *Maybe ten left, ten right. Bad girlie girls on right.* The hell hound grinned. *Cinders burn!*

Jus held up a hand to halt the hell hound's antics. The big man lifted up his hand, and a spell spread slowly out around him. A sphere of total silence radiated from the man, and he walked back to fold his companions in the spell.

There were two caves—one with three small entrances on the left, and one with a wider, more opulent single entrance on the right. The five companions moved together down the corridor, hugging one wall. Jus brought them swiftly, ushering Polk and Private Henry past and taking the last position as he covered the nearest cave mouth with his sword.

They were past the dangerous cavern mouths and already heading for safety, when suddenly a male drow carrying a basket of food came out into the main tunnel. He saw the Justicar only a few paces away, stared, and opened his mouth to scream.

No sound came. The spell made the drow blink, then he turned to run into the cave. Jus moved, but then something flashed past his flank. The drow jerked, spun, then smashed against the cave wall with a crossbow bolt protruding from his heart. Private Henry stared, his empty crossbow still held on target, amazed at himself, then could only watch as the perfectly matched team of Jus and Escalla sped into activity.

A second drow appeared, looking back over his shoulder and talking to someone behind him in the cave. His voice cut out in his own ears, and then his entire body fell severed diagonally through the waist as the Justicar's black blade sheared him in two. The drow fell, his hand spasming to fire his crossbow. The bolt sped into his home cave, struck sparks from the stone, and suddenly black figures surged upright in the gloom.

Behind Jus, Escalla shot toward the other cave. With the air of a master craftsman at work, Escalla fired her wand. A silent blast of frost solidified into an ice wall that sealed the opening to the cave. Escalla left only one small hole high up in one corner of the ice. As vaguely seen figures on the far side of the barrier began to appear, Escalla whistled happily, licked her index finger, and fired an ice storm through the little hole.

Violence broke out inside the sealed room, with figures jerking back and forth as shards tore into their flesh. With Jus now at the far side of the passage, Escalla had left the protection of the silence spell. As muffled screams of pain came from the cave, Private Henry stared at Escalla, utterly aghast.

She looked at him and shrugged. "I have a nasty side! What can I say?"

At the far side of the passage, all hell broke loose. A male drow charged from the cave mouth, saw Polk and Henry, and fired his hand crossbow. The shot went wide. The drow ran forward, his shout silenced, but six other drow came from the other caves and joined him in surging straight toward Private Henry.

Two died in a savage instant of horror, their blood misting as the Justicar struck from hiding. The drow turned, and Cinders shot a violent blast of flame straight into their eyes. The flame took one elf in the face, blasting the flesh from his skull. The other drow ducked wildly and turned, their black cloaks sweeping around to take the flame blast. Fireproof cloaks shielded the elves, but the instant of blindness cost the lead drow his life as Jus cleaved downward with his sword.

More drow came running from the caves. Already facing two enemies to his front, Jus poised, his sword ready, looking at the six elves behind him from the corner of his eye.

The drow hesitated, looking at the savage splay of dead around the Justicar. One of the elves hurled a javelin, while another fired a crossbow bolt. Jus scarcely seemed to move, and yet as he slid one step and turned, the bolt shot past him and the javelin clattered to the floor, split neatly in two by the ranger's black blade. The drow warriors drew short swords and bucklers from their belts, paused, then sped forward in a surge of maddened hate.

✻   ✻   ✻   ✻   ✻

Escalla clung to the wall above the cave mouth. Below her, two drow noblemen strode forth, one dressed in fur robes and the other armed with a pair of sinister silver swords. With a shout of triumph, Escalla flicked open her hands and fired. A lightning bolt stabbed downward, blasting the drow warrior from his feet, but failing to even scratch the elf in the fur robes. The warrior fell, and the fur-clad elf turned. Dodging sideways, Escalla fired a stream of her magic bees straight at the fur-clad foe. Again, the spell failed, the bees disappearing the instant before they hit.

The drow with the silver swords rose, snarling, but he went after the Justicar after a curt jerk of the noble's head sent him away. Dragging a hand crossbow from his belt, the remaining elf took aim at Escalla and opened fire.

Escalla tumbled wildly, head over heels, the crossbow bolt missing her by a hair. She whirled in her roll and fired her wand, and this time the spell blasted home. The elf slammed back against a wall, ripped by ice shards. An instant later, he lifted a hand and blasted his own ice storm straight toward the faerie. The impact smashed Escalla into the wall behind her, sending her tumbling to the ground.

✻   ✻   ✻   ✻   ✻

In the passageway beyond, Jus moved with a wild blur of steel. Drow leaped in and out, short swords and bucklers flashing. Jus spun and kicked one elf in the head, breaking the drow's jaw, then parried a short sword with his blade before running its owner through. The elf screamed a silent scream, staggering aside and gushing blood.

Short swords stabbed, and one ripped a mark across Jus's thigh an instant before the elf behind it fell back with his arms severed.

Cinders fired flame, and two elves staggered while others ducked beneath their cloaks. Steel flashed as the fight swirled in a maelstrom of blood.

* * * * *

Back down the tunnel, Escalla's enemy moved to cast a spell. Stunned, Escalla flickered into invisibility and shot to the ceiling. A lightning bolt blasted inches beneath her, hit the ice wall, and smashed back into the dark elf. Killed instantly, the creature fell steaming and hissing to the floor.

The ice wall cracked. Something struck it a blow from behind the melted impact point, and the entire sheet of ice began to break and fall. Escalla took one look, then threw herself behind a stalagmite.

"Jus! We got visitors!"

* * * * *

The drow bearing twin swords ran toward the Justicar, joining the only survivors—two scarred drow veterans. The nobleman signaled one to go left and one right while he struck sparks from his swords and faced the Justicar.

With his back against a wall, Jus stood with his sword on guard, Cinders wreathing the scene in sulphurous smoke. The ranger loomed above the elves like a sinister black giant. To his left and right stood drow with swords and bucklers. Before him stood their war leader with twin blades weaving. The three drow paced for a moment then sped suddenly backward as Jus lunged at one swordsman with his blade.

Evading the huge man, the drow lunged at Jus, parried the savage black sword with crossed weapons, then flew backward as Jus's kick crashed into him with enough force to shatter steel.

The elf leader instantly scythed high and low with his blades. Jus turned, still leaning sideways from his kick and parrying one blow and letting the other crash against his cuirass of dragon scales.

Sparks flew. The elf drew blood, but Jus spun, trapped the blade beneath his arm and hammered a blow down onto the drow's elbow. Bone broke, and the drow leader howled in silent agony.

Cinders blasted flame at the third elf, making the creature cower within his cloak and winning Jus an instant. The big man stood with legs bent, sweeping one arm up, back, and over to crash the elf leader across his knee. The drow's back broke, and as his victim fell Jus whirled to face the remaining elf.

A short sword ripped through Cinders and cut Jus's back, but the man smashed the skull hilt of his sword into the elf's teeth and whipped the blade in a savage blur, shearing open the drow's abdomen. As sheet ice shattered like an exploding wall of glass, Jus drove his black blade through the final swordsman, twisting the weapon free and beheading the dark elf as it fell.

The ice wall splintered, and a half-dozen female drow came raging into the corridor. Frost-burned and smothered with blood, they hurled themselves straight at the Justicar.

Escalla swung out of cover behind the elves and fired her wand. Two drow jerked and died, while others leaped untouched out of the storm. The drow whirled, saw Escalla, and opened fire with a shower of crossbow darts. Screaming in fright, Escalla covered her face with her arms, bolts smacking into her and ricocheting free—victims of her stoneskin spell.

Hugging the cave wall, Private Henry watched anxiously, panting as he saw the Justicar charge savagely into the attacking elves. A silver-haired head fell to the floor as the drow scattered to surround their foe. One leaped spectacularly above the fight, landing behind the Justicar. Pale with panic, Private Henry ran forward, dragging his unfamiliar sword from its sheath. He charged with the heavy blade held in front of him like a battering ram, crashing into the elf from behind. The drow whirled, Henry's sword jutting through her ribs, and felled the boy with a backhand blow of her fist. She loomed over him, grinning in insane bloodlust as she stabbed a short sword down at his chest again and again, the blade striking sparks as it struck against Escalla's stoneskin spell. Henry screamed and tried to fend her away with helpless hands. An instant later, her head snapped back with a crossbow bolt buried in her face. Private Henry looked up in shock to see Polk standing and reloading the crossbow. The teamster shook his head in annoyance at having to work so hard for his drink.

Female drow fought with a wild, manic indifference to life. They leaped like acrobats, spinning handstands and dodging madly from side to side. Looming like a bear amidst a flock of sparrows, Jus hacked one in mid flight, sending both halves of her smacking to the ground. He fought fast and furiously, kicking another, catching her by the skull and pulping her head against the cave walls.

Two elves held back behind the fight, both trying to cast spells, and both finding that the silence spell blocked their chants.

Escalla fired her wand again—the frost blast failing against one but staggering the other. As the last female warrior died, the two sorceresses flicked a look at Escalla, then leaped into the air, shooting like lightning bolts down the corridor in magic flight.

Jus dived forward, rolling to come up with his sword moving. As the sorceresses flew past, he whipped out his magic rope, making it crack like a lash at it fastened about the neck of one of the fleeing elves. The drow jerked like a victim on a noose, clawing at her throat.

Escalla shot past in hot pursuit of the remaining elf, who rolled to fire a spell at the faerie, snarling in anger as Escalla's shields wrenched the spell aside.

Escalla sped like a meteor, dodging spellfire left and right. She cranked the focus ring upon her wand and blasted a bolt down the corridor. The fleeing drow rolled, the bolt shot past beneath her, and the evil sorceress gave a cackling screech of mirth.

An instant later, the drow smashed into an ice wall at top speed. The crash broke half a dozen bones and sent her tumbling to the floor. Escalla fell on her like a diving hawk, screaming out a spell that blasted at the stunned drow. Once again, the magic seemed to die an instant before it hit.

Broken and staggering, the drow snarled and swept her cloak about her body. She shimmered and changed into a sinister gray manta that flew up into the air, fanged mouth open and screaming. The manta plunged down and folded around Escalla, intending to crush the faerie to death. The manta swirled, clamped its mantle around its prey, squeezed with all its might . . . and died.

Running with blood, the manta changed shape back into a drow sorceress. The drow's corpse lay curled about a deadly little shape— a steely urchin studded with vicious spikes. The spines had punctured the drow like a thousand knives. As the drow fell slowly to the floor, the urchin changed shape back into Escalla, an Escalla dressed in a few torn clothing threads and horribly drenched in dark elf blood.

"My clothes!" Wiping blood from her face, Escalla looked down at herself. She looked as if she had been swimming on a slaughterhouse floor. "You filthy drow bitch! Look what you made me do!"

The instant transformation had ripped Escalla's clothes apart. She threw the ruined scraps of her clothing away. Cursing and muttering, she began to search the dead, bleeding elf.

From far behind her came a thin little cry, the voice of Polk. "Girl, you all right?"

"I'm fine!" Escalla dropped her voice to a mutter. "Except for dripping with drow body fluids." She yelled across her shoulder down the tunnel. "I got her! How's Jus?"

"Poisoned!"

Gold glinted from the hair of the dead drow. A true kleptomaniac, Escalla swooped and plucked out a golden spider pin. Swearing like a dock worker, Escalla sped back to join her friends.

The tunnel section between the caves looked like a slaughter yard. Parts of dark elves lay amidst an ocean of blood—black and gleaming in the dim phosphorescent light.

With a look of raw fury frozen on his face, Jus sat slumped unconscious against a wall. Polk sat on his heels, looking puzzled. Private Henry wrung his hands in panic. Cinders merely grinned and wagged his tail.

Wincing, Escalla dropped to the floor. It felt like half her ribs were broken by the impact of the drow's ice spell. Hurting and dazed, she waved a hand at Polk and Henry. Dripping with filth and feeling violated, the faerie dragged herself over to Jus, took his pulse, then saw the bolt from a hand crossbow lying by the man's injured thigh.

"What happened?"

"The sorceress he caught on the rope attacked him!" Henry pulled at a drow's cloak to make a bandage, then hastily dropped it when he found it to be soaked with blood. "She stabbed him with a crossbow bolt."

Wiping her blood soaked hair back from her face, Escalla wearily trudged over to Jus. Her naked body dripped blood as she stepped onto him, and she saw Polk and Henry's eyes go wide in alarm.

"It's all right, guys. Drow blood, not mine." Escalla winced and held her ribs. "He's alive. Don't worry about it. Drow put a sleeping drug on their missile weapons. He'll come out of it in about ten minutes." The girl folded over, clutching herself. "Just time to . . . to check his pockets for small . . . small change."

Racing forward, Polk caught the girl as she fell. Lolling in agony, Escalla could only croak and close her eyes.

13

Cracked ribs, bruises, concussion . . .

This had not been one of Escalla's better days. Her stoneskin spell had stopped punctures but had transmitted the shock right though to the bones. Painfully awake at last, Escalla felt herself being tended to. Wounds were tended and her face wiped semi-clean. Sitting cradled in Jus's lap, Escalla smoldered, thinking dire thoughts about the drow. She opened one bloodshot eye and said, "So. Fire-proof cloaks, poisoned arrows, they use magic, move silently, and are immune to magic at least half of the time . . ." Extremely miffed, the girl lifted her arm and suffered to have another healing spell across the ribs. "Apart from that, we're pretty even."

Bandaged and grim, Jus merely kept on with his work, healing the faerie. "We got them."

"Yeah, and they almost got us!"

Unconcerned, Jus shrugged and said, " 'Almost' still makes them dead and us alive." He poured water onto a cloth and handed it to Escalla. "How do you feel?"

"Like crap!" With dried blood crusting her hair and skin, Escalla looked a mess. "My ribs are better though."

"Good."

Jus arose. He had a puncture in one thigh, as well as numerous gashes and painful, bloody cuts. He lowered Escalla to her feet and handed her a long strip of silken drow cloth as a dress. Escalla used it for cover as she tried to rub herself clean and shot a concerned look at the Justicar.

"Hey, man! You're still ripped to bits!"

"You needed the healing more than I." Jus moved slowly and heavily now that his wounds were stiff with pain. "I'll have more healing spells tomorrow."

"Damn!" Escalla threw her washcloth aside. "We can't go traipsing along these tunnels without you in full fighting trim. We'll get wiped out." The girl roughly tied the sheer black silk into a dress. "We're going to have to hole up for a day and let you rest."

The huge ranger sighed heavily, then looked at the drow corpses lying splayed and smeared about the tunnel.

"Not here. They might have a relief."

"There are side alcoves. We'll get in one, and I'll cover the entrance with an illusion spell." The girl flew up to hold Jus by the hand in concern. "You sure you're all right to walk?"

"I'll manage."

"Come on then. Let's get the loot sorted out, then we'll walk for half a mile and hide." The girl heaved an irritated sigh. "I feel like such an idiot. Virtually everything I threw at them was blocked."

"Change your strategy. Use spells that affect the area around the drow and not ones that attack the drow themselves."

"You got it." Escalla scowled and tried to think. "I've gotta hole up and redo my spell list."

Working with the diligence of a true monomaniac, Polk had been searching the drow lairs. Apparently the proper cataloging of spoils was a vital part of adventure. Polk sat cross legged amidst his chronicle and pens, carefully recounting every single sword blow, dodge, and spell. Escalla threw the man a happy little wave and was given a grumble in return.

"Hey, Polk! Nice crossbow shot, man. I didn't know you could shoot!"

"Had to save the boy." Polk sniffed in self importance as he went about his work. "The boy's no hero. Can't interfere with a hero, but the boy needed help."

Escalla kissed Polk upon the cheek and said, "Well thank you. Here's the magic bottle."

She placed the faerie bottle into Polk's lap—big and already brimming with a whiskey so concentrated that it could strip paint and raise the dead. The girl shot Polk a dire glance. "And no faerie wine! Especially not the sixty-three!"

Infinite happiness filled Polk's soul. He wrenched open the bottle, filled a tin mug, then drew in an important breath, rose, and presented the liquor to the Justicar. He poured more drinks for Escalla and for the teenage soldier, then contented himself with drinking straight from the bottle.

"Here's to adventure! Next time we'll bash a hundred more!"

The whiskey traveled down living gullets as though it had spines and claws. Private Henry almost coughed up a lung. He fought for breath, tears in his eyes, a look of horror on his face as he saw Escalla raise her little mug to him in salute and take a second draught.

"Here's to you, kid!"

Polk happily arranged items from the looted drow in a line along the floor. There were a few scant pieces of gold, a few platinum coins, short swords, daggers, bucklers, crossbows, poisoned crossbow bolts, and bloodstained clothes. Most intriguing of all were scroll tubes lined up side by side. Escalla raced over to pry open the tubes—only to be frozen in place by one hard glare from the Justicar. The ranger picked up the tubes one by one, checking them carefully. Cinders sniffed for magic then happily began to wag his tail.

Clean!

"Hoopy!" Escalla pounced, ripped the cap off a tube, and found only a piece of parchment covered with lines and squiggles. She hastily moved to the next tube, opened it, and found that it was the same.

"Aww man! These aren't scrolls!" She scowled petulantly at the parchments, turning them around and around. "Can't these drow even get treasure right?"

The Justicar winced as he sat down with the first piece of parchment spread out across his knees. He examined the carefully inked lines with notes and pointing arrows scribbled beside the diagrams in a different hand. He held the drawing up in the shine of Cinders's flames, checking carefully for secret messages and invisible ink.

Escalla wound up draped over his shoulder from behind, staring at the diagrams.

"What is that thing? Dark elf doodles?"

"No." Jus smoothed the parchment in grim distaste. It seemed to be made from human skin. "It's a map."

"Yeah?" To Escalla the squiggles hardly seemed map-like. "How do you figure that?"

"A simple one. A map of the underdark." The map was made of simple lines, interconnected with symbols marking many of the junctions. "See. This arch is the gate outside. This is the passageway we're in. The area marked here with an eye? It's this position here, the guard post."

"Hoopy." Escalla squinted carefully at the map. Polk and Private Henry gathered near. "Lotsa notes beside those symbols. Do you read Drow?"

"No. Do you have a spell or something that can do it?"

"Sure!" Escalla cast the appropriate spell. "There you go!"

They all craned forward with interest—even Polk, whose spelling skills were dubious at best, and Private Henry, who feared to admit that he couldn't read. Escalla ran her fingers over the lines of scribbled symbols, and for an instant thereafter, their meaning became sharp and clear.

"Main way—patrols, Eclavdra clan." The faerie read the symbols scribbled beside the main route marked on the map. "Here's us. Says, 'Post one. Incoming secret addits one and two. Faerie of the mother kin allowed to pass.'" The girl wrinkled her freckled nose. "Mother kin?"

"Follower of Lolth. Our quarry." The Justicar tapped the map. "Looks like the paths diverge just down here. What are the notes on the next junction?"

"Ah!" Escalla glared at the magically transformed writing, trying to make sense of it, then decided that drow simply couldn't spell. "Il-ilithids . . ." The girl jerked forward in alarm. *"Ilithids!"*

Standing awe-stricken behind the Justicar, Private Henry blinked like an owl. "What's an ilithid?"

"Mind flayers. Oh, they're great! You'll love 'em!" Escalla waved her hands theatrically about her head. "Imagine a super-powered mind-blasting psychopath that can stun your mind at will and wants to eat your raw, ungarnished brain!" The faerie jotted marks across the map. "This says, 'Ilithids'—*plural!*" The girl circled the location hard and sharp with a pen procured from Polk. "I wanna meet a bunch of ilithids like I want to be fed rot-grub. Definitely we go around!"

The Justicar looked at the maze of minor tunnels marked on the maps, each one marked with a danger symbol by the drow.

"The main path might be faster," he said, "if we can pass the mind flayers."

"Jus, *you* pass the mind flayers. Those of us with tasty delicious brains in our craniums might elect to just avoid the dinner invitation, all right?" The girl shot a grumbling look at the Justicar. "We go around!"

"All right."

"Anyway, faerie brains are more highly evolved than human ones. They're tastier."

With her spell slowly failing, Escalla shook her finger to jazz up the magic, then hurriedly went back to the map.

"There're other caves definitely blocking the way. Here's the first. 'Reptile caves—pass security level one.' I'm guessing that's where the trogs hang out." Escalla's finger traced paths and still more symbols changed. "Next zone down: 'Kuo-toa—security pass code two,' whatever that means."

"Evil sentient fish." Jus glowered a the map. "Go on."

"Well, that's about it." Escalla traced lines that finally led to a giant symbol far to the north: a huge cave topped with a drawing of a black spider. "The passages all pretty much lead there. I'm guessing that's home."

The locator needle seemed to agree with the map. Whoever carried the slowglass gem, he was heading northwest straight toward the drow citadel.

It would take a superhuman effort to make the journey, recover the slowglass, and fathom the motives of the murderer. Fortunately,

Escalla considered herself and her friends superhuman. She helped herself to a swig from the ever-full bottle—now mysteriously full of peach brandy—and clapped her hands as Jus noisily rolled up the map.

"All right people, let's move on!" The girl marched about the place like the leader of a circus troupe. "Henry, poison your crossbow bolts with the drow drugs! In fact, take the whole poison pot and dip your sword! Polk, let's get going!"

The drow had carried small brooches coded with patterns and squiggles. Jus knelt and seized a random selection, then began the hard march into the dark.

✳   ✳   ✳   ✳   ✳

Half an hour later, a tiny campfire made from lantern oil and fungi spread a yellow light about a nasty little cave. Dinner sizzled and gave off an amazingly offensive smell. Sitting cross legged in her black silk dress, her bottom planted upon Cinders, who lay staring in fascination at the fire, Escalla wrenched another piece off the roast and tried to fit it in her mouth.

"Look on the bright side! At least everybody gets a drumstick!"

Each sitting with a leg from a really big spider in their laps, both Polk and Private Henry managed to give watery smiles while wondering how to hide their food. Jus sat in silence, crunching upon spider meat. With his armor lying spread beside the fire, the Justicar was a mass of bandages.

The magic whiskey bottle wet the cloth Escalla used to dab his wounds. Jus heaved and bucked in pain, snarling imprecations at the faerie. She sat primly in place, holding her wash cloth and looking at the Justicar through hooded eyes.

"Don't be such a baby. We have to get these clean."

"They are clean!"

"They are not. These tunnels are filled with fungus. We'll clean you up and use nice fresh bandages, then in a few hours your healing spells will make you all better." Escalla moved with a matronly, possessive air as she tended the Justicar. "You're my pal, so we have to take good care of you."

Jus dragged his sword from his belt and lay it on the floor beside him where it could no longer jut into his ribs. Plumping up blankets on a nice dry patch of floor, Escalla made the man a bed.

"Now, you sleep. We need you at your best." The sight of a tiny faerie tucking in the large man seemed ludicrous, but Polk and Henry were too busy wrestling with their dinners to speak out. "Sleep tight!"

Lying painfully down, Jus gave a dissatisfied sigh. "Who's on guard?"

"I am!" Escalla forcibly closed Jus's eyes. "I have to stay up and relearn all my spells. Polk, Henry, and I will take care of it. So go to sleep and relax."

Busying herself about the campsite, Escalla dragged out her spell references, a scrap of parchment, and a pen. She perched a rather attractive pair of spectacles upon her nose and looked across the rims at Jus, gave him a rather sardonic, challenging little smile, and then set about her work. Her pen scratched, the fire crackled, and slowly the Justicar began to sleep.

Polk and Henry turned in, each wrapping themselves in drow cloaks to keep away the chill. They kept weapons close at hand and slept far away from the entrance. Private Henry watched Escalla, so prim and pretty in the firelight, as she jotted down her notes. He managed a nervous smile when the faerie caught his eye.

Escalla waved her pen.

"G'night, kid. It's all right." She tapped her tall, pointed faerie ears. "Anything comes waddling down the passageway, and I promise pooch and I'll scream."

The youth half wondered if it was a joke, but he decided not to look foolish and rolled over, too tired to stay awake.

The fire crackled. Escalla wrote, and slowly and surely her companions sank into a dead silent sleep. Cinders grinned. Escalla thoughtfully fingered his rents and cuts, then flipped through her little scrolls.

"Hey, pooch. Repair spell time?"

No. Makes Cinders sleepy. The hell hound's teeth gleamed. *Cinders stay ripped. Stay awake.*

"Don't worry about it. I'll be up for hours." Escalla smoothed out the dog's pelt then carefully spoke her spell and made the hide and fur go back to its usual pristine self. "There we go! Now you just lie there and let it do you good while I warm my faerie butt by the fire!"

The hell hound purred, the repair spell stealing through him from nose to tail in a warm delicious haze. His voice actually sounded sleepy as it drifted into Escalla's mind.

Nice faerie.

"You know it!" Escalla wriggled in Cinders's fur then leaned over to give the dog a kiss "Nighty night."

Night.

The tunnels were remarkably quiet. There was no time, no night, no day, no heat, and no rain. Water dripped, and the campfire slowly died. Keeping happily to her work, Escalla wrote and studied for an hour. While Jus slept, she dusted the big lug with a stoneskin spell, then made up her lost spells with another hour of careful thought. Finally she looked at her list and nodded carefully, stifling a yawn as she tried to see if there were any possibilities she had missed.

Another yawn came, this time wider than the last. "Spell shields, black tentacles, lightning bolts, couple of magic walls . . ."

Cinders's fur was obscenely soft and silky. Escalla lay with her head propped on her elbow, a little blanket drawn up over herself as she worked. "A few"—another yawn—"few utilities. A charm . . . charm monster spell."

It seemed a good idea to rest her eyes for a while, then awaken Polk for his turn on guard. Full of good intentions, Escalla never even felt herself slide beautifully off into the world of sleep.

The fire died down. The uneaten bits of roasted spider cooled. Cinders lay in a warm fuzzy daze, his tail occasionally twitching. In the caverns, all was peace and quiet as the water drip-drip-dripped endlessly from the mildewed walls.

After a long, peaceful time, the sound of movement came from the passageway. Bumbling along the tunnel came a single silly shape—a creature questing forward behind an absurd pair of long, thin feelers. Armored in a sturdy shell and searching the dark with addled eyes, the creature hunted after a particular delicious smell that seemed to quiver in the air.

The scent came from the travelers' cave. Edging forward, the creature pat-pat-patted with its feelers, tasting eagerly at the air. It stole forward just a little way, saw Escalla lying on the hell hound skin and the other figures wrapped in blankets by the fire. The creature shrank and kept perfectly still—timid and frightened—but the only sound was Escalla making little chipmunk noises in her sleep.

The scent struck—sharp and utterly delicious! Overcoming fear, the creature edged slowly forward, then suddenly saw its prize lying on the cave floor nearby. Its feelers reached out toward the Justicar. A long tail tipped with strange propellor-like blades waved happily in the darkness as the creature carefully began to feed.

Several minutes passed, then quite suddenly, Escalla shot bolt upright in bed, her eyes wide open and staring at the dark.

"Dad! The sculptures of me were all fakes. I swear!"

The creature froze, then bolted off in panic, its belly full and its legs galloping off into the gloom.

Far behind the fleeing creature, Escalla collapsed back in bed. Sleeping the deep sleep of the just, she snored raucously for many long and uneventful hours to come.

14

"ESCALLA!"

The noise shot Escalla up out of her bed, eyes wide open and her hands moving to snatch spellbooks, pens, and scrolls to look as though she were still working. She blinked about in a daze, only to see Jus looming over the dead campfire and wringing something in his hands. The faerie instantly turned invisible.

"It wasn't me! It was Polk!"

Polk awoke in a mad confusion of blankets. "It's a lie! A lie!"

"Of course it's a lie!" Jus whirled, uncannily able to see right through Escalla's invisibility. "You slept on guard!"

"It's not my fault! I was working! Everyone knows I fall asleep when I'm working!" Now near the ceiling, Escalla took shelter behind a stalactite. "Look. Everyone's still alive. What is your problem?"

Hundreds of pounds of stubble-headed fury paced like an enraged cave bear below Escalla's hiding place.

"*This* is the problem!" Jus waved the wolf-skull hilt of his sword. "My sword! Something's eaten the whole blade of my sword!"

The black blade was now nothing but a rusted stump about half a finger long. Escalla blinked back into view, hoping that calming words and a nervous grin were better than calming words alone.

"It wasn't my fault."

"Then whose fault was it?!?" Jus's bellow must have reached halfway to the drow citadel. "We left you in charge!"

"Well, Cinders was there!"

"Cinders is still humming away from some damned idiot's repair spell! We'll be lucky if he wakes up before lunchtime!"

Huge with anger, the Justicar paced back and forth, his furious eye always fixed upon Escalla.

"That sword saw me through a hundred fights. That sword wasn't stopped by any blade. That sword was the only thing I had to keep us alive long enough to beat your damned murder charge!"

Private Henry peeked out from behind a stalagmite. "Murder?"

"It's a bum rap!" Escalla shot a comment at the boy, then squeaked as Jus's hand fastened around her and dragged her down to face him. "All right, I made a teeny error of judgment! I was tired, man! Those drow really blasted me!" The girl clasped her hands. "I'm really sorry. Really really really sorry! Really really really really *amazingly* sorry! Now will you just calm down?"

Jus released the faerie and sat down, fuming angry and swearing at the dark. Polk cleared his throat to speak, but Escalla waved the man down before he could make a bad situation worse.

"Jus? We can get you another sword."

"We are in the bowels of the earth a hundred miles from anywhere!" Jus seethed, his head stubble standing up like porcupine quills. "Where were you planning on going shopping?"

"Hey! We've got swords! See! Lots of swords!" In a mad panic to head off Jus's rage, Escalla spilled captured drow short swords all over the floor. "See? These are swords."

The drow weapons were scarcely eighteen inches long. Jus picked one up, the weapon looking like a toothpick in his hand. He dropped it and sat down to brood, seething in annoyance at the whole wide world.

Escalla wrung her hands in misery and hovered at his side. "Jus. . . ?"

"I'm really mad, Escalla."

"I'll make it up to you. I promise! I'll find a better sword, a much much better one." The girl bit her thumb in shame. "And I'm really sorry about falling asleep. I stayed up for *hours* working, man. Honest."

He smoldered. Escalla ended up in his arms, trying her very best to be contrite.

"I promise you I'll do the next thr—err, two things you order me to do without question. All right?" Anxious and much cowed, Escalla sketched a little salute. "Promise."

Looking at the sad little stub of his sword—the wolf skull pommel still intact, but the blade a total ruin—Jus sank into a bear-like sulk.

"I pulled that sword out of my dead master's hands back in the Iuz wars. Killed the wight that was after me. Saved my life a thousand times." Bitterly unhappy, Jus sheathed the blade stub then jammed a drow dagger through his belt. "We'd better find some proper armament before we run into any more of our murderer's little friends."

There was a shy shuffle from behind. Looking up at the Justicar, Private Henry cleared his throat and timidly offered his sword.

"Sir? I'm really not much use with it." The boy unsheathed the first few inches of the blade and looked down at his feet. "I watched you fight. I . . . I could never be a fighter like that."

The Justicar looked down at the boy with a sudden grim pride. Rage and annoyance forgotten, he laid a hand on Private Henry's shoulder. "What's your name again, son?"

"Henry."

"Thank you, Henry." Jus hefted the boy's sword, then laid it back in Henry's hands. "Keep it. You'll need it. You kept a drow off my back. Well done."

Henry slumped in self-made misery. "It was only one, and she would have killed me if it wasn't for the faerie."

Perking instantly up, Escalla whirred over to the rescue.

"Spell! Ha! That's right! That was a *faerie* spell!" The girl dusted off Henry's helmet in pride. "Didn't they ever tell you about faerie magic? That spell is only effective if the recipient is pure of heart." Escalla smoothed the boy's hair and jerked his collar straight. "You've got the right stuff, kid. Magic never lies. Now let's get moving. We need your sharp eyes covering the rear while we go find Jus a new sword!"

Private Henry drew himself fully upright, reaching almost to Jus's chest. Full of pride and energy, he clapped a bolt into his crossbow, squared his helmet, and marched off into the passageway. Watching him go, Jus cradled Escalla in the crook of his arm.

"Was that true about that spell?"

"What, stoneskin?" Escalla pulled her nose. "Naah! But look how good it made him feel." The girl spread her wings and whirred into the air. "Come on, J-man! Time's wasting, and that slowglass is gettin' halfway to drow central!"

Jus sighed and hung back a few moments to use his healing spells to cure his wounds. Unarmed yet still dangerous, he stalked out of the cave mouth and moved into the dark.

They walked into the vile tunnel, water dripping and worms slithering wetly through the mold about them. Polk marched unsteadily, dwarfed by the pack of loot balanced on his shoulders. Somehow the little man never minded the load, being driven onward by sheer bloody-mindedness as he cleaved the dark like an icebreaker forging through a polar sea. Coming level with Escalla, he shot the girl a long glance, swelled his pigeon chest, and cleared his throat. "Discipline!"

"What?" Escalla eyed the man suspiciously. "Polk, have you been reading those stories about dryads again?"

"Discipline!" Polk sniffed, never to be swayed from his purpose once he had begun. "That's what you need. Rewards never come by accident. Since the fall of evil is a reward to the good, the good need discipline, application, a sense of responsibility!"

The faerie made a face and simply stopped listening. "Yeah yeah. Blah-blah-blah. The faerie fell asleep, so it's *her* fault Jus's sword got eaten!"

Walking just ahead of her, Jus raised one finger without bothering to look around. "Escalla."

"Yes?"

"Order number one. For the next hour, listen very closely to everything Polk has to say."

Escalla shot Jus a look that could kill, glowered, then sat herself atop Polk's backpack, propping her chin in her hands. Swelling grandly, Polk marched doggedly along behind the Justicar and tucked his thumbs into his braces.

"Well now! You see, back when I was a lad, schoolin' was different. *Focus*, that's what they gave us—focus and a sense of worth. Why, once I remember I gave my lunch to another little boy because his family was poor. Day after day I helped him out. No credit wanted! No fuss! In those days you spoke when you were spoken to! Kept your thoughts to yourself. Lesson *I* learned to heart!"

Escalla sighed, propped her elbows on her knees, and endured.

* * * * *

The locator needle pointed northwest. Ignoring side tunnels and slimy caves, the group moved northwards in skill and silence, watching carefully for sign of ambush. Their path continued sloping downward, descending in occasional steps and terraces where waterfalls of slime trickled slowly in the shadows.

Jus knelt to examine strange footprints he found gleaming wetly on the fungi here and there. None of the marks were fresh, but they gave a horrible feeling of presence, of a hidden life lurking always just out of sight.

Miles passed. It was a weird limbo in which time scarcely seemed to exist. One patch of fungi-smothered tunnel could have been any other, and the underdark was sealed away from the rhythms of night and day. Drifting from his peaceful haze, Cinders's eyes finally gleamed bright again. He wriggled himself into place across the Justicar's warm back and said, *Hi!*

"Hello." Jus carefully examined a hanging curtain of mold for danger, then led the party well away from the obstruction. "Nice rest?"

Nice! The hell hound wagged his tail, his grin gleaming like a nightmare. *Cinders better!*

"Well, wake up and keep your ears open." Jus cautiously steered Escalla away from an innocent looking covey of screamer fungi. "We're in trouble. I lost my sword."

Cinders help! His long black tail went wag-wag-wag. *Fun!*

The main pathway dissolved into a maze of interlocking caverns—some large, some small. Jus squatted down and had Escalla consult the locator needle, choosing a route that seemed to lead in the required direction. The team ducked one by one beneath a low ceiling and walked uncomfortably crab-wise between shallow pools of slime. They emerged into a new cave, where the lost tunnel reappeared.

Escalla heaved a sigh of relief at having found the right path again, waved the others to follow her, only to freeze, turn invisible, and dart madly back down amongst the mounds of bat dung.

"Down!"

Three shapes hovered in the gloom, bobbing malevolently up and down. They were huge, grim spheres, each one topped with a cluster of eye stalks and with one huge eye glaring off into the dark. Gaping mouths slashed across the arc of the spheres, mouths crammed with fangs that seemed to thirst for blood.

In a mad panic, Escalla grabbed Polk and Jus by the ears, trying to tow them back into the caves.

"Come on! *Gotta go!*" Her whisper hissed above the whir of busy little wings. *"Beholders!* Run like hell!"

The monsters moved, drifting slowly up and down. Hovering silently and lost in their own thoughts, the three beings stared off into the caves, having failed to catch sight of the tiny faerie. With her friends hidden safely in cover two dozen yards back in the caves, Escalla reappeared, plastered flat against the rocks and looking in fright toward the tunnel mouth. The girl worked the slide of her battle wand.

"Oh man, oh man! Paranoid xenophobic homicidal maniacs that shoot killer spells from every eye!" The girl looked left and right, trying to see a route past the lurking terrors up ahead. "We are dead!"

Jus stood up, tugged his armor straight, and settled his dagger in his belt. He strode straight down the passageway with his usual irresistible tread. Escalla could only gape in horror for a moment, then flew off madly in pursuit.

"Jus, get down!"

The three monsters were still there in the cave, circling and maneuvering slowly in the still air. Jus levered himself down a terrace and walked into the tunnel, marching over to the monsters and standing directly beneath the nearest one. He scratched the stubble of his chin, betraying amusement by shooting a sly look sideways to make sure Escalla was watching him. Intensely annoyed, Escalla emerged from behind the cover of a rock outcrop.

"Why aren't you dead, you shaven-headed git!"

Unconcerned, Jus stood beneath one of the monsters and cut himself a piece of spider meat, which he crammed into his mouth. He motioned to the monsters with his dagger, supremely unconcerned.

"Beholders are solitary psychopaths. Did you think there might be something weird about seeing *three* beholders together all at once?" The man spat a piece of spider chitin toward a nearby slug "They're gas spores."

"What?"

"A type of fungus. Dead ringers for beholders, except beholders are waaay too paranoid to ever be this close to one another."

Wings whirring and a disgusted scowl on her face, Escalla came out of the caves to glare at the floating gas spores. From a few inches away, she could clearly see that they were fakes—just blobs of fungi. Escalla aimed a kick at the nearest one, only to have Jus snatch her foot and tug her hastily away.

"Leave 'em be!"

"Why?"

"Poisonous. Touch it, and die young." The big man tugged Escalla's makeshift dress straight as he released her into the air. "They're a trap. Puncture the skin, and they explode."

"Oooh." Escalla instantly perked up her ears. "Really?"

"Really." Jus forcibly propelled the curious girl away from the spores. "The explosion of each individual spore is enough to turn you into a shadow on the wall. *Three* of them would be *apocalyptic*."

"Wow. Can I have one?"

"No."

"But—"

"No, Escalla."

"Ju-uuus—"

"No, Escalla. Absolutely not! End of discussion."

Jus gave a courtly bow, inviting Escalla to lead the way. "This is where the passage turns. It heads toward the troglodytes."

The faerie hmphed and acquiesced, but still remained obviously unconvinced.

As the party pressed on, they saw that the spores were growing from the body of a big lizard lying around the corner. The cadaver stretched almost twenty feet from nose to tail and wore a harness and a brand. Growing out of the damaged tarpaulins, packs, and rotten flesh were yet more floating spores—perhaps half a dozen bobbing booby traps, still tethered to the rotting corpse.

The spores remained hanging in the still, cool air, drifting slowly forward from time to time as gas trickled from tiny holes at their rear. Carried over Jus's shoulder, Escalla gazed back at them until they disappeared from view, watching past Private Henry as the boy walked nervously, cradling his crossbow.

The narrow, slimy tunnel curved and dipped, then suddenly opened onto a wider passageway. It was the old, familiar path that ran northwest, at least forty feet wide and user friendly. Escalla consulted the locator needle and pointed the way into the dim phosphorescent depths. She escaped from her perch upon Jus's shoulder, using her sharp ears and clever eyes to hunt for dangers lurking far ahead.

Danger soon appeared. Escalla's sensitive ears detected a scratching noise far ahead. Signaling the others to halt, the faerie turned invisible and flew softly forward down the passageway.

A few dozen yards beyond the adventurers, a dozen hideous monsters crouched in the dark. Working with great stealth, the savage creatures were pulling apart the rock wall with their claws.

Skeletal and horrific, the monsters were mere skin stretched over bone—human-like, but with bestial faces, and spreading a vicious stink of rotting flesh. At the rear of the pack, two of the creatures crouched over a long bundle wrapped in rags. The bundle seemed to pain them, for none would touch it willingly. The beasts seem to be squabbling over which of them should drag the heap of rags closer to the new hole in the wall.

Jus moved silently beside Escalla and joined her in watching the creatures. Escalla nodded her chin toward the beasts, wrinkling her nose in distaste.

"Ghouls."

Undead and carnivorous, the ghouls were also apparently working to a plan. Within the newly opened cave, a black pit could dimly be seen. The leader of the ghouls—a larger, wart-encrusted male—slashed at one of its subordinates, which loped into the cave and began sniffing like a dog. It peered into the pit then began snarling to the other ghouls outside.

The creatures crowded up to the cave entrance, the hindmost ghouls jerking their hands away from the rag bundle until forced to drag it closer to the cave. The bundle was unwrapped. The rags proved to be a torn battle flag. Working with fungi stalks as tools, the ghouls began prying and levering at the contents of the bundle, scattering away in panic as something metallic fell to the floor at their feet.

One ghoul tripped as it fled, then screamed, flashed, and blew apart in a choking cloud of dust. The other ghouls fled from the bundle until forced back by vicious blows from their leader.

The ghoul leader snarled at a subordinate, shoved it aside, then levered up something bright and golden with its fungus staff. For a brief instant, a sword glittered in the eerie light, and then the ghoul flung it down the pit. After a long, long moment, a faint metallic *clang* came from below. The ghouls bellowed and capered in glee.

Escalla looked up as a black shadow loomed nearby.

Drifting quietly in the air behind the ghouls was a great, brooding sphere. The object floated in midair—a menacing presence topped with eye stalks and a single huge eye just above its mouth. The sphere drifted unnoticed behind the ghouls, and Escalla felt a malicious little plan flooding through her mind.

"Hey, guys!" she whispered sharply. "Watch this!"

She fired her magic bees toward the sphere before Jus could stop her. The stream of magic missiles blasted into the giant sphere in a blaze of light. Instead of triggering a titanic explosion to destroy the ghouls, the spell set off a furious roar. The sphere whipped about to face the faerie, eyes red rimmed and fangs gaping. The big central eye blinked closed, and from an upper eyestalk a spell blast disintegrated ten square feet of passage wall. Jerked out of the way at the last instant, Escalla hung in Jus's grasp, staring in shock as the beholder shook the whole tunnel with its roar.

Ghouls screeched, leaping onto the sphere and sinking fangs and claws into its flesh. The beholder pounded itself against the wall, crushing ghouls and catching one of the undead creatures in its jaws. Bleeding, the beholder staggered as the ghoul leader jumped atop it and wrenched off several eyestalks. An instant later the ghoul was blasted into vapor by a shot from an eyestalk at its side.

The battle spilled back into the cave, injured ghouls falling screaming down the open pit and plunging to their doom. Jus pitched Escalla down the passage, grabbed Polk and Henry by the scruffs of their necks, and ran down the tunnel as if every legion of the Nine Hells were behind them.

A sharp zig-zag hid all sight of the fight, but howls and screams echoed through the gloom. Escalla whirled to a corner and clung to a stalactite in fright, covering the retreat of her friends with her wand.

Catching up with her, the Justicar shouted at her, "What are they when they're *alone*, Escalla?" Jus was not having one of his more enjoyable days. "They're *beholders*, Escalla!"

"All right! All right!" The girl angrily waved her hand. "It still worked! The ghouls are neutralized! The faerie scores again!"

Jus turned her around and pointed her northwest. "Move! If that beholder comes after us, we're toast!"

Weighed down by chain mail, Private Henry staggered and fell. Jus picked the boy up with one hand and set him on his feet. The boy looked back in terror as he ran.

"Is it coming?"

"Might not have seen us." The Justicar put himself at the boy's back. "If it comes, keep running! I'll buy you time!"

Escalla shot far ahead as they fled down the passageway. Something thundered in the tunnel far behind. Still invisible, Escalla looked behind her as she flew . . . and smacked straight into something hard.

Stunned, Escalla tumbled back and hit the ground. She half saw a gigantic figure towering over her invisible body—a big goblinoid creature that stank like a sewer. Confused, the monster staggered back and looked around for what had struck it. Squatting beside the first giant goblin was another, and another, and another . . .

A vast cavern opened beyond the monsters—a cavern that teemed with troglodytes by the score. The lizards sat in their scores at the cave center, tearing at bleeding chunks of food. A dozen giant goblin guards cradling huge clubs loomed at the tunnel entrance. The first rubbed its skull where Escalla had crashed into it.

Beyond the other monsters, pack lizards and drow merchants knelt reverently before a sinister, robed figure at the far side of the hall. The whole image hung frozen in time as Escalla stared, and then she heard the pounding of boots behind her as Jus, Polk, and Henry arrived upon the scene.

A hundred monsters turned to stare. Over by the kneeling drow, the tall figure dressed in black robes turned and brushed its cowl back across its shoulders.

There was no face, only a rotting skull with mad, staring eyes. Escalla took one look at the thing, screamed in panic, and shot backward past Polk and the others.

"*Lich!* Run, boys! Ruuuuun!"

Used to instant obedience, Private Henry turned and did what he was told. More bull headed, Polk and Jus stopped to judge for themselves. They stood for one tiny split second, staring at the cavern with its horde of enemies.

The lich, an undead sorcerer of terrifying power, stood at the center of the hall. Rotted jaws screeched with laughter as the monster threw its arms open, summoning a spell. Jus and Polk turned and ran.

Too late. The lich gave a vile scream as magic blasted through the cavern and into the tunnel mouth. A blazing wall of force sealed the tunnel shut, blocking Jus and Polk from escape and locking Henry and Escalla away from their friends.

The giant goblins smashed at Jus with their huge clubs. The ranger spun into the first blow and wrenched the monster off balance while crashing his elbow into its jaw. A kick from his heavy boots sent another monster reeling back. Jus finished by disarming the first monster and smashing its skull with one blow of its own club. He turned as Cinders blasted flames into the onrushing monsters and sent six of them staggering away with their flesh aflame.

A gigantic goblin picked up Polk and tossed the helpless teamster against a wall. He fell, was lifted by the hair, and then punched unconscious by one of the goblinoids. With hell hound flame sheeting all about him, Jus fell back against the force wall as a dozen monsters surged toward him like a tidal wave.

They were too close-packed to fight with clubs and claws. Jus roared, his rage making the whole tunnel shake as he crashed his clenched fist down onto a giant goblin's skull. His other hand crushed the windpipe of a troglodyte, the huge creature screaming and thrashing. The fangs of a fallen lizard snapped into Jus's calf. He raised a boot, smashed the creature's neck, then fell back to thud against the force wall as monsters climbed toward him in a swarm.

There must have been a hundred monsters, all surging into a screaming mob that choked the entrance to the cave.

Escalla fluttered madly above Private Henry on the other side of the magic wall. She fired a lightning bolt, the spell blasting into the wall without causing so much as a wrinkle in its shine. Two blasts from her frost wand stabbed into the wall and disappeared. The faerie saw Jus rock beneath the blow of a giant goblin's fist, and she tried prying at the edges of the force wall with her nails.

"Jus! Jus, I'm coming!"

"Go!" The Justicar bellowed at the faerie, wrenching a claw from around his throat and breaking a monster's elbow with one huge blow. *"Escalla, go!"*

"Jus!" Weeping helplessly, Escalla hammered uselessly at the edges of the force wall with her spells. *"Jus!"*

"GO!" Now almost buried under a wave of troglodytes, Jus roared as Cinders fired a last vicious blast of flames. "I order you to go! Save yourself and the boy!"

Something lanced through the screaming, ravening horde of monsters—a gigantic disembodied fist that snatched up the Justicar and pounded his head against the cavern ceiling. Unconscious, Jus was thrown to the floor, the huge hand hovering above. Linked to the lich by a tendril of force, the magic fist kept the other monsters at bay, shielding the fallen Justicar and Polk from harm. Escalla saw the lich turn to look right at her through her invisibility magic, saw the abomination lift up its hands to cast another spell—

With a helpless wail, the girl fired her favorite old stinking fog spell, filling the wide passageway with impenetrable clouds of murk. She snatched Henry by the scruff of his neck and dragged him fleeing back down the tunnel.

Behind her, the lich was laughing. Its wild cackle pursued Escalla into the caves long after the mere sound of it had faded and gone.

15

In a cavern somewhere near a rampaging beholder, Escalla crammed herself into a crevasse. With her fist jammed into her mouth, she wept in silence, her eyes wide and her face ashen, shivering in shock. Private Henry protected her, peering over the lip of the rock to watch for enemies. The boy was pale but behaving like a good soldier.

Escalla rocked back and forth, gripping her own skull as though it was about to blast apart. She had cast a shield against detection spells, and that was all that she could do. The lich was either coming after them or it wasn't.

And Jus was either dead or alive.

"Oh man. Oh man, oh man, oh man. I really fouled it this time."

Impossible to believe that once, long ago, she had wanted nothing more in life than to blow Jus apart, she now felt like her innards had been frozen to ice. Escalla stared into the dark, while her soul jerked and fluttered like a wounded butterfly.

There was a careful slither in the gloom. With his eyes on the caves, Private Henry slid down to Escalla's side.

"Miss? Um, my lady?" Private Henry swallowed, his crossbow pointing into the echoing caves. "Lady Escalla, I think that beholder is still out there."

Something howled deeper in the caves. It sounded like the beholder was once again on the prowl. Escalla's heart sank. Henry looked at her, lost and oh-so-terribly young, so Escalla deliberately sat herself up, wiped her hair back from her face and discovered that it hurt like hell to talk.

"Do you think they killed him?"

"What?" Henry's eyes blinked like an owl. "Mister Polk?"

"Yeah. Yeah, they got Polk, too." Running her fingers through soiled hair, Escalla tried to force her mind to think. "The lich was keeping them off him—the trogs and the big goblin things."

"Bugbears." Private Henry stared at shadows in the caves. "I saw a drawing of one once."

"Bugbears." Staring at remembered horrors, Escalla slowly shook her head. "There must have been a hundred of them."

"But they're alive!" Henry crept a little closer, anxious for reassurance. "You saw! You said the lich was keeping them alive."

"Yeah. Yeah, so I did." The faerie's whole body felt like ice— numb, chilled, and insensible. She had to *do* something, take positive action. Escalla shuddered and began making a plan.

A lich. Why did it have to be a lich? A sorcerer so powerful that it had spent an eternity rotting as its bones hardened with hate. It was probably the most savage monster in existence—intelligent, deadly, and apparently the master of a troglodyte tribe.

Escalla idly dangled her locator needle, staring at it blankly as she tried hard just to stay calm and *think*. The needle pointed northwest, away from the lich's caves, and quivered sightly as though the slow-glass was moving at the very limit of the locator's range.

The lich was out there, organizing its troops. *Here* was the ally Escalla's enemy had dealt with to find raiders to attack the surface world, but if the lich controlled the troglodytes, then why were the drow involved? What could a faerie possibly need from a city of dark elves?

The troglodytes were stealing living people. Perhaps that was why Jus and Polk were still alive.

Maybe.

"All right, Henry. We . . . we have to see where they are and what happened. Then we have to figure out our options once we see if they're . . . once we see if they're all right." Escalla tried to calm her ragged breathing and wipe the tears back from her face. "Just keep calm, all right? You're with the faerie. No one touches the faerie."

The girl had a useful spell up her sleeve—provided the lich wasn't just around the corner and about to blast them all into rich meaty chunks. She tried straightening her hair, sat erect, then forced herself to be calm.

"Henry?"

"Yes, my lady?"

"I have to concentrate, so just keep low and only disturb me if that beholder comes into this room."

"All right." The young soldier swallowed then crept back into place, trying to move the way the Justicar would. "Don't worry. I'll protect you."

"I know you will, Henry. Thanks."

Escalla took a deep breath and bowed her head. Sitting cross legged on the floor with a look of supreme concentration on her face, she opened her hands and quietly spoke a spell. Her point of view shifted to somewhere between her hands, the position wavering slightly until the spell steadied in her mind.

She turned slowly and looked up at herself. Her hair hung bedraggled, and her thin face was smeared with tears. The viewpoint bobbed and carefully rose, then Escalla turned and shot her viewpoint through the caves, leaving her mind and body safely behind.

The spell's eye moved forward swiftly through the caves and out into the main tunnel. It floated forward in eerie silence, able to see but not hear. Escalla slowed as she approached the entrance to the lich's cavern, feeling her way carefully forward. She wanted nothing to betray her spy spell. Jus would expect her to be as perfect as possible.

The entrance to the cave lay quiet. Huge bugbears—great hairy beings eight feet tall with stupid, pig-like eyes—leaned on their clubs and stared along the tunnel. Six were on guard at the tunnel mouth, with drow warriors tending a little fire behind them. Escalla hesitated, then drifted the spy spell past the guards. The bugbears never even twitched an ear as Escalla's viewpoint drifted by.

The main cavern was dangerously immense—a great arching space with an unsupported roof that dripped with slime. To the northeast and northwest, great tunnel roadways cleaved into the underdark. The vast central hall seemed to serve as a nexus point where drow caravans and travelers came to trade.

Beside the entrance to the northwest passageway, a hideous black presence materialized from the dark. The lich appeared, its rotting, skeletal face still hung with flaking strips of skin. With its magnificent black robes trailing all around it, the lich walked slowly forward, its steps so cold that they made the cave floor steam. The lich turned and stalked back toward its lair—troglodytes and bugbears bowing and cringing in submission as it passed. The drow watched coldly from the sidelines—dark, elegant, and vaguely amused by the spectacle of horrid death. Chilled, Escalla backed away, then whirled about and hastily sped after the lich.

Outside the lich's cave, a drow awaited. A huge pack lizard chewed on rotting meat behind the dark elf. Sitting beside the beast were a dozen spiritless creatures linked together by a chain, slaves apparently being traded to the drow. There were cowed, beaten bugbears, troglodytes, a pair of orcs, and a goblin child.

The lich leaned forward to speak to one of the drow. The dark elf nodded, paid a sum in precious gems, then walked back to the campsite while the lich returned to its cave. Torn with indecision over where to go, Escalla darted left, darted right, then shot after the lich and followed the dreadful being into its lair.

In a cavern lined with magic mouths that murmured and whispered in the very rock, Jus and Polk lay unconscious beside a pile of equipment. Jus still wore his armor, and no one had yet taken his magic ring. Two large troglodyte guards crouched beside them. The two humans were tied tight. The lich stooped over each man, staring, then spoke to the troglodytes and motioned toward the cave entrance.

The troglodytes bowed, lifted Jus between them, and carried him out to the slave merchants. The lich moved over to a shelf of rock, lay a hand in a niche, and drew forth a tiny folded piece of cloth. Opening a few folds of the cloth, it dropped the gems onto the fabric, and the gems seemed to disappear.

The lich peered into the cloth for an instant, replaced it in the niche, then lay down upon a shelf of rock and closed its eyes in repose. An instant later, an illusion spell snapped into place, hiding the lich from view.

Cinders lay in a heap in one corner, his mouth tied shut with Jus's own magic rope. Escalla hovered anxiously over the poor hell hound, seeing the dog's ears jerk and his head twitch as he saw her spell. Through his bindings, the black hell hound suddenly began to grin. Escalla bobbed up and down in encouragement, then as more troglodytes came to gather Polk, she flitted from the room.

Jus had been carried to the caravan and laid beside the slaves. The drow themselves were relaxing and eating. Boxes were being unloaded from their pack lizard, while a few more slaves were beginning to arrive. The drow were all supremely unhurried, passing their time torturing minor lifeforms and drinking thick black wine.

The spell began to flicker and fade. Escalla took one last scan of the route into the cave, drew one long, deep breath, then opened her eyes and found herself sitting cross legged at the bottom of the crevasse.

Henry lay motionless in cover, frightened yet still soldiering on. Rubbing her temples to clear a swimming sense of vertigo, the faerie blinked and then called out to the boy, "Hey, Henry!"

The boy slid back down to Escalla's side, keeping his face turned to the cave above, and sat at her side. "Did you see them?"

"Yeah. They're alive." Escalla sniffed, hoping that the bad smell in the air wasn't her. "The lich is selling them to the drow as slaves. Must be why the trogs raid the upper world. Looks like the slave caravan won't be heading out for a while."

"Where will it go?"

"Probably northwest. But to follow it, we'd still have to get past the lich and all his friends." Escalla felt tired and worn. The relief at seeing Jus alive had yet to settle her soul. "I could do with some ideas. Where's Enid when I need her?"

Private Henry blinked owlishly in the dark. "Who's Enid?"

"Gynosphinx. Freckles, perfectly spoken, polite and with a mind like an encyclopedia. You'll like her." The dear, quiet, lovely sphinx would have been such a comfort. "I'd say we have about an hour to effect a rescue before those drow get on the road."

Off in the deeper caves, the beholder gave an echoing growl. Perfectly trusting, Private Henry settled down to look at Escalla in joy.

"So that's it! They're alive! And you have a plan, right?"

"Sure!" Escalla blinked. Jus was alive! She sat a little straighter, her mind racing in a hundred directions and arriving nowhere at all. "Sure. Yeah, I have a plan, and it's a hoopy one, too! Best if I keep it secret for now, though. I'll fill you in on a need-to-know basis."

Infinitely relieved, Private Henry sat and hugged his crossbow for joy. "I knew it! The Justicar can't be defeated by a bunch of damned trogs!"

"Yeah, well, let's just say he's gathering his resources to help us with our efforts." Escalla lay back against the rock wall and stared at the ceiling, wincing as she tried to find inspiration. "We'll have to get moving quick."

"Just say the word!" Henry was so full of trust that Escalla could have killed him. "What do we do first?"

The faerie slapped a few half baked ideas together in the vague hope that they might stick.

"Well, kid, look on it as a five point plan." Escalla sat up, knowing that she was heading for a hellstorm of trouble. "First we get a new weapon for Jus, then we sneak into the lich's caves, then we take out most of the trogs, then we kill the lich. After that, we free Jus, Polk, and Cinders, then run off into the tunnels."

With a happy sigh of relief, Henry stood up and began to climb out of the crevasse.

"Thank the gods!" Henry reached the cave floor and gallantly offered his hand to haul the little faerie up onto her feet. "For a while, I thought we were in trouble!"

"Yeah, silly you." Escalla tapped her fingers together, trying to make vague ideas feel better than they looked. "As I said, the details will be revealed, ah, as we need to know."

The faerie heard the beholder growling off in the caves and fetched her battle wand.

"Come on, kid. Adventure calls."

Followed by the absurdly happy soldier, Escalla fluttered off into the shadows. Private Henry checked his crossbow, set his helmet to a jaunty angle, then marched off in pursuit of the smartest, prettiest, most competent girl he had ever clapped his eyes upon.

✳   ✳   ✳   ✳   ✳

A beholder's life was apparently a merry one. Having slaughtered a horde of ghouls, the beholder now amused itself with the corpses of the deceased. It had gnawed the faces off one or two and dragged out the intestines of others to create a vile, nose-blistering stench. All about the pit that the ghouls had uncovered, body parts lay scattered. Bleeding a noisome green ooze from a few cuts and severed eyestalks, the beholder hovered above its kills, chewing on a severed hand and scowling in thought.

Escalla's plans were detailed, concise, and foolproof. In accordance with these directives, something went "chink" against the beholder's armored shell, rebounded, and fell rattling to the floor. Utterly unharmed, the beholder swiveled around to look at the offending object. Lying on the floor, the drugged crossbow bolt lay pointing back down the corridor like an accusing finger.

Still frozen with his empty crossbow pointed at the beholder, Private Henry crouched behind a pile of rubble. The boy squeaked, the beholder roared, and a beam lashed out to blast a huge chunk from the rocks overhead. Henry ducked and fled like a hare. The boy's wail of panic brought the beholder shooting out of its cave like a cork popping from a bottle.

Spells shot from the beholder's upper eyestalks, blasting rock as Henry wove madly through the caves. With a shuddering roar, the beholder flew down the tunnels. As the monster flashed past, Escalla swung out of hiding. The girl gave a nasty little grin and fired her very best charm monster spell right into the beholder's unprotected back.

The magic stabbed straight toward the beholder's shell—a shell no longer guarded by its anti-magic front eye. As the spell struck home, Escalla hopped up and down and did a little dance of glee.

"Gotcha!"

The beholder screeched to a stop, whipped around, and gave a violent roar. Escalla stared for one brief instant, then screamed like a peeled weasel and flew madly up through the stalagmites. Death and disintegration beams blasted rock right at her heels. Utterly unaffected by her spell, the beholder barreled after her like a runaway wagon, smashing into stalagmites and shattering them like glass.

Tunnels and caverns opened up at every side. Escalla blurred inside a cave and rolled madly aside as a death beam stabbed half an inch below her nose. She saw a side opening and made toward it to escape, only to have a disintegration beam from the monster blast into the arch and bring the whole cave mouth thundering down in an avalanche. Trapped, Escalla squealed and wrenched aside. An instant later the beholder lunged into the cave after her, its central eye open and all magic instantly dispelled.

Even without its magic eyes, the beholder was well adapted for chewing faeries. With its jaws gaping, it charged straight at Escalla. The girl planted her back onto the wall, coiled her legs beneath her and launched herself away an instant before the beholder smashed against the wall. Finding long tufts of ragged hair hanging beneath the beholder's belly, Escalla latched onto the hair and hung dangling like a puppet. Above her, the beholder roared and bashed itself against the walls, angrily trying to shake the little faerie free. It tried to blast her with its eyestalks, but was unable to see beneath its own fat shell. Escalla wailed and held on for dear life as the beholder began to buck wildly in an attempt to shake her loose.

A crossbow bolt flashed past a hair's breadth beneath Escalla's bottom. Hanging on to the beholder, the girl managed to look back and see Private Henry and his trusty crossbow.

"Are you crazy?"

"Sorry!"

Flung madly left and right, Escalla screeched and held on tight. The beholder went on a wild ride to dislodge the hanging faerie. Careering madly down the tunnels, it bashed against the walls, knocking the breath from Escalla and making her see stars. Racing through caves, it smashed its belly against the ground. Escalla flapped her wings in panic, towed along just inches behind the bottom of the monstrous sphere.

The beholder dragged her painfully across rubble, through a stream, and then ploughed her through a fresh dung pile. As Escalla emerged, choked and spluttering, the beholder roared and burst through a pile of old dry bones.

Jerked and flung madly about beneath the monster, Escalla managed to wipe dung from her face and give a snarl of rage.

"You goggle eyed git! You'll pay for that!"

The beholder had traveled full circuit through the caves. It blundered into the cavern filled with dismembered ghouls and then tried to bounce like a ball and squish Escalla into the filthy guts of its last prey. Escalla flung herself left and right, swinging on the beholder's dangling hairs, felt herself land in something best left unidentified, then flailed out with one hand and caught hold of a prize.

A crossbow bolt!

Frustrated at its inability to dislodge the troublesome faerie, the beholder saw a long line of stalagmites down a side tunnel and roared with glee as it raced toward the stone spikes. Escalla took one sharp glance at the onrushing doom, hefted the drugged arrow, lined it up on a bleeding claw gouge in the beholder's carapace and rammed the weapon home.

"Take this!"

Above her, the beholder gave a scream of rage then quite suddenly took on an odd expression. With eyes wide in shock, it went plunging down to the ground. Escalla flew tumbling free an instant before the creature hit the ground. The beholder bounced onward like a titanic ball straight down the passageway.

Ten stalagmites stood in its way. Nine fell immediately with the blast of impact. The tenth cracked at its base and wobbled uncertainly in a spin. As Escalla climbed to her feet, the final stalagmite toppled and fell, landing with a crash upon the motionless beholder.

"Yes!"

Escalla leaped into the air and gave a highly immodest scream of victory. With one fist raised, she suddenly paused, sniffed, and made a little face of dismay.

"Ewww!" Blood, bat dung, mildew, and beholder fluids had wreaked havoc with her grooming. "We have to get that hell hound back and get me a bath!"

Running dazedly in pursuit, Private Henry blundered toward Escalla. Weighed down by chainmail and carrying his crossbow, the boy screeched to a halt and folded over with a stitch, too crippled by exhaustion to make any meaningful comment. He waved a hand at the beholder, wheezing something as he tried to catch his breath. Bruised, battered, but triumphant, Escalla slapped her hands, gave the boy a thumbs up and turned to view her prize.

"Knocked 'im out!"

The beholder had been paralyzed by drugs provided courtesy of the drow. The monster lay with its eyestalks stiff and staring into blank space. Escalla gave it a kick in what should have been its side, closed its upper eye stalks for it, then pranced and posed up and down in front of the creature's one main eye. She slapped her backside in its torn silks for the monster's delectation.

"Ha! Here it is, faerie butt, primo, perfect, untouched prime!" Escalla put her bottom almost between the monster's jaws. "Oh all right, you can eat me! Ooops! Paralyzed! What a shame!" The girl turned a pirouette and ended up leaning casually on the huge carnivorous sphere. "I'm so hot! I may have to start donating my old clothes to temple shrines!"

Peering over the top of the monster, Private Henry seemed a tad confused.

"My lady?"

"Quiet, kid! I'm having a moment, here!"

Collapsing to sit on the stump of a shattered stalagmite, Henry could only sit in a daze and stare at the monster.

"So this was part of the plan?"

"Part one of a beautiful plan!" Escalla lounged atop the angry beholder. "Flawless execution, kid! It's a joy to behold!"

"Are we ready to go yet?"

"Almost!" Escalla happily patted the paralyzed beholder. "I guess we've got at least three hours before ol' friendly here begins to wake up, so let's get this show on the road!" She patted the beholder's armored hide. "Grand Rescue Plan phase one: First, catch your beholder!"

* * * * *

Phase two was perhaps a tad less structured than phase one. Still, it held a certain amount of promise. Escalla unshipped one of her magic lights and left Private Henry watching nervously from afar as she drifted carefully back into the cavern of dead ghouls.

The ghouls had been very concerned with tossing objects down into the pit at the center of the cave. Escalla shined her light down into the pit and saw a rough stone chimney shaft that dwindled hundreds of feet down into the darkness below. The girl took a brief look about the cave making sure that the ghouls were definitely dead, then jumped down the shaft.

The shaft was only two feet wide—too small for any normal humanoid to scale. With her frost wand on guard, Escalla whirred carefully down one hundred feet, then two, then three. Big orange fungi jutting from the walls showed wounds where something falling from above had ploughed through the fleshy plants. Finally the faerie saw her light shining on an open space below. She stopped herself at the threshold, peering into a surprisingly attractive little cave.

Huge toadstools fully ten feet tall stood beneath the shaft. Beneath them, bones had been spread nicely about the place, thoroughly picked clean. Bumbling around among the bones was a strange creature the size of a large dog—a creature with long feelers and a tail tipped with a paddlelike-blade.

Escalla felt quite pleased.

"Oooo! Rust monster!"

The monster in question was standing upon its hind legs and trying to reach something caught atop one of the toadstools. Escalla looked carefully below, saw a sheathed sword wrapped in rags lying half impaled into a toadstool cap, and then fluttered into the cave.

The rust monster was friendly enough. Swooping down, Escalla gave the rust monster a pat on its head. It craned upward and petted her with its feelers, seeking a taste of metal. Disappointed, the rust monster abandoned her and went back to clumsily trying to reach the toadstool top.

Escalla beat him to it. She flew up and landed beside the sword, walking around and around it with a proprietal glee. It was long and heavy—a sword of the kind the Justicar seemed to like. The sheath had been painted bright colors, and the sword had been wrapped in the torn and bloodied banner of a nobleman. Escalla tossed the rags aside, took a good look at her prize, and rubbed her hands together in satisfaction.

Long rust monster feelers came probing over the edge of the toadstool, and Escalla irritably kicked them away.

"Scram! Go on!"

Time was wasting. Escalla decided to free the sword and get it back upstairs where it could be put to use, but in tugging the weapon free from the toadstool, she almost gave herself a hernia. With a blade almost twice as long as she was tall, the sword was heavy enough to crush Escalla flat.

"This thing weighs a ton!" The girl kicked petulantly at the sword and hurt her foot. "Trust me to find a fat sword!"

I should hardly think anyone smeared in bat dung was in a position to be insulting!

The voice had the prim, lofty tone of a school Ma'am. Escalla whipped about, scratching her bottom with one hand while pointing her wand with the other.

"All right, who's the loud mouth with the death wish?"

It is I. Words seemed to form in Escalla's mind—a phenomenon familiar to anyone who normally hung out with sentient hell hound skins. *And kindly refrain from scratching yourself like that in public!*

The sword was shivering slightly in Escalla's grasp, irritating her skin and making a slight humming noise. The faerie sighed and turned a world-wise eye upon the blade.

"Oh goody. Talking cutlery with an etiquette fetish."

It costs very little to keep up standards. The sword seemed to sniff in prim disdain. *You seem a tad young to be wandering on your own. Does your father know you dress like that in public?*

"Yeah! Dung stains and skin abrasions are all the rage this year!" Escalla sat down and glared at the sword. "So Spiky, what's your story!"

With enormous dignity, the sword cleared its throat. Had it been a mortal, it would have placed spectacles upon its nose. *I am the sword Benelux.*

"Beni-what?" Escalla scratched between her antennae.

Benelux! It is an onomatopoeic word from the old Flannic tongue, derivative of— The sword suddenly made an irritated noise. *It doesn't matter! In any case, I am an enchanted blade, lost here through the worthless incompetence of my subordinates.*

Escalla drolly rested her chin in her hand as she sat. "Meaning your owner you lost a fight and got pasted."

If you must put it so crudely . . . yes.

Annoyed by the sword, Escalla slipped into sarcasm as her first, best defense against authority. "So who was your owner? Who pasted him, and what's *your* claim to fame?"

I don't reveal my powers to just anyone who asks. The sword gave a superior little snort. *I am the weapon of champions! I am not for the use of any scruffy, winged little vagabond who happens to go past.*

"Well, that's all right." Escalla gave a shrug and began hauling the weapon over to the edge of the toadstool. "We're kinda encumbered right now, anyway. I don't think we have much room in the party for a sword who failed at sword fighting." As the rust monster pranced happily down below, Escalla dragged the sword closer to the toadstool's brim. "Can't just leave you to fret and die, though. Kindest to get it over quickly, I guess."

No! The sword squealed in fright. *I can be useful!*

"Useful how?" Escalla propped the sword up and leaned on it. "Come on. Tell Escalla!"

I'm more than just enchanted. The sword went into an awful sulk. *I cut things!*

"Oh, *real* unusual power."

I cut them really well! The sword had become peevish. *I'm always sharp.*

"A a real labor saver. What? There's a whetstone built into your sheath? I met a gnome with one of those once." Escalla peered into the sword sheath. "Hoopy!"

Sharper than that! A sneer crept into the sword's voice. *I was forged from pure metal from the positive energy plane.*

"Do tell." Escalla matched sarcasm for arrogance. "Meaning?"

Meaning that I have an adverse effect upon things of darkness and creatures that draw power from the negative energy planes.

"Ooo! Like ghouls?"

Yes.

"And ghosts and wights and mummies?"

Yes.

"And demonic spider queens and liches?"

Yes! Thoroughly annoyed, the sword had lost its temper. *Negative energy influenced creatures.*

"Hoopy!"

The sword made a sneer. *I had no idea education standards had dropped this low.*

Giving the sword a wry look, Escalla pulled her nose. "Hey, Spiky! Do you get out much—you know, hang out with other swords and stuff? Or don't *they* like you either?"

I can afford to be choosy. The sword gathered its dignity. *My last owner was a perfect gentleman. I must say, you are hardly an adequate substitute.*

"Lady, do I look like I'm going to be waving you around my head and smiting the smitable?" Kicking away a probing rust monster antennae, the faerie struggled to drag the huge sword to a safer place. "I've got you in mind for a friend of mine."

Full of suspicion, the sword hummed and hawed. *What sort of friend?*

"Oh, a warrior for good, upholds justice rather than the law, death on wheels, cleaves things apart, that sort of thing."

Is he skilled?

"I hope to kiss a duck the guy's skilled!" Escalla dropped the sword. "You'll like him! Remember when you were a little kid at school?"

I am a magic sword. I was never a child at school.

Escalla ground her teeth. "Then remember when you were a little baby poniard in the cutlery barrel?"

No.

"Hey! Just gimme the benefit of some creative self-projection here!" Escalla slapped the sword's sheath in annoyance. "Remember when you were young and other critters came to bully you? Remember how you wished some big kid would just stroll in out of the blue, scare the bad guys off, and look after you?"

The sword's voice sniffed in suspicion. *You're saying your friend is similar to that big child?*

"Yes!" Grabbing the sword sheath, Escalla dragged it underneath the shaft. "If that kid was about six foot six, shaven headed, could tear mountain lions in half with his bare hands, and hung out with sentient hell hound hides."

The sword seemed confused. *That doesn't seem a close match to your comparison.*

"So few metaphors stand up to close examination." The girl waved her hands in annoyance. "Are you coming to help my friend fight for justice, or are you staying for lunch with mister rust monster over there?"

Supremely calm, the sword gave a huff. *I believe I shall ascend and render assistance to your friend.*

"Great. Could you quit grousing and try giving me a hand here?"

Prim and proper, the sword gave a snort. *What is it now? What do you need?*

"Well, if you don't want to end up as rust monster food . . ."

Escalla swatted at a probing rust monster antennae yet again. "I suggest you help me make a plan to get you up this shaft!"

You could use the rope over there in one corner of the cave. The sword sighed. *Just give it to your friend and have him pull me up.*

"What rope?"

The one over by the backpack full of scrolls.

With an unkind glare at the sword, Escalla wandered over to the edge of the toadstool. Amongst a collection of dismembered skeletal remains lay a backpack, a rope, and a broken lantern with all the metal bits missing.

"Stay here!"

Escalla whirred over to the rope and managed to retrieve it. With much picking, she peeled away enough hemp stands to make a three-hundred-foot long strip of hairy string. She tied one end about the sword, scared the rust monster away with an illusion spell, then zipped up the shaft to find Private Henry anxiously waiting for her return.

The girl handed Henry the end of the string and said, "Heave ho. Company's coming!"

"Company?" The young soldier blinked. "What sort of company, ma'am?"

"Irritating company!" Escalla dived back down the shaft. "There's a blabber-mouthed sword on the end of the string. Bring it up when I give you two tugs. Lower the line again once you're done. There's scrolls or something down there, too."

The transfer took about ten long minutes—time that Benelux spent lecturing empty air on the shortcomings of the new generation of adventurers. With the sword's voice dwindling above her, Escalla took stock of the spells written on a newfound scroll, gave a happy smile as she saw some useful new magic, then sped up the shaft in pursuit of Benelux.

Up at the head of the shaft, Henry sat with the sword in his lap, looking chastened and bemused. Benelux was in full flow, informing the boy of the shortcomings of his uniform, when Escalla appeared and slapped the weapon on its overly ornate, enameled sheath.

"Hey, Spiky! Meet Private Henry of the Keoland border guard."

Indeed. The sword was indignant. *Surely you do not plan to put me in the hands of this child?*

"Nope. Henry has enough troubles of his own."

The beholder lay paralyzed at the rear of the cave, looking angry but incapable of doing much about it. Escalla summoned her old trusty Tensor's Floating Disk spell beneath the beholder. The spell bore the monster on a bobbing plate of magic force. Escalla had Henry toss the sword behind the beholder, and the faerie happily sat astride the monster and rode the whole contraption down the passageways.

"The grand plan! Step one: Catch a beholder. Step two: Get a sword." Pumping her fist like a cavalry general signaling the charge, Escalla sent her ponderous cargo floating off down the corridor. "All right, Henry, let's do a quick stage three, then get this show on the road!"

Stepping confidently behind her and looking the part of a conqueror, Private Henry checked his crossbow, drew himself straight, and followed Escalla as the disk drifted off to who-knew-where. The caverns lay empty, the dead ghouls decomposed, and Escalla's voice argued with the magic sword as she drifted off into the dark halls.

16

In a dark universe of fear, all manner of hideous creatures had set their minds to inventing tortures to inflict on living souls.

There were tests.

There were punishments.

There were foul torments so horrific that even their creators screamed at the very thought of them.

There were mind-wrenching terrors so foul that even the lords of the Abyss dared not speak their names . . .

. . . And then there was being tied back to back with Polk the Teamster.

Two hours, and Polk was still talking.

". . . see, a *real* hero *anticipates* trouble, son, has a sixth sense— warnings from the gods, uncanny awareness, a taste for subtle hints. . . ! That's your problem, son. No sense for danger. No ability to know when death is imminent!"

Polk leaned his head back against the stalagmite at his back. Behind him, Jus tried to heave on his own ropes and use the pressure to strangle Polk to death, but the bugbears had used too many knots and turns. Jerking at his ropes in fury, Jus flung his head about to try and catch sight of Polk behind him.

"Polk, *shut up.*"

"See? Now I knew you were going to say that. That's anticipation, son! That's what you have to learn." Polk sighed sorrowfully and contemplated the sad state of the world. "Guess I still have to train you. Guess the fault's all mine. I see errors, son, and I'm too forgiving, too quiet! I just let 'em slide. I don't comment—too polite, that's always been my failing. Never say an unkind word. Try to let fellers figure things out for themselves. A doctrine of non-interference, son! That's my way. I'm too quiet!"

Jerking back and forth to try and break his ropes, Jus breathed heavily, his eyes bloodshot with an utterly volcanic rage.

"Polk, enough."

"Well, that's nice of you to say, son. I see what you're getting at. The way I teach you is good enough for normal folks, but you're just a bit slow on the uptake, thick as a plank . . ." Polk gave a concerned shake of his head. "Ain't *your* fault, son! All great heroes have a few failings. It's just up to people like me to make allowances. It's my own mistake. I didn't take you properly in hand. 'Let the young feller learn from his own mistakes', I said. 'Experience is the best teacher', I said." The teamster gave a tragic sigh. "I should have been more forthright, guided you better. Now we're just gonna be fed to a demonic demigod, and that's that."

His hands tied behind his back, Jus flexed his fingers with the need to crush and rend.

"What?"

"Fed to demons, son. These drow are agents of evil. Stands to reason they have demonic overlords. Stands to reason overlords have to be fed." Clucking his tongue, Polk leaned around the pillar to look back at the Justicar. "Son, that's what I mean. You ain't got a logical mind."

They both sat roped back to back, tied to a huge, solid stalagmite. Bruised, cut, and gouged, the Justicar was still smothered with blood. Savage and dangerous, the Justicar watched events in the lich's caverns with predatory interest.

They were tied beside a slave caravan. A line of dispirited bugbears, goblins, and troglodytes—apparently failed tribe members—were chained in a line beside a reeking pack lizard. Drow merchants and guards lounged nearby, breathing perfumes, drinking wines, and idling away their time. The merchant leader walked languidly behind his men, seeming utterly unconcerned. Jus took stock of each drow, the position of their weapons, and the location of intervening cover.

The lich's cave, a dark cavern opening from which hundreds of soft voices were murmuring, stood only thirty feet away to the north. Beyond that, the main cavern was relatively empty. Four bugbears stood guard at the southern entrance—the one through which Escalla would come when she started her rescue. The rest of the cave sloped away eastward where it became warrens for the mutually hostile tribes of bugbears and troglodytes. The two species were ferociously antagonistic. Raw terror kept the stupid creatures in line—terror and a greed for the rewards brought by service to the drow.

There were signs that another previous caravan had left only hours before. Tracks and less wholesome spoor betrayed that Sour Patch's lost population had been brought here and then moved on. Conceivably this second, smaller slave train was heading in the same direction.

A hooting noise began to grow and swell. Around the cavern, colors shifted as troglodytes dropped their protective coloring. The chameleons emerged from their guard posts on the walls and leaped clumsily to the floor, expanding throat pouches to give off deep, ear-splitting *booms*.

A huge troglodyte chieftain paced out from the warren caves. Twenty warriors came with him—all huge lizards draped with belts made from badly flayed goblin skins, some with the wet red skulls of victims still hanging in their hands. They dragged prisoners along with them—six gnolls and a hobgoblin, all gouged, bleeding, and nearly dead.

Scores of angry bugbears flowed out from the other warren caves, following the troglodytes. Surly and snarling with jealousy, they eyed the bleeding prisoners. Leaving the slave caravan, the drow merchants walked over to meet the troglodyte leader and began talking in a braying, barking tongue.

Troglodytes offered their captives to the drow, pointing at the slave caravan. The prisoners were clearly too badly injured to march to the caravan's destination. The drow used gestures to reject the goods. Roaring in anger, the troglodyte chieftain turned and bellowed to his followers, who instantly gripped the captives and tore the creatures apart with their bare hands. Screams echoed through the tunnels, and the troglodytes closed in like piranha to feed on screaming, shrieking flesh.

Polk shrank back against his stalagmite in horror as he watched the captives being eaten alive. "Ah, son? Have you an escape plan of your own? Because mine still needs a little bit of work."

"Polk, *quiet.*" The Justicar tensed, leaning forward to gaze at the southern tunnel entrance. "Do what I damned well tell you the moment it starts."

Polk blinked and looked around at the Justicar.

"It?"

*   *   *   *   *

Lurching up the southern passageway came a large pack lizard—a big thing covered in mildewed scales and occasional fungus growths. The creature was led by a solitary drow—a thin, somewhat tall creature armed with a heavy crossbow and with an unusually long sword slung over its back. Watching the drow come closer to their cave, four bugbears at the cavern entrance came to their feet.

As the solitary drow trader approached, a bugbear halted him with an upraised hand and spoke in its guttural, snarling tongue. The drow looked at the floor stiffly and gave a grunt, shrugging his shoulders. The bugbear nodded as if in agreement, then presented its hand toward the drow, palm upward.

The drow hesitated, looked confused, and then put a platinum coin into the bugbear's hand. The gigantic goblinoid blinked at the coin, looked pleased, pocketed the trinket, then presented its hand once again.

The creature jiggled its hand and snarled out a few words, then pointed to the drow's cloak pin. Alarmed, the drow began to pat its pockets in confusion. It turned to face the pack lizard, careful not to touch the thing, since it was only a flimsy illusion spell case over a floating, misshapen string of shapes tied up in an old tarpaulin.

Pretending to search its own robes, the drow hissed a whisper into empty air.

"Why does it want to look at my cloak pin?"

"Cloak pin?" Invisible and sitting astride the floating canvas sausage, Escalla felt a flash of inspiration. "Oh! I think he wants your identification!"

"Identification?" Transformed into drow shape by one of Escalla's spells, Private Henry quailed. "I don't have any identification!"

"Lessee . . . we found some weird stuff" Escalla remembered the gold hairpin filched from the drow sorceress who had turned into a manta ray. The faerie extracted the pin and slipped it into Henry's hands. "There you go! Give this a try."

His ashen pallor making his black skin gray, Henry turned and placed the golden pin in the hands of the bugbear. The huge goblinoid took one look at the spider symbol upon the pin and instantly fell to its knees. Its companions clumsily followed suit, holding their bloodstained clubs against their chests in salute. Henry accepted the pin back from the guard, raised his hand in a vague attempt at benediction, then towed his rather awkward pack lizard past the guardpost and into the caves.

"There we are—simple!" Escalla, utterly invisible and therefore not sweating in fear, waved to drow guards and merchants. "You see Jus over there?"

Carefully ignoring the pack lizard and Henry, Jus sat tied to a stalagmite near the lich's cave. Polk had been tied to the opposite side of the same stone pillar, and the little man's mouth was moving as he showered an unwanted soliloquy on empty air. Pulling his long, stark white locks from his face, the dark elf that was Private Henry peered over at his friends.

"Are they all right?"

"Pretty much. Polk just has to hope Jus doesn't get one hand free." Escalla nudged the boy with her battle wand. "All the trogs and bugbears seem to be gathering at the warrens. Let's get baby over there as innocently as possible."

The long canvas sausage, lumped and ugly, was covered by one of Escalla's better illusion spells. Even so, the bobbing train of floating shapes were a poor simulation of a giant pack lizard's gait. Private Henry towed the ungainly mass along through the air behind him.

Perhaps forty troglodytes snarled and fought over a vile, blood-filthy feast. Other troglodytes had gathered behind by the score, booming huge calls that shuddered through the air. Swarms of bug-bears clustered nearby, glaring in naked hunger and envy at the feast.

Henry brought his lizard close to the flesh eating, blood spat-tered mob. Pale with fright, the boy fumbled, then tied the leash of his lizard to a stalactite only a few feet behind the snarling, jeering mobs of monsters. He breathed raggedly, his eyes bright with fright, and then felt an invisible kiss on his cheek.

"You all right, Hen?"

"Just fine."

"Alrighty!" Escalla's wings whirred like a dragonfly. "Just stroll over to Jus and wait for the fun!"

Henry tried to hold his loaded crossbow as innocently as possible. Wearing somewhat un-elven garments, he had already attracted side-wise glances from the drow. The magic sword Benelux gleamed gaudy and golden as it hung over his shoulder. The boy, trying to look non-chalant, began to make the long walk toward Jus and Polk.

A drow straightened his belt and began to make a determined course toward Henry. The deception could only last a few more sec-onds. Slapping her hands together, Escalla flew through the belly of her illusory lizard and began unplucking knots of hairy string. She whistled as she worked, the noise unheard over the roar and snarl of feeding troglodytes and the insults hurled by bugbear hordes.

The last knot untied, the tarpaulin jerked away and fell. As the paralyzed beholder thudded to the ground, Escalla tossed a magic floating disc beneath it and sent it scooting off to the north. Behind it, the canvas sausage suddenly disintegrated. Escalla turned and fled faster than any faerie had ever gone before.

The illusory pack lizard stretched, then came apart. In the packed central mob of feeders, food, audience, and jeering crowds, some heads turned—and then screamed in terror. Spreading up from the bursting body of the pack lizard came great bobbing, floating spheres—fleshy globes crowned with eyes on stalks and with fanged, snarling mouths.

The spheres began to scoot in all directions, propelled by internal gasses. The jammed hordes of bugbears and lizards froze in shock until a little voice pealed out across the cave.

"Hey, boys!" Thirty yards away, Escalla posed with a swarm of golden bees circling one fingertip. "Wanna see my party trick?"

Magic missiles flew out from Escalla's fingertips and thudded into all eight floating gas spheres. The universe seemed to take a breath of shock. The troglodyte chieftain had time to swell his throat in the beginnings of a scream, and then one end of the cavern disappeared in a thunderous blast of light.

The gas spores detonated in an instant, each one exploding in a titanic fireball. Bugbears and lizards nearest to the spheres were atomized, while others flew backward as the flesh was blasted from their bones. The explosions rocked the cavern, shattering the ceiling of the warrens and bringing rock falls avalanching down. The ground shuddered. Ceilings collapsed. A few surviving monsters staggered, burned and screaming through the dust, to be crushed by rock falls cascading from above. The distant tribal warren dissolved as thousands of tons of rock collapsed in a massive cloud of debris.

Escalla gave a victory scream. With dust choking the air around her, she sat atop the paralyzed beholder, riding it like a juggernaut as it sped along on its floating disk. The girl fired a spell past Private Henry, turning cavern stone to bubbling mud and sinking drow to their deaths. Wide-eyed, the boy pelted toward the Justicar.

Drowning dark elves fired wild shots from their crossbows. Henry skidded to a halt beside Jus and Polk just as a crossbow bolt whizzed overhead to strike sparks from the cave wall. The boy dragged out a knife and hacked at the ropes binding Jus and Polk. Strands fell, and then suddenly Henry jerked in pain, a poisoned drow dart grazing the skin of his thigh. Escalla's stoneskin spell had failed. Jus tore free and snatched the boy's dagger from his grasp, hurling the knife straight into the archer's groin.

Henry fell, alive but paralyzed. Jus reached for the sword at the boy's belt, only to have a nasal female voice bellow at him from midair.

Not that one, fool!

The sword across Henry's shoulders shot half out of its sheath. The handle was gaudy with jeweled unicorns, but the blade itself shone a brilliant white as though the blade were made from living light. Jus gripped the weapon and slid it free, feeling its pure, pleasurable weight singing in his hands.

Drow merchants leaped over their pack lizards, screaming in battle rage. Jus turned. In one split second he cut the legs from a drow in midair, decapitated another as it landed, and cut a swath in another that sprayed a fountain of blood. The last drow fired a crossbow. Jus angled the sword to send the crossbow bolt flickering off into the dark, saw the drow's eyes wince as the sword's light flashed in its eyes, then an instant later plunged the blade right through the creature's guts. The drow folded, screaming out a spell. Its wound closed, the drow staggered back, only to be sheared in two by one massive, roaring swing of the pure white blade.

Body parts were still hitting the ground as Jus whirled and looked for targets. Echoing in his mind, the sword's voice seemed a tad stunned.

You'll be the Justicar. I, ah, I'm pleased to meet you.

Bugbears and troglodytes were staggering from the rubble. More drow guards were racing to the spot. Jus saw Escalla atop her strange floating mount, then the girl pointed behind him to the lich's cave.

"Jus!"

A blast of ice-cold air swept forth, and the lich strode out of its lair. In one chilling glance the entity took in the disaster and destruction, then saw the Justicar standing in a ring of butchered drow. The monster gave a feral hiss, body crouching like a beast as it opened hands that streamed with magic spells.

From behind it, a raucous little voice screamed out across the cave. "Hey, handsome!"

The lich whirled. Two dozen yards away, a faerie in a ragged black silk dress sat astride a beholder. With a nasty laugh, Escalla wrenched open the lid of the beholder's huge central eye, unveiling the monster's angry glare.

A spell was already formed in the lich's rotting mouth. It screamed the symbols of a death spell only to have the magic disappear. The beholder's gaze shot out its ray of force, nullifying the lich's magic and stripping it of its powers.

Jus raged forward, the white sword streaming with light, and the lich turned and ripped a small rod from the sleeve of its robe. Jus streaked his sword blade down, and the lich whipped up its hand, the rod shooting out to become a staff smothered in blood red runes. The sword blow was parried, but the sheer force of it blasted the lich back against the cavern wall. Screaming in fury, the undead sorcerer threw itself at Jus, the runestaff lunging for the ranger's eyes.

The white blade flashed, sparks spitting as it hit the staff. Inhumanly fast, demonically strong, the lich fought with its staff, blurring blow after blow at Jus, each stroke met instantly by the human's sword.

The lich leaped and lunged.

Jus parried the blow.

As the staff tip hit the floor, energy exploded outward, blasting chunks of rock apart. Light flashed and an insane scream of anger echoed through the halls. The lich staggered, a wound cut into its side, its flesh seeming to explode as its own substance began to disintegrate.

With the sword cut still spreading destruction into its mummified flesh, the monster roared and launched a series of mad attacks. It whirled, the staff striking, rock exploding and sparks flying as Jus fell back toward Escalla. Huge and solid, the ranger retreated, his sword moving in sharp, short motions, never once making an attack. Even so, the man began to slip his parries.

Seeing a sudden opening, the lich roared and lunged its staff forward at Jus's heart, power raging along the runes and ready to blow living flesh apart. Already moving, his bait taken, Jus spun on his axis, brushed the staff with his sword and sent it skimming a hair's breath past his chest. In a white blur, the sword swiped the lich's head from its neck.

The sword screamed in triumph, utterly amazed. *Well struck! Well struck!* The weapon crowed in delight. *Sir, I believe we shall get along famously!*

The lich's body staggered forward, whirled, and then latched a hand onto Jus's arm. Flesh smoked as the freezing grasp took hold. Jus snarled and hacked the hand from its arm, leaving the claws locked in his tunic. Its flesh burned, boiling with little explosions where the white blade had cut. Jus roared and smashed his sword down through the headless body, cleaving it to the pelvis. He kept the blade twisting inside the body, the undead flesh burning. A scream shattered the air, and a wraith-like swirl of energy punched into the air. Abandoning its body, the soul of the lich fled to sanctuary.

Leaping down from the beholder, Escalla shouted, "Hey, Jus! Great rescue, huh?" She waved a hand proudly at the beholder. "And look! It followed me home. Can I keep him?" She grinned, then heard the beholder on its floating disk give a groggy growl. "Oh crap!"

The girl whirled, spread her hands and sent the beholder, disk and all, spinning off toward the collapsing warrens. Flying toward Jus, the girl gave a panicked little yell. "Jus, we're in trouble!"

"Where's Cinders?"

"I'll get him!" The girl fired her wand and sealed side caverns with walls of ice. "Get Henry and Polk, then run northwest!"

Jus obeyed, lumbering off to heave Henry over one shoulder and drag Polk to his feet. He shoved Polk ahead and ran into the tunnels.

Escalla fired a last blast from her wand, swore as she saw the charge counter drooping dangerously low, then swooped low over the cavern floor.

The lich's body had stopped disintegrating. The undead corpse lay hacked and twisted, half dissolved and still smoldering. Escalla took one look at the creature's rune staff, touched a control and it snapped back to the size of a toothpick. The faerie gleefully jammed it through the belt of her robe. Whirling, she sped into the lich's lair and stared about in confusion at a cave entirely wallpapered with living mouths.

"Cinders?"

Here.

The hell hound skin lay bundled uncomfortably near a pile of loot. Polk's backpack, bits of drowish cloth . . . it all lay there in a heap. Escalla sped over to the lich's secret hiding place and dug her hand into the crevice. She pulled out a carefully folded piece of black cloth and began to shake it open.

Out in the caverns, the beholder roared in rage. There was an explosion as some kind of magic blasted through the caves. In a panicked rush, Escalla unfolded the cloth disk, accidentally holding it upside down. A bizarre pile of junk instantly came crashing to the ground, scattering jewels all across the floor.

"No no no!"

Cinders's red glare flicked toward the door. *Faerie hurry!*

"I'm doin' it! I'm doin' it!"

With a wail, Escalla dragged the hole over toward Jus's backpack, planted her back against the bag and heaved it in. The backpack tumbled into the portable hole with a crash, and Escalla ran over to do the same with Polk's luggage.

Polk's pack felt as if it weighed a hundred tons. Escalla almost ruptured herself trying to shift it, then she looked at the backpack and saw that it was bulging with drow swords, shields, chainmail, cloaks . . . The girl snarled, tore open the lacings, and accidentally spilled Polk's luggage across the floor. As she picked up the magic bottle, she suddenly felt a chill run down her spine.

The floor had opened. Lying behind her was a coffin recess, and in the coffin a mummified corpse lay with a crystal in its clawed hands. The lich's soul stole out from the stone, occupying its spare body. The cadaver sat up, mad eyes opening. It whipped its head about to stare at the faerie and opened its skeletal jaws in an enraged scream.

"Sacred wine!" Escalla shouted into the magic bottle. "Sacred wine!"

The bottle suddenly began to gush. Escalla flung holy wine over the lich's face, and the monster screamed and began to dissolve. The monster screeched and thrashed, hurling its magic crystal. Escalla hit the crystal with the lich's own staff, shattering it like glass and thus ending any hopes for the lich's return.

Tossing the magic flask into the portable hole, she grabbed hold of Cinders, and ran as if every hungry denizen of the Nine Hells were right behind her.

Outside the lich's cave, the beholder rampaged in a mad dance of destruction. Roofs were collapsing, and rocks showered down everywhere. Escalla folded up the portable hole, shoved it through her belt, and dived beneath the hell hound skin. She ran like a mad thing, holding Cinders's head over her own. The result was like watching a fireside rug zooming off to hunt for prey.

Escalla raced along the northwest passageway. Behind her, the beholder roared, still unmoving, but able now to thrash its many eyes. Spells lashed out to rake the caves, keeping rock falls thundering from the ceiling high above.

Jus stood waiting in the dark, sheltering behind a rock as beholder spells blasted through the air. Passing the paralyzed Private Henry to Polk, Jus reached down to save Escalla from drowning underneath Cinders's fur.

"Cinders!"

Friend! The hell hound happily wagged his tail. *Happy.*

The sword in Jus's hand made a sound uncannily like clearing her throat. Jus held the sword out at arm's length to stare at the blade and asked, "Escalla, where did you get this?"

"Found it!" The faerie installed herself upon Jus's shoulders. "Shiny, huh? I told you I'd find you one!"

Somewhat annoyed, the sword gave a self important sniff. *My name is Benelux. I am made from metallic light forged upon the positive energy plane. Most pleased to meet you.*

"Justicar." Jus looked at the blade in bemusement. "Nice knowing you."

Fairly happy with her day, Escalla shrugged expressively shrug. "I call 'er Spiky!" The girl whirred upward, dragging her friends down the passageway. "Guys? I think the beholder is about to vaporize the last of the trogs. We should probably get moving before he uses us for after dinner mints."

The faerie sped off down the tunnel. With the beholder causing a slaughterhouse somewhere behind them, Jus and Polk hastened to follow the girl's lead. Jus slung Cinders abut his shoulders, picked up Private Henry beneath one arm, and marched off into the dark. Gleaming bright in his hand, the unsheathed sword flooded the passageway with light.

Benelux's voice echoed happily as the adventurers walked. *I say, you there! Canine! Have we been introduced?*

No. The dog skin wagged its tail. *Cinders.*

Benelux. How do you do? The sword sniffed suspiciously. *Are you certain you are a fit addition to this party?*

Cinders wag-wag-wagged his tail.

Benelux seemed indignant. *Ye gods, you might be a mongrel! I can hardly keep company with a mongrel! The Justicar is a swordsman, and swordsmen by definition are gentlemen. He will no doubt be as uncomfortable with the situation as I.*

With his big grin gleaming, Cinders's sniggered in the gloom. *Sword funny!*

I beg your pardon!

Funny funny! The hell hound waggled his ears. *Cinders new friend.*

As the group jogged off down the tunnel, Benelux addressed the Justicar. *Sir, I have grave doubts about the decorum of this party.*

Ignoring it all, Jus merely walked faster. Far behind him, distant walls crumbled as the beholder rampaged through the lich's lair.

17

"Oh! Oh yeah! Yeah! Harder! *Harder!*" Lying on her stomach on Cinders, Escalla ploughed her fingers into his fur and clenched her toes. "Yeah! Oh push! Yeah!"

Lying face down on Cinders, scrubbed clean and awaiting her fire-beetle roast, Escalla groaned and sighed as Jus massaged her back with one careful finger and his thumbs. Escalla drummed her fist on the floor in fits of ecstasy. Still paralyzed, Private Henry sat propped in a corner and could only stare. Polk had been reunited with his whiskey bottle and was already giving the day's horrors a rosy glow. Jus, now repaired and wiped clean, sat beside the steaming cooking pot that had served as Escalla's bath, attending to the girl. Knowing his friend far better than she thought, he rewarded her for the rescue in the most practical way.

"Oooooh!" Escalla slumped in a post-massage daze. "Ooooh, I love you!"

Jus gave a slow, knowing smile and let the comment slip. Escalla sighed, unaware that she had ever spoken.

Propped within swift reach of the Justicar, Benelux made disapproving sounds as Escalla's noises went on.

Sir Justicar! This faerie of yours, is she always this noisy?

"I'm a screamer! What can I say?" Escalla answered the sword without real malice. "You never get polished or anything?"

I have a permanent shine. Benelux sniffed in cold disapproval. *Expressions of pleasure are undignified.*

"Yeah, but they add to the fun." Escalla turned to jelly as Jus hit the right spot just in the hollow of her neck. "Ooo yeah."

A tireless man with strong hands, Jus showed no signs of slowing in his work.

"Benelux, true worth is never obvious. Find the good in other people and work outward from there."

Hmph! The sword's flawless blade gleamed. *Of course worth is obvious, because true worth is never slack. The wise must share their wisdom, for the general elevation of all. Polk understands!* The sword had apparently not yet heard Polk humming his rather off-color song about the princess and the gnome. *This girl needs improvement. I intend to provide suitable advice.*

"Oh, be my guest." Jus worked carefully on Escalla's feet, making the girl claw the giggling hell hound and scream like a happy banshee. "But there are some battles best not fought."

Benelux made a noise of scorn. *You are clearly tired, sir. A true gentleman must realize that good fights are necessary fights.*

"No argument there."

Private Henry tried to talk but could only mumble. Escalla looked up and patted the boy on one boot. He was at least back in his own physical shape. White hair had hardly suited him.

"You all right, Hen?"

"Mrl murgle mungle."

"Hoopy!" Escalla smiled then hissed as her calves were massaged. "You'd think drow would carry the antidote to that stuff."

Looking happily up from his bottle, Polk wreathed himself in smiles. "There must be antidote there. Elves are elves. Ain't all elves logical?"

"Polk, they're dark elves. If they were animals, they'd be pond dwellers who eat their own young."

The teamster looked about the little cavern in clear, undiluted joy and said, "We now have one portable hole, ten feet deep by ten feet wide."

He folded up the portable hole and took charge of it himself, putting it in his breast pocket with a satisfied pat. Reaching for his bottle, he gave a toast to victory.

"I knew you could all handle it. Just needed the right coaching. A prod. A push toward glory!" The little man crowed in triumph, puffing out his meager pigeon chest. "That's what Good does. It overcomes! It triumphs in adversity! The more the obstacles, the greater the victory."

"Yeah *right*." Escalla was almost asleep, but nevertheless managed to look up at the Justicar. "Hey, Jus? He thought we weren't coming to rescue you, didn't he?"

"Yes."

"Polk, say, 'I have just been rescued by a teenaged boy and a faerie'!"

Annoyed, Polk sniffed through his great hatchet nose. "I have just been rescued by a teenaged boy and a faerie."

"Good!" Rolling over, Escalla held up on self-righteous little finger. "Now say 'I, Polk, hereby declare that I owe the faerie a total of seven hours of foot rubs, to be delivered at the rate of one half-hour per evening for the next two weeks.' " The faerie hovered overhead as Polk irritably muttered the promise. "Good! And Private Henry hereby requires a really big chapter in your chronicles, all about how he blitzed a beholder and became a total hero." The girl rubbed her eyes, more than ready for sleep. "Are we all happy?"

The sword Benelux snorted. *No.*

"Is everyone *important* happy?" Escalla gave a titanic yawn. "Then let's get some sleep." The girl rolled herself up in silks and nuzzled happily down into Cinders's soft black fur. "You guys had a hard day. I'll take first watch."

She was asleep in moments. Jus tucked her in, patted Cinders on the head and served out dinner to his companions. He popped a coal into Cinders's mouth, put Henry in a comfortable position away from the fire, then watched as the adventurers slowly drifted off to sleep.

Escalla rolled over in her bed, fast asleep, and quietly murmured Jus's name. The big man sat beside her, looking down at the little form with its strangely innocent little smile.

Jus quietly bent over and kissed Escalla in her sleep. He stroked her hair then sat down to keep watch over his friends.

Behind him, Cinders grinned his piranha grin and quietly thumped his tail.

❖   ❖   ❖   ❖   ❖

"You!"

Lord Ushan burst into the pearlwood chambers, his robes swirling with illusory flame. He pointed one finger in accusation at Lord Faen. "Clan Nightshade kills a scion of the Seelie Court, and yet you elect to sit here as their guest!"

Closing one of Clan Nightshade's books, Lord Faen raised his brows and replied, "This is common enough knowledge. I have no reason to depart." Lord Faen tilted his head to gaze at Lord Ushan thoughtfully. "You seem to have been sadly out of touch."

"I have estates to govern! Bifrost, Beastlands, Elysium! Girl or no girl, some of us still have to rule!"

"Estates. How interesting." Lord Faen arose and walked quietly over to the windows, looking out across Lord Charn's lake. It all had a wonderfully rustic appeal. "Nightshade's invitation to us all is still in force. I would consider it rude to reject them at this time."

Furious, Lord Ushan paced back and forth. His orc servants waited with eyes downcast in the corridors beyond. He took his staff of office from one girl's hand then whirled on Faen in a rage.

"This is collusion! By staying in this . . . this primal filth, you give royal approval of assassination! Does the Erlking not care that Cavalier Tarquil is dead?"

"Yes. Poor Tarquil." Faen stroked his goatee. "Still, at least his problems with vendettas are now over. It must have eased life in Clan Sable to have the boy turn up his toes."

Turning stiff, Ushan coldly glared at the other lord and whispered, "Have a care, Faen. Tarquil was not the only duelist in Clan Sable."

"I'm sure of it." Unconcerned, Lord Faen sat down. "Still, we are all touched by your loss. Is there to be a service in Tarquil's memory? I really should attend. Tell me, will you reincarnate the boy?"

"We will take a clone from his remains."

"Ah. Of course."

Faen returned to his book. Ushan watched him, flexing his hands indecisively about his staff, then turned back to his serving girls.

"Find the murderer, Faen."

"It is a very large universe, Ushan." Lord Faen fluffed out the pages of his book again. "Still, I am continually amazed at the things that turn up when you least expect them."

18

The underdark was unpleasant—wet, stinking, mold encrusted, and the phosphorescent light tended to make people's teeth look violet. The sorry thing to say was that after a few days, Jus almost felt used to it. From time to time, noises far ahead gave warning hints of danger. The party hid themselves in side caves, screened by one of Escalla's illusions as slow moving drow caravans plodded past. There were occasional monster tracks and occasional patches of deadly molds that Jus simply spotted and avoided. If one moved carefully and cleverly, it was quite possible to survive.

For a while. A very little while. Some of the monster tracks were . . . *impressive*.

For her part, Escalla seemed relatively unconcerned. Dressed in her latest attempt to make proper clothing out of black drow silks, she sat cross legged atop Jus's head making herself a pair of long, fingerless gloves.

"Look, guys! When it gets warm, drow silk actually stretches! This stuff fits sheer." The girl leaned over to look joyously into Jus's face. "Isn't that hoopy?"

"Yup."

New clothes had kept Escalla fascinated for at least half an hour—half an hour that would have been better spent scouting for danger up ahead.

"Don't you think it's hoopy?"

"It's hoopy." The Justicar managed to reach a finger up and place it on the girl's lips. "Now shush."

After long miles of travel, the tunnels had suddenly become more chill. The scent of fresh water filled the air—a strangely clean, refreshing scent. With the tunnels echoing more and more loudly to the rush of a nearby stream, Jus shrugged the girl off and loosed the sword Benelux in its sheath.

The sword cleared its voice in prim suspicion. *What is it?*

"A river." Jus found the sword vaguely annoying, but then again, he found a lot of things vaguely annoying. "Fresh water, fairly clean."

Excellent! Brimming with satisfaction, the sword seemed to glow. *Perhaps we might find a trading establishment—a tavern, a town, even a small port—where more suitable garments might be purchased, something fitting your new status as companions of the magic sword.*

"Is she still blathering?" Escalla flew over to slap the sword's sheath. "You know, for someone who tolerates unicorn art, you sure are free in handing out fashion advice!"

Young lady—Benelux gave a cool sniff—*there is a certain element of the common about you.*

"Oh, ain't too much about me you could call common!" Somehow Escalla managed to strike a sultry pose whilst in flight.

Polk rummaged around in his belt pouch for something to eat. "Yep! The girl's got class!"

"Class!" Escalla pinged her finger against the sword. The girl patted the scroll case that now hung between her wings. "Spells and wings, and a figure that sings. No one touches the faerie!"

Jus planted himself flat against an outcrop of rock, cautiously peering around a corner toward the unseen darkness ahead. Without looking back, he forestalled an angry retort from the magic sword.

"What was on those scrolls you found back where you caught that beholder?"

The girl beamed as she patted the scroll tube that hung between her wings. "A few cool spells! Earthy kinda ones. Flesh to stone. Stone to mud. Pass wall. All pretty hoopy, huh?"

"Are they useful?"

"More or less. I'm gonna copy some of them into my spellbook, so I need to make ink. Can you let me know next time we find a trickle of water or something?"

Jus nodded his chin forward at the underdark. "How about *that* one?"

The passageway had grown more dank, and clean moisture had cleared away much of the phosphorescent moss. Before the party ran a vast, dark rushing river that filled the caverns with a glorious surge of sound.

At the far side of the river, perhaps a hundred feet away, the passageway continued on toward the drow city—and according to the locator needle, toward Escalla's slowglass bauble.

The river flowed powerfully, icy cold and pitch black. It blocked all possible progress. Escalla simply hovered and stared. Polk blinked, and Private Henry edged fearfully closer to the water until physically yanked back from the edge by Jus's powerful hand.

Escalla blew out an annoyed breath and planted her fists upon her little hips.

"Well poo!" The girl shook her head. "You know, I have *got* to find a way to make you people fly."

There was no bridge, and the powerful current meant that there was no way to simply swim across. Escalla unshipped her wand, checked the charge and made a dissatisfied little noise.

"No way I can make an ice bridge all the way across. I've only got two more shots with this thing if I'm lucky. Remind me to recharge it when we get home." She whirred upward, deliberately keeping well above the water. "I'll go over the other side and just take a look. Maybe there's a really big drawbridge or something."

The faerie disappeared in the dark. Anxious about letting the girl go alone, Jus kept a grip on the hilt of his sword and paced the banks. In the river, a fin briefly broke the surface—a fin from a fish that must have been at least thirty feet long.

After a while, drifting faintly above the roar of the water, Escalla's distant voice came from the dark. "Hey, guys! There's some kinda giant fish man over here!"

Jus surged forward to the edge of the riverbank in alarm. "Is he attacking you?"

"No!"

"What's he doing?"

"Knitting lace. He's pretty good!" Escalla's voice could barely be heard over the rush of water "All right, he's seen me. He looks like he wants me to talk to him!"

Pacing, the Justicar bellowed hard to make himself heard. "Don't get too close!"

"Jus, he's a fish. I don't really think I want to swap addresses or anything."

While they waited, Polk finished gnawing on a spider leg and Cinders sucked loudly on a piece of old coal.

Finally Escalla called over to them from the other bank, "He's saying something! I can't figure it out."

"What?" Jus pushed Cinders's back from his helm, trying to hear the girl properly. "Don't you have a spell for translating languages?"

"Well duh! Be handy if I'd bothered to memorize it!"

"Why didn't you memorize it?"

"*Well*, excuse *me!*" True to form, Escalla lost her temper. "Since everything we've met so far has tried to eat us or enslave us, I kinda thought spells for blowing things up might be a bit more useful!" After a moment, the girl called back again. "All right, he's offering to ferry you guys over if you pay him."

Jus gave a puzzled frown. "How do you know that?"

"Because he's standing in a big boat and shaking a money box at me!" The faerie's temper was never good when she was being harassed. "Just get some money out and get to the damned shore!"

Polk looked at Jus, who looked at Henry. Cinders looked happy, and the sword lacked the ability to show much of an expression at all. With a mutual shrug, the party walked down the harsh gravel beach and waited by the shore.

A shape swiftly materialized out of the gloom. A large, flat barge drifted across the current. Standing at the rear and plying a single oar loomed a titanic, vicious looking creature that set the whole party on guard.

Fully eight feet tall, the creature was a monstrous humanoid fish. A huge jaw crammed with fangs gleamed sickly yellow in the light.

The creature stared at its passengers out of eyes the size of dinner plates. The scaled horror was powerful enough to shove its boat across the river without the slightest show of strain.

The boat grounded against the gravel with a crash. Hovering well out of reach of the fish man, Escalla gave her friends a gleeful wave.

"Guys, this is Thoopshib the ferryman!" The faerie gave an amazingly false smile. "Thoopshib, these are the guys. Guys, keep smiling and just start putting money in the box until he looks happy." The faerie wavered. "Well, happi*er*, at least."

A money box was presented. Digging into the loot gathered from the lich, Polk produced a handful of money. The fish man walked awkwardly over to the shore, its whole massive frame alive with an impression of carnivorous strength. A clawed hand held out a money box, and Polk fussily counted platinum coins into the box one by one until the monster seemed satisfied.

The sum offered was probably sufficient to buy a boat of their own. Thankfully, no one saw fit to mention the fact. Jus stepped onto the barge—watched closely by the creature, who recognized a being at least as deadly as itself—then helped Polk and Henry climb aboard.

Cinders sniffed the reek of fish and seemed gloriously happy. *Kuo-toa fish!* The dog's manic grin gleamed as little flames wisped from his nose. *Big stink! Very tasty! Fish scream when burn!*

There had been very little arson in Cinders's life of late. He wagged his tail in anticipation. *Fish live in school. One fish, two fish, red fish, burn fish! Burn-burn-burn-burn-burn!*

"Let's not burn any boats while we're still on them." Jus kept his voice low, his face calm and his hand near his sword. "Just get ready to blast it if it tries to rock the boat."

With Escalla flying cover overhead, the ferryman would hardly dare. Henry shot a glance at the faerie, then looked back at the savage ferryman and tried not to stare.

"What is it?" the boy asked.

"Cinders says it's a kuo-toa," Jus replied.

"A kuo-toa?" The boy swallowed. "How does he know?"

"Cinders is a hell hound. He's been around."

Private Henry shot a nervous glance toward the grinning Cinders. "I thought hell hounds were evil?"

"He's not evil. He just needed a good home." Jus gave one of Cinders's forelegs a pat. "But he's right. Fish fear creatures that use flame."

The barge surged forward through the water, heading toward the far bank.

Private Henry looked about nervously and cleared his throat. "Sir?"

"Yes."

"What's a kuo-toa?"

The Justicar carefully avoided looking at the ferryman, while keeping the creature very clearly in the corner of his eye. "*That* is. They're often assassins—very, very dangerous."

From above the boat, Escalla gave a snort. "Assassins, huh? Masters of poison? Like cone shells?"

Jus looked up at Escalla with a shared smile. "*Exactly.*"

The barge grounded at the far bank, and the passengers hastily removed themselves onto the shore. Escalla thoughtfully watched the kuo-toa and raised her hand to give it a friendly wave. The creature actually seemed to like her. It spoke—its voice huge and guttural—and nodded its head at her in apparent approval.

Jus was kneeling in the river gravel, looking at a broad swathe of footprints trailing up from the ferry and into the tunnel mouth. Escalla, Polk, and Henry immediately came over to watch the ranger at his work.

"Tracks?"

"Human—two hundred or more, probably chained at the ankles. See the short steps?" Jus touched the gravel and watched it slide. "This is only about three hours old."

Trying to emulate the Justicar, Henry inspected a footprint of his own—this time the mark of a slim drow boot. "Is it the hostages from Sour Patch?"

"Has to be." Moving two hundred captives along the main

tunnels had left constant spoor. "No troglodytes with them any-more. They're being driven by drow."

Escalla knelt beside Jus and pulled out the locator needle, which still pointed resolutely to the northwest. The girl shrugged then put the magic trinket away.

"Well, I gather there's more like Mister Thoopshib here just a ways along the tunnel." The girl returned another wave from the ferryman. "You know, he seems pretty happy for a carnivorous assassin."

"He likes you."

"Yeah. How about that?" Escalla frowned. "Matter of fact, I think he thinks he *knows* me."

The party turned and regarded the kuo-toa, who stood staring at them with his unwinking fish eyes.

The light dawned somewhere deep inside Polk's skull.

"You mean he's seen another faerie? He's met the murderer as he passed this way?"

"Got it, Polk!" Escalla tapped her chin in thought. "He obviously thinks we're one and the same."

"Guess you all look the same to him, huh?"

"No accounting for eyesight." Escalla brushed back her shim-mering blonde hair. "This is getting interesting. Come on. Let's see if I've got any *other* friends just down the lane."

* * * * *

The long passageway continued, now chilled by the breeze that flowed from the icy river. Other paths joined the main tunnel, and the air took on a distinctly fishy smell. Only Cinders seemed pleased. The rest of the party wrinkled their noses and tried not to gag as the reek thickened until it almost brought tears to the eyes.

Flying cautiously beside Jus, Escalla's tall ears pricked up at the same moment that Cinders gave a warning growl. Far down the passageway, lurching shapes began to appear. Escalla turned invisible as the remainder of the party faded into hiding against the tunnel walls. Looking over her companions, the faerie moved carefully down the tunnel to investigate the oncoming shadows.

A dozen fish men walked along the passageway in a weird hopping gait. They were led by a vast, powerful kuo-toa, its skin a ghastly white, and its hide covered in thousands of knotted scars. The creatures' huge eyes flickered to stare at the invisible faerie, and the fish creatures instantly readied their harpoons.

With her cover somehow blown, Escalla dropped her invisibility. Hiding behind a stalactite, she poked her head out and examined the kuo-toa, then cautiously waved her hand.

"Um, hello."

She had a fireball spell ready to make instant fish fry, but much to her surprise, the kuo-toa leader gave a croak of something almost like relief. The creature lowered its weapon—almost certainly defusing a spell of its own—and lifted a hand toward Escalla in a grave gesture. The beast held out its hand with its middle fingers separated into a v-shape.

Always affable when allowed, Escalla copied the gesture with her own small fingers and repeated, "Hello."

Eight feet tall, fanged and clawed, an eater of human flesh and a drinker of blood, the kuo-toa leader bobbed its head in deference. The girl tried to make a placatory gesture, and the other fish men sank down in ritual obeisance.

From the corridor behind Escalla, Jus's voice called out calmly and quietly, "Are you all right?"

"Yeah. It's more kuo-toa." Escalla kept her face affable, motioning to the fish creatures in what she hoped was a friendly way. "There's about a dozen of them, and they're getting along with me just dandy. Everyone come out and be perfectly calm."

The kuo-toa leader gurgled something to its followers, and the fish men resumed their ungainly march down the passageway. On seeing Escalla's companions, the creatures saluted casually with the middle fingers of their hands spread wide, a salute both uncomfortable and strangely silly. Jus gravely returned the gesture.

Polk and Henry did the same, and the creatures continued on their way toward the river and the ferryman.

Jerking with ill temper, the sword Benelux gave a cold growl. *Kuo-toa. Assassins! Murderers! We should find their nest and eliminate them all!*

"We have a prior task." Jus settled the sword through his belt. "Racial genocide is not my mission."

Do you call yourself a warrior for law?

"No. I'm only interested in Justice." The Justicar took Escalla onto his shoulder as he spoke. "These fish men have done nothing worthy of my attention."

From Jus's shoulder, Escalla stretched and yawned.

"Hey, Spiky! Ease up!" Escalla peered down at the sword. "You'll get wrinkles. You have to expand your emotional horizons. Make a promise to tell yourself a few jokes in between kills. It worked for me!"

Benelux merely seethed.

Jus tugged at Escalla's foot, quietening her down as the tunnel opened out into a titanic, echoing cave. An open space more than a hundred yards wide yawned in the gloom. A weird blue light swam like reflections in an ancient sea, and an alien world took hold upon the underdark.

A sinister, stepped pyramid arose at the center of the cavern. The mound served to raise a horrible idol high above the cavern floor—a blood spattered thing shaped like a naked woman with the head and pincers of a lobster. The claws were opened in the same gaping salute used by the kuo-toa in the halls. A still-bleeding human heart was wedged into one of the claws, and an ocean of blood seemed to have poured down the pyramid. Guarding the approaches to the idol were kuo-toa priests and warriors, creatures who even now tore the eyes and organs out of human victims who had slid lifeless down the blood-soaked stairs.

Escalla stared, quite ashen, and felt her skin turn strangely numb. "*Now* they may have just crossed the line."

Private Henry crept forward, staring at the shrine—the corpses and the fish men feeding wetly on their prey. The boy's hands gripped more tightly at his crossbow.

"Human sacrifice. . . ?"

"Human sacrifice." Jus seemed to swell, his huge, bristling frame turning carnivorous and savage. To the Justicar, no crime was worse than preying on the weak. The kuo-toa suddenly seemed in need of *Judgment*.

Escalla saw Jus's stance and felt a cold chill of panic as she expected him to begin slaughtering the kuo-toa. There were a dozen in sight, but countless carved doorways opened onto temples, barracks rooms, and even palaces.

"Jus! Deep breath! Don't go all apocalyptic on me!" The faerie whacked Jus across the helmet. "I need to clear my name here! This is a prime place for evidence collection!"

"I know."

"Kill fish later. Help disturbingly attractive yet strangely innocent faerie now." Hastily ushering the group into cover behind an outcrop of fungi, Escalla gathered Henry by her side. "Henry, Spiky, brief recap. Yours truly here has been wrongfully framed and accused of a crime. We're here to prevent a miscarriage of justice and protect one of the world's most priceless beings from harm— namely *me!*"

Do tell. Benelux seemed to glow with pure sarcasm. *Who would ever have placed you as a criminal?*

"Hey! This is serious!" Escalla whacked at the sword's sheath. "A faerie cavalier has been offed, and whoever did it is a faerie who likes using the underdark as a private holiday home. Whoever murdered Cavalier Tarquil used a marine cone shell. If these fish men down here are an assassin cult, this is probably the place the cone shell came from."

Brilliant. The magic sword gave a sniff. *With wisdom like that, you should bottle it.*

"I'm warning you!" The faerie faced the sword, her antennae stiff and her little fists balled. "I can still find a rust monster! So just shut up and keep your eyes open for evidence. We're looking for clues— anything to show that someone's been getting his murder equipment from the kuo-toa!"

Hmph! The sword gave a droll little sneer. *Such as a signed receipt in triplicate?* "One cone shell, please return by Godsday."

"Sounds ideal." Escalla gave a snort, then hitched up the belt of her little black dress. "Jus, if you had a lending library for cone shells, where would it be?"

"Somewhere near where assassins are trained." The Justicar loomed in the tunnel like a feral nightmare. "Look for a marine . water pool. All the other water here is fresh."

"Hoopy." The faerie briskly clapped her hands and rose up into the air. "Well, let's just go into the shrine and act like we're here as guests. No one has seemed interested in stopping us so far."

Private Henry gave a nervous blink. "The fish seem to like you."

"Just as long as that doesn't involve feeding on my intestines, I'm happy." Escalla led the way into the terrifying cavern. "Follow me, people, and try to look like we see human sacrifices twice a day. Jus, no sword stuff until we get some evidence in my hot little hands."

From a side passage, more kuo-toa appeared. The creatures approached the guards at the pyramid's base, exchanged the strange salute, tossed money into a giant clam shell, then removed little tokens that were hung about their necks with string. One of the visitors moved to a second shell and seemed to pay far more money. The guards hooted in approval and hung the donor with a somewhat flashier token—a bright red crab claw. The visitors immediately proceeded to climb the pyramid to pay homage to the idol.

The guards looked over at Escalla, Jus, Polk, and Henry, fixing them with their huge, emotionless eyes. The fish men made no immediate move to sound an alarm. Girding her narrow waist and hoisting her rather understated bosom, Escalla steeled herself for the ordeal to come.

"Here goes."

She flew over to the kuo-toa, opening her hand in the local salute. The kuo-toa responded, and one guard addressed her in a language made mostly up out of jaw clicks and gashing teeth. Escalla kept her smile and gave an easy wave of her hand.

"Sure!"

The kuo-toa spoke again, and Escalla fluttered over to the big clamshell basins.

"I totally agree! But it might rain on Moonday. Best cover up once that bad weather sets in!" The girl waved a rather nervous, reluctant Polk forward. The teamster was looking up at a seven-foot tall kuo-toa that was eating wet chunks of a human liver. "Polk! Get your shanks over here and get the purse open!"

"Portable hole."

"Whatever! Just get us some cash!"

Escalla peered into the more expensive of the two offering basins, then stuck her head into the portable hole after Polk had partly unfolded it. She flew inside, entirely disappearing from the outside world as she entered a weird little space about ten feet square. Sure enough, rolling about in one corner of the hole there were a few small gems and baubles. Escalla grabbed a few of the less impressive items and popped back out into the light. She dropped a pair of little pearls into the basin, trying to indicate that she was paying for her entire group. The kuo-toa gave the same savage hoots of approval, then proceeded to hang stinking crab claws about the necks of everyone present. Escalla took one sniff of the partly mummified claw and a pained expression crept onto her face.

"Why, *thank* you." She gave a watery smile. "I'll treasure it always."

The guards opened the way to the pyramid and idol. There seemed to be no way to avoid it. Mincing past a collection of human remains, Escalla slowly flew out over a moat filled with giant leeches that were kept at bay only by a narrow little wire mesh fence. Jus glanced at the leeches, dragged a protesting Polk into the water with him, and waded toward the pyramid with Private Henry splashing clumsily at his heels. Revolting leeches fully three feet long reared from the water outside the fence, their sucker mouths probing and puckering, sending Escalla whizzing high above Jus with her legs tucked up out of harm's way. She flew backward, her eyes on the leeches, and so managed to bump her backside into something sticky, hot and wet.

She had reached the pyramid. Escalla stared rigidly ahead of herself, reaching behind her rear. Something wet, congealing and hot clung to her bottom—and a big, dripping, solid *something* was right at her back.

"Jus, it's a corpse, isn't it?"

"Yes." The sound of his voice revealed that his fury was barely in check.

"I think I just shoved my bum into its chest cavity."

"Yup." Jus climbed slowly and steadily up the pyramid. "Looks like it."

"I'm gonna puke!"

"Don't." His face savage and his black hell hound skin bristling, Jus clambered heavily up to join his friend. "Do nothing suspicious, not until it's time to fight."

The pyramid steps were awash with blood. A foul cascade had poured down from the base of the huge idol above, dripping over the steps and oozing slowly into the moat below.

At the upper platform of the pyramid, the lobster-headed idol loomed. Blood had been smeared over its claws and breasts, and a heart had been placed in each open claw. A clamshell at the monstrous image's feet held votive offerings. There were shells and basalt figurines, images carved from bone or chunks of brilliant coral. Hanging upside down on the edge of the platform was a sprawling corpse, a figure whose whole chest had been torn open to feed the monstrous goddess above.

The last group of kuo-toa pilgrims had already departed, heading down the far side of the pyramid. Jus swiftly knelt beside the corpse, wiped blood from its still-warm face, and stared at it in thought.

Escalla had painfully levered herself free, fighting an urge to scream.

"You, ah, you found . . . found something?"

"It's one of the half-orcs from Sour Patch." Jus turned the dead creature's face. "Still bruised from where I hit him."

"Oh." Escalla had worries of her own but felt somehow vaguely responsible for Sour Patch. "Do you think the slaves all ended up here?"

"Doubtful. The drow are in charge of them." Jus let the half-orc's head slump back onto the cold stone steps. "They may have given some of the captives as a bribe to the kuo-toa."

"So some might still be alive here?"

"Perhaps." The Justicar could hardly hold out much hope. "Cinders?"

Smell kuo-toa. The hell hound's eyes seemed more cunning, more feral when he hunted prey. *Smell drow. Human smell a bit. Little bit smell.*

Standing to look out across the cavern below, Escalla watched the guards at the northwest tunnel exit. The girl turned, flicked her glance across the votive bowl before the idol, then reluctantly edged closer and peered inside.

Quick as a weasel, she darted her hand in and snatched a trinket from the edge of the seashell.

"Hey!" The girl held a treasure in her hands. "Look. A votive!" The other adventurers surrounded her as she showed them her prize. "It's hair, *faerie* hair."

The lock of hair shone like pale gold. The strands were long and fine, and tied about an elven finger bone. Escalla held the hair up against her own. They were almost a match, shade for shade. The girl's humor left her face as she stared at the hair strands in thought.

"Now we're getting warm."

The Justicar squatted down beside Escalla, his hand resting on her back. Grave, intelligent eyes watched Escalla with her find. "Could you link it to a specific person?"

"No." The faerie carefully stored the evidence away. "Not in a court of law. Who's to believe me when I say I found it down here? But it's giving me some crystal clear ideas."

Polk and Henry were waiting. With a glance over her shoulder, Escalla leaned in to whisper in Jus's ear. "Keep Cinders watching out for any sign of a faerie." The girl flicked a glance at Henry. "And, ah, let's keep it happy. The kid's been looking a little pale."

Escalla seemed white as a ghost herself. Jus let her feel a warm squeeze of his hand. Cinders teeth gleamed in manic goodwill as the ranger rose. He turned to talk quietly with Private Henry. Escalla drew in a breath and turned around to survey the cave.

She felt her antennae freeze.

Two titanic kuo-toan priests stood at the edge of the platform, staring wordlessly at the party through their huge fishy eyes. Sheathed in blood, the monsters stood in silence. Escalla waved to them, received no response, then cleared her throat to attract the attention of the menfolk just behind her.

"Ah, guys? Guys, we may have a problem."

Apparently suspicious of why the party was loitering, the two huge kuo-toa had come to escort them off the altar. Still, they ignored all of the travelers save Escalla. To the faerie, they spoke in their snapping, vicious tongue, crouching like mad carnivorous nightmares over the dainty faerie. The kuo-toa bid Escalla a farewell, then turned and left their guests standing alone and unguarded in the room.

The northern side of the huge temple had been carefully sculpted into palatial apartments. The rooms were perfectly squared with high ceilings rippled by an eerie underwater light. Walking slowly up sand-scattered steps, the Justicar and his companions might have been in a palace under the sea. Jus walked over shells and dried seaweed, past the gnawed remains of grizzly cannibalistic meals, and halted at the edges of the hall.

Escape lay only thirty yards away. The northwest tunnel opened into the underdark but was guarded by a team of kuo-toan warriors. On the sands just outside the palatial apartments, a group of them sparred carefully with weapons while a gnarled instructor taught the arts of the backstab and the garotte. The creatures paid no attention to the visitors behind them. Escalla looked about uncertainly, shrugged, then pointed to an entrance just beyond.

The new room had definite possibilities. At the far wall, two tall statues of the lobster-headed goddess flanked an ugly throne that had been studded with pearls. The throne depicted fish skulls and and drowning humans being torn apart by crabs. The walls were carved into horrible bas-reliefs, the rippling lighting had taken on a darker, more sinister hue.

Sitting on a platform smothered with blood, the throne faced the massive temple cave. It clearly gave a wonderful view of sacrifices, executions, and the occasional leech attack. Escalla edged forward to the threshold. There were kuo-toa soldiers crouching in the corners of the room. One thin, misshapen creature crouching at the foot of the throne held a conch shell trumpet. Pillars carved to look like columns of fish-infested skulls held aloft the ceiling. Six taller, grimmer guards lurked by the columns—all watching Escalla and her companions in silence as the girl crept timidly into the room.

Escalla rapped her knuckles against the doorframe, clearing her throat and giving a smile as she caught the attention of the guards.

"Um, hello." Escalla advanced a little farther into the room. The fish simply stared, their fangs gleaming and their faces devoid of emotion.

At the foot of the throne, a huge clamshell pool glinted in the light. Within it, tiny fishes swam, and brilliant sea shells gleamed. The shells caught Escalla's eye. The girl edged a tad closer, gave a nervous, placatory wave to the guards, and peered into the pool.

"Jus, what do cone shells look like?"

"They're sea shells, and they're conical."

"That's *great*, Jus." Unamused, Escalla put her fists on her hips as she hovered, glaring back at her friend. "Can you tell when a shell is venomous, or can't you?"

"Just hold it to your ear." The Justicar walked forward, apparently ignoring the guards. "If you hear the ocean, it's harmless. If it kills you, it was a cone shell."

"Funny."

Funny! Cinders's grin twinkled like jagged mountain peaks.

The pool held quite a few interesting life forms—tiny blue ringed octopi and sea snails with conical shells. Giving the pool a cautious glance, the Justicar kept carefully clear.

"Don't fall in."

"Well *duh!*" The faerie made a droll little face. "Any other good advice?"

"Yes. Go talk to the chamberlain."

Stealing silently in from a side entrance way, a hunched, thin kuo-toa came onto the dais. The creature's eyes swiveled independently, taking in Polk and Henry, Escalla and the Justicar. The black presence of Cinders and the faerie's golden hair seemed to impress the creature, and it made a simple little spell pass with its hand.

The creature spoke, its cruel fangs clacking. A disembodied voice, eerily suave, feminine, and calm, drifted out from somewhere in midair. *"Greetings, air child. We had not looked for your return so soon."*

Biting her lip, Escalla decided that the creature was talking to her. "Well, I just can't keep away! You know how I love this temple."

The fish creature bobbed, its savage voice gargling. It made motions with its hands, and the female voice echoed from above. *"Your gift of sacrifices has gained you great credit with us. May we assist you?"*

Escalla took on a sly look, hid it with a false blonde innocence, and clasped her hands together. "Well yes. Just a little thing for now." Escalla blinked brightly. "Do you remember me borrowing a deadly cone shell from you a while ago?"

"Yes." The fish creature bobbed. *"In return, you paid us with the hearts of many upworld slaves."*

"Oh, how very . . . outgoing of me." Escalla looked a little sick. "Anyway, silly me—must have slipped my mind—but can I just trouble you for a receipt?" The girl gave a polite little clasp of her hands. "It's for my records, you know?"

Not quite comprehending, the kuo-toa simply stared. Escalla signaled Polk for a piece of parchment and a pen, then flew over to present them to the fish creature. "It's an upworld thing! Sorry. Don't mean to be a bother."

"It is necessary?"

"I'm a faerie. Would I lie to you?" Escalla put the pen into the creature's clawed hands. "So if you could just write out my name and the exchange deal . . . you know, 'We, the temple of the sea goddess, acknowledge that we gave a venomous cone shell to so-and-so for the purposes of an assassination . . .' That kind of thing."

"So-and-so?"

"You know . . . my name." A true mistress of fast talk, Escalla was beside the kuo-toa, helping it write out the receipt. "Just scribble it in there. My full name. Nice and legal."

The kuo-toa scribbled its foul script, then paused. *"Please write in your name."*

"No, you do it. Just put it in here."

"I do not recall your alien name. Please refresh my memory."

Frustrated, Escalla tried fishing for ideas. "Well, it's just I forget what name I left with you guys. I have so many! Let's see what jogs your memory." Escalla tried her mother's name. "Let's try Ifurela, Lady Nightshade. No? How about Tielle?" The girl watched carefully, but the kuo-toa never twitched. "Lord Faen? Lord Ushan?"

With a sinking feeling, Jus made ready to strike with his sword. Above him, Cinders was stoking his flames. Escalla waved her hands, making less and less as she went on.

"Otiluke? Tensor? Bigby?" The girl threw up her hands. "Come on. Gimme something to work with here!"

The kuo-toa turned and began to write. Relieved, Escalla fell back toward her friends and whispered avidly in their ears, "He's doing it! I mean, *she's* doing it! We're getting a receipt!" The girl gave a huge gesture of relief. "So that's it! We get the receipt, and we run for home. No drow city!"

With his eyes nervously fixed on the kuo-toa, Henry cleared his throat. "What about the captives from Sour Patch?"

"Yeah, too bad about that reward." Escalla shot a guilty glance at Jus and Henry. "Ah, I mean too bad about all those poor souls, but they're in the clutches of the drow, man. Nothing we can do about it. Can't be helped!"

"We're going after them." The Justicar stood with his feet planted and his eyes seeing every tiny little movement in the room. "We need to know why your murderer is taking human slaves." The big man's voice echoed like the slamming of a tomb. "They have a date with Justice."

Escalla seethed, going into a grumbling sulk. "I just *knew* he was going to say that!"

Benelux gave a self-righteous glow. *I knew it also. He is made of purer stuff than you.*

Further retort was halted as the kuo-toa held up the finished receipt and stared at it with its eerie eyes. The creature came toward Escalla, who rubbed her hands in anticipation.

"Here we go!" Posing, Escalla elegantly reached out for the slip of parchment. "And now, for your listening pleasure, ladies and gentlemen, the murderer is. . . !"

A huge bubbling roar came from the far side of the room. Escalla whipped about to see a mammoth kuo-toa dressed in golden chains. Standing in a secret door that opened beside the throne, the monster's voice thundered and was echoed calmly by the disembodied voice above.

"This is not the faerie that we have trained! This one is male. It has no mammary glands!" The kuo-toa scribe whirled, staring at Escalla, the receipt crushed hard in its hand. Outraged, Escalla lost her temper.

"What do you mean no mammary glands! Hey! You fish reject, what the hell do you think *these* are?"

"You are a different faerie." The newcomer angrily waved a claw. *"Why are you here?"*

Stumped for ideas, Escalla turned to face her friends. "Got me there. Guys, anyone got anything more to say?"

Wag-wag-wagging his tail, Cinders grinned in glee. *Yes.*

"What?"

BURN!

His first blast smashed three kuo-toa off their feet. The creatures screamed as the noxious oil on their scales caught fire. Gleefully thundering a vast column of flame into the kuo-toa, Cinders made a noise of insane enthusiasm, sweeping fire all across the enemy.

"At least he has no problem with commitment!" Escalla blasted a fireball into a knot of onrushing guards. "That's great, pooch! That was real subtle!"

Burn! Burn fish! Burn palace! Burn idol! Burn cave! Cinders fur stood on end, flame streaming from happy teeth. *Burn!*

The scribe screamed and launched himself into the air, clawed hands reaching to rip Escalla from the sky. The girl's eyes bulged as she was snatched and squeezed like a grape. An instant later, the scribe's hands were severed by Jus's sword. Croaking, Escalla thudded to the ground, her ribs almost crushed and the dead hands still pinning her tight.

Above her, Private Henry screamed a panicked war cry and parried a harpoon that would have pinned Escalla to the floor. Angrily fighting free, Escalla struggled out of the dead grasp and spat her hair out of her mouth. Something blurred past her, a spear smashed sparks from a pillar beside Henry, and Escalla fired another fireball in reply.

Jus had already taken the arm off a huge kuo-toa, kicking backward to smash another monster's knee as he whirled. Behind him, Polk made the brilliant move of opening his portable hole, diving inside, and reaching back out to fold up the hole.

Two of the lesser guards hurled themselves at Private Henry. Rushing at him, the monsters hurled heavy harpoons straight at the boy. Imitating the Justicar, the boy managed to smash one huge spear out of the air. The second missile tore the whole sleeve of his mail shirt, ripping a line of blood along his arm. With a roar the boy whirled and swung his sword. To his astonishment, the sword blade bit into flesh, and the fish bellowed in agonized rage. It struck at the boy, had its blow blocked, then whirled backward as Henry cleaved his blade down into the monster's skull.

Overjoyed, Henry turned to the next monster and struck wildly down. His sword blade hit the kuo-toa's shield—and suddenly stuck fast to a layer of glue. The kuo-toa roared and twisted the weapon from his grasp, raising a spear to plunge it through the boy.

The kuo-toa's head suddenly exploded as Escalla smacked it neatly with her pencil-slim lich staff. The corpse jerked like a mad puppet, leaving Escalla staring at the magic staff in astonishment.

"Hot damn!" The girl reached out a hand to the dazed Private Henry. "You all right?"

"Um . . ."

"Yeah. All glory to King Um! Whatever, kid. Now's *not* the time!"

Escalla picked up Polk's folded portable hole and shoved it down her cleavage. "Time to run!" A horn was blowing, summoning more kuo-toa. "Jus! Pack it up, man. Time to flee!"

Roaring and cursing, Jus was surrounded by kuo-toa guards, all of them reeling away from the white blade. One lunged in with a pole arm, lost the business end of the weapon to Jus's sword, then jerked as a massive blow opened its guts. Another slashed with its claws, ripping Jus's shoulder. As Cinders sheeted fire to incinerate a ring of guards, Jus trapped his attacker's hand, slammed one hand against the monster's arm and snapped its elbow. It fell back, screaming as Benelux ripped through its chest. The sword twisted, whipped out, and flicked up looking for targets all in a single horrid blur.

The kuo-toa leader had already disappeared through a secret door beside his throne. With guards thundering in from the temple outside, the secret passageway seemed like a good idea. Jus threw himself at the door even as it slid closed, shattering the panels and making the kuo-toa leader reel back in fright. The creature leaped down a set of stairs with powerful shoves of its stumpy legs. Jus loomed in the door, terrifying with his brilliant sword, blood-smeared armor, and smoking hell hound skin.

"Move!" Jus bellowed to his companions. "We're going this way!"

Jus shoved in through the door, and Private Henry instantly followed at his heel. Escalla made to follow, then suddenly blinked and swerved back into the throne room.

"Wait! The receipt!"

The piece of parchment lay on the floor beside the scribe's severed hands. Escalla dived toward the receipt—only to look up in shock to see thirty enraged kuo-toa charging straight for her. A massive barrage of harpoons showered toward her. She threw her hand up in a spell, her magic shield snapping up an instant before the rusty harpoons arrived. The shield staggered as spears struck like a thunderstorm, spraying sparks and snapping points. One harpoon punched through the shield, and Escalla screamed, twisted aside, and had the middle ripped out of her dress. With the kuo-toa lunging toward her, the girl hurled herself backward in panic, screeching in frustration as the monsters overran the receipt. She flew backward through the secret door, harpoons ricocheting madly from her shield.

She bumped into Henry's back. The boy was stuck halfway down the stairs. As a dozen kuo-toa charged for them, Escalla blasted her black tentacles spell into the passage entrance, blocking the doorway with tendrils that caught hold of screaming kuo-toa and tossed the creatures aside.

"Jus! We've got company!"

The spell would last for a few minutes, no more. Escalla blundered about in a blur of wings until she dragged out her little lightstone. The sounds of screaming, throttled kuo-toa, thrashing tentacles, and alarm horns made conversation almost impossible.

"What's the hold up, Hen?"

"A door just slammed! The Justicar is on the other side of it!" Henry pressed his ear against a wooden door that blocked the passageway. "I can hear movement but can't hear fighting. He won't answer when I call!"

"Great." Harpoons clanged from the magic shield, tentacles thrashed, and kuo-toa roared. With hundreds of angry monsters at her heels, Escalla yanked her light stone out of her cleavage to look at the door, noticing the folded up portable hole between her breasts as she did so.

"Polk! You still in there?"

"Yep!"

"Are you peeking?"

"*Yep!*"

"Polk, I'm gonna give you such a pinch when we get outta here!" Escalla yelled into the dark. "Jus, come on man, open the door! What's the hold up?"

*　*　*　*　*

On the other side of the door, the Justicar's eyes bulged. The garotte around his neck jerked tight, and his fingers bled as he tried to pry the wire from his throat. The kuo-toa snarled, heaving backward on the garotte to try and tear Jus's head off his shoulders. High priest of an assassin cult, the kuo-toa hissed with the pleasure of the kill. Jus tried to rear and slam the monster against the walls, but the creature outweighed him, shoving him against a pillar and heaving viciously at the ranger's neck.

Jus tried to punch backward with his fist but struck only the harsh hide of the monster's arms. His elbow viciously slammed backward and failed to connect. He tried to rake his boot sole down the monster's shins, but the creature hopped and stepped away. With his air shut off, Jus staggered and heaved, while at his belt Benelux cried out excitedly with advice.

Drop your weight! Turn into him! The sword jittered like a school marm. *Look out! Don't let him bite your head!*

From the other side of the door, a little fist began pounding at the door.

"Jus! Jus, I mean it! This isn't funny! There's about a million fish out here!"

Whipping his free hand down to his side, Jus tried to draw his sword. The weapon was too long to free from its scabbard until Jus loosed the first few inches, gripped the blade in his gauntlet and whipped the weapon clear.

A spell exploded somewhere on Escalla's side of the corridor.

"Jus, open the door! *Open the door!*"

The Justicar rammed the sword hilt back, crashing the pommel into the kuo-toa's skull. The fish snarled and ducked, the next blow glancing off its angled skull. Jus reversed the blade and stabbed backward past his flank, slamming the weapon home and drawing a wild roar from the kuo-toa. Still the wounded creature held on, arching backward with renewed frenzy as it tried to tear the Justicar's head off. Cinders thrashed to no avail, and blood poured from Jus's upper hand. The wire garotte had cut through his leather gauntlets to slice into the flesh of his hand like a giant razor blade.

Jus stabbed backward again—the sword skipped clear of fish scales—and then again, this time jamming into flesh. The kuo-toa screamed, released its garotte, and smashed down with its hand.

Benelux clanged protesting to the floor, struck out of Jus's bleeding grasp. Still holding the ranger from behind, the kuo-toa tried to strangle him with its bare hands. It bit at his head, getting a mouthful of Cinders's fur and breaking teeth on Jus's metal helm. The Justicar gave a vicious noise and grabbed the kuo-toa's hand, snapping a finger and bringing yet another bellow of pain and rage. He broke a second finger, then a third, breathing at last through a throat that felt ragged with pain.

Behind him, the door exploded inward, flying to pieces, revealing a furious Escalla hovering in midair with magic still boiling around her fist.

"*I said open the damned door!*" Pausing in mid yell, the girl saw the kuo-toa strangling Jus from behind. "Hang on!"

A flame bolt ploughed into the kuo-toa's back, blasting open flesh and scales. With a roar of agony, the monster released Jus and whirled aside. An ice blast from Escalla's wand hit it in the chest and sent the creature skidding across the floor. Jus dived, the sword Benelux sweeping up in his hands as he snatched it from the floor. A crossbow bolt from Private Henry stabbed into the monster's thigh. The creature made a swift look to a box in one corner of the room. It opened its arms, screamed the syllables of a spell, and a magic gate flashed into being.

Jus and Escalla both lunged forward, Escalla smashing her lich staff into the creature's back. An instant later, Jus gave a hoarse roar and speared his sword through the creature's skull. Still screaming, its body flopping with horrid vitality, the kuo-toa leader took one step forward, drawing Jus and Escalla to the threshold of the gate.

Jus and Escalla stared for a brief moment into a watery universe of palaces and kelp. Enthroned on a couch of pearls sat a titanic being, a creature with a naked human female's torso and the head and arms of a lobster. Surrounded by countless thousands of priests, kuo-toa, carnivorous sea beasts, and lesser gods, the entity turned to look at the intruders at her door.

The dead priest tumbled forward into the water. Escalla gave the sea goddess a nervous little wave.

"This one's broken! We were just returning it!"

The sea goddess roared.

Jus lunged back into the secret room, snatching Escalla out of the gateway an instant before it crashed shut.

The room was chaos. Kuo-toa raved, harpoons clanged against the walls, and the place stank like a slaughterhouse. Chained to the walls were the rotting bodies of half a dozen armored gnomes, their weapons and treasures at their feet. Rot-grubs still writhed through the corpses moving in and out of eye sockets.

Private Henry was madly turning the windlass of his crossbow, a quarrel held between his teeth. The magic tentacles were failing, and kuo-toa struggled past. Fingers shaking, Henry slapped in the quarrel and shot the leader, making the creature tumble and fall. His crossbow was empty, and still more kuo-toa charged into the room.

Desperately searching for an escape, the young soldier saw a crossbow lying among the weapons piled at the dead gnomes' feet. He snatched it up and stared helplessly at the alien shape of the weapon. He made to fetch his own weapon back, but the kuo-toa surged forward with a hissing roar. Escalla pushed the boy back, opening her hands and sending a dense poisonous fog thundering out to fill the other room.

"Jus, find a damned exit! Hurry!"

There seemed to be no other doors. Looking swiftly at the walls, the Justicar lumbered over to the far end of the room, his bleeding fingers probing at his bruised throat as he ran. Every breath was agony. He threw a healing spell to repair the worst of the pain.

"Cinders, look for doors! That fish came here as an escape route!"

The hell hound wailed unhappily, fish-spittle dripping down his fur. *Big fish bit me! Fur all gooey!*

"We'll wash it later! Look for doors!" Jus whirled, slamming his sword pommel against a wall of solid stone to test for hollow spaces beyond.

Benelux gave a squawk of panic and outrage. *I say! Careful!* The sword screeched as she was used as a hammer yet again. *Stop! No! Wait! One of my pommel pins is shaky!*

Jus swore, striking chips from the stone as he hammered at the carved walls. With kuo-toa raving and blindly hurling spears, Escalla pushed Henry back toward the far wall, made to follow, caught sight of the kuo-toa priest's box, and instantly swerved aside. The lid already stood open, and all sorts of glittery stuff could be seen inside. Escalla dived straight into the chest and began burrowing like a crazed little mole through coins, pearls, and knickknacks.

"Polk?"

"Yep?"

"Incoming!"

With the portable hole partly open, Escalla burrowed into the treasure trove, stuffing away anything light enough for her to shift. Pearls, loose change, a mummified thought-eater, a dead cone shell . . . Polk screeched as dross and rubbish showered him in his hidey hole.

Far across the room, Jus turned and bellowed hoarsely in rage, "Get out of there! Move!"

"But there's still stuff here!"

"Do it!"

A kuo-toa staggered wheezing and reeling through the poisoned fog. The creature held a long staff tipped with pincers. It saw Escalla even as she flicked into invisibility. Lunging at her with the staff, it caught her tight. Escalla squealed, kicking her heels as she became visible once again. The girl sent an electrical shock chasing down the staff and into the fish monster's hands, causing absolutely no effect at all.

At the far wall, Jus bashed his sword hilt against solid rock, then suddenly heard the answering echo of a hollow space. He banged the sword on the wall again, and the pommel broke. Benelux screeched in dismay as the gaudy golden unicorn pommel, now sadly battered out of shape, fell clanging to the ground. Jus cursed, half turned, and caught sight of Escalla being shaken like a leaf on the end of a kuo-toa pincer staff.

"Escalla!"

The kuo-toa slammed the faerie against a wall. She fired magic golden bees at her captor, but the swarm bounced and scattered from the monster's hide. Another bash against the wall rattled Escalla's teeth. Now chittering mad, she gave a snarl of rage and raised her hand, preparing her most savage fireball spell.

Jus took one look at the building storm and screamed, "Escalla, no!"

The spell detonated, catching Escalla's captor in the back and blasting it apart. The explosion whirled Escalla like a leaf, sending her wailing through the air.

"Waaaaaaaaah!"

The girl flew through the air, landing bottom-first upon a carving of an angler fish. The carving's dorsal ridge felt indelicate enough to make Escalla's eyes start from their sockets. She grabbed the carving to slide free, hung for a moment on a lever, and then fell as the lever shifted and a grating nose began from somewhere inside the walls.

The wall beside Jus and Henry slid open, revealing a set of steps leading west. Jus lunged toward Escalla, grabbed the stunned faerie by the scruff of her wings, and ran toward the closing door.

A shimmering gateway was opening in the room behind them. Apparently the sea goddess was miffed. Kuo-toa fought their way into the room through Escalla's poisoned cloud, some dying, some wheezing, and others foaming with rage. The Justicar dived and rolled through the swiftly narrowing doorway just before the sliding door slammed shut. Coming to his feet, he tucked the faerie under his arm, Polk still giving muffled yells from down her cleavage. With the battered sword in his hand, Jus pushed past Henry and led the retreat.

With her pommel shattered, Benelux made outraged noises, but Jus was long past caring. A doorway sealed the top of the new stairway. Jus crashed into it with his shoulder, breaking the door off its rails. He burst into the passageway that led into the underdark. A single kuo-toa was running past, heading for the temple beyond. Jus caught it with a savage flail of his unbalanced sword, sending the creature reeling into the wall where he stabbed it through the gills.

Five more kuo-toa stood just inside an entrance that led back into the temple. They turned, roared, and snatched up their harpoons to attack Jus's unprotected back.

Reeling out of the stairs, Private Henry screeched a thin noise of panic as he tugged and struggled at his captured crossbow. The huge boxy mechanism fumbled in his grasp. Spell runes flashed, the boy pressed one with his thumb, and suddenly the weapon bucked like a maniac. A blurred stream of crossbow bolts ripped into the kuo-toa, the crossbow flashing as spells blurred its mechanism back and forth. Henry stared in shock as the kuo-toa spun with bolts ramming into them. Still hanging over Jus's shoulder, Escalla looked back at the boy and gave a dazed thumbs up as she saw him fire.

"Hoopy!"

The entire temple had been roused. Jus began running up the northwestern tunnel, heading into the dark. Jolting up and down, Escalla fired her ice wand behind the party—the last shot from her wand, which finally sputtered out and died. The spell stabbed back down the tunnel and made a wall of ice, blocking the angry kuo-toa from pursuit. Escalla shook her wand and cursed, slinging it across her back upon its strap.

"That's it! The wand's out until I get it recharged!"

There were hundreds of angry foes just behind them. It might take five minutes for them to break the ice wall or five hours. Escalla could not afford to wait and see. She summoned her floating disk spell beneath Jus's feet. The big man blinked in astonishment, then grabbed Henry as they began to whiz speedily down the tunnel.

Escalla led the way. Her ribs were crushed; she was ripped and battered. With hundreds of baying enemies just behind her, she chose to look down at herself and make a little rant of outrage.

"They tore my dress! Those fish tore my dress!" The girl had worked for hours to make something out of the drow fabrics. "What the hell does the underdark have against my clothes?"

The faerie's slim little middle was now bared, framed by ragged strips of silk. She flew upside down and backward, peering at herself as she flew, somehow missing a stalactite in her path.

"Actually . . . I think I can work with this!"

"Escalla!" Jus managed to get the girl's attention back onto the road just in time to make the disk dodge wildly through a forest of stalagmites and then plunge down a limestone cascade. Jus and Henry lay flat on the disk, holding on like grim death. The disc dodged, twisted, then turned, narrowly missing rock pillars and walls. A stream of carnivorous stalactites came showering down, missing the floating disc by a hand's breadth as it plunged down a slippery chute of stone.

Blank with fright, Jus ducked beneath a gibbering stirge.

"Escalla? *Escalla!"* The disc tilted sideways and shot through a tiny cave mouth. "Escalla, is this thing safe?"

"Sure it's safe! I'm totally unharmed!" Ahead, the passageway branched then branched again. "Hey! Does anyone remember that map we found?"

She chose the narrowest passage, a tiny thing only a few feet wide. The floating disk blurred over a forest of shrieker fungi, the huge toadstools wailing like banshees as the party passed, awakening monstrous shapes burrowing in the muck nearby. The companions left the cacophony far behind as they wound through twists and turns, ducking beneath low ceilings that almost skinned Cinders off the Justicar's back. They dodged right and left through a maze of caves, muddling their trail.

Quite suddenly, the disk spell dissipated. Hanging in midair and still shooting forward, Jus and Henry blinked then went crashing to the ground. Escalla heard the noise and doubled back, hovering above the two men and managing to look immensely pleased.

"Hoopy! I never had one last that long before! We must have come four miles!"

Motion sick, slashed, half choked and dangerously annoyed, Jus arose, straightened Cinders on his head, and dusted himself off.

"Polk?"

From inside the portable hole, a muffled voice replied, "Yes, son! What is it?"

"Get out of there!"

"I'm just sorting a few things!" The hole unfolded. Escalla threw it away in alarm, and Polk's head emerged. "I'm writing us a schedule! We need organization and planning. That's the backbone of any good adventure!"

"Right." Jus fetched Escalla, inspected her, then sank a healing spell into her ribs to clear up her bruises and scrapes. "Have you got the map?"

"Lich took it," Polk replied.

He shrugged, then clambered out of the unfolded hole. Inside the pit, a scatter of pearls, gems, bent copper coins, and old keys glittered in the gloomy light. The teamster heaved out his chronicles, slung them safely over his back, then took a sharp look at Escalla's face.

"You all right, girl?"

"I'm fine."

"Did you know you've got some freckles down your front?"

Escalla hovered, regarding Polk through lofty eyes. "Polk, a woman without freckles is like a night without stars!" The tiny faerie posed sweetly, them smacked the human up the side of his head. "Show's over! We need to hole up for a while. Let's find a stream, get some water, then get moving!"

A side cavern gave access to a freezing cold, clear little river, a stream haunted by eerie eyeless fish and transparent shrimp. Helping herself to a cup of water, Escalla shook her head and dabbed at her countless bruises, cuts, and scrapes.

"Damn! Why didn't my stoneskin work? That was a perfectly good spell!"

Sitting beside her and carefully filling his water bottle, Jus shot the girl a droll glance. "Did the beholder ever look at you?"

"Oh. Oh yeah." Crestfallen, Escalla helped herself to a mug of water. "I can't be expected to remember everything." She sipped her water, made a face, then held out her little cup for Polk to sweeten from his magic whiskey bottle. "Well, we can't go to the drow without all of us having stoneskin put on us. We'll get creamed!"

"How long would it take to conjure the spells?"

"Ah, well, I'll have to rest overnight." The girl thoughtfully ticked off each stage upon her fingers. "Probably enchant you and me tomorrow, rest another night, then do Polk and Henry the next day."

The Justicar corked his water bottle and shrugged. "The kuo-toa will be following us right now."

"Point taken." The girl stood and tossed her empty frost wand inside. She settled her scroll tube across her back and polished off the little lich staff. "I guess we'd better go."

The party gathered themselves. Henry stood peering into his new crossbow, which seemed to fit about a dozen crossbow bolts into a magazine at the top—a problem, since he now only had twelve quarrels left in his quiver. The boy examined the whole mechanism in puzzlement.

Escalla perched on his shoulder and said, "Guess it's a type of haste spell on the thing. Hoopy." The faerie patted Henry on the head. "Don't lose it!"

Polk bumbled past, his book open as he began scribbling his own version of the fight. He licked the nib of his pen and looked thoughtful, failing to see the glowing caterpillar that had taken up residence on his hat.

"Come on. We're behind schedule." The man shot a look at Escalla, then scribbled on his page. "How do you spell 'svelte hellion'?"

Escalla gave a warning snarl. "Polk, if you're planning on writing about my cleavage, you can forget it."

20

When the party found a suitable campsite and stopped to rest, the only one unhappy with affairs was Benelux. The sword sulked in silence, but no one paid her any attention. The sword's ornaments had been made from gold, with an eye for decoration rather than function. Her gold pommel was now gone, and her elaborate golden crossguard was battered and scarred. She finally made a petulant noise and spoke up as Jus laid her out on the ground.

Well? Have you a repair spell? Are you fixing me? I'm in ruins! I cannot be seen in public like this!

"We're fixing you." Jus sat with the sword over his knees, using an old pair of pliers from his pouch to unfix the weapon's broken handle. The blade gleamed, its tang white and perfect.

Exposed, Benelux gave a little screech of shock. *Sir, I'm naked! Have you no sense of shame?*

"Sorry." Jus polished the weapon on a piece of black drow cloak. "Just wait a minute."

Have you the means to fix me?

"Definitely."

Escalla came tripping innocently over from the portable hole. "We can fix you. Just close your eyes or whatever, and it'll be a surprise!"

I insist upon fittings suitable to my high station. The sword gave a sniff. *I have appearances to keep.*

"Oh boy, have I got a fashion look for you!" The girl held the hilt of Jus's old skull pommeled sword hidden behind her back. "We've got the perfect thing right here!"

Somewhat mollified, Benelux gave a sniff. *Will I look dignified?*

"It'll be great!" Escalla gave a shrug as innocent as the dawn. "Trust me. I'm a faerie!"

✿   ✿   ✿   ✿   ✿

In the underdark, time never seemed to pass. The water and the cold, the echoes and the darkness, all blended into a never ending daze. Sleeping and waking came and went unregulated by night and day. The party camped at need on shelves of rock or hid in dripping caves.

Jus and Henry awoke from their latest sleep to find that Escalla had gone.

Her beaver skins lay where she had left them, but her scroll case and staff were missing. Kicking Polk awake, the men arose, packed the bags, and sped into the main tunnel. Several minutes of frantic searching revealed nothing but empty spaces until Jus spied a trail of hardtack crumbs.

In a passageway beside the main tunnel, Escalla sat happily upon a toadstool, fanning her little wings. Surrounding her was a ring of giant ants, each insect fully two feet long, armored and armed with formidable stings. Escalla twined antennae with the leader, laughed, and apparently told a joke that the ants appreciated. She patted them on their shells as the creatures went their way, giving a piece of spider jerky to each one as a parting gift. As the last ants scuttled off, the girl looked around to see Jus, Polk, and Henry gazing at her with hooded, unamused eyes.

Wondering at their expressions, Escalla gave a shrug. "So I like bugs!" The girl waved her hands. "Like my magic bees weren't a clue?"

Jus walked toward the girl, his tread heavy, and gave a tired sigh. "We've been looking for you for ten minutes."

"I was just down here. I gassed out a nest of gremlins for the ants, and they came to say thank you." Escalla handed a tiny leg bone to Cinders. "Here you go, pooch! Compliments of the chef."

Mmm! The hell hound mumbled the bone in his mouth. *Good gremlin!*

Jus sat down beside the girl, unsuccessfully pretending that he had not been worried sick. "Don't run off alone."

"It was ants, man! Ants are hoopy!" The girl paused. "And bees."

"Escalla."

"What?" The girl collected herself. "Anyway, the ants said there's some stuff down this corridor to watch out for. Magic using two-leggers have blocked the next junction. Guess it must be drow."

"They don't know for sure?"

Raising one brow, the faerie looked as Jus as though he were insane. "Hey! They catch 'em and eat 'em. They don't interrogate the beggars!"

Jus shook his head. "Nice."

"They're *ants*, man!" Escalla gave a shrug. "Didn't you ever have an ant farm when you were a kid?"

"Why would I want to grow ants?"

"For fun!"

Jus simply looked at her. "Escalla, oversized carnivorous insects are not *fun*. Oversized carnivorous insects are *alarming*."

"Oh?" Scratching her head, Escalla puzzled over the strange ways of the world. "Eerie!"

Laying the subject aside for now, Escalla produced the indicator needle from her pouch. As always, the needle pointed northwest. This time, however, a faint quiver in the needle made it tickle in Escalla's hand. The Justicar watched the motion for a moment and then nodded in slow satisfaction.

"Stationary target. Ten-mile range."

"Really?"

"Really." Peering through a cave mouth into the main passageway beyond, Jus led the way into the gloom. "Let's get moving."

Polk followed the Justicar, carefully recording the route. Henry brought up the rear, his crossbow at the ready. Escalla looked over her companions in satisfaction, dusted a speck of lichen from Cinders's freshly brushed fur, then flew down to salute the skull-pommeled sword at Jus's hip.

"How's life on this beautiful subterranean morning?"

I am not talking to you. The sword was in a most offended huff. *You tricked me.*

"What trick?" Escalla opened her hands, admiring the sword. The wolf-skull pommel, the stark black grips . . . it all looked wonderfully grim. "It's dire, it's dark, it's minimalist. It's a statement! This is a sword for striking fear into . . . into . . . into folk who need to be fear strucken!" The faerie fluttered along beside the sword. "This is *your* look. I swear!"

The sword remained indignantly silent.

Unperturbed, Escalla shrugged and flew ahead to scout for danger. As the party moved on, Benelux snorted then muttered in ill temper. *Justicar? I am beginning to feel your companion the faerie is perhaps a tad* tarnished.

"Yup." The big man never once took his eyes away from scanning the gloom. "Tarnished in some ways and surprisingly pure in others."

Polk snickered, and from the corridor ahead, Escalla's angry voice drifted back. "I heard that!"

Cinders gave a brilliant grin. *Funny!*

*　　❋　　❋　　❋　　❋　　❋*

Half a mile beyond the ants, the tunnel opened out into a great echoing cavern filled with ghastly phosphorescent light. A fortified wall ran across the cave, pierced by a gate studded with bronze spikes. Guards patrolled the wall above, and more guards stood at the gate. They were drow—ebony skinned, silver haired, and sinister.

Jus lay flat in cover with Henry at his side, both carefully scanning the distant scene. Behind them, Escalla watched master and student at their work.

"A guard post has at least four times as many soldiers as you can see." Jus carefully pointed out the hidden spy holes in the distant wall. "There's probably thirty drow soldiers with commanders, a priest, and a powerful sorcerer as back-up."

Trying to count the drow, Henry bit his lip. "How do we kill them all?"

"No point." Jus shrugged. "Escalla, what have we got spell wise? You had some scrolls?"

"Yeah. All earth ones. Stone to flesh, flesh to stone, dig, pass wall. That kind of thing." The faerie patted the scroll case slung across her back. "I can make a hole through the wall, but we'd still be seen."

Behind Jus, Benelux made an irritated little noise and spoke to Polk. *The drow city is nearby, and that means there's work to do.* The sword wriggled unhappily in its sheath. *We can't fight stone walls. I do wish they'd just find a way to sneak past.*

"They'd never consider it! No, it'll be a frontal attack, blades swinging—courage against all odds!" Polk gave a self important puff of his chest. "These people are adventurers. They're the slayers of Keraptis, conquerors of White Plume Mountain, masters of the underdark!"

Escalla appeared, peeking over Polk's shoulder as he spoke. "Polk, have you got those gee-gaws we found on the drow guard post back before the trogs? You know, those spider amulets?"

"Yes! Yes I do!" Polk had proudly organized the portable hole's storage space and had inventoried every single item. "Six medallions, black, spider images on the reverse!"

"Hoopy!" Escalla held out her hand. "Pass 'em over! I'm gonna talk our way past these guards."

Polk and Benelux gave an almost identical squawk—*"Talk?"*—but had no choice in the matter.

The faerie led the way into the middle of the cavern. Polk hung at the rear, kicking toadstools. Escalla flew straight up to the drow, tipped them a salute, and presented them with one of the black medallions. Her other hand was behind her back, readying a spell.

A drow passed a detection spell over the girl, seeking to discern whether she was a secret agent of purity and goodness. The spell inevitably came up blank. The drow consulted one another, made a note in a record book, then opened up the gates to let the party through.

Walking past the guards, Polk shot a sidewise look at the dark elves and then glared at the other adventurers.

"That's it?" the teamster whispered hoarsely. "We're just walkin' though?"

"Yep!" Escalla tied the spider medallion about her neck. Her suspicions were growing richer. "And the drow were amazingly unsurprised to see a faerie pass them by. How about that?"

"We're just leaving then?"

"Polk, there are waaay more drow in the world that we have time to bump off! Now if you want to get to the drow city, just shut up and march."

*   *   *   *   *

The long tunnels were joined now by other paths. A reeking drow merchant caravan plodded past, guarded by warriors and trailing a swarm of flies. Cinders growled as he passed the drow, and Jus firmly kept the hell hound's snout pointing toward the walls.

Dark elves glared as the party passed. Escalla nodded and waved in response, her grin staying even as she sweated in fright.

"Oooh, we are going to get so killed!" The drow caravan had an armed escort of a dozen trolls—massive green creatures that dragged their knuckles as they walked. Escalla gave them a tinkling little wave. "I'm gonna kick the arse of that Seelie Court when we get home."

Jus kept a quiet eye on the disappearing drow. He walked slowly and carefully, one hand resting upon Benelux, his eyes spearing every shadow. Above his head, Cinders's red eyes gleamed as they searched into the dark.

The tunnels were now a well traveled road with the marks of thousands of marching, hopping, or dragging feet. Walls grew farther apart, the glowing fungi seemed deliberately tended, and nightmarish streaks of phosphorescent minerals added their pulsing light. The miles went slowly past, and then quite suddenly the tunnel walls simply disappeared.

Standing in a great, gloomy silence, Escalla, the Justicar, Polk, Cinders, and Private Henry gazed upon the vault of the drow.

It was a vast, empty space in which echoes simply died. A cliff wall soared into unknown distances above, dwarfing the adventurers below. A roof arched upward, disappearing into the distance a thousand yards above, the ceiling's arc shown by nebulous sprays and swirls of colors stolen from a madman's dreams.

The caverns stretched for untold miles. Overhead, a great bloated node of minerals stole a lurid glow across the scene. Light the color of blood seeped across the rocks, making each formation shimmer with sickly colors all its own. There were pale blues and acid yellows. Clouds of blue spores drifted from titanic mushrooms that loomed into the sky.

Half hidden in the eerie hush, noises drifted in the gloom: distant night creatures gave screams and cries or wept like children and sighed awful promises. There was no wind. The air never stirred, and the false stars upon the ceiling were dead and cold.

The light made all shapes flat and lifeless and turned familiar colors into startling new hues. Escalla hovered, staring at the hideous kingdom, and her bared skin shone a cadaverous lavender-blue. The Justicar turned to look at her and slowly raised a smile.

"Lavender?" Jus seemed amused. "Heh."

"Lavender!" Recoiling in panic, Escalla almost expired in shame. She was utterly appalled as she looked at her own usually milk-white flesh. "Lavender! Aww man! What sort of style credibility is lavender?" Escalla whirled, trying to see her rear.

The cave gave an impression of vast, terrifying space, yet the light was dim enough to make vision fail to see more than a few hundred yards. A path of crushed crystal ran out of the tunnel. Overhung with stinking toadstools in which gibbering little creatures lurked, the path shone a horrible violet-blue. Jus stepped cautiously onto the crystals, felt them crunch like bird skulls underfoot, then led the way forward into the emptiness.

The huge, dark figure of the Justicar seemed utterly indestructible. Having hesitated at the threshold, Escalla and Private

Henry moved instantly onward in the Justicar's wake. Simply being near him seemed protection against the horrors of the unseen. Standing and writing in his book of chronicles, Polk finished a paragraph with satisfaction, looked up to find that he was standing alone, and ran after the other explorers as fast as he could.

A tower loomed above the path—a savage shape framed by impaled corpses that were gnawed and worried by jabbering creatures of the dark. Lit by stars that were not stars, the carnivorous beasts tore strips of flesh from corpses and cackled as they ate.

The magic sword at Jus's side stirred softly in its scabbard. *Undead.*

"I see them." Jus kept his voice low. "We're too near the tower to risk killing them."

Ah. The sword seemed thoughtful. *I take it we shall pursue such aims later? If so, I believe I can coach you in appropriate heroic rhetoric.*

"I look forward to it."

A checkpoint barred the road ahead. Drow stood to watch the party approach, while others leaned over the parapets of the tower. A freshly impaled victim still jerked and twitched beside the road, blood pouring out to seep through the glowing crystal path. Jus looked upon the sight and bristled like a vast, dark animal.

"We have a very great deal of work to do."

Drow soldiers stirred—males left to do the dirty work while their dark sisters indulged their appetites in the tower.

Escalla whirred forward, producing her black medallion for the guards, and announced, "Greetings."

The senior guard looked at Escalla as though she were filth from underneath a stone. The drow took the medallion, tossed it into a basket, then wiped his hands upon a cloth as though they were suddenly unclean. The elf's voice, oddly accented, dripped with scorn, soft and sibilant, sweet as poisoned syrup and utterly foul. "Why have you come?"

It was Escalla's moment to shine. Dressed in artfully torn black silks, she arrogantly threw back her long blonde hair and disdainfully looked the dark elf up and down.

"I have business. Business far too complex for a mere elf to understand." The girl flicked a hand toward the other adventurers. "These three humans are my retainers."

Escalla very deliberately ran her fingers into her hair, lifting her glorious golden locks. The spider pin gleamed, and the drow instantly stiffened and backed a step away. Weapons wavered and then pointed aside.

"Go." Looking as though the words choked him, the chief drow motioned for his men to let the travelers pass. "Go along the right hand path to the city. Do not deviate."

"As you wish." Escalla made a wave as she turned away, muttering beneath her breath. "And a nice day to you, you walking sphincter!"

Followed by her entourage, Escalla began to move away.

As he passed, the Justicar turned, vast and deadly, and looked coldly down at the drow.

"When did a convoy of two hundred slaves pass here?"

The drow sneered.

Escalla snapped an icy glare at the elves. "Answer him."

Reluctantly, the elf shot a glance at Escalla's golden hair pin then looked away. "Yesterday. The ceremony will not be for another four hours. Cross the river to the temple." The drow wrote a description of the visitors into a book and slammed the cover shut. "Go. The presence of lower creatures is offensive."

Cinders grinned at the very flammable elves, his teeth promising a later meeting, and then Escalla grabbed Jus and dragged him away. As they moved down the road, Escalla let the man's bulk hide her from the elves.

"I thought they were going to go for you, man. That gold pin saved the day."

A dozen armed elves stood by the roadside, crowding close enough to be threatening, their weapons only just pointed aside. Escalla led the way ahead of her retainers, giving a cold, disdainful sniff toward the watching elves. She whispered to her friends as they passed slowly through the gauntlet toward the open mushroom fields.

"It's all right. Just be natural." Escalla glared coldly at a drow who stood watching her pass beside a huge alarm gong. "We're evil. We eat broken glass and wire for breakfast. We do bad things to wood-land wildlife."

Burn elves now! Funny!

"Pooch, be good, or I'll smack your nose!"

Walking past the drow, Jus came level with the faerie. "They have a ceremony planned. The traitor faerie is probably involved somehow."

Escalla kept her face neutral in case the elves were watching. "I *know* that, Jus. Great! So we're heading for their main temple?"

"Looks like it." The Justicar settled his armor across his shoul-ders. "We can't get back out the same tunnel we used to get here. Any idea how we find a route to the surface once we're done?"

"No idea in the world." Escalla seemed amazingly unconcerned. "Let's just wing it. We'll figure something out!"

The Justicar shot a look at the girl, who replied with an open little shrug, "Trust me. I'm a faerie!"

The road took a bend around an outcrop of rock. Safely out of sight of the guards at last, Escalla breathed a sigh of relief and whirred down to stand encircled by her friends. She pulled out the locator needle, which now bucked like a beetle dancing a country jig. The needle pointed northeast, toward the farthest reaches of the drow cavern. Henry, Polk, Jus, and Cinders joined the girl in bend-ing over the needle in thought.

"All right, so the slowglass is here. Maybe the murderer is even here." Escalla sat down on the gravel with a frown. "Now we ask why. Jus, you're the investigator guy."

The Justicar turned to look over the vast reaches of the drow homeland. The venous light made distances impossible to judge. To either side of the roadway, forests of titanic toadstools loomed, the dark spaces alive with horrible, cautious movements.

The drow city was to the north, miles away and unseen, yet spreading a dark presence and a spreading scent of blood. The Justicar, apparently unafraid, rested his hand upon his sword and gazed toward the drow citadel.

"Tell me: Lolth was an ally of a faerie goddess, the Queen of Wind and Woe?"

"Oh, it's not a happy story." Escalla flew up to perch upon the ranger's shoulders, resting her elbow upon Cinders's furry skull. "Ancient history. A faerie sorceress slew a god and stole his power, then began to carve an empire through half a dozen planes. The fallout split the faerie races—most of them for the worse. Pixies and other species are all our degenerate cousins." Escalla made a disapproving face. "Anyway, Clan Nightshade trapped her, and it's nothing to be all that proud of. We were on her side, then turned coat and betrayed her. I mean, she was out of her mind. Guess the ancestors figured she had to go before it went too far." The girl wasted little time apologizing for faerie kind; she rarely met a faerie that she liked. "Anyway, she was too tough to take out in combat, so they tricked her. Turns out there's a Clan Nightshade trait for being tricksters or something."

Jus pulled at his nose. "I hadn't noticed."

"Yeah, well, it got the faerie goddess sealed in Pandemonium, and only Clan Nightshade knows where to find the key." The faerie shrugged. "It's been about, aaah, twenty thousand years since she went in the box. I imagine the old wench is a tad pissed at us by now."

Nodding slowly, the Justicar absently stroked his friend's feet with one hand. "By killing your fiancé, someone's trying to delay your clan's acceptance back into faerie society."

Listening intently, Private Henry blinked from one partner to the other. "Because they have their own plans to release the Faerie Queen of Wind and Woe?"

Escalla looked at Jus. Jus looked at Escalla, and Polk looked at no one in particular. The faerie girl blankly nodded in agreement as she ran the thought through her head. "Sounds like you got it, Hen!"

"What would happen?" Henry shrugged in confusion at his friends. "If she got out, I mean, would it be bad?"

Escalla looked at Jus then turned around, looking a wee bit pained. "Um, in her time, this bitch took on whole pantheons—and that was before she had twenty thousand years to spend getting *really* vindictive."

"Oh." Henry blinked, unsure whether he had actually been given an answer. "Not good?"

"Oh, *definitely* not good!"

Everyone looked northward toward the city of the drow. Thin, distant screams carried in the air, a moaning sob that made everyone's hair stand on end. Escalla wilted, looking north, and was dead certain that she was not about to enjoy her day.

"All right, so someone is looking to unleash the Faerie Queen of Wind and Woe. The only way to do that is to seize the Nightshade key."

Watching the darkness, Jus loosened his sword. "How would an enemy seize the key?"

"It's hidden in an energy pocket. Take a real planet buster of a spell to retrieve it! Even then, the key's useless until you activate it. You need Nightshade's ruling family to do it. The key has two eyes. Each eye faces a different way. Each eye has to simultaneously see one of *us*—a true member of the ruling family beckoning it to open. And an illusion spell instantly sets off an alarm." The girl shrugged. "Even if one of us was loony enough to try it, you'd never get a second member of the family to go along."

"Yes." The Justicar nodded. "But if you used slowglass, could you record a visual image and play it back into the eye?"

Escalla froze. Suddenly she looked quite sick and tired.

"Oh great." Her antennae dropped as the thought struck home like a soiled knife. "Oh, that's just frazzin' great!" Escalla kicked a toadstool over, sending the fungus cap flying off into the dark. "Slowglass! I thought they were giving it to me just because it was expensive." The girl swore like a teamster.

As a teamster himself, Polk could only blink in surprise at her technical knowledge and take a pull from his magic whiskey flask. "Girl, now hold on! Don't stand there jawin'! It's fate! Destiny! You were *meant* to be here!"

The Justicar glowered down at Polk through lowered brows.

"Don't get started on predestination, Polk!"

"But it has to be destiny!" The teamster opened his hands, appalled that his chosen heroes could fight against tradition so constantly. "And what's predestination got to do with it? Did you make that up of your own free will?"

"Polk!" Escalla snapped as she paced angrily up and down. "No philosophy with the Justicar. You'll burn out your brain!" Escalla paced, angered, agitated, and seething with energy. She'd been had, and the thought of being duped had set her aflame. "Let's say we've got a murder plot that's part of an attempt to free the faerie goddess. They haven't won yet. We can still bust up the works." Escalla shook her head bitterly. "Breaking into the key's hiding place . . . a spell that size requires a ton of energy. I mean a *huge* amount of energy." The girl never once took her eyes from the north. "I'm getting a real bad feeling about what all those captured Keolanders are for."

21

After several hours of walking, the darkness ahead finally began to resolve into a single, massive wall.

A city nearly filled the northern sector of the cavern, a city of pus-white walls encrusted with strange minerals. The walls glowed like a corpse glimpsed sinking in the murky depths—a pale shape, cold and unwholesome, that sent a shudder through the soul.

The city towers rose hundreds of feet into the air. There were sky bridges and spires, tall spines capped with impaled corpses, and buildings fashioned into leering demon masks. The walls of the city seemed to shift and move, as though pulsing with living, corrupted blood.

A city. There would be thousands of drow, any number of them capable of casting spells to root out an intruder. Escalla stared uneasily. Beside her, Jus stood and gazed upon the city in cold appraisal.

After a moment, the Justicar looked at the locator needle. It pointed northeast past the eastern edge of the city and toward the rear cavern wall. Collecting his friends, he moved off to the east, skirting the city walls and keeping carefully to the cover of toadstool groves.

Agog, Polk hurried forward and pointed toward the city. "We're not goin' in?" The man seemed disappointed. "I thought we were going in."

Jus looked down at the irritating little man and scowled. "Polk, we are not tourists."

"But it would look good in the chronicle! How can I tell people we *almost* reached the city of the drow?"

Escalla glowered at Polk then removed the man's hat and peered inside. "Polk, I think this thing is restricting the blood supply to your brain."

"Eh?"

"Nothing." Escalla replaced the hat and pulled it down tight. "If you're that keen on entering the place, be my guest."

"You're not going to come?"

"Polk, I'll kiss a duck before I put my silken little faerie butt inside those city walls."

Jus kept the walls in sight, following them for almost a mile until they finally curved away toward a great pale cliff. Flowing between the city and the cliff face, there was a black river, its water gleaming like liquid metal in the hideous light.

Jus ducked into cover and looked carefully at the cliff and the plateaus above the city. Escalla joined her friend's side, checked the locator needle, and pointed up the cliff.

"There. Real close. The needle's going mad."

"Then that's it." Jus looked at the cliff face on the far side of the river. "We'll head to the cliff face, climb it, and bypass the city."

Listening in, Polk tugged at his collar then stuttered forward in fright.

"So son, ah, did the river just happen to escape you? The black river? The evil, black, sinister, underground river?"

Shooting a sidewise look at Polk, Jus raised his brows. "Don't like getting wet?"

"Son! Big things with teeth live in rivers—especially in *underground* rivers!"

"I thought fighting toothy things was heroic, Polk?"

"Not when it's in the water!" Polk stamped his foot. "As senior tactical advisor, I'm putting my foot down."

Jus looked at the man, feeling tired, then pointed at the forest of toadstools all around them.

"We're going to float over on a mushroom cap, Polk. Only an idiot swims rivers in the underdark."

"Oh." Polk sniffed, then decided to take a look at a giant

toadstool. "Well all right them. Good to see my advice is always followed."

"Right." Jus wearily waved his party onward. "Come on. We'll get out of sight of the city walls."

This was Jus in his element. He led his companions stealthily down toward the shore, selected a giant toadstool as a boat, and unsheathed his sword. Benelux made a glad battle cry and flashed brilliantly with light, only to see the entire party scowling at her in annoyance.

The sword hurriedly shut off its light and said, *Sorry.*

Jus grunted in reply and tipped the toadstool over, severing the stalk where it joined the cap and making a paddle by carving the stalk with two long swipes of the hideously sharp sword. He pushed everyone in and paddled the makeshift raft into the water. The river wasn't wide and was soon crossed.

Jus left his companions standing and staring in amazement as he attacked the cliff face with astonishing speed. The man moved like a mountain goat, lunging upward from crag to crag. When a spider the size of a cat lunged out of a crevice at him, the ranger pulped it with one single massive blow of his fist. Watching admiringly from below, Escalla could only shake her head in love and pride.

"Oh man, he is *so* harsh!"

Finally, a rope came spilling from above. Jus's magic rope—taken from another enemy in a far distant place—lengthened and spilled to the ground. Henry and Escalla looked at one another in agreement, then chased Polk up the rope. It was no easy task.

At the top of the cliff, Polk fumed and glared, looking at Escalla in hurt betrayal.

"No need to push! I was going!"

"Yep, and now you're here." Escalla hovered where she could keep an eye on Henry as he climbed. "Hey, Cinders! See anything?"

Cave. Lots drow. The black hell hound skin gleamed beneath the dim, hellish lights. *Smell spiders.*

"Spiders. Great." Escalla needlessly gave help to Henry as the boy crossed the cliff's edge. "That sounds real fun."

Puzzled, the Justicar scowled. "I thought you liked bugs?"

"I'm starting to get an overdose." The faerie made a face in disgust. "Face it, man, this arachnid diet you've had me on just isn't good for anybody."

Cinders's nose pointed north. Across the flat plateaus, dim shapes of towers could be seen, each one swimming with eerie lights. Keeping low, the party sped northward, hugging ripples in the cave floor and moving in silence.

Beyond the towers, the cavern wall was pierced by a horrible tunnel mouth—a vast carving of a spider that seemed to suck the cavern roads into its maw. Escalla looked up at the spider's mouth, spared a swift glance across the plateaus, then shuddered as a shiver crossed her spine.

"I guess this must lead to the temple?"

"I guess."

Jus was lying flat just ahead of Henry and Polk, carefully scanning the tunnel mouth for the faintest sign of guardians. Escalla sat beside Jus, ludicrously tiny next to his armored bulk. With her long hair stirring in a strange breeze from the tunnel, Escalla stared wide eyed into the dark and swallowed.

"I think Lolth's in there."

"I know."

The faerie wilted, suddenly feeling sick. She leaned her head against Jus's shoulder and held onto his arm.

"Jus? I am just *so* sorry I had to drag you here."

"Sorry?" Jus turned, a strangely puzzled look crossing his face before he softened with a strange, sad little smile. "Someone has to look after you."

"Yeah." Escalla ruefully gave the man a smile. "Hey, Jus?"

"What?"

"Present for my man." The girl threw dust over Jus's shoulders, a stoneskin spell shimmering as it took effect. "Stay safe."

"Thanks." Jus loosened his sword in its sheath. "I love you."

"Yeah, I know."

The big ranger and tiny faerie clasped hands, squeezed, then released each other. They rose up and began to move toward the tunnel mouth.

Behind them, a grinning Private Henry nudged Polk as he watched Escalla and the Justicar. Hefting his crossbow, the boy rose to his feet, followed his friends, and then idly glanced over to one side.

Sitting in a shadowy crevasse, a drow looked at him. Henry's jaw dropped, and the elf's eyes widened in shock. The drow took one look at the party and gave a sudden panicked cry. Something big erupted from the shadows in the cave behind her. Emerging into the meager light, a troll reared from the darkness and slashed at Escalla with its claws, the creature's talons striking sparks as they crashed against her stoneskin spell.

Henry dived, already streaking sideways to cover the faerie. He screamed and pulled the trigger of his crossbow. The machine kicked like a mad thing, blasting a dozen crossbow bolts straight into the monster's flesh. The beast reeled but remained very much alive and angry. Henry dragged out his sword and flailed at its hide, driving the staggering monster back toward the tunnel mouth.

Seeing her pet guardian on the retreat, the drow flung up a hand and total darkness descended—a darkness obliterated a second later by Jus's magic light stone. The drow had already turned to run. Jus whip-cracked his enchanted rope, bringing the drow down in a screaming heap. The creature fumbled for its hand crossbow and fired a shot that was parried aside by a lightning-fast flicker of the Justicar's sword. An instant later, the elf's head fell to the ground.

The troll roared, its wounds already healing closed. The creature bashed at Henry, who blocked the monster's claws with his sword even as the barrage sent him to the ground. Jus reared up behind the troll, his sword held high and his face terrifying. The magic sword screamed in strange joy as it cleaved down through the troll's shoulder and into the chest, sending it crashing to the ground.

"Cinders!"

The monster had already begun to rise. Grinning gleefully, the hell hound blasted flame into the troll. Fire ripped the flesh off its bones, making the troll bubble like a torch as it finally died.

"Jus!" Escalla screamed.

Two hundred yards away, a female drow sat upon a huge lizard. The dark elf stared blankly at the adventurers, then turned and fled toward the towers. Escalla shot off in pursuit, only to see the drow spring into the air and turn into a flying manta. The sorceress flew hard and fast toward safety. Unable to catch the drow, Escalla sped back and helped Henry back to his feet.

"Boys, we're gonna have company!"

The Justicar looked back toward the disappearing manta. With his hell hound over his back and his white blade gleaming, the big man turned, leaped over the burning troll, and sped down the spider tunnel. Escalla blinked then slapped Polk and Henry, shoving them in Jus's wake.

A long tunnel sheathed in horrific bas relief wound through solid rock like a monstrous black gullet. With his magic sword sheeting light into the darkness, the Justicar ran fast and hard, Cinders streaming flames and smoke behind. Jus sped through tunnels and over a stream. The tunnel walls spread out to become a vile promenade a hundred yards wide. Scenes of slaughter and perversion were carved into the walls, blurring past like a nightmare as the ranger charged through, but so far, the tunnels remained strangely empty of drow.

The tunnel ran for a thousand yards, and then a thousand more. Thundering forward, Jus never slowed his pace. Far behind him, Private Henry and Polk fell behind, struggling forward and reeling in a daze of exhaustion.

The tunnel finally ended in a vile riot of sculpted spiders and orgiastic rites. Sitting at the tunnel mouth, a female drow had half risen to make a challenge when Jus smacked her in the guts with his sword, cutting the dark elf in half. A second elf turned to scream a warning to a vast temple building just beyond. Her head fell from her neck before she could even scream.

Jus erupted out of the tunnel and saw another drow staring at him from ten feet away. The magic rope snapped out. Jus jerked the drow toward him and broke the creature's neck with one vicious twist of his hands. His long-contained fury finally released, the Justicar was already on the move, tossing his prey aside as he sped into the cover of ornate gardens of fungi and bone.

"Whoa!"

Escalla flew out of the corridor, bypassed the three dead drow, and urged Polk and Henry onward to glory. The two humans collapsed, wheezing painfully and almost ready to vomit. Laden down with chainmail, Henry had almost killed himself on the one mile run, but he still carried his crossbow in his hands.

Panting hard, the party drew in the sight of a horrible new cave. Red light, thick as blood clots, spilled outward, hazing the cavern like a hideous living mist. It revealed a large cavern, perhaps a mile wide—a place that seeped poison like a canker buried deep in the heart of the Flanaess. The place seethed with evil, a presence foul enough to stain and thick enough to cut.

Buildings stood nearby, vile colonnades of stone carved until it seemed the walls were made of flayed corpses, screaming skulls, and grasping claws. Far beyond, at the heart of the huge cavern, a trumpet's call set the cavern shuddering. A sudden flash of light—dark purple like fluid from a severed vein—spurted upward from an unseen point at the center of the cave. With it came an ocean of terrified human screams.

Jus rose from cover, paused, and let Cinders glare at the terrain. *Spiders. Steel. Cooking smells. No drow.*

"Right." Jus flicked a glance at the buildings jutting out from the colonnade. "Military barracks, empty ones. Something's going on."

The group moved around the barracks, crouching low. Escalla faded to invisibility, lofting high to gaze farther into the awful cave. After a few moments, the group cleared the barracks, and Escalla's voice came drifting down from above.

"Oh crap."

Dropping Polk and Henry into cover behind a ridge of glowing minerals, Jus looked sharply upward.

"What?"

"Guys, you know those missing Keolanders?" Escalla's voice seemed dazed. "I think we just found them."

The mineral ridge looked down upon a vast purple pit that swirled and pulsed like blood. A stockade surrounded the pit, and chained in rows were hundreds, perhaps thousands, of screaming prisoners. There were humans from Keoland, elves and half-orcs, halflings and gnomes. Drow agents had spent months plundering the world above, seizing victims for a hellish feast of living blood.

A vast temple stood at the far end of the cave, a temple shaped like the egg of a titanic spider. Beside the temple doors, two drow blew upon huge horns. A thin, exquisite drow priestess came strolling from the temple, her naked body smeared with runes painted in sacrificial blood. A dozen priestesses followed her, accompanied by loping centaur creatures that were part drow and part spider. Perhaps a hundred drow gathered at the temple steps, screaming out a hideous hymn to their goddess.

Staring out over the struggling slaves, Jus felt Escalla's little hand upon his arm. "There! It's a faerie!"

Escalla pointed across the valley. Flying from the temple came a tiny shape, a faerie masked and robed in white. Jus took one look at the creature and gave a cold growl. "That's our target."

Escalla cracked her knuckles, ready for action. "Yep. Got it!"

The enemy faerie wore a stylized white mask, blank except for painted tears. White robes hid the faerie's body.

Staring across the valley at the other faerie, the Justicar narrowed his eyes. "Who is it?"

"In that gear? Could be anybody."

Escalla seemed far more interested in the preparations being made near the temple steps. A vast golden bowl had been set before an engraved slab of stone. A huge archway of bones had been raised beside the golden bowl, the structure braced by ropes and chains. Escalla took one look at the arrangements and swore.

"Damn!"

"What?"

"See that?" The girl pointed to the arch of bones where the enemy faerie hovered, painting runes with a small brush. "They're making their own gate! They can tap into the faerie gates and have Lolth retrieve the faerie key."

Flat against the ground and almost invisible, the Justicar hissed as he weighed the scene below. "They can make their own gateways?"

"In theory, sure." Escalla made a frustrated noise. "Hell of a spell, though!" Almost all of the drow priestesses now flanked the archway, eyes closed and hands linked, their throats screaming terrible syllables. "See? Ha! It's going to take every mage they've got to break into where *they're* going."

Henry peeked over a clump of lichen, stared, and said, "Where are they going?"

"Don't ask!" The girl had her eyes on the temple door. "Oh my gods! Get down!"

From the gates of the drow temple, a sinister black light spilled forth. A visible cloud of evil stole slowly down the steps. The elves' chanting took on a dead, tinny sound, as though the music died as it crossed into another world.

Lolth, Mistress of Spiders, had taken on a form of flesh to enter the mortal world. Probing slowly from the yawning temple doors came a long, hideous black leg, almost pencil thin, and then another, and another. Creeping forth with mincing steps, the demon queen of spiders moved out to survey her prey.

The sheer evil of the creature struck like an icy knife. Black and gleaming, the gigantic spider loomed above the drow. Where a spider's face should have been, the face of a beautiful dark elf woman peered forth, her face leering as she saw the slaves penned in their thousands at the temple gates. The captives tried to shrink away, the motion looking like a tide surging through a formless sea.

And then the screaming began.

Drow warriors dragged a captive to the temple steps and threw him across the obsidian altar. A priestess gave an orgiastic scream and sawed the prisoner's head off slowly with a ceremonial knife. Blood spurted steaming into the giant sacrificial bowl as the head was cast aside. The jerking corpse was strung up above the bow to drain its blood, while another prisoner was dragged swiftly into place and killed with savage speed. Fifty other screaming, fighting captives were dragged forward to await death in line, while the demon goddess cackled in laughter. Lolth dipped her face into the bowl and drank with manic thirst. The spider seemed to shimmer as hot blood filled her with its power.

Escalla and Henry had frozen. Only Jus and Cinders reacted, the hell hound and master both giving a killing snarl. Jus tried to surge forward to take the white sword to Lolth, but Escalla hurtled into his path.

"Stop! Jus, no! Not like this! Please!" The screams of the doomed and dying ran hideous through the cave. Escalla ran her hands through her hair, trying to think. "All right, all right! Jus, this is not for you!" A demon! A demon queen! The spider lady was swelling with power as she drank her hellish draught. One twitch from Lolth, and Escalla and her friends would be smears on the wall. "Jus, I'll stop Lolth! You free the prisoners and try to clear the gate! The gate's our only way out! I'll come and help you when I can."

Screams and howls sounded as the obsidian knife sawed through victims. Lolth slurped and drank, consuming gallons of blood. Her head whirling in panic, Escalla tried to think of a scam, a trick, a brilliant ploy.

Sudden inspiration struck. The faerie dived down, relieved Polk of a flask from his belt, then hovered high.

"Oh, I'm gonna regret this!" The girl took a big deep breath. "All right, people, plan resolves! Let's get moving!"

A distant hunting horn sounded down the tunnel that led to the main drow cave. The companions whipped their heads around to stare at the tunnel mouth nearby. There was a distant noise of movement, an echo of running feet as drow from the plateaus came to destroy the intruders who had violated the temple grounds.

Rising, Henry stared toward the tunnel and licked his lips. He put his crossbow down and clumsily drew his sword.

"You two deal with the demon," the young soldier said. "Polk and . . . and I will hold the tunnel mouth." The boy flicked a pleading look toward Jus when the big man turned to stare. "You can't free those people if you're attacked from behind."

Jus gave the boy one long, searching look, then nodded and placed one hand upon the boy's shoulder. Huge with anger, Jus spared one look at the main temple with its shocking scenes of sacrifice, then waved the others to stay put as he flowed into the barracks and its colonnade. Red eyes gleaming, Cinders switched his ears left and right, leering in anticipation, then slowly let his black fur rise.

The hell hound worked in perfect unison with his partner. Standing in the middle of the dark colonnade, Jus swirled. Flame whiplashed out of Cinders's jaws, blasting into the huge black widow spiders that nested in the shadows. Big as melons, the foul creatures exploded and died even as they leapt straight at the Justicar's face. Cinders snarled in glee, blasting the last survivors as they lunged into the attack. Teeth bared, the hell hound watched his enemies burn and gave a feral growl.

Aside from the smoldering spiders, the barracks were empty, but the supply rooms were not. Jus tossed aside baskets, threw jewels and treasures to the ground, uninterested in meaningless baubles. He found the tools he needed stacked box by box in a room filled with swords and shields. Crates of quarrels for the elves' crossbows lay stacked beside a wall. Heaving two huge boxes onto his shoulders, Jus stalked out of the flames and curling spider corpses toward his friends, then slammed his treasures to the ground.

The big man threw open the ammunition boxes. Each one contained perhaps a hundred small crossbow quarrels, each one tipped with deadly poisons.

The Justicar set the boxes in place and said, "Here are your tools."

Henry threw himself into place opposite the tunnel mouth, cramming a handful of the small crossbow bolts into his magazine. Jus dragged rocks to fence the boy in with cover, made sure there was a line of retreat into more cover, then tore the lids away from the ammunition cases.

"Polk! Polk, come here!"

The teamster started forward in confusion. Jus grabbed the man and positioned him beside Henry.

"Polk, you stay here and load for Henry. Whatever happens, you keep feeding crossbow bolts into that weapon. You hold them as long as you can, but if it gets too much, I want you both inside that portable hole!" The Justicar wiped clean a streak of rusty earth to the front of their position, swiping it free of dirt. "Here's a drow cloak. It's flame proof. Keep that iron ore deposit in front of you in case they fire a lightning bolt."

"Yes, sir," said Henry.

Jus squeezed the boy on the shoulder with one big hand, gave him a long, hard look of trust that made Henry feel ten feet tall. The boy lay flat over his sights, legs braced against a stone to fight the recoil, and readied himself to make his stand. Jus tucked a last few stones into place around Polk, slapped the little man on the back, then sped away toward the palisade and its horde of guards.

The sacrifices shrieked and died. Escalla hovered, unwilling to leave the boy, then flew down to draw two magic symbols on the ground to either side of the tunnel mouth. She sped back, gave the boy a kiss, and threw a pinch of diamond dust into the air.

"Here's a stoneskin spell and a protection against charm spells. Good luck!" Escalla smacked Polk on the backside, then unsheathed her sinister lich staff and spread it out into a faerie-sized quarterstaff. Polk looked up at her, grim and pale, and gave her a wave. Escalla lifted her staff and began to fly away.

"Polk! Fight the good fight, man!" The girl backpedaled in midair, following after Jus. "Won't be long! I'll buy you a drink when we get back!"

Polk and Henry lay in cover. Without Jus and Escalla nearby, the underdark suddenly seemed ominously still. The sound of feet pounded down the long, dark tunnel, hunting horns sounded, and still the shrieking, bloody sacrifice went on.

22

Sliced flesh made a sound like crisp, wet melon—a sound that carried even over the terror, the shrieks, and the screams of sacrifices. Leering over the palisade, a female drow laughed at the prisoners below. The woman watched Lolth feeding, adding her screeching voice to the hellish hymns. She babbled in excitement to two other guards beside her . . . then her entire body suddenly fell in two.

A second guard turned in shock an instant before four feet of white hot metal ploughed through his guts. Benelux screeched in fury as Jus kicked the corpse free of the blade and rammed the sword hilt backward to smash the wolf-skull pommel into the third elf's face. The drow reeled backward, teeth broken. Jus kicked the creature's knees, crashing the drow to the ground before hacking its head off in one terrible blur of speed.

The drow hymns continued, screaming and horrible. Horns bellowed, victims raved in fear, and the slaughter of the three guards went utterly unnoticed in the cacophony.

Jus crouched amidst the spreading blood of his victims, the hell hound snarling from his helmet in a lusting feral glee. Escalla joined him as the man leaped the fence to sink down behind a surging mob of prisoners.

Escalla clung hand in hand with the Justicar. At the altar, huge spider-centaurs cavorted around their queen. Lolth reared, foul and massive, her size growing as her bulk took on a hellish radiance. Giant black widow spiders the size of small dogs boiled all over the temple steps, climbing over shrieking prisoners near the altar stone. Lolth drank and drank from the giant bowl with a thirst that never slaked, surging with energy stolen from countless slaughtered lives.

Hidden by hundreds of chained prisoners, Escalla went to work. The captives were all shackled by one single chain per row of twenty, the chain running through manacles fixed to their right ankles. Shivering in shock, the prisoners stared at the huge, blood-spattered man in the black hell hound skin that crouched amongst them—then gaped as Jus rose to hack a huge white sword down into a passing drow. The drow screamed and died, unnoticed by his comrades amongst the chaos.

The nearest prisoners were the kidnap victims from Sour Patch. A half-orc goggled as he recognized Escalla and the Justicar. Escalla saw a chained, pale figure gaping at her, the human's face smothered in pimples. Escalla clapped the man's jaw shut as she passed him by.

"Magic wishing weasel, son! Your wish is our command! Escapes from certain doom half price all this week."

Captives saw Jus standing over the butchered drow, and all of them instantly tried to surge pleading toward him.

The huge warrior bellowed and shoved the nearest men down. "Still! Stay still! Don't move!" One blow of his magic sword hacked through the nearest chain. "Drag the chain free, but stay where you damned-well are!"

Another chain sprang free as Jus crashed the white blade down. Benelux pulsed and glowed with an excited stream of light.

Oh, I so enjoy the way we work together!

The prisoners stayed in place as the captives at the far end of the line began to drag the huge chain out of long line of manacles. Jus hacked lengths of chain into sections, passing them to prisoners to use as flails.

"You have a choice: die like dogs on the altar, or kill the drow!" The Justicar hurled lengths of chain to the eager half-orcs at his side. "We outnumber them twenty to one. Charge when I say charge, or just lie here and die!"

Overhead, the gate spell crashed into life, the arch of bone glowing and shimmering as a path was forced into another world.

Escalla looked at the black widows swarming up the temple steps.

"When we get outta here, we're going somewhere totally devoid of damned spiders!" Cursing, Escalla stripped herself naked right before the prisoners' eyes. She tossed her scroll case to the Justicar and shouted, "You idiots do what Jus tells you if you want to stay alive!"

As Jus worked his way through dense packs of prisoners, freeing the rows one by one, the distant drow choirs increased the tempo of their maddened hymn. Escalla made a flash of light as she changed her shape into a big spider, making human captives cringe away from her in panic. The spider picked up the lich staff and Polk's bottle in one clawed leg, then turned and sped toward the mistress of the drow.

"Outta the way, people! Come on! Spider comin' through. *Move!*"

Escalla the spider scuttled through the ranks of prisoners nearest to the altar. Halflings were being dragged toward the altar stone by a dozen guards. The priestesses beside the bone gate finally unlinked their hands, drained by the effort of casting their spell. The white-robed faerie stood before the gate, arms open in a gesture of supreme triumph. Behind the faerie, Lolth plunged her whole head into the vast, deep bowl of blood, storing up life energy to allow her to seize the Nightshade key.

Escalla the spider leaped onto a drow's back, dodged a horde of black widows who tried to drag her along in their dance, and leaped over to a spider-centaur's back. Awkwardly clutching her bottle and staff, she tried to hide herself amongst the chaos. A halfling was flung on the altar and horribly killed, the death sawing right through Escalla's bones. She paused, uncorked Polk's magic whiskey bottle, and then bellowed down into the open neck.

"Faerie wine! Faerie wine! *Vintage sixty-three!*"

The bottle began to gush with wine. Escalla joined a cluster of excited black widows that surged to the side of the blood bowl as the latest corpse was strung up above. Sixty corpses now lay in a heap beside the altar, the bodies sliding and tangling. Drow worked fast, killing, hanging, cutting free—a frenzy of activity. Escalla jumped onto the bowl's rim, saw Lolth as the monster plunged her head deep and drank, then hurled the magic whiskey bottle into the blood. The enchanted wine spread through the blood in an invisible swirl.

A drow high priestess half-caught the splash of the bottle being tossed into the bowl. Whirling, the priestess saw a spider clutching a rune staff perched at the edge of the bowl. The woman froze, and an instant later Escalla had leaped onto her face and bit with poisoned fangs. The drow fired a wild spell, hitting another drow who screamed and simply withered away to ash. Crashing the runestaff into the drow's face, Escalla blasted the woman's head apart.

"Hands off! No one touches the faerie!"

The dead drow flew back across the temple steps. Back in faerie form, naked and drenched in blood, Escalla looked up, her lich staff smoking in her hands. Above her, a row of headless corpses poured blood into the golden bowl. At the bone arch, a masked faerie in white stared at her, utterly appalled. Drow priestesses, still dazed, turned to look at the intruder in shock. Guards paused in mid cut as they butchered screaming victims. Surrounded by stares, Escalla wiped blood from her face.

"You people have pissed me off *for the last damned time!*"

Escalla thundered a magic cloud across the drow. The temple steps were instantly swept with boiling venomous steam. Drow screamed and died, drow ducked and dived, priestesses sheltered behind magic spells or crawled hacking on the ground. Naked, bloodstained, and screaming in battle frenzy, Escalla lunged at the enemy faerie as the creature whirled to flee.

* * * * *

From the prison pen, the Justicar gave a huge bellow of rage. He whiplashed his magic rope and dragged one drow screaming down into the mob, where captives pounded the creature into a bloody pulp. Other drow fired crossbows, and Jus parried three bolts in a blur of steel. The drow stopped to reload, and Jus crashed his blade into the palisade, blasting through the palings. Two thousand enraged prisoners surged behind him in a mob that boiled with rage.

Crossbows hammered a storm of steel at the Justicar. Quarrels ricocheted from his stoneskin spell, then the white blade ploughed through the drow. Blood exploded as elves died, and then the prisoners smashed into their guards in a maddened storm of steel. Chains flailed, and drow screamed.

At the heart of the maelstrom, Jus caught a drow sword as it flashed toward him and severed the drow's arm. Waving his sword, the big man bellowed and led an enraged wave toward the temple steps. A hundred guards were staggering, reeling, and dying as they left Escalla's deadly cloud.

Prisoners crashed into the drow with a noise like exploding worlds. Steel and flesh crashed home, the prisoners clawing into the drow like a tidal wave of rage.

Jus bellowed through the cavern, making the whole temple shudder, *"Kill them! Kill them all!"*

Chains, fists, and swords struck home. Drow fought in a mad panic. Somewhere in the distance, a wild stutter sounded as Henry's crossbow began firing at something. Jus stormed up the steps as lightning bolts ploughed into the human mob, the drow screaming in frenzy and rushing down the temple steps to meet fists and rage with steel. The Justicar parried a spell, the white sword smashing lightning back into the drow, then hacked madly into the drow sorcerers.

Blood flowed, hundreds died, and still Lolth drank. With her head buried deep in the steaming, bloody foam, the demon mistress ignored the chaos around her as she slaked a thirst and began to glow with unholy power.

* * * * *

At the tunnel entrance, the echo of charging feet had become an unending drum roll. Polk lifted his head, pitched a magic light stone through the entrance, and saw at least a dozen drow racing toward them.

"Here they come!"

The sudden light bought them a moment as the drow slowed to shield their eyes. Private Henry opened fire—spaced, careful shots, each one of them a tribute to his two long weeks of military service. The first shot spat sparks from a drow's mail armor. The second pierced his target, the drugged quarrel paralyzing his victim almost before the creature screamed. Third and fourth shots flickered through the air, making one drow curse and clutch his thigh before he collapsed.

The fire came sharp and fast. Sure that half a dozen crossbow-men covered the entrance, the remaining drow fell back into the shadows, awaiting enough reinforcements to carry out a headlong rush.

Polk shoved crossbow bolts into the top of Henry's magazine. He kept one worried eye upon the tunnel mouth as everything suddenly turned still and silent.

"We got three of them." Jubilant, Polk stared at the tunnel. "Do you think that's it?"

The temple cavern behind them suddenly shook as thousands of human voices rose in a battle roar. Amongst it all, the massive bellow of the Justicar and the screaming of his sword almost tore the rocks apart. As if on signal, a solid rain of crossbow bolts tore wildly from the tunnel, the bolts striking rocks near Polk and flying uselessly through the sky. With a manic scream, a dozen drow came charging from the passage, throwing bows aside and drawing swords as they howled in bloodcurdling hate. Henry fired his crossbow, the weapon whirring as a solid sheet of arrows blasted a drow leader off his feet.

The bolts flew into the tunnel in a terrifying swarm. A drow officer lifted his sword and screamed as he charged. Suddenly a stream of death ripped across his chest, and the drow spun in a mist of blood. Three more elves raced past the corpse, only to jerk back with arrows jutting from their flesh.

Quarrel after quarrel spat sparks and ricocheted madly from drow armor. Missed shots ploughed across stone and spun from tunnel walls. More dark elves ran forward, armor making bolts bounce and flicker aside. One warrior jerked back with a bolt through his eye. Others took shots in the chest and thigh, cursing then screaming foully as the drugged points struck them down.

A score of drow hurtled into the field of fire. Henry swerved his crossbow left and fought the thunderous recoil. The weapon bucked and raved, quarrels blasting toward the onrushing drow. Lying awkwardly on his side, Polk panted in panic, cramming handful after handful of bolts into the magazine. The arched bow blurred white hot, the string thudding like a drum. Blood and sparks and ringing metal turned the cave into a churning storm of chaos as the drow ran forward, screamed, and died.

The drow fell back. From behind them, leaders struck with whips and spells to drive the laggard onward. Sheltering in the recesses of the tunnel walls, drow fired random crossbow shots that smacked into the rocks beside Polk and Henry or flew wide.

Shoving through her followers came a tall drow sorceress dressed in blood red mail. She ran forward, buckler held high to deflect a rain of Henry's crossbow darts. Other elves ran behind, using her as cover, then streaked away from the deathtrap of the cave mouth. One of them sped over Escalla's magic runes, and a massive blast of flame shot upward and blew the drow apart. A survivor staggered to his feet, and Polk shot the creature with a hand crossbow. Drow soldiers shrank back into the safety of the cave mouth, lying flat behind the bodies of the dead and paralyzed.

Still standing amidst a rain of fire, the sorceress snarled and launched a lightning bolt. The spell shot toward Polk and Henry, hitting the metallic ores in front of them and arcing uselessly into the ground. She screamed in fury even as a fresh stutter of crossbow bolts began smacking into armored elves and forcing them to ground.

The woman screamed at her cowardly followers, ripped spell energies out of her black soul, and flung them at her foes. A fireball thundered, the flames engulfing Polk and Henry utterly. The sorceress rose, half turned to wave her forces forward, and gave a mad ululating cry. A dozen drow stormed forward, only to halt in shock as a lethal rain of crossbow bolts blurred into their ranks again.

Black cloaks smoking, Polk and Henry were back in action, the crossbow hammering home a stream of fire. The sorceress staggered as three bolts hit her armor and flew away. Then one dart speared through her naked thigh, and the drugged tip instantly took hold. Jerking forward, the paralyzed drow crashed to the ground, her spell staff and her buckler rolling in the dirt. Her warriors fell back, firing wild shots from hand crossbows, and suddenly the air was starkly still.

Panting and swearing, Polk kicked one empty crate of crossbow bolts away and tipped the other on its side. He filled Henry's magazine, cursing dully and monotonously, his eyes glazed with panic, while somewhere behind them the cavern echoed to countless hundreds of battle screams.

*   *   *   *   *

Temple steps were awash with blood. Freed captives rolled on the ground, dying on the fangs of black widow spiders or tearing the arachnids apart limb from limb. With captured swords, lengths of chain, or bare fists and nails they threw themselves upon the drow, who fell back toward the altar in fear. Drow soldiers fired wildly into the enraged crowd, only to be pulled down by the onrushing waves. Spells flickered and blasted—pinpricks to a mob driven wild with fear that took its last refuge in blood-red rage.

Their fury had solidified into a huge blood spattered form. With his hell hound sheeting flames into the drow, Jus fought like a dark, roaring god. Swordsmen leaped howling at him, turning somersaults as they flew over the battling crowds. The Justicar cut the guts out from one in midair, hacking another down as he fell from above. The white blade ignored drow enchantments and alloys, shearing through metal, flesh, and bone as though they were wet paper.

Driven by one man's fury, the sword sheared a drow priestess in half, showering drow with blood as the ranger clawed his way into the midst of the exhausted drow clergy. Charm spells spattered away from him, canceled by his old bone ring. A curse spell twisted away from him as he roared in massive anger. An instant later, a priestess lay screaming as she died, but a second drew a mace to fight hand to hand. The mace was parried, struck from her hand, and her arms severed in four blindingly fast bows, leaving the vile cleric screaming as she fell through the ring of drow and into the bowl of blood.

Surviving drow had made a ring about their demon queen, but the gigantic spider still had her head below the blood and was drinking deep. Buying time as their queen charged herself with power, the drow roared defiance and hacked into the human swarm. Blood flew in red streams from both drow and captives.

Jus launched himself at the elven lines, smashing home with hell hound flames blasting before him. The huge man crashed into elves, scattering them, and the mob surged forward through the breech to drag drow to the ground.

The high priestess gathered thirty desperate followers and made a counter attack. Raising her hand, the priestess began to scream out the syllables of a spell. Jus heard the spell, turned, and caught the priestess's eye as she gasped in an instant need to kill.

Jus looked at the woman and gave one low, predatory growl.

Screaming in hate, the priestess launched a spell. A lightning bolt blasted toward the Justicar. The man swung out with his sword, striking the bolt aside and ploughing it into the drow. Dark elves were blasted from their feet while others ducked, magically immune.

The mob hesitated, fearing to come too close to Lolth. Taking the fight to the enemy, Jus hurtled himself at the high priestess, who drew out a long staff that trailed writhing tentacles. With a manic scream, the woman ran headlong through the corpses, wild with the need to tear open the Justicar's heart.

*   *   *   *   *

"Bastard!"

Naked and bloodstained, Escalla flung herself at the enemy faerie, who stood beside the bone gateway. Masked in white, it had a clear stone on a ragged string hung about its neck—the slowglass gem! The masked faerie spared a glance at Lolth, who kept feeding, building up the power that could crush the intruders and seize the Nightshade key. The faerie whirled, saw Escalla's rush, and shot out a magic shield to hold off the inevitable blast of spells.

Screaming in fury, Escalla blurred forward with accelerated speed and ploughed through the shield, crashing full tilt into her enemy's chest. The white-clad faerie flew backward, slamming against the temple gates and tumbling into the pitch-black interior. With a wild scream, Escalla sped forward in pursuit, moving almost faster than the eye could see. She shot like a meteor above Jus and the drow, leaving a monster summoning spell sparkling in her wake. A swarm of giant damselflies flashed into existence behind her—creatures that plunged down onto giant black widow spiders, plucked them up into the air, and began eating the arachnids greedily.

Still moving blindingly fast, Escalla sped through the temple doors. An ice spell blasted at her, ripping the flesh from her bones and smashing her to the floor. As she screeched and writhed, the other faerie whirled down from the ceiling, blasting a fireball down to incinerate Escalla's remains to ash. Scorched bones hissed, an obscene parody of Escalla's beauty. The enemy faerie stood over the corpse, then turned back in triumph to glance toward the demon queen.

Leaning against a nearby column, Escalla waved to catch the enemy faerie's eye.

"Hey, moron!"

An ice blast of Escalla's own punched through the other faerie's shields. Ripped and torn, the other creature dived aside, a spell flashing to repair wounds before the creature even hit the ground. Escalla walked forward, laughing as the dazed faerie crawled across the floor.

"Simalcra are so hoopy, huh?" Escalla's opponent had the typical fault of all court-raised faeries: just not enough experience from the school of hard knocks. "Aw, and I bet that was your best combat spell!"

Whirling in silent rage, the other faerie fired another ice blast. Escalla was blown apart—the pieces falling to the earth, turning to singing cockroaches and running around and around the floor. A nasty little peal of laughter came from somewhere in the shadows above the door.

Escalla appeared, now masked by magic shields of her own.

"Nope! Guess you had one more!" The naked girl gave a smile filled with pointy teeth. "Simalcra are just too, too hoopy."

A lightning bolt thundering off her magic shield, Escalla lunged with the lich staff pointed straight ahead. The enemy faerie threw itself aside, and a chunk of masonry exploded as the staff struck home. Escalla whirled, but her enemy sped deeper into the temple. She threw the staff like a javelin, the weapon missing by a hair as the enemy faerie fled madly away. Swooping to retrieve her weapon, Escalla flew hot on her enemy's tail.

The other faerie twisted through huge hallways lined with spider sculptures. In a vast room filled with gigantic spider webs, the enemy faerie dived wildly toward a little door. Escalla ripped a spell past her enemy, and a wall of flames blocked the path. With a wild scream, Escalla ploughed toward her foe, holding the staff before her like a spear.

The other faerie blasted out a cloud of choking fog. Escalla shot through, felt a shape whir below her, and lashed out with one hard little foot. A mask cracked as she kicked the enemy faerie in the face, and then suddenly the other creature turned on Escalla like a shark.

Too close for staffs or spells, the two faeries fought blindly, kicking and tearing at each other, but Escalla's blood-slippery skin gave her enemy no chance to grip. They grappled in midair, falling wildly through the fog. Escalla managed to grip the string around her enemy's neck and rip it free, the slowglass gem falling to the ground.

Nails tried to rip Escalla's face. She struck madly with her lich staff but missed, and the other faerie punched back. Escalla crashed into a springy surface, saw the other faerie lunging straight toward her with a dagger, and managed to plant both feet in the other creature's chest. Her enemy tumbled backward and rebounded from a pillar, slamming face down into the spider web just below Escalla's heels.

Clouds dissipated. Both faeries hung in the giant spiders' web, stuck fast and buzzing wildly with rage. An instant later, giant black widow spiders emerged from the upper corners of the room. They stared at the prey through unwinking eyes and began to creep relentlessly along the strands of web. Escalla took one look at the spiders and felt her skin begin to crawl.

"Oh crap!"

Pointing one finger, Escalla fired little swarms of golden bees. The spellfire snapped and rebounded off the webs, failing to so much as break a strand. Escalla cursed, swiped clumsily with her lich staff, and blasted one sticky rope of spider web free. The black widows bounced madly on the web, running forward as they felt their prey beginning to escape.

Below Escalla, the other faerie jerked in a frenzy of panic. Escalla was breaking free strand by strand, and the black widows were racing in for the kill. The enemy faerie tore itself free, hanging by a single hand that was stuck tight. Flapping in frenzy, the faerie tried to break free.

Spiders gathered for a death lunge, Escalla broke another strand, and the masked faerie opened fire with a spell. Flesh blasted apart, and suddenly the masked faerie was flying free. Reeling in agony, the creature sped away out of the temple, leaving Escalla staring after it in shock.

The other faerie had deliberately blown off its own hand at the wrist. The severed hand still bounced and clung to the spiders webs. Hacking herself loose, Escalla fired a lightning bolt through the nearest spiders and cleared the web, then used the lich staff to cut the severed hand free. The faerie whirled, then looked down to hunt for the fallen slowglass gem . . . only to see the whole floor of the hall sparkling brightly with mountains of gold and jewels.

It was the temple's treasure horde!

With a staff in one hand and a severed trophy in the other, Escalla stared. Fifty black widow spiders surged toward her from all sides. The slowglass gem gleamed and sparkled just below her, bracketed by enough treasure to buy a kingdom. Out of time, Escalla could only look about and flap her wings in woe.

"Oooh, shoot!"

Escalla dived, plucked up the slowglass gem, and shoved it in her mouth. With her mouth and hands full, the girl shot faster than a crossbow bolt out of the temple, leaving enraged spiders following fast behind.

✷ ✷ ✷ ✷ ✷

Outside the temple, Jus fought beneath a diving umbrella of damselflies that struck and swerved at the drow—sometimes dying, sometimes killing. The drow high priestess screamed in fury and lashed at the Justicar with a rod that sprouted flailing tentacles. The strands struck home in a wild blur, whipping out to bind legs and arms, stinging with acid wherever they touched. Jus jerked in fury pain, trying to wrench himself free. A mace crashed against his shoulders, nearly cracking his spine. Jus kicked out viciously, connected with a kneecap, and brought the drow priestess crashing to the ground. Before he could finish her, he felt a blade rip into him from behind, then another crashed against his armor of dragon scales. The Justicar managed to tear the tentacles free and hurl the weapon aside, when suddenly the whole world exploded in his face. The drow priestess managed to slap a hand against the Justicar, and magic gave a hideous, brilliant flash.

And Jus was blind.

His eyesight simply disappeared, leaving him in total darkness. Jus reeled back, slinging the tentacle staff far away and sweeping the sword Benelux up on guard.

"Cinders! Can you see?"

Can see! The hell hound had fought in tandem with the Justicar for many long, hard years. *High left!*

Jus whipped his sword high left in a parry, and the weapon rang. Jus stepped back, sensed movement at his side, and smashed his sword down. The blade bit into something that screamed, and then Cinders barked a warning from above.

High-low! Jus sped his sword up in a parry, caught an attack, then blocked a stab lower down. *High-low-high! Left foot! Rear high! Low left!*

Jus fought purely by instinct. He felt motions beside him and whirled the sword up to meet each strike as Cinders yapped out commands. The stoneskin spell wore away under the assault of a dozen swords. He almost stumbled over a corpse then lashed out wildly to catch a sword that stabbed for his heart. He crashed his blade past the incoming weapon, ramming home with huge force. A dark elf screamed as Jus twisted the weapon and ripped it free.

He parried madly as a fresh rush of blows crashed home. A mace hammered against his sword hilt and almost struck the sword out of Jus's hands.

Lower! Lower! Benelux screeched in fright, as she only just managed to catch an elven blade. *Dog, call the shots properly!*

Is properly!

You're not doing it right! No, left!

"SHUT UP!" Jus roared at his two companions. Fighting purely by instinct and skill, Jus barely managed to put his weapon in the way of an attack. "Cinders, you help!"

All around him, he heard shrieking and dying. The drow still held a line protecting Lolth as the titanic spider drank. The battle would be lost in seconds. The moment the demon queen decided to lift her head out of the bowl, the captives and their rescuers would have no hope. Why she had drunk so long in the middle of a battle was anybody's guess.

Jus spun, crashed his sword down on something—felt a presence behind him and to the left—and smashed his elbow into a drow face. As a sword clanged off his dragon scales, the Justicar shouted, "Cinders! Where's the high priestess?"

Left front—three yards. Cinders heaved then blasted flames forward in a thunderous tidal wave of heat. *Path open! Go!*

Jus leaped forward, his sword smashing down and meeting nothing. Jus sensed something slashing at his face, ducked to his knees, and swung. His sword rang against a metal buckler, the huge force of his blow making his enemy crash to the ground.

The screams and howls of dying humans, half-orcs, elves, and halflings sounded in a mad chorus. Drow war cries screeched and echoed in the hellish light. Through it all, a strangely beautiful female voice managed to shout at the Justicar.

"You cannot see, human! You are doomed!"

Jus closed in upon the voice, deliberately keeping himself turned slightly away as though unable to find his enemy. He moved his sword point uncertainly.

"I know enough. You have been *judged*."

"You are the Justicar—the hand of justice!" Sneering, the drow high priestess shifted, moving to one side.

Jus flicked his head and turned, again slightly out of line.

"You cannot see!" she screamed in triumph as she attacked.

Jus threw himself flat, spinning with his sword scything across the ground. The blade sheared through ankles, and the ranger heard a scream of agony. He rolled, rose, and slammed his sword through the stunned priestess, killing her instantly.

"Justice *is* blind."

23

Shooting out of the temple, Escalla saw the other faerie plunge straight through the bone gateway. In flicker of light, her quarry was gone. Furious but unwilling to leave her friends, Escalla stared ghast at the carnage before her.

The temple steps were awash with blood. A hundred drow were dead, and easily twice as many humans. The damselflies had torn apart the black widows and the spider centaurs. A knot of drow priests and warriors were gathering around Lolth. The drow took heart as hunting horns sounded from the entrance to the distant caves. Escalla hoped Henry and Polk had the sense to get out of there.

Seeking the ranger, Escalla saw Jus staggering near the altar, his stoneskin spell long spent and blood running down both arms. The huge man suddenly staggered as a hand crossbow bolt struck him from behind, piercing Cinders's fur but failing to penetrate the dragon scale coat below. Jus whirled blindly, his sword up and circling as drow closed in.

Escalla began to throw a spell, but the gem in her mouth stopped her from uttering the incantation. Her hands were full and drow surged below. With a painful gulp, Escalla swallowed the slow-glass gem, turned a little green, then sped to the rescue of her friend.

"Jus!"

Escalla flamed destruction from above, making a circle of fire about the Justicar. She landed amidst the flames, clinging to the battered ranger. "Jus, are you hit? What's wrong?"

"Blind! Spell." Jus staggered as he nearly tripped over the high priestess—one of the most extravagantly bisected corpses Escalla had ever seen. More crossbows fired from the drow toward the mob of former captives, and Escalla interposed a shield that made the darts leap and bound away. More horns and war cries sounded as a horde of drow warriors rampaged down the tunnel toward Polk and Henry.

And Lolth finally moved.

Wrapped in clouds of shimmering black power, the demon queen raised her head from the bowl and gave a long, slow roar. Escalla stared, Cinders gaped, and the mob all froze in fear. The demon goddess was greeted by a wild cheer from her surviving guards, who all shook their weapons in salute toward their queen.

Lolth looked across the carnage, stared blearily at the dead and dying, and then collapsed on the ground with one almighty drunken wail.

Drunk as the proverbial skunk on about a thousand bottles of the dreaded vintage sixty-three, Lolth groaned and flopped about, then screamed in agony as convulsions seized her. Drow beside her shrieked and died as she lashed out at them with her mind, blasting skulls apart and sending dark elves streaming into the temple to hide. Escalla saw the drow turn and run, and she canceled her fire-wall. She seized a human who knelt strangling a long-dead drow. The man looked up as Escalla dragged him by the hair.

"Take the Justicar and go through the bone gate!" Escalla put Jus's arm over the pimple man and yelled, "Get out through the bone gate! Run! Run!"

For a moment, Jus resisted, shouting, "No! Polk and Henry!"

"I'll get 'em!" Escalla replied. "You hold the exit!"

Jus nodded grimly, and the mob turned like a living tide toward the gateway. Escalla heard screams and horn blasts from the distant tunnels and sped back to assist Polk and Henry's last stand.

* * * * *

At the tunnel mouth, Henry swerved his crossbow from left to right, the dwindling ammunition pouring into the magazine as fast as it could move. Crossbow bolts hammered into drow as they churned in confusion. Return fire rang and howled as it careened from rocks and rebounded from Henry's stoneskin. The magic was fading, and now Henry's helmet rang as a crossbow bolt struck the metal crown, making his ears ring.

Still the magic crossbow snarled, sheeting darts into the enemy. Enemy fire whirred from the tunnel as drow held up the bodies of dead or paralyzed comrades to use as shields. The drow shuffled forward inch by inch, awkwardly closing the range. Two broke and sped to the left, hitting the last of Escalla's traps and blowing themselves ceiling high. Others ran past the smoking remains, leaped over a pile of rocks, and began racing to Henry's position. The soldier whipped his crossbow about to blast a dozen shots at them as they ran. One elf fell, but the other threw himself flat and began worming through cover.

Switching targets had let other drow rush closer. A dozen cringed behind their horrific shields as Henry shifted fire, and the boy was forced to hammer the advancing elves once more.

Inch by inch, Henry and Polk were losing. The drow were gathering and signing to one another, almost confident enough to rush the deadly crossbow. Polk searched the bottom of the ammunition box, whipped out the last dozen crossbow bolts, and slapped them in place. "Almost out!"

Blurring insanely fast, the magic crossbow's string suddenly snapped in two. Smoking, the pieces hung limp as Polk and Henry stared.

A sudden scream of victory came from the single drow on the flanks, and the dark elf charged Henry with two short swords clashing. Henry rolled, freeing his sword just as the Justicar had shown him, rolling and hacking upward into the drow's knee. Hamstrung, the drow fell. Henry screamed in fright and stabbed his sword down like an ice pick, the point skipping and sparking off the drow's armor time and time again.

Desperate, the dark elf kicked Henry, and the boy fell. Turning, the drow raised both swords over Henry's chest.

Henry roared furiously, bellowing like the Justicar and unleashing a vast strength brought on by terror and desperation. Rolling, he smashed his sword through the drow's chest, carving right through into its evil heart. The drow fell on him, both swords striking stone to either side of Henry's head.

The boy shoved the corpse away even as the elves at the tunnel mouth charged in one screaming, frenzied mass. A solid rain of crossbow bolts hissed forward. Polk whirled the portable hole outward like a cape, and the incoming darts flew harmlessly into the hole. Polk then grabbed the boy and ran.

"Strategic withdrawal, son!" Polk bellowed out like a wild bull as he ran. "Justicar! *We have a problem!*"

More drow sped fast along the flanks to cut the retreating humans off. Henry pushed Polk back to run for safety just as a random dart pierced his calf from behind. Henry arched and froze.

Polk turned, saw the boy stiff and paralyzed, then grabbed Henry by the arm as the boy collapsed.

"Son!"

The teamster shoved Henry into the portable hole and threw the magic crossbow after him. A drow sprang like a mad locust straight at Polk's back. The teamster turned and drew his last loaded hand crossbow, shooting the drow through the face.

The dark elf warrior fell lifeless to the stone floor, but a female drow leaped over the corpse and struck with her short sword. The blade speared straight through Polk's chest. The teamster gasped and teetered even as something flashed past his shoulder to explode like a bomb, crashing the drow off her feet.

"Bitch!"

Frenziedly beating her enemy to death, Escalla jammed her lich staff into the creature's open mouth and triggered the weapon's power. The drow detonated, and Escalla tumbled on the blast, showered by yet more gore.

Polk teetered, gasping and choking on his own blood, then fell. Escalla opened the portable hole under him even as a dozen crossbow shots hissed past her. With Polk inside, the faerie towed the hole awkwardly behind her as she fled, dragging it like a blanket.

✿　✿　✿　✿　✿

Half a mile away, a solid column of refugees poured through the bone gate, occasionally trampling one of their own number. Lolth staggered and lurched into the columns of her own temple, clutching her face and screaming like a soul in torment. Drow fell, telepathically suffering their goddess's hangover. Escalla found Jus hovering beside the gate and blinking blankly as though it would clear his blindness. Escalla grabbed the man by the elbow and led him to the archway.

Jus stared about as he heard the sound of onrushing hordes of drow. "Are Polk and Henry safe?"

"I've got them! It's not good." Escalla shoved the portable hole into Jus's hands. "But they must have killed at least a hundred drow!"

"Good men."

"Polk's hit bad!" Escalla screamed. "Real bad, Jus!"

"How many are left?"

"Huh?" Escalla gave Jus a confused look.

"How many captives? I can't leave until they're all out!"

Escalla did a quick estimate. "A few moments! When I say go, then get through quick!"

Lolth blundered closer, trying to focus on the departing sacrifices. More and more drow were flooding from the tunnel, charging toward the temple gates. Moving fast, Escalla dipped down and rapped her knuckles upon Benelux's hilt.

"Hey, Spiky! Where did you say you were forged?"

The positive energy plane! The sword gave a self important cough. *The pure energy that formed the building blocks of all matter, the—*

"Is it hot?" Escalla cut her off.

Hot? Benelux swelled with grandeur. *Imagine the inside of a vast, undying, ever-churning sun. Imagine pure light and heat eternally exploding upward like a fountain of power! Imagine——!*

"All right, that's hot. That's perfect!" Escalla chased the last few dozen prisoners through the bone gate. "People, *we are leaving!*"

Escalla looked around desperately. The last battered refugee in sight stumbled through. If there were more, they were on their own. She couldn't wait any longer.

Escalla shoved Jus forward, and he disappeared. Seeing her prey escaping, Lolth reared and screamed. The demon's head swam to the nightmarish effects of vintage sixty-three. Lurching sideways, all eight legs churning and slipping, the colossal spider blundered through her own altar, sending the bowl of blood clanging to the ground. The temple guards had fled, but the drow from the main caverns were closing fast. Escalla gave a last look over the underdark, tucked severed hand and lich staff underneath her arm, then quickly sped away.

She shot through the great bone arch, popped out of a mirror, and bounced upon a trampled, crushed, and altogether broken bed. She flew out the room's shattered windows to wave to a faerie who stood goggling at the vast crowd of refugees milling on his lawns.

Naked, blood smothered, and carrying a severed hand, Escalla gave the faerie a salute.

"Hey, Dad! Did you miss me?"

* * * * *

The blindness was clearing.

Jus blinked, holding onto a broken balustrade as he stared at once beautiful gardens that were now trampled flat by two thousand panicked feet. Refugees had swarmed over the lawns, where a dozen faerie sorcerers held them in a magic fence. Lord Charn hovered, tearing his hair out, appalled at the destruction to his home.

The splinter and crash of breaking woodwork sounded as one last refugee thundered through the magic portal—a gateway that exited from an ornate mirror mounted on Escalla's bedroom wall.

Velvet curtains had been torn down as a solid battering ram of humans, elves, halflings, half-orcs, and even a dwarf or two had charged over a balcony and into the sylvan gardens beyond.

The Justicar blinked, and the last of the blindness fell away. Seeing Escalla hanging bloody and disheveled at his side, he said, "We're in the faerie lands!"

"Yep!"

"This is your old bedroom!"

"The Nightshade key is kept in Dad's vault just down the hall." Escalla looked at Jus's dubious face. "Hey, man! I'm the heir! Of course the key's hidden in the palace. Dad and I were always looking after it!"

Jus angrily wiped his eyes and asked, "Who knew the key was here?"

"Dad, me . . . maybe Mom and Sis." The girl shoved the severed hand down the portable hole. "Now hurry! Get this mirror onto the lawn before Lolth comes through. There's about a hundred million drow charging straight toward the gate!"

Escalla's father appeared, looking stunned. He opened his hands and demanded an explanation.

Jus looked at the mirror—a vast heavy thing of silver, framed with gold, and fixed to the wall. He gripped the frame and heaved, plaster cracking and exploding as he tore the mirror from the wall. With a roar, the huge man dragged the mirror free and held it above his head.

"Where to?"

"Grove of the planes!" Escalla cleared the way, bellowing at faeries who had come swarming in droves toward the room. "Outta the way! Demon goddess comin' through! Move-move-*move!*"

Jus leaped from the balcony, slamming to the grass a dozen feet below. With the huge mirror held above him, he charged through the hordes, who screamed in terror as one gargantuan spider leg began to probe slowly out of the mirror's face. Jus jumped a fence and thundered into the plane tree grove at the heart of the gardens.

Escalla whirred madly back and forth trying to look at every tree.

She scrunched her fingers inside her hair and tried to think. More and more spider leg began to shove through the mirror. "Crap! Which tree? Which tree?" One tree had pure white flowers. "This one!"

The mirror went clanging down to lean against a tree. Escalla hovered frantically beside the arch made by the branches of the pure white fruit tree.

"Jus, the sword! The tree is triggered only by something from the home plane!" Escalla recoiled from the mirror, screeching as Lolth poked her front legs through. "Just the tip! Hurry! Hurry!"

Drawing his sword, the Justicar took aim, then sliced the blade in a blinding arc. There merest hair's breadth of the tip whisked beneath the archway, and instantly a glowing plane of force sparkled beneath the arch. With titanic spider legs shoving through the mirror, Jus picked the mirror up, roared like a giant, and hurled it toward the magic trees.

Lolth's face emerged through the mirror, the demon screaming in anger as she finally caught sight of her prey. The scream turned to a wail of absolute despair and horror as the mirror shot through the archway and plunged straight into the plane of positive energy.

The mirror disappeared. Benelux gibbered, having lost a six-teenth of an inch from her tip. Jus and Escalla stared at the glowing magic archway and panted, watching blankly to make sure all was well.

"Well, that's that!" Escalla seemed a tad dazed. "Guess that's Lolth unable to manifest for about a hundred weeks!"

Jus blinked. "Is that good?"

"It's so-so."

The tree suddenly shuddered violently, then shuddered again. The force field changed to fiery red, then shook as the whole tree almost tore itself out of the ground.

Cinders stiffened his tail and whined, *Run bye bye now!*

Jus coughed. "Can things get out that gate?"

"Like if all that energy in Lolth exploded?" Escalla drifted away from the quaking tree. "Um, a strategic retreat is probably—"

Something blasted like a volcano deep inside the plane of elemental light. Jus turned and ran like hell, Escalla only slightly ahead of him. Behind them, the grove of plane trees exploded, trees blasting apart. Energy flashed, and suddenly there was nothing but a shiny-sided crater of molten glass fifty feet across where the grove had once stood. A cloud of flames rose into the sky, showering ashes across the staring faces of two thousand refugees and several hundred faeries.

Lurid red flames lit faerieland. Burning brands showered down over the palace and the gardens. Into the silence, Cinders's voice carried to every single ear as the hell hound breathed out in awe.

Spider go bang! The black dog wagged his tail. *Hoopy.*

24

By evening, things were calmer. Illusion spells covered the worst of the damage to Clan Nightshade's palace, and Lord Nightshade and Lord Faen had tended to the eighteen hundred and eleven surviving refugees. Wounds were tended, and a faerie feast had been prepared—a feast devoid of faerie wines, particularly vintage sixty-three.

Sitting at a huge campfire roasting a dozen giant frogs, the Justicar sat with Cinders at his side, watched in awe-stricken silence by countless nearby refugees. The pimple smothered boy and a half dozen survivors from Sour Patch all hovered in the shadows of the trees nearby, all looking for some way to do the big ranger a favor. Jus merely did what had to be done and tried to keep his temper as far too many hands tried to pass the salt.

Benelux lay bared across Cinders's fur and had gone into a blubbering great sulk.

It's a liberty! The female voice had kept its tirade going for at least half an hour. *You could have killed me!*

Jus spared the sword a hostile glare. "It was only the tip."

That tip was shaped by a titan! Benelux wailed in loss. *Where can we find a hand skilled enough to repair my damaged beauty?*

Jus turned one of the frogs, which sizzled greasily above the campfire. "Faeries said they could fix it."

Faeries? Benelux bridled. *Are they properly qualified?*

"I guess."

Well, see to it that they are swordsmiths—not blacksmiths. The magic sword gave a sniff. *I do not want myself pawed by just any faerie!*

Jus sheathed the weapon and shut it up. For a few moments, peace reigned until Escalla came wearily traipsing down the hill.

She looked a little pale and worse for wear. She wore stockings, elbow-length gloves, and a bodice made of black silk with a skirt deliberately cut short from a faerie dress. Washed and scrubbed, she still looked like hell. The faerie kept one hand on her stomach as she walked into the light.

"Hey, boys."

Hi! Cinders's tail wagged a hello. *Frog onna fire!*

"Hoopy." Escalla came over to sit upon the plush, soft hell hound fur. She leaned on her lich staff and looked plain tired. "Well, the trial's set for an hour from now. All the right invitations are out."

Looking levelly at the faerie, Jus smoothed her a place at his side. "Have they tried to arrest you?"

"Killing Lolth tends to make people a tad nervous about your powers." The girl gave a sour smile. "Heh. I'm still kind of officially under house arrest. They've sent out couriers to bring in the hunting teams." Escalla helped herself to campside tea. "My sister and my mother are back. Not a word said. Keeping to their rooms."

"Of course." The Justicar served Escalla food from the fire. "Is Clan Sable still here?"

"They will be. The faerie clans are coming here now. Apparently we've got King Oberon coming along as referee. Guess we've got an hour before show time." Escalla looked down at her food then put a hand on her belly. "Ooooh, I feel awful."

"Really?" Jus looked at her. "Is the slowglass safe?"

"Yep." Escalla looked a tad green. "I, ah, passed it in as evidence."

An embarrassed silence reigned. The faerie realm was filled with the babble voices, the smell of campfires, and the sound of shocked people trying to convince themselves they were still alive. Faerie warriors watched over their "guests"—surprisingly polite, all things considered. Gates flashed all over the palace as more and more faeries began to arrive, the sound of clarions becoming monotonous as the Seelie Court gathered for the trial.

Prodding at the leg of giant frog that roasted over his campfire, Jus stared at the flames and asked, "How's Polk?"

"He, ah, h-he—" Escalla's bottom lip quivered. She swallowed and went on. "He didn't make it. He died, Jus."

The Justicar stood, actually mad—no, *furious.* Burning with utter rage, he slowly clenched his fists and paced round the fire. Escalla sat by the fire and gazed at the coals.

"There wasn't anything we could do. That drow got him right through the heart." The girl rubbed at her eyes. "The kid's with him. He's bruised all to hell and a bit cut up, but otherwise he's fine. They made a good team, you know?"

Upset, angry that he was upset, and annoyed at being angry about being upset, Jus stopped pacing and swiped at his eyes.

"They did well. They really did." Jus cleared his throat—a cold seemed to be making him sound a little hoarse. "Can your people fix it?"

Escalla sighed and gave a nod. "Probably. Dad put a priest on it. Said we'll probably have him back from the dead by tomorrow morning . . . if all goes well."

"Good."

From the palace, horns blew an insistent little fanfare, summoning the court of faerie law. Jus signaled some nearby refugees that they were welcome to the campfire and the food, then gathered up his gear.

Jus's calm eyes turned to look long and thoughtfully at Escalla.

"Are you all right?"

"I'm fine." Escalla took charge of her staff, scroll tube, and the portable hole as Jus swept Cinders into place around his shoulders. The girl let Jus lift her up and set her on his shoulder. He rested his face against her flank for a moment, and the girl gave his big, stubble covered head a hug.

"All right, J-man. Let's do it!"

✶　✶　✶　✶　✶

The central ballroom of Clan Nightshade's palace had again filled with faerie aristocracy. Chairs were arranged into a vast ring about the floor, and chandeliers blazed brightly above. Banners from ancient conflicts hung in splendor beside paintings so perfect that they had lives all their own. As hundreds of gorgeously costumed faeries flew in through the doors to take their seats, Jus and Escalla walked slowly inside with Henry trailing awe-struck in their wake.

All speech stopped. All eyes instantly turned to stare at the rebel Escalla and the huge figure of the Justicar.

At one end of the ballroom, a throne had been arranged. A wing of crimson-armored guards knelt beside a lean, cool figure who sat upon the throne. The Justicar walked across the open ballroom and delivered a long, grave bow to the Erlking, Oberon. Escalla joined him, giving a cool nod. Henry bobbed like a child's toy, bowing again and again until Escalla dragged him away to the sidelines where the boy could do no harm.

Hundreds of faeries—both exiles and the Seelie Court—had gathered. Into the hush, Lord Faen strode forward, his two-foot height proud and haughty as he thudded his staff of office against the floor.

"All hear! This court extraordinary is now in session!" The old faerie signed to warriors beside the windows and doors. *"Seal!"*

Red-armored royal guards slammed the windows and the doors, then rolled magic seals across them. Power flashed, and the rooms were shut tight against intrusion or escape.

Lord Faen turned, ignoring the operation. Before him in the front rows of the audience sat Lord Ushan of Sable, his flame red robes now black in mourning. The Lady Nightshade, pale, beautiful, and severe, sat beside Lord Nightshade and their youngest daughter Tielle. Young duelists, clan heads and courtiers, all made a solid wall of faerie might that awaited the evening drama. Lord Faen finished his circle of the floor then walked back toward the throne.

"It pleases his Highness the Consort-Royal to declare this court in session. Let no spell be cast without permission, on pain of retribution. Let no blows be struck. Let all who have business before this court state their cases and be satisfied." The faerie lord made a single bow toward the Erlking. "My Lord Oberon, Clan Nightshade embraces the spirit of the Seelie Court and petitions your judgment."

Lord Ushan gave an angry start, only to be held in place by a hand idly raised by Oberon himself. Thin and attenuated like an exotic mantis, the Erlking was clearly different from the faeries around him. Oberon looked coolly at Lord Faen and then Lord Nightshade. When he spoke, the Erlking's voice was surprisingly cool and soft.

"What does Nightshade desire of us?"

Charn, Lord Nightshade stood and said, "Your Highness, Nightshade asks that this court determine the guilt and identity of the murderer of the Cavalier Tarquil Sable."

With a roar, Lord Ushan sprang to his feet.

"No! Improperly worded!" The Lord's robes changed color—back to their usual sea of flames. "We have a culprit already in custody. This court should be sitting to determine punishment for the girl Escalla Brightflower Nightshade."

Lord Faen turned a glacial gaze upon Lord Ushan and replied, "The wording was exactly correct. You are out of order. This court sits to determine the murderer of the Cavalier Tarquil Sable—and also to assess sundry other crimes." Lord Faen turned to Oberon. "Highness?"

The Erlking raised one fingertip and said, "Begin."

With his wings stiff and his antennae erect, Lord Faen began a slow path past Lord Ushan, Lady Nightshade, and the glaring, sneering Tielle.

"My lords and ladies, upon the death of Cavalier Tarquil, evidence showed that a faerie was the most obvious candidate for murderer. An outside specialist was therefore commissioned by the crown to pursue evidence and collect facts. This commission has been duly carried out." Faen pointed with the butt of his staff. "The Justicar will present the facts that he has gathered. Attend him."

Again Ushan gave a cry of dismay. "This under-creature is a companion to Nightshade's daughter!"

"He has served us with extraordinary courage and diligence—up to and including confronting the demon queen Lolth on our behalf." Lord Faen turned his back upon Ushan. "Unlike faerie lords, the Justicar holds truth above all honor. He has no objection to submitting to truth spells. Cast one now and be satisfied."

With a snap of his robes, Lord Ushan did exactly that. With a truth spell in place, he sourly sat down.

The Justicar walked slowly forward—three times taller then the faeries, his heavy boots and hell hound skin seeming stark and pitiless. The human rested one hand on his sword and addressed the throne.

"The body of the Cavalier Tarquil was found with a poisoned goblet at his side. Apparent cause of death was from imbibing poison." The Justicar turned to pace slowly across the room. "My own subsequent examination of the corpse revealed anomalies. An injected poison had been administered within the victim's hairline. The puncture wound had been missed by previous investigation. However, the wound had not bled at all."

A thin faerie lady with delicate turquoise skin raised a fan quietly to the Justicar and asked, "Justicar, this is significant? Why would a wound not bleed?"

"Blood had already pooled at the victim's front, my lady, where the Cavalier had been lying face down." The Justicar bowed calmly over the little woman. "This is a sign that the body had been at least three hours dead by the time the puncture wound was made."

"Ah." The blue lady twirled her fan in puzzlement. "Double poison? Someone making sure of their mark?"

"Perhaps, my lady." The Justicar kept his voice deep and civil. "In any case, the Lady Escalla entered the room at one point during the evening while the body was present. She wore a slowglass necklace—immune to illusion. We have retrieved this slowglass and can now show this court the events of that night."

Carried carefully by royal guards, the slowglass gem—newly cleaned and polished—was borne into the room. Lord Faen bowed toward the throne.

"Lenses can project images from the slowglass onto the wall, my king. Light caught in the slowglass will leak outward only once. A time spell allows us to accelerate or stop time for the slowglass, but please pay close attention to the images. We cannot replay an event once the light has fled."

A harsh laugh came from the audience where Tielle, Escalla's sister, lounged scornfully back in her seat. "Your slowglass could show nothing but actors in a play! There is no guarantee that what we see is what happened that night!"

The old faerie lord flicked his level gaze at Tielle. "This slow-glass has been retrieved at enormous risk. There are certain aspects of the scene about to be played that are unlikely to be faked." Lord Faen motioned to his assistants. "We shall be able to judge for ourselves."

The Justicar knelt so that his bulk would not inconvenience the audience. When the Erlking gave permission, spells were thrown. Time accelerated for the slowglass gem, the images trapped within shining outward through a magic lens to shimmer in midair. Lord Faen stood leaning on his staff, watching days speed past in seconds, finally holding up his hand as the images began to show familiar events.

The faerie lord watched carefully as recoded events began to unfold.

"This is about three weeks ago," said Faen. "The slowglass gem lies in a jeweler's strongbox. Ah! Here we have the gem being traded to Lady Nightshade. Tielle inspects it. Here it is mounted on a neck-lace. Money is paid, and the gem comes here to the palace. Ah, Cav-alier Tarquil!" The now dead cavalier's image froze as the sorcerer froze the time spell. Tarquil peered straight toward the gem, dangling it at arm's length as he inspected it with a sly smile.

"Continue!"

The images moved once more. Lord Faen stroked his goatee as he watched Clan Nightshade's plots and plans. "Now they enter the Dreadwood Forest and the camp of Escalla and her companions. Here the necklace is placed in Lady Escalla's baggage. What joy as she discovers it the next day!" Events played themselves fast and sure, the court craning forward to make sure no details escaped their eye. "Here we have the gem held up before Escalla—well dressed for once. She makes a welcoming gesture—interesting!" Faen nodded, then held up his hand. "Ha! Nighttime at the palace! Escalla looks into the gem, then slings it about her neck. Stop! Let the gem play events at their real speed."

The gem's viewpoint was occasionally alarming. At the moment, it showed a scene bracketed by Escalla's meager cleavage as she flew down a starlit path. The girl apparently wore a lacy silk dress and little else. A few titters from the audience were met by a dire glare from Escalla, who paced impatiently back and forth in the middle of the ballroom floor.

The images showed Escalla approaching the balcony of her old bedroom. Cavalier Tarquil's bodyguard gave a knowing look and deliberately walked away. The view lofted over the balcony, through gauzy curtains and into Escalla's old bedroom. A reflected image in the mirror showed Escalla standing in her dress, the slowglass gem sparkling about her neck.

The gem's point of view wobbled and shifted as Escalla hung the necklace over a the door handle. Coming back into the gem's view, Escalla turned, surveyed the still form of Tarquil—

—And then began doing a strip tease.

"Stop!" The Justicar leaned in to stare hard at every single aspect of the scene. He pointed to the still form of Cavalier Tarquil, lying sleeping on his face amidst his cups. "Continue."

The slowglass gem could see both Escalla and Tarquil. The image of the nearly naked Escalla blew the gem a kiss, waving and grinning and setting the entire faerie court agog. Faerie lords guffawed. Faerie princes raised their brows appreciatively. Faerie ladies tittered. At the middle of the ballroom floor, Escalla turned beet red and clenched her fists in rage.

"Hey! It seemed a good idea at the time, all right?"

The projected image of Escalla was slapping her bottom and dancing up and down beside the still form of Tarquil. A magician slowed the action to catch Escalla mid sashay, slapping her rear and giving the slowglass gem a nasty piece of sign language.

Red with fury, Escalla stamped her foot on the ballroom floor. "*All right!* Enough with the slappy dance already! They get the idea!"

Court ladies laughed, and Escalla folded up her arms and seethed.

Stroking his stubbled chin, Jus fixed his puzzled eye upon the girl and asked, "What were you doing?"

"Showing him the goods he was going to miss out on!" Escalla waved hands in anger. "Hey! I have a nasty side!"

In the air above the ballroom floor, the nearly naked image of Escalla blew a final kiss to the sleeping Tarquil, who still lay unmoving. Escalla triggered the magic gateway in her room and dived through with an admirable athletic clench of her rump and flip of her heels.

The Justicar turned to Lord Faen and said, "Freeze time." The images froze. "The images are clear. At no point did Escalla touch or even approach the Cavalier."

A faerie lord from the Seelie Court, a weird creature with long antennae, gave a lazy flip of his hand. "She may have done this as a show! She may have deliberately hung the slowglass gem there as evidence, then arranged another way to kill the Cavalier."

The Justicar gave a nod. "She may. One hour from the time of her disappearance from the palace, Escalla was in company with myself and her father. Lord Faen can confirm this."

With a flip of his long hand, Oberon gestured to Lord Ushan. "My Lord, you are satisfied that this human speaks the truth?"

Looking as though he would rather choke, Lord Ushan gave a chop of his hand. "He speaks truth, my lord! But—"

"*Excellent.*" Oberon leaned back upon one elbow in his chair, thoughtful eyes resting upon the Justicar. "Justicar, continue."

Jus signaled to the faeries controlling the slowglass, and the images reeled on. "There will be another visitor to the room sometime within the next hour of elapsed time."

Tarquil lay perfectly still, utterly unmoving. The entire court frowned, noting the unseemly stillness of the victim. Someone cleared a throat to speak, when suddenly an image appeared. A new figure had entered Tarquil's sleeping chambers.

The figure stole in through a magic gateway made by the fireplace arch. White robed and masked in a blank faceplate painted with mocking tears, the image carried itself with incriminating stealth.

Jus froze the scene.

"As it pleases the court, this individual—or an identically dressed one—was later found to be a consort of the demon queen Lolth, who we almost had as your uninvited guest here this morning."

The scene played on, and the entire court leaned forward to stare.

The masked faerie pulled something palm sized from its pouch, holding it with enormous care. Creeping carefully over to Tarquil, the assassin cautiously pressed its gloved hand into the sleeping cavalier's hair, held the position, and then withdrew.

The masked figure put its weapon into its pouch and drew the heavy leather glove from its hand. A silver ring sparkled briefly on the assassin's hand. Jus froze the image, looked at the ring, then watched as the masked faerie kicked at Escalla's discarded dress. With an air of triumph, the masked face peered directly at the slowglass gem, heard a noise, ripped the gem free, and shoved it into the front of the robes.

Down *cleavage*. Jus pointed at dim white shapes preserved in the image.

"*Female.* Breasts bound flat with bandages for disguise. Far, far larger breasts that Escalla's."

"Hey!" Escalla looked betrayed. "I have understated elegance!"

"Understated enough to be identifiable." The Justicar dismissed the pictures above. He nodded to Escalla who began rummaging inside a portable hole. "My Lord and Ladies. Commissioned by Lord Faen to pursue the stolen slowglass gem, I pursued the gem through magic gates into the underdark. This slowglass bauble is a rather expensive gem, and so coveted that the thief saw fit to wear it as a necklace, even though it only hung from a piece of string." Jus stroked his chin quietly.

"From this point, the slowglass will show the thief's journey through the underdark—a journey through drow checkpoints and a lich's lair, through a kuo-toan temple, and into the city of the drow themselves. The gem thief has been working to a larger plan, a plan to use Lolth as an instrument to release the faerie Queen of Wind and Woe from imprisonment."

The entire faerie court immediately froze.

The Justicar merely shrugged and continued, "The images here will show the summonation ceremonies. Escalla and my party were able to interfere. The masked faerie lost the slowglass in combat with Escalla."

Escalla's mother had sat like a creature with a vile smell beneath her nose throughout the entire trial. Sitting erect, the woman made a show of wiping clean her hands. "A waste of our time. Your assassin is still masked! There is no way to ascertain her identity!"

"Oh but there is!" Escalla hovering in midair before the assembled court. With a theatrical sweep, she addressed the entire room. "The thief made a mistake! You saw it in the image. We need to find someone who always wears a silver spider ring!"

Tielle immediately put her left hand beneath her dress. Lord Faen, Jus, and Escalla turned to look at the girl and raised their brows. Escalla flew over to join her family, while Lord Faen turned back to the Erlking.

"My King, evidence seems to point well away from Escalla Nightshade."

"Granted," Oberon replied gravely.

"Oh hoopy!" Escalla clasped full hands to her bosom in joy, then tossed something in the air. "Hey, sis! *Catch!*"

A beautiful conical shell fell into Tielle's lap. Tielle gave a screech of raw fear and hurled the thing off her lap, leaping away in terror.

Hovering above, Escalla flexed her fingers as though unsheathing claws.

"It's only a little seashell, an empty one from a kuo-toan temple." Escalla picked up the shell and held it to her ear with a look of concentration on her face, as though she were talking to the mollusk inside. "What? What was that? Tarquil's assassin used a kuo-toan cone shell? But we never mentioned that to anyone but Daddy and Lord Faen!" Escalla turned big wide eyes upon Tielle. "What? How would Tielle recognize a kuo-toan cone shell unless she was the assassin? I dunno. Let's ask her!"

Waving at her sister, Escalla pulled a severed hand out from behind her back—a hand wearing a silver ring.

"Hey, dimwit! You lost it back at the temple, ring and all! We even got it on the slowglass!" Escalla shook the feminine hand back and forth in a wave. "Gotcha!"

Tielle shrank back in her seat, then shoved both of her hands into the air. "I have two hands."

"Yep, and a regeneration spell only takes about a minute." Escalla twirled the severed hand in the air. "If I get a clone spell cast on this, you think you'll be twins?"

Tielle didn't hesitate an instant. With a screech, the girl blasted a black bolt of energy—not at Escalla but at Oberon, who sat staring on his throne.

Jus whirled, the white sword streaking from its sheath. White light met black in a screaming howl of agony, sparks spraying all across the hall. The black bolt sheared in two, each part ploughing through the palace walls to either side of the Erlking. Jus sank into guard position, his magic sword smoking black as it dissipated the deadly force still clinging to the blade. Cinders snarled, hissing smoke, and the Justicar launched toward Tielle.

As the entire court erupted in chaos, Tielle turned, ripped a flower from a vase, and threw it through a fireplace. A magic gateway flashed into place. She dived and rolled, plunging through the portal an instant before the Justicar's sword blurred through the empty space. The gateway had gone—open and shut in a single instant.

"Damn!"

The court was still sealed tight by the guards' spells. Escalla ripped open the scrolls in the case on her back—treasures from the underdark—and trilled out the passwall spell. A hole appeared, leading onto the lawns crowded with refugees. Tielle emerged from a gazebo and instantly dived toward a garden patch, searching for herbs to use as keys for her escape.

Escalla snarled through the air and hit her sister full tilt, both of them tumbling end over end across the grass. Hundreds of refugees stood and stared.

In the palace hall, guards had clustered about the Erlking, too shocked to follow in pursuit. Only Lord Nightshade, Lord Faen, and a few courtiers had followed into the night.

Escalla's scroll tube went flying. Hair ripped, and lich staff tumbled. Tielle drew a dagger but took a right-cross from Escalla's fist that threw her back against a tree. Tielle turned, seized an orchid, and tossed it toward a garden arch. A gate sizzled into existence, but Escalla smashed a branch across Tielle's head before she could fly free.

Jus lumbered down the lawn. Other faeries followed, slow and dazed. Tielle and Escalla fought in bitter fury, punching spells at one another that were too weak to pierce through each other's defensive screens. Each had exhausted all their best spells battling in the under-dark. Escalla now took the fight where it belonged. She kicked her sister in the chest, sending her ploughing through the grass.

"Bitch!"

"Sniveling little daddy's girl!" Tielle wiped blood back from her nose. "When I'm queen I'll have them rip your guts apart!"

Escalla swore and threw a spell—a minor little thing that rico-cheted from Tielle's defensive shields. Tielle laughed and backpedaled gaily through the air, one eye on the gateway shimmering in the dark.

"Time to bid your comic spells farewell!" The girl spread her wings wide. "Lolth will be back, and I'll be with her! Time to shoot off and away!"

Jus and the faerie guards were coming fast. As Escalla made a lunge for her fallen lich staff, Tielle tipped a mocking salute to one and all and headed for escape.

From behind, Escalla's voice came loud and clear. "Nope! Time to die and get buried!"

Tielle whipped her head about. Escalla stood in the grass, lich staff at her feet and an open scroll in her hands. "Hey! You like comical magic? *Top this!*" Escalla trilled spell syllables, unleashing power stored in the scroll. "Flesh to stone!"

Tielle screamed and tried to plunge through the gate, but the powerful spell blasted into her from behind. As Jus, Henry, and a dozen faeries thundered onto the scene, Tielle's body jerked and turned to stone, slamming down to the ground.

Escalla stalked forward, looking extremely miffed.

"Framing me was the worst idea you ever had, bitch!" Escalla flicked out the scroll. "Spell number two—for those of you who have come through this with a sense of humor—*stone to mud!*"

Frozen in a pose of horror, Tielle's petrified shape instantly dissolved into a pool of mud. Escalla steepled her fingers as she surveyed the results.

"Aaaand for my grand finale, let us just cancel out that flesh to stone spell, huh?"

The result was a big pink pool with a pair of blinking eyes staring up from the mess. Escalla bit her thumb at her sister, then turned about to see Henry and the Justicar staring at her wide-eyed. Escalla could only roll up her scrolls and shrug.

"Like I said, I have a nasty side!"

A splendid day began in the Dreadwood. Sun streamed through the trees, lighting upon ruined village roofs and mossy giants' bones. Woodsmoke carried the scent of bacon in the air. A few faerie courtiers walked along or fluttered above the paths, peering at the astonishing sights of an unknown world. Drifting over it all came the sound of happy feminine singing—a voice that had not a worry in the world.

Enid the sphinx, freckle-spattered and eternally polite, came loping from the old tavern, batting at a rolled up ball of parchment with her paws. She stopped as she saw a ten-foot hole sitting in the middle of the path, and minced over to peer into the depths.

The hole was deep and looked remarkably comfortable. It had been lined with polished bookshelves that smelled pleasantly of beeswax. Hundreds of books and scrolls were neatly stored in place. Enid's entire library lay in the middle of the shelves, surrounded by scores upon scores of new books.

Still singing happily, Escalla came flying out of the tavern. She wore new clothing—black elven chain mail so fine that it felt like sheer black silk, gloves and leggings, skirt and halter, all as stylish as a faerie could wish. Followed by a floating disk that bore two dozen fresh new books, Escalla whirred over to Enid and waved.

"Hey, Enid! It's for you. Like it?"

"Like it?" Enid peered down into the hole with wide eyes. "Are those books all for me?"

"Books, maps, scrolls, riddles, lost languages . . . I even swiped some from a lich, so be careful with those! Bought the rest in town.

Keoland paid a reward for returning their lost population." Escalla tugged at one corner of the hole and lifted it up. "And it all folds up like a handkerchief! We can carry it with us wherever we go." Escalla tucked the folded portable hole into Enid's pretty collar. "Here. From us to you—a gift for our friend."

Escalla hugged the huge sphinx, who nuzzled happily and purred. Heaving a sigh and enjoying the sunshine, Escalla looked over the crumbling old village. With her lich staff at her belt and her recharged ice wand in one hand, Escalla lifted into the air on silver wings.

"Polk! Come on, man. We're going! And don't forget the map!"

A snort came in reply, and an annoyed voice echoed from inside the shadows of the inn. "I can't bring the damned map! You know danged well I can't! Someone else will have to!"

"Just carry the damned thing and stop grousing!" Escalla waved her arms in irritation. "Look man, you're a hero back from the dead! Faerie magic—lifetime warrantee! Can't you just be a *little* bit pleased?"

A big hairy badger waddled out of the door and glared up at Escalla. "You did this on purpose!"

"I did not!" Escalla bridled, the picture of absolute innocence. "Would I do that to you? Hey, man! It was faerie magic! How was I supposed to remember that they can only do reincarnation spells?"

"It ain't funny!" As a badger, Polk made an impressive sight—fat, hairy, and with a regal waddle to his walk. "I can't even pour my own beer!"

"We'll put it in a bowl for you! At least they made it so you can talk. What's your problem?" Ever helpful, Escalla brought the case to Enid for judgment. "Enid, does this suit him or what?"

The sphinx wrinkled up her pretty nose as she bowed down to inspect the sulking badger. "Well, I must say I like the stripes!"

"See! She likes the stripes!" Escalla waved a hand at Enid. "Think of the advantages. No more clothing expenses, hours of happy excavation, and you get to sleep in all winter!"

Polk glared at Escalla and licked his chops. "I said it ain't funny."

"All right, here's a plan." Escalla sat cross legged on Enid's furry back. "We'll go find someone human who has a proper raise dead spell. Then we'll just kill you again, and get them to raise you back!"

Polk bristled in annoyance. "I'd still come back as a badger! I come back as what I was when I died!"

"Well, then we could reincarnate you again!" Escalla seemed utterly enthused by the idea. "I mean, a badger is only one random choice out of many! Maybe you'll come out as something even hoopier? How about a giant woodlouse? Or you could be a beaver and do woodwork in your spare time."

"No, thank you." Polk sniffed in enormous self-importance. "Badgers got dignity, and from here on, if you don't do what I tell you, I'll give you all fleas."

Escalla froze. "Do badgers have musk glands?"

"You'll find out." Polk waddled over to Enid's back and clambered aboard. "So we're leaving? Where's lunch? Where'd the Justicar go? I want to fill him in on all my newfound woods-wisdom. Bein' a badger gives a man a whole new range of skills!"

❖   ❖   ❖   ❖   ❖

Walking quietly through the forest, Lord Faen, Lord Nightshade, and the Justicar reached a meadow filled with buttercups. The brilliant yellow flowers glittered in the morning sun, the winter cold giving way to a warm and mellow spring. The Justicar found a mossy log and spread Cinders out beneath a sunbeam. He popped a piece of coal into the hell hound's mouth, and the dog sucked happily and thumped his tail against the bark.

'nk you!

"You're welcome."

The big man scratched fingers across his freshly shaven head, his dragon scales armor gleaming in the sun. The newly repaired magic sword at his belt gave a sniff and wriggled in her sheath.

At least justice has been done. The sword's voice brimmed with self esteem. *A Justicar! A dealer of justice! Ours is a most satisfying profession.*

"Quite." The Justicar poured good dark ale from his own flask, passing little thimble cups to Lord Faen and Escalla's father. The two faeries sat cross legged on the mossy log, frowning as they tested the alien drink and finding the earthy taste a bit puzzling. Lord Nightshade drained his cup then held it out for more, while Lord Faen quietly put his own drink aside.

Patting Cinders between the ears, the Justicar watched the two faerie lords as he refilled the small thimble-cup.

"Did you find him?"

Who? Benelux jittered in her sheath. *Who? Who?*

Lord Nightshade spared the sword a long suffering glance and turned to the Justicar. "He was found sheltering on a Clan Sable estate in the middle of Elysium. I believe a full confession will not be necessary."

Who was found in Elysium? Benelux rattled her sheath in anger. *I say! If we are going to be a partnership, you must allow me into your confidence! How else can you benefit from my wealth of good advice?*

"The murderer." Jus sighed and poured himself an ale. "He was found in Elysium."

Benelux jittered. *But . . . but the murderer was that wretched girl, the one who tried to unleash that demon! The one who looks like your partner—only with bigger breasts!*

"You can't murder something that's already dead." Lord Faen decided to risk the beer and took a sip. "The body had been dead for hours before the cone shell was used. Remember the pooled blood? The unbleeding wound? No. Tielle wasted her efforts there. Tarquil had been gone for hours."

The Justicar spared a droll glance down at his sword. "You found nothing odd in the fact that Tarquil slept peacefully right through a striptease?"

I know nothing about such things. The sword gave a prim little sniff. *I suppose it might be possible.*

"Escalla dancing half-naked is a pretty good recipe for waking someone up." The Justicar drank from his flask. "No. The body had already been poisoned. Escalla was framed. Tielle's assassination attempt was simple coincidence. She wanted to stop Clan Night-shade from returning to the Seelie Court before she could finish her plans to release the Queen of Wind and Woe."

Annoyed, Benelux jiggled up and down. *So who killed Tarquil?*

Jus, Lord Faen, and Lord Nightshade all looked at the sword as though she were an idiot.

"Why, Tarquil did!" said Faen.

There was a long, somewhat smug silence between the three men. Finally Lord Nightshade helped himself to another beer.

"You see, my dear, Tarquil's life was hanging on a thread. Too many vendettas had been declared upon him. It seemed a good idea to lie low. His uncle, Lord Ushan, wanted the alliance with Clan Nightshade stopped, so they concocted this little affair. They cloned Tarquil and killed the copy, hoping to frame Escalla for Tarquil's murder. In a few years, Tarquil would have reappeared claiming to be a clone, inherited his own estates, but still would not have been legally responsible for the deaths his previous self had caused in duels." Escalla's father brimmed with richly deserved satisfaction. "A horrible scandal if it should come out. Clan Sable is therefore giving us full support for our return to the Seelie Court, as well as aban-doning a few strategic offices to other, wiser heads . . ."

Benelux hummed and hawed. *But what of Tarquil? He planned to frame Escalla. Surely some sort of justice must be done?*

"Ah." Faen stroked at his goatee. "Well, we wondered about that. Unfortunately, someone broke into his prison, polymorphed him into a mouse, and punted him though a faerie gate that leads to the beast kingdom of cats. He was last seen in a scrying spell, running like a champion!" Faen scowled. "Which reminds me. Where was your daughter last night, Lord Nightshade?"

"I have two daughters," Charn replied innocently. "Which one do you mean?"

"Why, Escalla, of course, the one still in solid form."

"Safely at her prayers, Lord Faen."

"Ah, quite so." The goateed faerie smiled knowingly.

Tielle had been carried off in a bucket to be imprisoned by the

Seelie Court. She was alive but was going through some bad days.

Lolth had lost her current body on this plane, and it would take months for her to make another, by which time her hangover might even have gone. Certainly the Nightshade key would have been re-hidden by then. All's well that ends well.

Jus corked his drinking flask and said, "I must insist you abandon your plans to force Escalla into marriage. She served the court well. She deserves her own will in the matter."

"Oh yes, of course. Our stock is rather high in court right now." Nightshade gave a genial smile. "The Erlking thinks rather highly of us. My wife's claws are clipped. Life will be a bit more . . . effervescent from now on."

"You will be returning to the Seelie Court?"

"In a sense. The Seelie Court is coming out of retirement. There will be more faeries wandering the worlds from this point on." Nightshade looked at Faen, and both men shared a nod. "Though cautiously at first."

Lord Nightshade stood, his hands in his back as he stretched his wings. Faen joined him, and Jus swept Cinders back across his own shoulders. Faen fluttered up over the buttercups, where he had a fine view of the ruined village just below. Enid and Escalla were eating bacon from a frying pan, Escalla laughing and beautiful with her hair bright golden in the sun.

Lord Nightshade watched his daughter with a rueful little smile.

"Escalla will not be returning to the court." Charn looked at the Justicar and shrugged. "What was this place she wants to see? *Hogwart?*"

"Hommlet, my lord." The Justicar gave a bow. "And then horizons far beyond."

"Then we shall meet again." Nightshade took the Justicar's hand and pressed it with his own. "You'll do right. I can tell."

"Good-bye, my lord."

"Good-bye, my son."

Lord Nightshade produced a little box and gave it to the Justicar—parting gifts to see Jus and Escalla on their way. The two faeries stood and watched as the big human and his hell hound strode through the buttercups to where Henry awaited them. Now dressed in faerie-made armor and bearing a sword made by faerie smiths (along with his deadly crossbow), the boy ran up to Jus, who clasped him warmly by the shoulder and led him back into the village.

Enid the sphinx waved a paw back toward the two faerie lords. Escalla turned and gave a long look at her father, flashed him a strangely understanding smile, and waved farewell. Side by side, Escalla, the Justicar, Henry, and Enid marched up the road into the north, with Polk the badger happily holding their road map upside down.

As the travelers disappeared from view, Lord Faen rested his hand upon Lord Nightshade's shoulder.

"Quite a remarkable girl, your eldest daughter. Not quite . . . genteel, but a certain lively spark. I believe I shall miss her. I do wish her well on her travels."

"I shall miss her, too." Lord Nightshade heaved a sigh and plucked himself a buttercup. "Still, she grows and grows. I have such hopes for her."

"Yes." Faen walked side by side with Nightshade as both men moved back into the forest. "What was that you gave them as parting gifts just now?"

"Oh, for him, a longevity potion. For her, I thought she should keep her wedding dress. You never know when a girl might need it."

"Oh?" Faen led the way beneath a drifting cloud of thistledown. "Just her dress?"

"And a dozen growth potions—you know, faerie-to-human size. Plus the recipe. That sort of thing."

"Oh?" Faen activated a magic gate and seemed a tad puzzled. "How did you know she wanted that?"

"A little dog told me."

Enter the magical land of the Flanaess, world of adventure!

GREYHAWK is the setting of the role-playing game
DUNGEONS & DRAGONS. Each of these novels is based on a classic
D&D adventure module.

Against the Giants
Ru Emerson

A village burns while its attackers flee into the night. Enraged, the king
of Keoland orders an aging warrior to lead a band of adventurers on a
retaliatory strike. As they prepare to enter the heart of the monsters'
lair, each knows only the bravest will survive.

White Plume Mountain
Paul Kidd

A ranger, a faerie, and a sentient hell hound pelt with a penchant for
pyromania. These three companions must enter the most trap-laden,
monster-infested place this side of Acererak's tomb: White Plume
Mountain.

Descent into the Depths of the Earth
Paul Kidd

Fresh from their encounter with White Plume Mountain, the Justicar
and Escalla depart for the town of Hommlet. But life around a faerie is
never exactly . . . stable. Before he knows it, to save her life the Justicar
is on his way into the depths of the earth to fight hobgoblins, drow,
and the queen of the demonweb pits.

Available June 2000

☢ T A ☢ ● ☢ ☢ I V ☢®

R.A. Salvatore
Servant of the Shard

The exciting climax of the story of the Crystal Shard

In 1988 R.A. Salvatore burst onto the fantasy scene with a novel about a powerful magical artifact—the Crystal Shard. Now, more than a decade later, he brings the story of the Shard to its shattering conclusion.

From the dark, twisted streets of Calimport to the lofty passes of the Snowflake Mountains, from flashing swords to sizzling spells, this is R.A. Salvatore at his best.

Available October 2000